Praise for Flora Collins

"Flora Collins is a sure-handed and inventive suspense novelist."
—Adriana Trigiani, bestselling author of *The Good Left Undone*

On *Nanny Dearest*

"A slick thriller." —*CrimeReads*

"A seesaw of rising tension that ultimately delivers a raw, crashing conclusion... Collins's debut illustrates the sometimes obsessive and terrifying nature of love and the shattering consequences of its betrayal." —*Library Journal*

"A well-crafted debut... Horrifying... Psychological thriller fans won't be disappointed." —*Publishers Weekly*

"Unsettling, compelling, elegantly paced—Flora Collins's debut is a slick, contemporary novel that explores the wispy, nagging memories of childhood, the dark side of relationships, and the unrelenting desire to be loved."
—Julia Heaberlin, bestselling author of *We Are All the Same in the Dark*

"A powerful debut about the fine line between love and obsession... Haunting." —Miranda Smith, author of *What I Know*

"You won't be able to put this book down."
—Emily Freud, author of *My Best Friend's Secret*

Also by Flora Collins

Nanny Dearest

A

SMALL

AFFAIR

FLORA COLLINS

mira

mira™

Recycling programs
for this product may
not exist in your area.

ISBN-13: 978-0-7783-8693-3

A Small Affair

Copyright © 2022 by Flora Collins

For questions and comments about the quality of this book, please contact us at
CustomerService@Harlequin.com.

Mira
22 Adelaide St. West, 41st Floor
Toronto, Ontario M5H 4E3, Canada
BookClubbish.com

Printed in U.S.A.

3 1984 00413 0215

To Andrew, my best friend and the closest thing I have to a husband. Always and forever grateful that our "marriage" has yet to be tabloid fodder.

A

SMALL

AFFAIR

PART
ONE

One year ago

WE MET ON an app, one of those achingly boring, exclusive ones. White text on a black background. Where you have to work in a certain industry, have a certain type of education, a *pedigree* to differentiate yourself from the riffraff.

Oddly, or perhaps not oddly at all, I remember the exact moment we matched. I was on my couch under a heavy knit green blanket, my legs splayed across my best friend and roommate's legs. We were watching *Real Housewives*—though which franchise, I can't recall—ignoring each other, ignoring the TV. Classic millennials on our phones, doom scrolling.

I wish with all my might I could do that again. Sit next to Quinn on that olive green couch we'd found in a West Village Housing Works and ignore each other without these ghosts separating us, sitting on my chest. Incapacitating me. Incapacitating all my relationships.

"Ugh, can you move your legs? Mine are asleep," Quinn whined, throwing his end of the blanket in my face and getting up on unsteady feet, stretching. He padded across to our small kitchen and took out a beer, watched me on my phone, my face lit by the glare of the TV.

I looked up. "Want to help? I'm back on the apps." Quinn set his beer down and clapped his hands. Quinn didn't date much. He'd been on and off with his partner, Sam, for seven years now, since we were sophomores in college. Right then they were off, had been off for the past six months or so. I knew it would only be so long until they got back together; they rarely dated other people. It was like they were actually meant for each other.

But he loved to live vicariously through me. Loved to vet and interrogate all the guys who had come home with me over the years, commenting on their clothes, their hair, their smell, their faces, forcing me to tell every minute detail about the sex, the morning after, whether they snuggled me up close at night. Whether they followed my instructions in bed, asked what I wanted, needed.

So I wasn't surprised when he plopped back down on the couch, grabbed my phone away from me and began to swipe.

"All these people have liked you?" he asked, eyes roving over the screen. I nodded. "Damn, Vera, you haven't been on this app in ages, have you? You have like fifty likes." I nodded again. I hadn't gone out with anyone in a few months, mostly because of new responsibilities at work. It wasn't even like I felt incapacitated by those responsibilities; I just had no wish to spread my enthusiasm for work thin. Dating forced me to spread it thin, and if I were being honest, the whole *process* of dating made me utterly exhausted.

But now I had a handle on everything. I was ready to start anew, begin the process yet again like every other mad straight woman always assuming the next man will be different. And I was bored. I hate that most of all, that I was *bored*. My whole life in pieces because I didn't buy a good enough vibrator.

"So you get to 'like' them back? And that's a match?"

"Yes. If you gave me my phone, I could show you." But it was no use; he was already at it. "You know, we have different tastes. You keep swiping *no* on people I think are cute."

But Quinn kept the phone. "Babe, I have better taste than you. Just trust me." And I did.

In a few minutes he passed back my phone. He'd only "liked" three people back: a tall, built guy with too many selfies. A dweeby-looking dude with excellent education credentials, but barely any neck.

And Him. Tom Newburn. Older, the oldest end of the spectrum I'd set. Thirty-seven—ten years older than I was then. Square jaw. Slicked back, dark hair. Shapely lips. One child. Liberal.

Within minutes, he'd messaged me. And it occurred to me, as my phone buzzed with a notification, that there was no way to tell when he'd "liked" me first, that he could have been waiting for months, since the moment I'd first logged off the app. And just like that, he pounced the moment I "liked" him back.

Are you a fan of Eyes Wide Shut?

And that made me smile, because that was my answer to the prompt "What's one thing you can never stop talking about?" And I'd said: "Nicole Kidman's poison-green Galliano for Dior dress from the 1997 Oscars." It was a cheeky answer for a straight woman to give; it easily filtered out the men who would automatically dismiss me as a "fashion chick" and swipe left.

I typed out a reply. Then deleted it. Typed it out again. Quinn wasn't paying attention to me anymore; he was back on his own phone. I didn't want his opinion, anyway.

Yes, but I prefer To Die For *if you really want vintage Kidman.*

That was the beginning of the end, I guess.

2

Present day

IN MY MOTHER'S guest bedroom, all I do is sit and think.

Mom never had great taste. And somehow even in this gorgeous landscape, with a view of the mountains, the house itself seems stale and brittle. The cherry-patterned wallpaper is garish, yet somehow faded, though she's only lived in this house for a few years. The curtains are brown and made of hemp, thin as well as ugly. The kissing swans lamp on the bedside table is one she found at a flea market. One swan's eye is chipped.

I'm used to staring at her, the one-eyed swan. I hardly leave this room some days and I know she isn't judging me. Like even my closest friends are.

After all that happened in the city, I needed to escape. I'd grown up in Westchester, a breath away from Manhattan, but when my parents divorced in my early twenties, my dad moved to Seattle and my mom sold the Westchester house and bought this smaller one farther north, in the Hudson Valley.

Mom was almost too happy to take me in. My brothers were long gone—Oliver, living abroad and Theo, in the Midwest. I had collapsed at her feet the moment I stepped over her threshold, choking on the sage she had used to cleanse the house.

She had hugged me, told me it was all going to be okay, patted my cheek, sprayed my pillow with lavender for a good night's sleep. And it worked.

It wasn't until a few nights later, when we were having a late-night cup of expensive, loose-leafed tea, that I remembered why I rarely came up here. Why my mother, with all her supposed good intentions and New Agey "vibes," could be such a damn bitch.

She laid her hand on mine. "I know how you're feeling, baby. *No one* was happy with me after what happened with your father. I was public enemy number one. Remember, your brothers didn't talk to me for three whole months afterward?" She clucked her tongue and I quickly slipped my hand out from under hers, anger simmering at my temples.

"You don't have any idea how I feel. You *knowingly* cheated on Dad with Mike. Mike *knowingly* cheated on Linda with you. You and Dad got a *divorce*, but you did not have fucking blood on your hands." I scraped my chair back, the tea wobbling over and spilling onto the ugly tiled floor, and I went up to my hideous, cherry-lined room and cried. Cried until my head pulsed with it.

As a rule, I don't cry. The sheer effort required to produce tears is too strenuous for me. And when I first heard the news that destroyed my life as I knew it, I didn't cry then either, not at first. It took days for my eyes to shine, to leak. Even sitting at the precinct, being interviewed, I kept a poker face. Refusing to show any kind of perceived weakness, even at that point.

Someone, somewhere, probably on Twitter, called me a stone-cold bitch, sociopathic. But I do possess emotion. I just push it all down, down into the darkest, most unvisited depths of myself: sadness; self-doubt; any kind of wavering emotion that could catch me off balance. Perhaps it was a survival technique. But I've never been in therapy, so who really knows.

Now I'm soft, gummy almost with my feelings. Sometimes I can't control my mind at all; no matter what I do it's just endless, flashing reminders of the *New York Post* headlines, the descriptions, in scintillating, precise detail, my brain a super-cut on repeat.

The odd thing is, it's not the scenarios that my imagination flashes back to me; my mind doesn't project me to the scene of the crime. What flickers through my head are the banner headlines, the bold type, the black italics on my phone screen. I can get lost among the lettering, in the negative space. Even a year later.

I was told not to read any of it.

But of course I did. Of course I did.

3

One year ago

OUR FIRST DATE was at Piccolo Cucina on the Lower
East Side. It was early spring. I wore a long-sleeved black dress
with delicate embroidered flowers and painted my nails my
signature burgundy, coffin shaped. I put my hair up halfway,
lined my eyes. Wore expensive underwear, pink and diaphanous, and black patent stiletto sandals.

He was late and I didn't register when he got to our table.
I was too busy on my phone, catching up on work emails. It
took me a moment to feel him there, to sense that someone
was watching me. When I looked up, he was already smiling.

He wore a navy suit jacket, a light blue button-down shirt
with gold cuff links. Khakis, chinos. He filled it all out nicely.
His hair was combed back. The shirt brought the blue out in
his eyes, faint but there. His face was moisturized; his lips, too,

in a supple, subtle way. Like he took care of himself without any prodding. He looked familiar somehow, maybe an amalgamation of so many good-looking, interchangeable white men whose eyes I've had to meet across Manhattan restaurant tables.

"Have you been waiting long?" he asked as he slid into the small wooden chair across from me.

I slipped my phone into my purse, clicking on the Do Not Disturb tab so the chimes wouldn't interrupt our meal. "I was beginning to think you forgot." I smiled slyly and took a sip of water.

"Forget you? Never." And he waved a waiter over, ordered a bottle of Cabernet.

He asked me about myself and listened. He ordered the tuna. I ordered pasta with ricotta and eggplant. I hadn't eaten since lunch. By glass of wine number two, I was tipsy, letting him in.

"I really liked my childhood. It was quite idyllic, actually. My brothers are four and nine years older than I am, so they could be kind of mean, but always in a loving way. There was never any real tension among the three of us. My mom stayed home. My dad went into the city every day for work, but was always back by six. We had family dinners every night at six-thirty. There were kids my age all over the neighborhood, so I never felt lonely. I miss the house where I grew up. Sometimes I go visit it. It's only twenty minutes away from Grand Central Station. This young, hip family owns it now. Their kids are called, like, Leaf and Orange. Their parents painted the names on this little backyard playground. Do you think it's creepy that I know?" I giggled.

He smiled back, took a sip of his own wine. "Not at all. You're just observant. And nostalgic. Nothing wrong with being nostalgic."

He'd cofounded a logistics tech start-up called SNAPea. He lived in Brooklyn Heights, a different neighborhood from most of his colleagues but he'd loved how picturesque it was, the fermented history in its pretty little sidewalks. He'd grown up in Connecticut. He had one daughter, a three-year-old called Penelope. He was separated from his wife, in the midst of a divorce. "Does that freak you out?" he said, spearing his tuna with his fork.

"Does what freak me out?" My face was glowing at this point, red with drink.

"That I have a kid. That I was married."

I shook my head. "As long as you don't have a second or third secret family, then we're all good."

He laughed. "You're kind of dark, aren't you?" I winked, nodded.

He asked me about my job, which was a win in his favor. A lot of men were quick to dismiss working in fashion, as if there wasn't a whole complicated, intellectual, economic side of it. As if it didn't take talent, drive, a discerning eye *and* business acumen to make it in such a competitive industry.

I was the director of sales at a small, but growing apparel company called Magdelena, named after the founder's grandmother. I loved working there. I breathed it, burrowed myself in it; nothing I did had felt quite right until I landed that job, like I'd been waiting for my life to start. I loved the challenge of expanding the company to new retailers, new marketplaces, the rush of elation when I landed a new buyer. The puzzle solving of creating marketing strategies and watching them take off. The control I had, like I was a small god continuously molding this label into what I thought it could be. The twinge of superiority that came from knowing the company would be a household name in a few years. I loved Huda, the founder, who knew every *Vogue* cover from the magazine's founding to the present day, who made the warmest ginger cookies and the strongest elderflower gin drinks. I loved the clothes, too. Comfortable and chic, forgiving shapes and material. Sophisticated color combinations, sensuous textures and completely seasonless. Things I actually wore in real life.

I had wanted to work there so badly that I found the other girl interviewing for the job, who had gotten as far along in the process as I had, someone whom I actually had met a couple of times through mutual friends. On the night before our final round, I texted her, asking to get a drink, to make a truce of sorts, to celebrate our mutual success thus far. As I knew it would, one drink turned to seven and the poor girl ghosted her 9:00 a.m. interview.

I don't tell Tom this, of course.

I pitied people who didn't love their bosses, whose Sundays were filled with worry and regret about what the coming week would hold. Huda always said that we grew together; when she'd hired me three years earlier, we had been a team of three: her, me and Landen, who took care of all the back-end stuff for the website. Now we were a team of ten. I'd had an intern the previous summer for the first time. There were talks of a brick-and-mortar store opening up in Soho. Though I had less work-life balance than most, it didn't matter. I loved what I did.

"It's so lucky you have a passion. That's what most people need to get through this life. Money is nice. A family is better. But having a passion is what really makes you tick." He stirred his cocktail. We'd moved on from wine.

"So what's yours?" I asked, letting my sandaled foot touch his under the table, a childish but intimate gesture.

"I think that's my problem. I don't have one. I never had one. I just wanted to work as hard as possible, make a lot of money." And he locked eyes with me, holding my gaze as the waiter brought us the check, took our empty glasses.

When we slipped out into the cool April air, he asked if he could hold my hand. He asked if he could kiss me, his lips soft and welcoming. He asked if I'd like to go home with him. He got a yellow cab and I held his soft-knuckled hand as we crossed the Brooklyn Bridge. It was sweet. *He* was sweet.

We only had two more dates after that.

4

Present day

"BITCH, YOU KEEP getting mail," Quinn chirps over Face-Time, giving me a great view of his chin.

"*Bitch*, just throw it out. It's all junk, anyway." I lean the phone against a bedpost and lie on my stomach.

"No, like legit mail. Not just from, like, Spectrum. Come down here and get it." Quinn pouts, his bottom lip looking enormous from this angle. Quinn has the sweetest face, puffy lips and brown emotive eyes, close-cropped dark hair to show it all off even better.

"It's probably more love letters, from all my fans." I smile. There had been a lot of those in the early days. The paparazzi got wind of where I lived in Crown Heights, and thus the public suddenly had access to me, too. When I moved out, I told Quinn to find a place in Washington Heights or something, move to the opposite end of the city. But he refused; he liked our apartment, his ensuite toilet and the skylight in the living room. Who cared if a few weirdos showed up once in a while with death threats for his old roommate?

"I'm not opening your mail for you unless you ask me to, remember?" He puts the phone faceup so all I see is his ceiling. "But I do have to swipe it before that sneaky bitch Hamano sees it. She is relentless with her questions about you. I'm like, call her up yourself. Vera's still *alive*." I giggle. Quinn is the only person who can make me laugh, about this or anything else, anymore. It's so perverted, so dark. But our humor always has been that way. It's when I'm off the phone with him, that I'm sucked back in, that I remember nothing, *nothing* is remotely funny about this. About who I am now.

After I moved out, I started subletting my room to this woman Hamano, who Quinn knew from an LGBTQ Half Asian Pacific-American affinity group he's part of. She was positively starry-eyed when Quinn eventually told her who I was, why I had suddenly departed from the city in the middle of the month. She asked Quinn all about me, all day long, until finally he told her to shut the fuck up or move elsewhere. Clearly, his threats weren't as effective as he'd originally thought if she was *still* asking about me.

"What did she want to know this time? My shoe size or my social security number?" There had been so many trolls in the early days. Men, obsessed with the idea of a woman so beguiling that it would cause Tom to do what he did. Women calling me a gold-digging slut. More men attempting to stalk me at the apartment. Even *more* men trying to find "fun" facts about me; my high school yearbook photos uploaded onto Reddit and dissected by old classmates whom I used to lord over as queen bee. Death threats to my brothers. Death threats to my brothers' kids. A pile of literal dog shit sent to my old office building. So-called witches tweeting at me, asking what spell I'd put Tom under.

Five phone numbers later, after countless letters had been dropped off at my apartment building, graffiti sprayed outside of Magdelena's offices—"cunt killer," which I personally found uncreative and factually incorrect; I had not *killed* anyone's *cunt*—and a full deletion of my social media, I'd moved out.

Quinn said the letters had stopped coming. That everyone, besides Hamano, had basically lost interest in me. I'm surprised when he waves a white envelope on camera, my name clearly written in girlie, looped cursive. There is no return address.

But there's a postmark. And it's from a town I recognize. I swallow back some bile and try for a smile, but suddenly my teeth ache.

"This came yesterday. I swear Hamano was about to tear it open and pretend she didn't see your name very clearly written right here." He points a red polished nail at my name and it's dizzying. "But I snatched it from her. Anyway, I refuse to open it, because that's a criminal offense. So I'm using it as bait for you to come down here to see *moi*." He bats his lashes.

"Throw it away. I mean it." I must sound harsher than usual because Quinn's face softens and he lowers the envelope out of the camera's frame.

"Okay, okay. Whatever the lady wants," he says, trying to lighten the mood. "But please come and see me. Pleeeease. Your bestest friend in the wooorld." He pouts again, and one stray tear trails down his cheek. Quinn has many talents and one of them is crying on command.

With the envelope out of the frame, I can finally breathe. I smile for real this time, and in a moment of gratitude, I acquiesce. "Okay. *Okay*. But none of our usual haunts. Bronx Botanical Gardens on Saturday." Quinn whoops, agrees and his phone slips out of his hand, onto the hardwood floor, and for a moment all I see on his end is darkness.

5

One year ago

I WAS NEVER the sort of woman to cyberstalk my boyfriends' exes. Or really do much social media stalking in general.

I know that a lot of women, before a first date, search the person on Google, Facebook, Twitter, LinkedIn, all the sites where one can find information in this day and age. I get it; we need to take every precaution possible as women. One friend found a date's father's obituary, got too drunk and asked him if he was in therapy for such an unexpected death. The date had looked at her quizzically, with confusion and then disgust, until she realized that he hadn't mentioned that information. Needless to say, they didn't go on a second date.

I preferred a blank slate. I wanted Tom to tell me everything I needed to know autonomously, build up my own image of him. It was more interesting to date that way, without all the preconceived notions I would have had if I searched for him online. He could show me whatever side of himself that he wanted and I would gradually fill in the blanks. Getting to know him wouldn't be tainted by canned information.

That first night, we arrived at his Brooklyn Heights brownstone, red brick with a black oak door, a tall stoop leading up to it. He ushered me into a foyer with high ceilings, reflective walls, splashy art providing the only color against a minimalist palette. We went to his industrial-sized kitchen with a giant stove, an outsize honed-granite island. He offered me a seat on one of its chrome-and-leather stools and poured us each a glass of scotch in cut-crystal tumblers. The ice cubes were perfectly square and crystal clear too, no cloudy cubes in this house.

It wasn't that I was unduly impressed. I'd been in too many enormous, eye-wateringly expensive houses and apartments in New York by that point. I had had nights with men in several-thousand-dollar-a-night hotel suites, men from far-off, unknown locations, spending an evening in the city before they jetted back to Europe or South America or California. My college boyfriend lived on Fifth Avenue. His liveried doorman called me Miss MacDonald.

But with Tom, it was different. Even the nouveau riche possess a learned, blasé way of commenting on their obscene wealth; they swaggered more than their old-money counterparts, but they knew that any display of giddiness or boastfulness was unseemly. Tom, however, exulted in it. He wanted to show off all this extravagance. It was as if he had just won the house as a prize, fully furnished, and wanted to parade his trophy before my eyes. I thought it was sweet, endearing even, that he had the temerity to be so vulnerable. Most men, especially men of power, shy away from any emotion close to excitement.

"Let me give you a tour!" he said, shaking the ice in his

glass. He took my hand and guided me out of the kitchen, into the living room. There were portraits on these walls of his daughter, of his ex-wife, and instead of ducking my head in embarrassment, I went up and took a closer peek. "Apologies for that. This is still half her house, after all." The ex-wife was pretty, tall and dirty blond, a tender smile. Their daughter looked like him.

"It's no problem," I said, before he led me away to another room, a dining room, and then a den, a windowless home office he called his tomb that included an old gas fireplace with a marble surround, wainscoted wooden paneling, slightly cheesy, over-restored nineteenth century hunting-party paintings, each lit with its own brass picture lamp. A mounted fox head or two would have been at home in that space.

Toward the back of the house was a garden. He turned on the lights and we peered through the sliding doors at a swing, a red wagon left overturned near some dying, browned hydrangeas that should have been clipped over the winter months. It occurred to me, then, that though he was giving me a tour, there had been few words spoken. No stories of the architectural history of his house, of the origin of the furniture he collected, of the art on his walls. But I didn't mind. Something about the silence was comforting.

We went upstairs, then, to his library, stacked with coffee-table books, novels on the shelves still crisp and unread. He put on some music, something almost hip like Beach House, and he started talking again.

"What do you think?" he asked, taking a sip of his scotch.

I smirked. "It should be bigger."

His eyebrows danced in shock, before I let a liquid smile appear on my lips. "Oh, good one," he chuckled softly.

"You're so proud of it."

He took off his jacket, ran a hand through his hair. "I am.

I mean, to be perfectly honest, I don't know much about the *things* in this place. We—my ex and I—hired an interior designer to take care of all that. But it's cool, isn't it? This sound system, too, is unbelievable. Sometimes I lie here, on this couch, and put the music on top volume and close my eyes. It almost feels like I'm tripping, to have all those reverberations running through me. The whole home is soundproofed, too, so I never get any complaints."

I'd tuned him out at this point. He looked so cute, so exposed, even in his own home. His dark hair was in little spikes, his button-down rumpled. I stopped him midsentence with a kiss, bit his bottom lip, heard him moan slightly as we began to undress each other.

We didn't finish the house tour. He never showed me what was upstairs. And I didn't care to ask. Maybe, maybe if, when he fell asleep on the couch spooning me, his breathing heavy and loud, his stubble tickling my cheek, I had gently gotten up and tiptoed across the library floor, felt my way up the stairs and onto the third floor, things would be different.

But then again, maybe not. Maybe I only ever saw what I wanted to see. And in some ways, that's the hardest part of all.

6

Present day

I WAKE EVERY morning at six to the whir of my mother's blender. She makes something with lots of kale, collagen, bee pollen. Something that I know people pay at least fifteen dollars for in the city. When I first moved in, I would grumble, throw a pillow over my head and hope to fall back asleep. Sleep was so crucial then. It was my only escape from the frantic thoughts that wouldn't stop churning through my head, no matter what distraction.

But now I welcome the sound. It's like an alarm clock, and anyway, there's no way my mom would have the self-awareness to stop her crack-of-dawn smoothie-making. Most mornings I pad downstairs, make some coffee and sit with her, let her prattle on about how the creamer in the coffee is going to give me cancer, that she's thinking of going to a silent retreat for a week in the Catskills, that if I just learn how to meditate away my pain, my shame, all will be well again. "Nothing in this life is permanent," she likes to chirp.

"How did you sleep?" She's dressed in an embroidered ankle-length caftan, her graying brown hair up in a bun, glasses askew on her nose. "Is the lavender spray still working well?"

I nod and start the coffee maker, something I had to buy because she gave up caffeine three years ago. "All good, Mom. All good." I mix my cancerous creamer into the roast and sit next to her. Outside, the sky is breaking, a breathtaking watercolor of orange and yellow gilding the landscape.

"What's on the agenda today?" She takes a sip of her green drink from a metal straw. She asks me this every morning, even though the answer is always the same: stare at the wall for a while, try to read a book, watch a season of *The Office*. Take another nap. In my old life, I was never someone who dreamt of free time, who relished sitting around and doing nothing. I needed to busy my mind, to always have a project, something to work on, to manage. I would cancel on friends constantly to stay late at the office, preferring the solitude of the empty floor, the dimmed lighting, the hum of the building ventilation system, to most people's company. And there was always more to do, more wholesalers to follow up with, new media requests, expense reports to be submitted, new items to launch online with copy written by an outsourced marketing company but perfected by me.

Magdelena wasn't my baby, but sometimes I felt like its parent. I called it my goddaughter and, in my quieter, slightly resentful moments I would tell myself it was the goddaughter whom I'd adopted. Because even Huda didn't stay as late as I did.

Now, in my new life, with nothing to do, I feel like I'm decaying, like I'm entering a vegetative state that I will never leave. That the frenetic portions of me I reveled in are so dormant that

I'll never be able to resurrect them. If I think too much, let my mind wander, I sometimes imagine my iMessages chirping, people, not a ton, but a few wanting to see me, inviting me places, yearning for my presence, my expertise.

But today is different. "I'm going into the city." Her eyes widen and she claps her hands, her many rings banging against each other.

"Good for *you*! Can you pick up some stuff for me? I can give you a list." I resist the urge to roll my eyes.

"I'm not going to Manhattan, Mom. It's a quick trip." She purses her lips in annoyance and slurps back the rest of the smoothie.

"You should move back there," she says nonchalantly, avoiding my eyes, fiddling with her rings. "I've been trying to *reach* you for months now and I just can't. Your aura is all over the place. I think you need a change of setting."

I grit my teeth. "This *is* my change of setting."

"Yes, but you've been here months now and you won't *go* anywhere with me. Not to yoga, not to lunch. Not even to the movies. No one is going to recognize you here, I promise you that." She begins to run the water. No dirty dishes allowed to sit idly in this house.

I rub my eyes, because I know her endgame. "Fine, *fine*. I'll pick up your stuff. Make me a list and I'll do my best, 'kay?" She turns from the sink and smiles.

"When do you leave?" And I tell her. She offers to drop me off at the train station. A small win. I'll go to Manhattan first, I decide, then make my way up to the Botanical Gardens later in the day.

Around 7:00 a.m., my mom does her second morning meditation. This is usually when I stare at the wall for a few hours, but this morning, energized by the draw of the city, I do something else, something perhaps equally sad and masochistic: I shoot my old boss, Huda, a text.

★ ★ ★

I had spent the previous night googling Magdelena. Of course, I had kept some tabs on the company even after losing my job. Apart from that tiny reversal of having my face and name associated with the company, they had been steadily growing. Features in *Vogue*, *The Cut*, the *New York Times*. A small but hopeful show during New York Fashion Week this past February. An updated Shopify site.

Things were glowing over there. And I should be part of that glow. I *was* that glow for the past few years. Huda had said so many times that I was the one who had made it all happen, that I was her secret ingredient. I ran a tight ship. When I got my first intern, I was a strict boss, maybe too strict, but it made the company skyrocket, let Huda shine while I smiled on the sidelines.

And then I was booted without any credit.

Mom's manipulative trick to get me into Manhattan was the final nudge for me, a sign, as she would call it, that I couldn't wait any longer to confront Huda. So as the train rickets its way down the track, I stare at my phone, waiting for the three dots to appear, showing that she's responding. I know it's a Saturday, but she'll definitely be at the Union Square office. And I know she's seen my message. In the old days, not a minute would go by without a response from her. Once, she took an urgent call from me midcoitus, about a wholesale account for a small boutique in Miami. Now she is ignoring me, and I almost send her a selfie of me on the train to dangle that *yes, bitch, I'm coming. Whether you like it or not.*

It's not until I'm at Grand Central Terminal, detraining, that I finally hear the ping I've been waiting for.

Sure. I have thirty minutes at 12. See you at the Starbucks on Fifteenth.

★ ★ ★

She's late to the meeting, an obvious power move on her part. I pick a table facing the entrance and sip my green tea latte, not even pretending to be busy on my phone or reading a book. I want her to know, from the moment she walks in, that I mean business. I have the file, revenue sheets, articles, meeting notes from the past few years. Physical evidence of my dignity, my worth, all in print on Mom's recycled paper.

When she finally comes in, she's hard to miss, as always. At six feet, Huda towers over most of the men in her vicinity. Her dark hair is chopped into a pixie cut and she's wearing a black sheath dress—ours, I mean *hers*—with a teddy coat, even though it's pushing seventy degrees outside. She has red-heeled booties on, too, adding even more inches to her height.

Since Magdelena has grown, Huda has only gotten more intimidating to look at, a more cliché "fashion" type than I know she actually is. If I were still her employee, if she were still asking me for advice, I would tell her to tone it down. Magdelena is about inclusivity, about stretching what it means to "look" high fashion. I wonder, not for the first time, who she is getting guidance from, who her confidante is now that I'm gone. She has so many more employees now that it could be anyone.

She bypasses the ordering station and immediately sits down, rearranging her long legs to fit around the small table and chairs. She keeps her sunglasses and coat on, too, as if to let me know that she's short on time, that I'm not important enough to merit even a mere thirty minutes.

How things have changed.

"Vera. How are you? How is your mother's?" She purses her lips, her voice cool and steady. No "good to see you."

I know she's not bullshitting her promise to leave in thirty minutes, so I spare the niceties. "It sucks. I want my job back and here's how and why." I open the folder and produce the data I've gathered, flipping the folder and sliding it over to her to review. "It has been eight months since you formally let me go. I've followed Magdelena's growth and I'm impressed. The show looked great. I know your goal was always a write-up in the *Times* Styles Section, so congratulations on that." She offers me the tiniest smile. "The new pant line is superb, too, the techno knit ones, with drawstring waists." I pause, letting my compliments wash over her before I go in for the kill.

"But you need me." I tap the folder. "You're still growing, yes, but as you'll notice in the graph on page five, your social numbers have plateaued since I left. Instagram is stagnant and you're being knocked off in cheaper fabrications. With Barneys closing, you obviously had to rethink some of your accounts. And I admire the ecomm push. I do. But the site isn't up to the standards that it should be for the brand's global reach right now. You need to pivot distribution centers. I'm sure the shopping cart abandonment is through the roof right now with your shipping times." I rattle on, leafing through the pages I've put together, the graphs and plans for growth I'd spent the past week typing out.

Finally, I sit back, take a sip and look Huda in the eyes, or at least where I think her eyes are behind her sunglasses. "Look. As I said, it's been eight months. I'm not self-centered enough to believe that anyone is thinking about what happened anymore. It's not like I'm a criminal. I didn't *do* anything, Huda. If you want, I'd even work remotely from my mom's for a while. I don't have to go into the office." I pause, searching her face.

She sighs, pushing the folder back to me, and crosses her arms. A sad, pitiful smile flickers on her lips. "Thank you for putting this together. It must have taken a lot of work. But, Vera, we replaced you. You know that. There's no position open right now." She bites her lip. "And besides. It just doesn't look good for the company. I mean, firing and rehiring like that just shows a lack of commitment, a wayward message. It wouldn't look good to our current team."

I feel a needling behind my eyes. So swallowing whatever pride I have left, I start to beg. "How about freelance? You can cut my salary, cut my days. Anything. I just need something to *do*. No one will hire me. And you *know* me, Huda. You know how hard I work. You know I basically built this brand—"

It was the wrong approach, that last part, and Huda curls her lips into a pout. "Yes, you contributed a lot to Magdelena. But God, Vera, you made us lose out on a huge investment round." She spits the last part and I quake, my hand clenching the table for support. "Yes, you're smart and capable. But you let your personal life spill out for the whole world to see. And I don't condone that. My employees are *scared* of what your reputation could do to the company. They're a little afraid of you, too. Even if there was a chance of you coming back, I couldn't do it. It would undermine the balance, the equanimity of the entire team. I can't have my employees *afraid* of coming to work every day. I can't sacrifice our feminist messaging by hiring you. I just can't." She combs her fingers through her hair and repositions herself, toes pointing toward the exit.

Her tone softens. "We had a great run together, Vera. I cared about you. I *still* care about you. But as the CEO I have to make tough decisions, and one of them was letting you go. Permanently. You did get a severance package. I'm sure you'll land on your feet. As I said, you're smart, you're capable." She stands up, pushing her chair delicately into the table. "And now I have to go. Best to you, Vera." And she leaves, her boots click-clacking against the floor, the folder that I spent so many hours on lying on the table in front of me. She didn't even bother to take it.

"Fuck you," I shout at her receding back, garnering the attention of a few other Starbucks patrons. The barista on call gives me a *please let yourself out* look. And I do, stuffing the folder into the nearest garbage can.

★ ★ ★

By the time I get up to the Bronx Botanical Gardens, I'm
still livid. Shopping for my mother's dumb herbal tinctures
and overpriced tea leaves didn't help much.

I find Quinn in the rose garden, where we'd planned to
meet, AirPods in, a lilac-colored bucket hat on his head. I
come up to him from behind, reach up and put my hands on
his shoulders so he jumps a little before turning around. He
pushes me back slightly. "Jesus, V. Way to be a freak." He takes
out his AirPods and embraces me. No longer accustomed to
physical affection from anyone except my mother, I stiffen and
he steps away. "Okay, someone woke up on the wrong side of
their mother's guest twin bed this morning."

I roll my eyes. "Nice to see you, too." He studies me, one
perfectly plucked eyebrow rising underneath the brim of his hat.

"The country has not done you good. You're like the first
person who somehow comes back from fresh air looking paler
and more distraught than before."

"Yeah well, I'm not leaving there anytime soon." And I tell
him about my meeting with Huda.

Quinn grimaces. "Oh, God, Vera. There are gentler ways
to beg for your job back. Why do you always have to act like
you're better than everyone at their own job? It's not cute."

I follow him through the garden, not even bothering to
admire the landscape around us. "Because I *am* better than
everyone at *a lot of* things."

He shakes his head. "Defense mechanism."

"What, like you're such a saint? You haven't seen me in
months and the first thing you're doing is berating me." I follow him out of the rose garden and toward the conifers.

"Because you look angry! You have that pinched look between your brows. You're going to get premature wrinkles
that way, you know."

I tug on his backpack, forcing him to stop short on his

walk. "You know how goddamn tired I am of people saying I'm *angry* or *mean*."

He turns around and sighs. "You're right, you're right. I'm sorry. You don't deserve that." And he has to mean it. Because that was one of the many accusations hurled against me. That I was cunning. Cruel. Overly ambitious. Someone with a short temper and a need for things to go her way. None of which was wrong, exactly. I'd always prided myself on my steadfastness, my sharp tongue and inability to bullshit. It's what got me hired at Magdelena, what made me rise so meteorically in an industry that spat people out before they even got a toe in the door. So what if, while I was growing up, people thought I was a mean girl; I didn't care about being nice, especially if someone was wasting my time. But like everything else, all those qualities came back to bite me in the ass.

"Tell me about you," I say. And Quinn obliges. He's a journalist, on staff at a popular media company. His boss keeps assigning him inane topics, silly hot takes on social media trends, interviews with dewy-eyed skincare gurus. He went rogue and wrote this one explosive piece about Korean-pop "schools," these intensely grueling institutions wannabe K-Pop stars go to in Seoul to be transformed into BTS or BLACK-PINK. He had even gotten some interviews with a couple of fledgling wannabe pop stars while visiting cousins in Seoul. But his boss wouldn't publish it. Unlike me, Quinn is not the type to ask for what he wants or admit to resentment when he doesn't get it.

"Did you read my latest on that fitness influencer Marjorie Gerald's kid? Her parents are literally buying her a kitchenware line and saying she designed it, that she's some certifiable cooking genius. She's six!" Quinn shakes his head and takes a quick puff on his Juul. "These crazy rich Brooklyn families, man. I thought I dealt with entitlement when I was in the service industry, but this is a whole other level." He rambles on and I listen, my eyes roving over the crowds at the garden today. Being in the city again, spotting varied faces that don't share DNA with me is bizarre after so many months of seeing no one.

A woman is ahead of us on the path, one hand on her belly, the other clutching a towheaded child. There's a jolt in my brain, a quick flash of Penelope, her brown eyes, full lashes. Of Odilie. Their portraits on the wall in his brownstone. Her picture in the paper. Her pictures online. Her pictures next to mine. I stop in my tracks, close my eyes, clench my fists. My stomach burning, my heart hot.

It must take Quinn a few moments to realize I'm not following him anymore, because the next thing I know a gruff stranger's voice is in my ear asking me to move, people are trying to get by. And then my eyes are open and Quinn is leading me to a bench.

"Fuck. What happened, Vera?"

I shake my head, rubbing my temples with my index fingers. "I don't know. I'm just fucked up. Let's move on. Forget about it." But he takes my hand and pulls me back down as I try to stand up.

"I have something for you, actually. I'm not sure if it'll help."

I grin. "A sedative? I though you weaned yourself off of Xanax a while ago."

He scratches the back of his neck and brings his backpack to his lap, rummaging around in it, slipping out a familiar white envelope. And my heart is in my throat.

"Why the fuck did you bring that here? I told you to throw it away." I scoot away from him on the bench and get up, start to walk quickly away from him, almost colliding with a stroller, another mother cooing at her toddler.

Quinn catches up with me in no time. "Because of that reaction. I think you need to read it."

I fold my arms, glaring at him. "Fuck off, Quinn. I don't need to do anything. And fuck you for taking my mail without asking."

He rubs his face, moving us back toward the side of the path as the mom gives us an alarmed look. "I read it, Vera. You need to read it, too. I think it will help. You obviously know who it's from."

I snatch the envelope from him, wrinkling the paper in the process, filled with rage that he's making me do this, but I know I'll never hear the end of it if I don't. He's carefully slit it open along the top fold, but I tear into it like an animal, anyway. I would use my teeth if I could.

I watch the Michigan postmark tear apart, flutter down to the ground. I don't bother to pick it up.

The letter is on pretty good stock. Not the most expensive, but hefty nonetheless. I focus on this instead of the words, my hands shaking, the flora surrounding me swimming in my peripheral vision.

A Remembrance Ceremony. A celebration of her life, one year after her death. Odilie Newburn, the typeface precious and pink, curly, like an invitation to a baby shower, a wedding.

I tear it up, let the pieces fall among the flowers.

7

One year ago

I CAME HOME after that first date in the early hours of the morning, the sky a breathy blue, the 4 train empty. I had to be in the office in four hours and I'd barely slept, my back cramping from the couch we'd both passed out on.

But I wasn't tired.

Instead, I gently removed my clothes and lay on my duvet spread-eagle, one hand gently placed across my vulva, playing with the thick tuft of pubic hair I'd left toward the top, and looked up at the shadows shifting on my ceiling.

It had been a good night. Drowsy and gentle, rough when I wanted it. Playful, even. More intimate, somehow, than other one-night stands I'd had. The silver-framed photos on a table of his daughter. The pillows picked out by his ex-wife's decorator.

He was helpless, too—before he fell asleep, fast and neat, no sloppy snoring or drool. He said he was lonely, a whisper of a confession, before he slipped his arms around me, cuddled me close like we were young lovers in a college twin, kissed my spine and made me shiver.

I slipped out without saying goodbye, his chiseled face so placid in the twinkling dawn light, his trousers and Brooks Brothers button-down thrown ruthlessly in the corner of the room. His hands clasped across his chest, tightly, as if holding on to a secret.

Eventually, I began hearing the sounds of Quinn waking up, loud cursing as he dropped something on the floor of our kitchen. He startled when I padded in, folding myself into the sofa.

"You just came home, didn't you?"

I nodded, twisting my hair, watching as he stirred sugar into his coffee. "And you didn't say goodbye to him." I nodded again and he clucked his tongue in agitation. "Men aren't as hardened as you think they are. It's nice to make your departure known every once in a while." He poured me a cup of coffee with a drop of cream and handed it over.

"Vulnerability with these guys takes too much effort." I sipped, burned my tongue. "Besides, it's not like I've done an Irish exit recently. I haven't gone on a date in months."

Quinn fiddled with his phone, putting on an NPR podcast through our speakers. It occurred to me that I was disrupting his routine, the quiet hour he cherished before he had to get showered and dressed. "Yes, but before that. You were on dates three, four times a week. And how many did you ghost?"

He was right. But who had the time in this city to prolong a song and dance that took so much energy? If you don't want to see someone again, ghosting was the quickest way to get that point across. I didn't feel great about it. But that was why

I had taken my break from dating in the first place. Regardless of what I did or didn't do, it was always too exhausting.

"How was dinner with Sam and that gang?" I asked, changing the subject. Quinn had seen our old college crew the night before: Sam, his on-again, off-again partner, Evan and Claudia, a group of grungy hipsters who had never grown up, still bumming cigarettes on the back patio of Three Diamond Door every Saturday night, washing their sheets once a month. Giving each other stick-and-poke tattoos and STIs, sometimes at the same time.

"Sam has some artist in residency thing in Hudson starting next week. Maybe you could visit them when you see your mom. Claudia and Evan are the usual. They did ayahuasca together last summer and are convinced they're soul mates." Quinn gave me a little shrug.

"Wasn't Claudia a strict lesbian as of last year?"

Quinn finished his coffee, discreetly turned up the sound of the podcast as if to tell me to shut up. "Sexuality is fluid. They seem happy, I guess? You should come out next time. They asked about you."

I loved Evan and Claudia and Sam. I'd had my fun with them when we were in college; my own stick-and-poke tattoo of an obtuse angle on my left ankle, drug-fueled nights and shaved-head moments. But now it felt like I'd outgrown them. Work in some ways had made my life so small. The people I socialized with dwindled down to Quinn, to Huda. In some ways, though, I cherished that. I liked my own time. I liked my own company. Quinn sometimes said that if he didn't live with me, he knew he wouldn't see me at all.

He accused me, many, many times, of prioritizing work over almost everything, ignoring people with whom I'd had a certain intimacy the moment something else came along, when other goals and distractions overshadowed whatever fulfillment I got from spending time with them. I could be dismissive.

I didn't much care for friends. I wasn't a girl's girl; in fact, other women usually became catty or jealous of me, because of my personality or looks or ambition, who knows. All my closest female friendships had disintegrated over the years, women becoming initially infatuated by my confidence, wanting, perhaps, to *be* me, instead of befriending me. Then becoming angry with me because their boyfriend flirted with me or because I was too honest when they asked my opinion about an outfit or hair color or a personal project they were working on. I wasn't great at being supportive. Once Magdelena began to blow up, other women seemed like competition to me, anyway, potential backstabbers, threats to my growing power. No one was going to undermine or stand in the way of what I'd started to build.

Maintaining friendships, especially with other women in the fashion industry, sabotaged my time, my single-minded pursuit of success.

Quinn and I had something different, though, an extra layer of softness, a security in our relationship that I had with few others. Freshman year at NYU, we had met at a grimy frat party, a far cry from a campus school's raging kegger, but full of hormonal, predatory teen boys nonetheless. Quinn had noticed one guy getting into my space, continually touching my arm, my ass, despite my protestations. Quinn didn't know me, didn't know the guy, but told him to back off, asked me if I was okay.

We'd spent the rest of the night together, sharing fries across the table at a twenty-four-hour diner. After years of being the queen bee in high school, I wanted genuine companionship. I was tired of lording myself over people, having people please me instead of being honest with me. Quinn was my first experiment. From then on, we were inseparable. He was quippy and smart and not intimidated by me; he was the first person who ever called me on my bullshit, saw through my callousness. When he came out as queer to his family, I went to his home in New Jersey and held his hand as he faced his devout Christian parents on their living room sofa.

When he began seeing Sam, I learned along with him about the gender spectrum, about what it meant to date a Black nonbinary person and helped him broach tough conversations with Sam. Quinn, in turn, introduced Sam and me to his father's Korean roots, teaching us how to cook *sundubu-jjigae* and *hoeddeok* and introducing us to writers like Ch'oe Yun and Shin Kyung-sook.

Later, he cheered me on as I pivoted away from the fine arts and applied for internships in fashion, eventually for jobs. When I told him how I screwed over my competition for the Magdelena job he wasn't happy, but he didn't reprimand me, either. He let me be myself, blind ambition and all.

And once we were out of school and work became my life, I didn't feel the need to see much of anyone else, not Claudia or Evan or Sam, even. So in response to hearing that they were asking after me, I said, "I'm glad they're curious."

Quinn dropped his mug into the sink, the ceramic clattering loudly against the metal. "You can use the shower if you want. I'm going to make breakfast." And I was dismissed.

I didn't think about Tom or the date for the rest of the day. Huda called me at 7:30 and told me she needed me to take an 8:00 a.m. call with a Japanese wholesale client because she would be at the dentist. From there, the day descended into its usual madness, my phone's constant chirps and pings and the chatter of our small, cramped office providing the sensory overload that I'd grown used to.

An investment meeting was moved to two weeks later, screwing up our calendar for the month. A few orders were lost leaving our new fulfillment provider, creating not only a customer service hassle but also a headache for our inventory processing software. Huda came in still high from nitrous oxide, and accidentally sent the wrong mock-ups of the fall collection to a top client.

By the time an assistant sent me a spreadsheet organized by first name instead of last, I was on my last nerve, not caring to hide my contempt as I explained her mistake. To my horror, she began to cry, dainty droplets running down her reddening nose.

When she came to me, later in the day, eyes dried and nose powdered, I wondered if she expected me to apologize. I knew I should, and I squeezed my temples, forcing myself to relax, to put on a smile and apologize to her. "V-Vera?" she said timidly, twisting her honey hair with a fingertip. "These were dropped off downstairs for you." And she scurried away from my desk before I could ask anything else of her.

It was an invitation to a private showing of the latest Mark Ryden exhibition. For the first time all day I let myself smile genuinely.

8

Present day

"WHY WOULD YOU do this to me?" For the second time today I'm getting confrontational in a coffee shop. I glare at Quinn from across the table of Pine Tree Café, an un-touched matcha latte sitting between us. "Do you know what it's like to see her name? Do you know how many times a day I want to hurt myself because something reminds me of her? She's everywhere, always. She's my ghost. Jesus Christ, Quinn. What were you thinking? You should have burned it the moment you saw it."

He glances down in shame, taking a spoon to his latte and mixing in the foam. He pauses before speaking. "I think they're trying to make peace with you, Vee. They're telling you it's not your fault. Why else send that invitation?"

I grit my teeth. These are the moments, arduous and

weighted, when I remember how alone I am here. How there is no guidebook to what happened to me, no AA meetings for those who get caught in the crosshairs of violent crimes. That I have no community to turn to, to ask: How do you navigate a friend so naive, so unassuming and hopeful about humanity, that he thinks an invitation like this is an olive branch?

"No one cares about making me feel good, Quinn. Especially not her family. They sent it out of spite. Her sister probably wants to call me out in a eulogy and expose me as some homicidal, soulless whore."

He slurps some foam off the spoon. "Well, at least you look good in black. And you can run in heels so when the mob comes after you that won't be an issue, either." His quips don't make me smile, though, and he casts his eyes back down into his drink. But he looks up again just as quickly, composing himself. "What if it's not like that, though? What if they do want to reach out? What if they understand that this whole horror has caused you pain as well? This could help you, Vera."

I scoff. "I can see the *Post* headline now. Something about being attention seeking, never allowing the family to mourn in peace. A blurry picture of my thong showing through my dress."

Quinn sighs. "It's in the West Village. The invitation said no press. So what's the worst that can happen? We can go, stand at the back, and if someone is a dick we can leave." I give him another deadly glare. "I checked, Vera. After I opened the letter, I checked all the interviews the press did with Odilie's family, and even when coaxed, even when the opportunity was dangled right in front of them to disparage you, they never did. Not once."

My eyes widen and I start to quake again, my fingers tingling like at the onset of tears or a panic attack. After moving to my mom's, and thanks to Quinn blocking certain sites on my phone, I'd begun to avoid all of it, any new mentions or press. I already thought I knew what everyone believed me to be. I'd been smart and deleted my Instagram right away. But I saw it in my Twitter replies, the anonymous emails and letters I received. I saw it in the wary ambivalence of the cop who watched my building because of the press, the way he wouldn't look me in the eye.

Quinn can feel my pause, my momentary inability to respond. Still, he persists. "And besides, you have supporters. People who think you've been unfairly trampled by the media. I wouldn't say you're a trending hashtag or anything, but from what I've seen, it's far from unheard-of to have sympathy for you. You are a victim in all of this, too."

I close my eyes. Open them. "Do I have a fan page?" I ask wryly, and Quinn cracks a smile.

"Not quite, but we could probably make it happen." He finally takes a sip of his latte. "But seriously. I really don't think the family is out to get you. They're decent people who had the worst possible thing imaginable happen to them. And they understand that, in your own terms, this is the worst possible thing that's happened to you as well, even if it doesn't come close to losing a daughter, a sister. I took a photo of the invite, by the way. So even though you threw it away, we still have the information."

I lean back in my chair, almost tip it. "I'll think about it, okay?" And he nods, knowing that that's the best he's going to get for today. "Hamano is going to shit herself. Imagine if she had opened my mail instead of you? She would totally be showing up at this thing, ogling the family, Instagram-living the entire ceremony."

Quinn laughs. "God, I missed you."

When I get to my mom's later that evening, I have the house to myself. I'd called a cab to pick me up from the train station, and the respite from having her in my hair is more calming than I could have imagined.

I sideline all her weird vegan products and boil some pasta for dinner, dousing it with butter and parmesan before taking it up to my room.

This is my usual schedule, since Mom eats way too late for me and I refuse to share the charred cauliflower and bean puree dishes she is always pushing on me. I would eat at the table, but that just gives her more time to nudge me, to berate me and then to talk about herself, to compare some small conflict she has with my own endless inner discord.

My meeting with Huda seems like a week ago now and as I nibble my food, staring at the wall, at the swan lamp with the entwined necks and the chipped eye, there's the deep, jabbing reminder that I'm back at square one. No one is giving me my job back. No one is giving me my life back.

I remember, in the house in Westchester, forcing my big brothers to help me cut out the outfits I saw in magazines, pasting the pictures on sloppily drawn paper dolls I'd made, and then directing Oliver and Theo to parade my gang down the staircase banister, demanding they hold the dolls right, make sure their two-dimensional outfits found the best light.

As a teenager, I'd been a fine artist first with an expertise in collaging and figure drawing. I'd gone to NYU to earn a BFA. But my childhood love of fashion—the production, the aura and sensibility and mythologies around different designers and labels stayed with me and eventually became my new passion. I realized, during a summer internship at alice + olivia, that it was the process of it all, right down to the branding of the designers themselves, that really interested me. I knew I could make a career out of building up a brand, positioning it uniquely in a world already saturated with new, innovative companies. That was where the real authority lay; everyone thinks it's about the face of a brand, the designer, but the real power lies in the direction, the execution.

And I'd done that. I'd been Huda's fucking camel the past few years, carrying her load, doing all her work, building Magdelena into what it is today, with absolutely no thanks. No credit. Scrubbed away from the website the day I was fired.

For the alice + olivia internship, for all of my internships and jobs following that one, I'd done all I could to make myself the leading candidate whenever a bigger position opened up at that company or the next one. I was always the most polished, the most presentable, the most articulate, the hardest working. I developed new strengths, like becoming a data-analysis whiz and a spreadsheet queen. And always, I was the chosen one. Oh, I had my techniques. I gathered intel from eavesdropping, checking bosses' emails, figuring out who else might be hired on my team. I would research them, ensure that there was no way they could eclipse me. I'd mention in passing how *disorganized* I'd heard that other high-powered fashion person could be, or drop a hint about how a prospect had only gotten ahead because her daddy's law firm represented Condé Nast. I landed an "it girl" to be brand ambassador for a fledgling streetwear company I briefly worked for, because her agent had a huge crush on me, which I encouraged, of course. I routinely took advantage of coworkers' weaknesses. All to stay ahead, ensure my path. But who am I now?

I place my food at the foot of the bed and go to the dresser drawer and retrieve my piece and weed, pack a bowl. I sit back on the bed to smoke, watching the ghostly tendrils pirouette around me before evaporating. I sit, head against the wall, until my brain is a little muddled, my limbs languid.

And then I get my phone out and download Instagram.

I create a fake account and type Odilie Patterson Newburn in the search bar and wait to see what pops up.

Of course, there are a bunch of memorial pages. Strangers, sob sisters, people lurking on the sidelines who revel in reposting images of her. But finally, I find her account, the fifth hit, Odilie_000. The account is public, and the last post is of her in Michigan with Penelope, stooping down to give her daughter a kiss, the picture filtered subtly, tastefully. Her pregnant stomach protrudes the tiniest bit.

She has a few highlight reels, one titled Food Snaps, another titled Antigua, another titled Penelope <3. She has 8550 followers, which I'm guessing is about double what she had when she was alive, considering all the rubberneckers. She seems to have kept a pretty consistent style throughout her grid, similar colors and filters. Nothing feels out of place.

She posted at least once a week, which strikes me as bizarre given the advent of Stories. But they're all classic Instagram, especially back a few years ago: pretty sunsets, rosebushes, avocado toast, pink smoothies. It's all very wholesome with short, sweet captions filled with emojis. Comments from other women saying how great a photographer she is, even though anyone could do what she's doing with a good iPhone and the right filter.

There are a few pictures of Tom, which I rush past, that I refuse to keep my attention on for too long. "Hot couple alert!" reads one comment; someone years later responded, "This didn't age well." I scroll up again, briefly, to more recent years. The birth of Penelope, which, like Kylie Jenner's newborn post of her daughter, has the most likes of any of Odilie's posts I've seen aside from the final one of the two of them. In the neonate photo, Penelope's infant feet are clad in tiny pink slippers, her face rosy and wrinkled as a Craisin. Immediately after are photos of small Penelope, sound asleep in a bassinet.

The last in the series is a video of Tom holding her, rocking her, singing to her so softly I can't make out the song and I pause against my better judgment, my fingers ready but unable to flick out of the clip.

His arms caressing this fragile creature, they look so big, like slabs of meat, his whole chest so thick and brutish against this tiny, tiny human. The way he sways with her, like he doesn't quite know how to do it, moving his hips slowly like he's uncertain if he's ready for this, if this is the new life he wants to lead, with this tiny flesh bundle as the center of his universe. The universe that he probably dominated up until this point.

Or maybe I'm projecting.

I click out of the video and continue scrolling. More baby pictures, more stylized, colorful brunches where she's photographed alone in front of savory dishes. She doesn't seem to have many friends or doesn't want to present herself as someone reliant on them, rather; in many of her photos, I imagine they're the photographer, out of frame. If she is with other women, it's in a formal setting, like the pictures of her and Tom. Even her food pictures never include another plate, just the typical bird's-eye view of what I imagine are her meal, her drinks. Of course, the comments are flattering, but they're superficial, a lot like the "perfect couple" one I saw earlier; there aren't any hints at inside jokes or callbacks to other times. Her page, I realize, reminds me of a brand, the overly cheerful tone almost suitable for an inanimate *thing*, a kind of message that she wants to get across, revealing nothing about the person herself.

There's something eerie about that, almost chilling, and I decide to navigate out of the page, when I spot a flash of navy that makes me pause. It's from one of her later photos, the ones I haven't studied too carefully, and I click on it to enlarge it.

Odilie is standing in front of a mirror, her hair done up in a twist, her lips painted red, wearing a navy sheath dress.

The mirror is ornate, gold with a spiky rim, and the room behind her is vast. It doesn't seem like it's her home; at least I don't recognize it. But it does seem familiar to me. The whole photo seems familiar to me.

That dress, it's Magdelena, one of my favorites and one of our biggest sellers. It's stretchy and comfortable, wraps around the waist nicely with an adjustable self-belt, allows for a touch of cleavage with its low V-neck. I own it. I used to wear it all the time and I would recognize it anywhere, Huda's signature white patch pockets sewn on either side of the dress.

It's not that bizarre that Odilie would own this piece. It *was* a hit and Odilie was certainly in our demographic. But it's the place, too, that's bugging me. Something about the whole image is bugging me, like I've seen it all before, set on a different stage.

I exit out of it quickly and scroll down, all the way down to ten years ago, to her first block of posts, the colors so grainy and oversaturated I'm immediately transported to the early ages of the app. And then I've reached the end of her profile. So I'm forced to stop, sit back, my head on the window adjacent to the bed.

Now what? What was I doing? Why, suddenly, do I so desperately want to map out the life of a woman whose death ruined mine? But I know why; it's because of what Quinn said, the delusion of connection with her, with her family. I want to know her, perhaps, so attending her Remembrance Ceremony won't seem like such a farce.

Maybe I just want connection in general. At the end of it all, Quinn was the only person who really stuck by me. All those people I called friends, whom I worked with, whom I went to college with, disappeared at a time when I needed people on my side the most.

I take a pause and bring my pasta bowl down to the kitchen

to clean. I spot a bottle of wine tucked in the back of the fridge and serve myself a huge glass. I'm about to go upstairs to finish whatever I'd started, when Mom comes bursting through the door, smelling too strongly of the jasmine essential oil she's covered herself with today.

"Did you get what I asked for?" she says by way of greeting and I nod, eager to slink off to my room with the wine. "Great! Don't you want to hear about my date?" I'm about to say no, but she launches into it, sitting herself down, waving her bangled arms as she talks. They met in yoga, of course, he owns a restaurant in town, he paid for her dinner, they're astrologically well matched, he has a mustache, which she doesn't love, but her psychic told her she'd meet someone important this month, so it must be he.

"I wanted to go back to his place, but I told him I had a sick daughter at home, that I could *not* leave her for the night." She plays with her scarf, decorative, gauzy and colorful, not exactly made for warmth.

"Your sick daughter?" I snort.

Mom pouts. "Well, I didn't want to explain your whole situation."

"You should have just gone home with him." I pick my glass of wine back up and prepare to go upstairs.

"You know I'm not like that. Never on the first date." I stop, my shoulders flinching. It's such an obvious barb, a victim-blaming dismissal, just how I was portrayed in the press. But Mom doesn't even realize what she's said; that's how self-involved she is. Her own world, her own sense of self, always comes first.

She wasn't always like this. I mean, she has always been self-obsessed, maybe more vain or preoccupied with her own goings-on than most moms. I remember getting an A in physics, or making the winning goal at a soccer match, and her response would always be to praise herself for how good a parent she was.

But at least back then she was involved, more willing to sit with me and let me cry, tell her mundane things about school, my friends, my teachers and extracurriculars without interjecting. She attended all of our shows and games and exhibits. She pulled out all the stops for our birthdays, always knew exactly what we wanted for Christmas. She was present.

Since the affair and the divorce, though, she's shifted. Her charmingly eccentric obsession with tarot and ghosts and mediums that peppered my childhood turned into a cliché; another white woman trying to find purpose by changing her diet, investing in crystals, energy testing and ancient medicines, the last of which are either quackery or else completely appropriated from Indigenous cultures. It's like when she left my dad, she left behind any semblance of self-awareness.

The affair, thankfully, had taken place when I was already out of the house, in my last year of college. It was with my dad's best friend, Mike, whom I'd grown up knowing. A tall, portly guy who lived nearby in Westchester and worked in contracts law. My brothers and I don't know many details. We each received a call from my dad on the day he was moving out and then a few months later he was living in Seattle full-time, as far away from his ex-wife and ex-best friend as he could get. As far away from me, too, and that made me ache until it didn't.

I gulp down the wine and set the glass on my dresser, before crawling back into bed and waking up my laptop. I put on some music, a lyric-free band that I used to study to, and start my journey upward into Odilie's life, or the life that she wanted to present to the world, an illicit, yet possibly expiatory activity.

Younger Odilie is different. And I don't mean in the ten-year-age-difference kind of way. She's not the woman I saw glimpses of in photographs at his house, or online after her death—or even later in her feed. Her nose is wider, her lips thinner, her eyes hooded and rounder, her body much softer. When I squint, I can recognize her, somewhere in the depths of her old face. But if this wasn't her profile, I would never have known it was her.

The pictures of her are chaste. She has limp hair and no style. "Cheap prep" is what I would call it if I wanted to be cruel—Aéropostale polos, poorly fitted jeans—and she hunches in on herself, like she's not quite sure how to fit her body into space, like she wants to make herself smaller.

She grew up in Wyneck, a coastal town not far from New York City that is known for its wealthy summer residents, which I first learned only because of a throwaway line Tom said to me, about Wyneck and how much he hated it, hated having to go there and navigate the social scene, hated the sweat that collected under his shirt from the reverse-chic lack of central AC. Later, her parents moved to Michigan.

I let myself wonder, briefly, how he met her. If, eventually, she moved up to New York and found him there. If their worlds collided earlier than that, in Wyneck. I wonder if I'll be able to map it, if there will be an indicator of when they got into a relationship, when they got engaged. I'm sure there will be because what else is Instagram for?

One New Year's Eve, Odilie posts a very poor photo of fireworks. "Who wants to be my New Year's kiss?" It's cheekier, much more provocative than most of her captions, and I wonder if she was drunk when she wrote it, why she didn't delete it the next morning, what kind of message she's left by letting it linger there. There are a few comments, a couple by men who want Odilie to "find them in the New Year." Nothing from Tom, though. That chapter of her life hasn't started yet and I wonder when it will.

At 2:00 a.m. I finally place my phone down, my temples aching from staring at a screen for hours on end. And in that moment, in the darkness of my room, it floods back to me what I've been doing, whose life I've been meticulously combing through for the past few hours. I shut my eyes and lie down.

Why am I doing this? What do I gain from reliving the life of a woman who is dead? How could this possibly help get my life back on track? I turn toward the window, where my empty wineglass sits on the sill.

I can't untangle the reasoning, how I went so suddenly from cowering at a card postmarked Novi, to trying to know her, to understand her in all of her iterations, for the past decade. It's like what Quinn told me opened a well in me, a need to comprehend. Before, I had simply accepted the fact that this woman's life, and death, were attached to me for the rest of *my* life, like a necrotic appendage.

But somehow, humanizing her has paradoxically made me feel better. Like I'm bringing her alive again with a few clicks. And that's just it. At least where I'm at in her timeline now, she is only showing what she wants others to see. There is no sense of invasion, no feelings of excavating a corpse. All I have encountered is an average girl, with a somewhat boring life, who somehow made her way into the upper echelons of New York, into Tom Newburn's arms.

I roll over, close my eyes and hope that she doesn't show up in my dreams.

9

One year ago

I STILL DIDN'T text him after he sent me the invitation to the exhibit. I wanted to wait, to push him, make him salivate a little so that when I did return his message agreeing to go, he'd remember how much he wanted me. I stayed late at the office that night. Huda and I ordered food from Thai Villa, getting pad Thai sauce all over our desks and keyboards. Neither of us were clean eaters, ever.

I liked those nights when it was just Huda and me. It reminded me of the early days, the scrappy intimacy we shared, working out of her leased walk-up in Williamsburg before she moved to Manhattan and got a real office. Huda was married, but you wouldn't know it. Her husband was away half the year, working as a travel journalist, and when he did come home,

he was still a fairly mysterious figure. Always in Huda's background, shy and reticent around her friends and colleagues.
They'd married when they were very young, straight out of
college, but had known each other far longer, having grown
up in the same Greek Orthodox community. Huda would
say that she felt like she'd been married to him for her whole
lifetime, that the months they spent apart barely registered.

But like Quinn, she was always keen to know about my
dating life, so after we finished our work and made some gin
and tonics using the communal ice machine, she made me get
her up to speed. I'd told her I'd had a date that week.

"Ooh, I'm going to google him!" she squealed, wheeling
her chair over to the one giant desktop computer that was by
the intern station. Before I could protest, she had some Forbes
profile up. "OMG, he's hot. That chiseled jaw, wow. And
rich." She scrolled through the article before getting bored
and going back to his Google results.

"Stop. You know I hate to google them this early," I whined.
She clicked on one profile of him in Bloomberg and started
skimming.

"You know how nuts that is? What if he was a serial rap-
ist? Or dated someone you knew? You always have to check
these things." She went back to the Google search page again.

"I've made it this far unscathed. Besides, until recently, my
middle school poetry was like my first hit. I wouldn't want dates
prejudging me for that." But she was already clicking on a *Times*
article, which happened to be his marriage announcement.

She turned to face me. "You know about *this*, right?"

"Of course. They're separated. In the midst of a divorce."

She raised one eyebrow. "Are you sure?"

"Well, I slept over and there was no one else home. I guess
I have to take his word for it." But Huda was already going
onto Facebook, typing in his ex's name.

"OMG, I especially don't want to Facebook stalk *her*. That feels like a total invasion of privacy."

But Huda clicked. "Trust me, I'm doing you a favor." I turned away and went to fix us more drinks. Within a moment, though, she was calling me back over. "You're safe. He's being honest. He's not in her profile picture and she has no relationship info."

And a small part of my chest that didn't know I was worried, let alone *cared*, unclenched.

"You're going to be a stepmommy, though. He has a kid, if he hasn't shared that crucial piece of information yet." She clicked out of the profile, her mission completed.

"Shut up. We went on *one* date. You know how much of a slut I am." Huda snorted, took her cup out of my hand and downed a big gulp.

"Yeah, you do not like settling down. But maybe a once-married man is the one for you. He's mature, so he probably wants something more serious. He'll respect your career. He probably won't expect to see you every day, just how you like it." I grinned, sloppily, the drink going to my head. I always respected, even admired, Huda, but these were the moments during which I forgot our power dynamic completely, the fact that she had this knowledge about me, about my essence that usually only a close friend possesses. Some would say it was a dysfunctional work relationship. But I didn't care—yes, she was my boss. But she was also one of my best friends.

"You haven't texted him back, have you?" She gave me a sly grin and wheeled the ergonomic chair over to my desk, plucking my phone off the charger and typing in my password. She was already into my contacts by the time I got over there. "You don't even have his number saved? That is *cold*." She handed the phone to me. "Well, you're lucky. 'Cause if I'd found his contact I would have texted him for you."

"Trust me, I know you would have," I muttered and clicked on my iMessages, finding his number and tapping a few keys before putting my phone down again. "You win. I texted him, agreeing to go to the Mark Ryden show with him."

She squealed again. "He's the one. I can feel it."

I had mentioned to Tom how much I was dying to see the Mark Ryden show at the Paul Kasmin Gallery. That when I had gone, one Saturday afternoon with Huda, the place had been so packed that we could barely get a glimpse of any of the paintings before being shoved aside by a mob of tourists, iPhones lit up, so many voices making the space shrill with noise.

I had said it in passing, when he asked me who my favorite contemporary artists were. I'd made some joke about how I was betraying my gender by admiring Ryden instead of a female artist. He'd acknowledged the comment, but we'd moved on to another topic quickly, and I hadn't even remembered the conversation until that invitation for the private viewing appeared on my desk.

We were meeting for a drink beforehand and I found myself fussing around with my hair, my clothes, in the hours between work and our 8:00 p.m. meetup.

I stood in front of the three-way mirror in my bedroom, trying on and discarding dresses, jeans, skirts, boots, heels, trendy sneakers. I felt like I was in seventh grade, getting ready for a dance, before I hit puberty, before I became somewhat feared and popular.

I finally chose an upcycled, black vegan leather skirt from our last collection, ankle boots and a black-and-white silk vintage YSL blouse with pin dots. I made Quinn take pictures of me, tasteful and artful with the mirror reflecting dozens of versions of me, my red lips striking against my pale skin and with my espresso-brown hair falling in waves past my shoulders. Secure with herself. I opened Instagram to post the pictures.

Huda was making us boost our personal Instagram presences. She preferred traditional influencer pictures—of people at brunch, poolside, on West Village streets. I was a little more opaque with mine, more landscape shots, cool architecture, not as much of myself. I knew she would be happy with this post. She always said, "Vera, you exude such confidence. You should post more images of yourself on socials. If nothing else, it'll help the brand."

As I walked to the train, I watched the likes roll in. Huda had also forced me to make my account public, so a lot of them were from wannabe influencers, people who want free gifting from Magdelena, men from across the world whose DMs, asking me to meet them in Budapest, Tel Aviv, lingered in my inbox.

I got a few glances from men on the platform as we waited for the train together. Like most women, I'd been getting looks like that since I was a teen. But unlike some women, I was able to harness that power a little bit earlier, to recognize it and use it to my advantage. I knew I was pretty, beautiful even. As a little girl, I'd been told as much by shopkeepers at boutiques, by relatives at family holidays. Later, from older men after they'd had too much to drink. That knowledge was how I climbed to the top of my small high school's social ladder, the perennial popular girl destined to fall from grace, to topple mightily later in life. Except, I hadn't. Not yet.

I thought about this as the train jerked its way north, on my way to a date with a man ten years older than me, who was so clearly using his wealth and connections to woo me. I didn't speak to anyone from Westchester anymore. I had dismissed them as soon as I showed up at NYU. They were part of a Suburban Vera that I wanted to shed as I metamorphosed into City Vera. I followed a few of them on Instagram, though. Their lives seemed stable enough. Most of them worked in finance, or were marrying men working in finance, living lives less interesting than, but somewhat parallel to, mine in the city. What would they think of twenty-seven-year-old Vera, whose power and influence seemed only to be on the verge of growing greater?

Quinn always made fun of me for being popular in high school. I was the only one of our college friends who had been, and in the early years of our friendship he would introduce me as "Vera who was prom queen twice." I insisted that I wasn't mean, that I was a benevolent overlord to my Westchester disciples. But that wasn't true. If I wasn't an outright bully, I had definitely excluded people, wielded my power over them in order to assume authority. And I asked myself why? Why did I need to do that? Was I just another teen girl with a narcissistic mother who took out her anger and sadness on her more submissive peers? It all seemed so cliché, so *afternoon special* to me, far from what I wanted to think my psyche was like, that I tried not to dwell on it too much. I pushed it out of my head as I headed into Manhattan.

This time Tom showed up first, in another light blue Brooks Brothers button-down to bring out the blue in his eyes. I spotted him from outside, before he spotted me, sitting in the corner of the dimly lit restaurant, a bottle of champagne already cooling on the table. I took a breath before fully entering and watched him all alone. He wasn't fiddling with his phone or checking his watch. Instead, he was staring straight ahead, eyes alert and focused. But it was hard to read what he was looking at, besides the wood paneling of the bar.

I finally walked in and he found me instantly, before I even had time to pull my back straight, make my presence known in the room. He stood up when I got to the table and gave me a hug, his arms compressing me tightly against his chest, almost restrictive.

"Fancy seeing you here," he said, his lips quivering into a smile as we both sat down. I took a sip of the champagne sitting in front of me and smiled back. It was funny seeing his face again, a face I had seen and touched, but had already become a sort of blotted mirage in my memory. It seemed more off-kilter this time, less proportionate. I noticed the tiny twist at the end of his nose, the way his upper lip puffed out and overlapped his bottom lip. The tiny shaving nick below his left ear.

"I'm excited for this show. I'd never heard of Ryden before," he said, taking a drink from his own glass. "But I looked up his stuff. Kind of weird, isn't it? Wouldn't have pegged you as a devotée of weird neo-surrealism."

I blinked, the champagne bubbles watering my eyes. "That sounds quite dismissive, doesn't it?" I gazed at him over the rim, watched him squirm.

"No, no. I mean. I'm excited! You're just full of surprises, Vera. That's all." We continued to drink, trying to decide if we should order food or not. I asked him about his workweek; he said a few things that I barely listened to. He asked about mine and I gave the bare minimum answer. The champagne bottle was emptied. No food was ordered, and I found myself, for the second time, tipsier than I would have liked in front of this man I barely knew, who I wasn't even sure I liked.

"Nice exit the other night, by the way. Made me feel like I was in college again." He poured me the last of the champagne and I watched it fizz down into a mere drop. "I looked for you in the morning. I roamed the halls of the house, saying your name. It was very ghostly, very Victorian gothic. Vera echoes nicely in large Brooklyn brownstones, by the way."

I smiled, despite myself. "Yeah, I'm sorry about that. I'm

bad at mornings, you know?" A waiter came with the bill and Tom slid his Amex into the check sleeve. "There's too much intimacy in waking up next to someone you barely know. The morning breath, in a strange bed—or couch. We're both sober. Whatever fun we had the evening before has dwindled and been forgotten, replaced by whatever inane responsibilities we have that morning. It's a lot to navigate with someone you've known only a few hours." I watched the waiter take away the check.

"Well, what if you got to know me for longer than a few hours? Would you stay over then?" He looked at me inquisitively, the question so genuine that I had to catch myself before I blurted out something I may have regretted.

"How much would it matter to you?" I replied coquettishly.

He dropped his hand on the table, inching it closer to mine, his cuticles so well maintained, the nail beds scrubbed so clean, that it almost looked like he was wearing clear polish. "It would mean a lot."

I fumbled then, dropped my hand back to my lap, averted my gaze from his penetrative one. "You know, it's a little odd to be asking that on a second date."

He sat back, keeping his hand where it was on the table. "I know. But I'm almost forty. I'm not looking to play games. I'm sorry if that was too direct. I'm sorry if I'm awkward. I haven't dated in a while, as you can imagine."

And he did sound apologetic. His gaze fell to the floor; he rubbed the back of his head sheepishly. That was what took me in, made me walk my fingers over to his and graze them. The self-consciousness. Because what gave me more of a high than having the power? Sure, he was rich and good-looking. But he *was* fumbling. He was being too earnest. And that meant I could twist him any way I pleased. I was used to the loud, self-indulgent air that most men, especially the older

ones, give off. The arrogant self-preservation that they ex-
uded when they were called out for their shortcomings, their
vulnerability.

He was doing the opposite. That was what hooked me.

We left the restaurant, somehow hand in hand, the gallery
around the corner, a light misting of rain coating the sidewalks as we dashed over toward it. It felt romantic. And when
I looked at him, by the artificial light streaming through the
gallery windows, before we walked in, I barely noticed the
imperfections. His face was somehow symmetrical again, chiseled and precious and twinkling.

10

Present day

THE NEXT MORNING I awake dry-mouthed and dehydrated, the sticky wineglass hovering on the windowsill like a mocking reminder of indolence. I really hadn't drunk that much since coming to live here, so my tolerance is low. Apparently, one or two glasses is enough to do me in now.

The house itself is quiet like it was last night, and I wonder with a tug of trepidation if Mom is out again with her new beau. From the light shining in the window, I'd guess it's probably early afternoon already. I'd somehow slept through the blender's whirring and her departure. But I decide not to trudge downstairs, make my coffee. All my hands want to do is grab my phone and get back to my late-night activities, despite that ache I felt, the gnawing self-doubt about the reasons behind my fascination. Something about the new day forces me to put all of that aside, my brain refusing to relapse back into my guilt, resisting the impulse to examine this perversion.

I switch to my laptop, my hand still cramped from holding my phone and scrolling last night.

It's winter. Odilie posts photos of the snow, idyllic and otherworldly, outlining the trees, blanketing the roads. She posts a photo of spiked cider she's made, the blurry face of someone in the background, whom she calls her roommate in the caption, not tagged.

Odilie gets a new cell phone, an iPhone 4S. She takes a picture of it with her digital camera. I had the same one, much to the envy of my classmates.

Odilie posts a wider shot of herself behind a receptionist's desk, face peeping out, the desk itself still decorated with garlands and wreaths even though Christmas is long gone. I google the name of the office, hashtagged in the captions. A dental practice. The website shows a gleaming staff, all with straight, white teeth, a Wyneck address. I wonder if the 4.5 star Google review they get is accurate, whether it was a good place to work. Odilie doesn't post about it much after that. I wonder how long she stayed.

More photos of her weekends. Some goofy Apple Photo Booth photos. It's all so mundane, and yet I keep scrolling. She's still her old self in all of these photos, round with a choppy haircut and thin eyebrows. She gets a tattoo of a butterfly on her ankle.

Odilie dyes her hair a platinum blonde. Then she dyes the ends pink. Then, just as quickly, she goes back to brown.

Someone gets a dog, a Chihuahua called Cookie; Odilie poses with it. Then a few posts later there's another picture of Cookie, asking if anyone wants to take him in, the dog's eyes sad and wet.

Then, more meals, more landscape shots. The beach at sunset, a boat out on the water, the empty main street of Wyneck before all the summer residents flocked there, like the town is taking one last deep breath.

And then it's summer and I recognize her.

It's so sudden a change that I check the date of the photo posted, positive for a moment that I accidentally scrolled too far up. She's posing alone on the beach, the camera zoomed in on her face, her smile wide, teeth achingly white. The water is stormy behind her, though the sky is a clear blue.

Her lips, stretched into a grin, are what I notice first. They're plump and pink, almost juicy. She definitely got injections. The rest of her face is made up, her nose contoured, but not necessarily different. It's a lot closer to the nose she had when she died, but not quite. She clearly had more work done later, got the tip refined.

Her brows are filled out, too, her round eyes more pronounced. I can't tell if it's a fox-eye lift or if it's natural, but they're artfully shadowed; the shape is finally filling out her face in an alluring way.

But there are other things, too. She's fresh-faced, dewy even. Gone is the wobbly black eyeliner I've seen in most of her pictures. And her hair has highlights and is cut into a severe, shoulder-length bob.

Her body itself is all angles. No softness or roundness around her thighs and face. Her hands are bony, her oversize magenta nails almost clownish against the daintiness of her fingers.

She is still young, about twenty. And there's something so sickening, so strikingly sad, that she felt such an urge to reconfigure her face and body. The cosmetic surgery, the makeover, that I can understand. But her poor body looks sharp, her skin draped over jutting bones where there once were curves.

She looks like herself, though, much more like herself. If herself is the one splashed on the cover of the *Post*, on the nightly news, in a retweet comparing our faces. As if looking at her cherished, overrefined face next to mine would somehow make me admit to a wrongdoing the world believed me to have committed.

Her eyes, they're almost vacant, despite the toothy smile. She reminds me, I realize, of the women I grew up with in my hometown, who gave up their careers to raise children and resented it, but actually derived pleasure and meaning from the PTA meetings, the bake offs and Unitarian church services they attended. It's as if her direction, her goal in life, has taken another course.

But how? When did this happen?

The front door bangs open against the foyer wall and I bolt up, the laptop falling to the floor with a crash. I check the screen quickly, make sure everything is in working order, before I minimize the Instagram window as I hear Mom approach my room. It's like I'm in high school again.

"It's almost 4:00 p.m., Vera. Are you seriously still in bed?" Her voice screeches and I wince. She rarely raises her voice above the gentle yogi lilt she has taken on, so when she does, I know she has had a bad day, that her inner irritated bitch, the one I know is always hiding not very well under her performative, relaxed demeanor, has its claws out.

"What's up?" I say nonchalantly, not willing to engage with her judgment.

She stands in the doorway, her jacket still on, her hair done up in some bizarre topknot-adjacent look that would probably flatter someone about twenty to thirty years younger.

"Guess who I saw at the farmers market?" I wriggle my feet under the covers, the arches tensing with her tone. Of course, she doesn't let me guess. "Candace Roberts. Remember her?"

I don't, but I decide not to answer because I know she'll bulldoze over anything I have to say. "She was in your high school graduating class. She was part of that whole PTA fiasco your freshman year, if you recall?" She folds her arms and I wince again, the pang trembling to my toes.

Candace Roberts. *Candace Roberts.* She'd been my friend for about three weeks of freshman year when she first moved to Westchester from some unknown southern city. Or at least unknown to me at the time, though it was probably something like Atlanta.

My friends and I had invited her to a slumber party, our annual one at the start of the school year. But then two weeks in, she got her period for the first time and didn't know where the nurse's office was. So she walked around with a wad of toilet paper in her underwear and then that slid out in PE and she was toast. There was no way we could have a newbie, public period shedder at our slumber party. We said it was canceled.

Someone put up photos of the party on Facebook. In one of those photos, my friend Ashley had accidentally spilled red nail polish all over her pajama bottoms. And oh so cleverly I'd pointed out in a Facebook comment "Ha! Ash, you're such a Candace Roberts! She wasn't invited but she still showed up!" Of course it was a dog pile from there; the comment went semi-viral in our school, and again, Candace was tortured in the halls because of her menses mishap.

And my mom got a call from Candace's mom, yelling, calling us mean girls, saying that she was going to phone the school and tell them we were bullying her daughter. Of course, that only made her less popular. Soon she'd faded into obscurity, and from my brain apparently, for the past fourteen years.

My mom, though, harbored this deep resentment against that whole situation. She'd been demoted from the PTA, asked to be a note taker instead of a chairwoman. That was the real tragedy of the situation, in her mind. And nothing has changed since.

"Well, Candace and her husband bought a house around here. A weekend home. She's pregnant, too. They live on the Upper East Side. Her husband's a lawyer. She's glowing. But of course, she didn't even have to ask about you." Mom twists her face up into a grimace. "She didn't even pretend. She went right in and said, 'Oh, you must be so concerned about Vera. And to have lost that amazing job, too? Gosh, I can't *imagine* it. And what that poor woman's family went through! You just must be so, so concerned. I met James when we were in college, so I never had to go on those dating apps, thank *God*. Look at the kind of men you find there!'" Mom shuts up, finally, and shakes her head. I remain unmoving, breathless, waiting for her next barb.

"You know what, Vera? I've let you hide out here too long. You need to stand on your own two feet again, deal with this mess in your wake. A mess that *you* got yourself involved in with your bad judgment. You're twenty-eight years old for God's sake. No matter what you say, we all have a hand in the cards that we're dealt in this life and you fucked up. And by the way, your stupidity hasn't just impacted *you*." She pauses, huffs out the rest.

"How do you think it feels to see everyone else's daughters getting married and having their own kids? Getting on with their lives? It's so embarrassing. God, your brothers were just so much easier." She flings open the door and stalks out, stomping her way back downstairs. I hear the clang of the teakettle.

Before I can process any emotions, sit with Mom's words too long, I text Quinn.

Kick Hamano out. I'm coming home.

11

One year ago

THE MARK RYDEN show, without crowds, was exquisite. I spent what felt like hours marveling over every intricate detail, following every infinitesimal brushstroke. Tom didn't trail me around the gallery as I feared he would. Instead, he wandered off, studied the works that interested him. Not nearly as long or as carefully as I did, but I appreciated his independence.

Soon, though, after I'd walked around the space two or three times, he approached me. "They creep me out a bit. I mean I think I *get* it. But I wouldn't want one of these hanging in my home."

I nodded. "They're supposed to creep you out. But I know what you mean. I wouldn't necessarily place one on my bedroom wall, to spot in the dark. Those bulbous heads aren't for everyone." I drifted off to *Allegory of the Four Elements*, but this time I looked back at him, beckoning him to follow me. He stood beside me, and I felt him watching me study the work.

"If you could buy any of these, and *not* put it on your bedroom wall, which would you?" he asked, almost in a whisper, his breath hot on my ear. I paused, so aware of his body adjacent to mine, wanting both to take his hand again and shove him away. Ask for space and lean into him.

"I have a reproduction of *Rosie's Tea Party* that I've hung in the bathroom of my own apartment. It's kind of an inside joke between my roommate and me. He hates it and it's the first thing you see when you walk out of the shower. But that isn't my favorite." I twist around and head to the northern part of the gallery, around a corner and to one I've only allowed myself to look at once so far, so I could savor it later, spend several minutes lingering over it before we inevitably had to leave.

"This one. If I could buy any it would be this one." He stood where I was, planted his feet next to mine and looked up, mimicking my perspective, the tilt of my head. We gazed at it together. *Sophie's Bubbles.*

"Understood," he said after a while, putting his hands in his pockets, leaning back to take in the canvas.

"You going to buy it for me?" I asked, turning to face him, this time watching him study the work.

He chuckled. "I don't want to make any promises. But if that was your one wish, to touch this painting, I could probably make that happen for you."

I smirked at his pomposity. "Is there anything you *can't* do?" He stepped away from the painting, giving me a wide berth, and eyed me.

"Apparently get you to sleep over."

I took his hand again and whispered, "Let's go back now and we'll see how long I stay." I felt him shiver as my breath tickled his lobe. And we were off, into a cab, back to Brooklyn Heights.

★ ★ ★

It was the presumed power that I fed off, the glimpses of vulnerability from the kind of man whom I'd rarely seen show emotion, let alone candid interest in someone. I was a game player because I expected it, because I had never really known anything different. And I always believed that was where one's power in dating lay, one chess piece ahead of the other person. But I hadn't realized how incredible it was to *know* that person's feelings for you, and manipulate that vulnerability however I saw fit.

I stayed that night. When we got to the brownstone he made us martinis, plucking the olives out of a jar with a toothpick. We sat outside, in the little garden with the swing set, empty and desolate-looking under the moon. He spoke some more about his childhood. He grew up middle class in Connecticut. His mom was a physician's assistant, his dad "worked in insurance." He felt slighted and thus ostracized because he didn't get into the schools his brother had attended. He felt slighted and ostracized in general from being in the shadow of his big brother. He thought he had a mild form of dyslexia that was never diagnosed. He wasn't popular in high school, he said, or in college. But something changed when he entered the working world, in finance. By the time he started his own company, he had discovered a confidence and self-possession that he hadn't been able to attain in any other situation.

"Because you were destroying the world, finally. You had power," I said nonchalantly. He paused, imbibing that sentiment.

"I guess you're right."

I plucked the olive from his empty glass and slid it onto my tongue. "I'm always right." He leaned over and kissed me then, so, so gently that I almost thought it didn't happen, a mirage of a movement. But I pulled him closer, pressing harder, our teeth gnashing against each other. And then we were going upstairs, not to the second floor but to the third, to the master bedroom this time. The thought flickered, as I noticed the vanity, the screen in the corner painted with images of women bathing, that this was his ex-wife's domain. That she existed within the drawers and closets, if not at that moment, then at some moment not too long ago.

I pushed that thought away, luxuriating in the high thread count sheets, closing my eyes as he slid off my skirt, shutting out all corners of the room until all I could see was the light behind my eyelids, all I could feel were his movements, the tender ways with which he held my body, his breath brushing it. I'd never had sex with a man who enjoyed kissing to the degree that he did.

So I stayed. When, finally, he turned to me and said he was going to sleep, that I was welcome to join him, I obliged. The bed was comfortable. I felt at ease. He wrapped himself around me and then unraveled himself as he fell deeper into unconsciousness. I lay awake, noticing the outlines of the sparse furniture in the dark, but soon sleep took me, too.

I woke up the next morning alone in the bed, the sun drenching the sheets and pillows, my naked body. I watched shadows flit across my exposed torso, tore off the covers and felt the prickle of my hair standing on end as my body cooled down. I liked it there, without him, for the moment. It didn't occur to me to wonder where he'd gone and I didn't hear any noise from the bathroom, so I continued to stretch like a cat.

In the daylight the room appeared even more opulent and expertly designed. The bed's headboard, I noticed, was kelly green and plush velvet, the bedposts carved with an interlacing floral design, crawling up like ivy from the bed. The walls were painted an almost unsettling white, so bright and clean that it was an anomaly that anyone lived there. I guessed he had staff, people to come in every day to scrub the dirt off, repaint as needed.

I stood up, noticing the angora rug, as white as the walls, covering the floor at the foot of the bed. It felt so good on my bare feet, the softness seeping in between my toes. I could roll around on that and be happy, I thought, wrap it up and wear it as a shawl.

The only other pieces of furniture in the room were the vanity and screen I'd noticed the previous night. The vanity was huge, with a three-paneled mirror, clusters of brushes all organized by usage and height in various cases and jars. On the maplewood tabletop sat a perfume flask, purple crystal. I spritzed some on my wrist, inhaled the lavender scent. I pulled open one drawer, was met with a tray of lipstick in every shade of red imaginable, organized from the brightest to darkest.

I gently closed the drawer, tempted suddenly to go look into the closets located on the far side of the room, their handles big and bronze, incised ornamentally like the headboard. But that seemed like too much of an invasion, to go into another person's closet. I didn't want to know what his wife wore, what her sense of style was like. After sleeping in what used to be her bed, entwined in her sheets.

I stepped outside the room and opened the door just to the right.

It was his daughter's bedroom, painted a startling silver, shelves and crates filled with toys and games crammed into every nook and corner possible. It was clean, though, immaculately so, like the master bedroom, the woven rug in the middle with jumping sheep lint-free, no childlike stains.

Near the bed was a mobile with stars, multicolored and metallic, like a Dorothy Gillespie sculpture but less bristly. I touched one, hesitantly, watched the individual dangling star swing in space, catch the light from the window.

And then I felt a hand on the small of my back and I turned around, to him.

I remembered, then, that I was still nude save for my underwear. He was dressed in an expensive-looking sweatshirt, nice-fitting jeans, scruff on his face and a greasy paper bag in his hand.

"I thought you had left," he said, kissing my forehead. "That I'd failed."

"I was giving myself a tour. I didn't know where you'd gone."

He shook the paper bag, the smell of bacon wafting out. "Breakfast. You looked pretty sound asleep." And I followed him back into the master bedroom, the breakfast soon forgotten as we got back into bed, the rest of the morning slow and luxurious, tantalizing and gratifying.

It didn't occur to me then, that the vanity so plump with cosmetics, could be a warning sign. That a child who apparently lived with her mother, wouldn't want to take more of her things with her. For all my streetwise knowledge, my self-defense skills, it didn't matter. I wanted what I wanted in those moments and I devoured it, without a second thought.

12

Present day

WE GIVE HAMANO a week to leave.

We aren't cruel about it. We actively help her find a place. She's subleasing anyway, with the original stipulation that I could come back at any time. I don't feel bad.

Mom gives me money. She wants me out of her hair so badly that she just forks over enough to pay for a few months' rent, and then some. I didn't ask. In fact, we don't speak again after she exploded at me. I just check my bank account the following day and suddenly there's money in it, transferred from hers.

Within the week we give Hamano to move out, I pack. I avoid my computer except to network, look for job leads. I take with me things I should have removed long ago, old clothes and books and magazines I coveted as a kid, that Mom has put in storage in her attic. I don't want to come back here. I don't want any excuse to face her again.

I get groceries delivered to me and make a filet mignon in her vegan kitchen, refusing to air out the smell. I fry up eggs, let giant wheels of brie grow runny on her counters. When she lights incense, I cough loudly. When she sprays her essential oils, I open a window. I play loud, angry late 2000s rock and roll when she does her yoga, a far cry from the pop-y, upbeat music I'd actually listened to during that era. It's such a pure, clichéd form of teenage rebellion that I dance, too; dance in ways I haven't moved my body for months.

She doesn't approach me or confront me about any of it. We can tell when the other is coming down the hall, in the kitchen, so it's easy to avoid each other. For those days before I'm finally out, we're just two bubbles, never touching lest the other one bursts.

I've never fought with her like this before. Even as a teen, silence was never my strong suit. But her words, the blame she's so eager to use as a barb, they've seared me so much more than the same ones printed over and over again in all those rags ever did. They were from my own mother. And hurled at me when I had just begun to unpack whether they were really true.

I text my brothers, in Chicago and London. Our communication is sparse. Of course, they reached out when it all happened, especially when people on Twitter began threatening their children, but beyond asking me if I'm okay, we haven't been keeping in touch.

She'll calm down and apologize, says my oldest brother, Oliver, in London with his British wife and twin babies. Theo, who has been living with the same girlfriend for close to a decade now, is more straight up. *She's batshit. She's always been batshit. Don't take anything she says personally. I know it's hard. Sharon hasn't spoken to her in a year because she complained, loudly and*

*meanly, about us not getting pregnant. Stay strong. You're welcome
to come out here and stay with us for a little while.*

I would almost take him up on the offer, too. But even
after everything, I can't imagine leaving New York quite yet.
I just can't.

I call my dad in Seattle one evening. It was a strange decision, when he moved out there. I'd never even heard of him
liking the Pacific Northwest, let alone wanting to live there.
But he was retired and after the situation with my mom and
Mike, I guess he wanted a clean break. He says he loves Seattle,
that there's a calm to it that he could never find in New York.
That the air is fresher. He made friends easily. He's dated, too.
And I'm happy for him. But it does hurt, sometimes, that he
moved so far away.

My dad has always been even-keeled, to a fault. Soft-spoken
and gentle, loving but a little distant. He echoes Theo's thoughts
about having me come stay with him and I decline.

"Your mother, she's lonely, I think. All of you kids are living your own lives. The boys are away. But you know how
she is. She feels a certain way then she gets tired of it just as
quickly. She welcomed you with open arms and then decided
she couldn't support you anymore. It's not about you, sweetie.
These are just her ways. She'll eventually apologize. She probably felt guilty the moment after you had your fight, but pride
is preventing her from doing the right thing." He pauses. I
hear him take a sip of water.

"And you. Are you okay?" His voice strains. He'd been so
tactful about my whole situation, never asking outright about
anything that happened, always sidestepping any overt mention of that nightmare. Thankfully, the online trolls mostly
kept away from him, probably because he is so offline that it
was harder to dox him.

"I'm okay, Dad. I'm okay," I answer. I hear him pause again, the beat of silence allowing him to form his next words.

"Nothing that happened was your fault, Vivi. You know that, right? You'll get up on your feet again. Life will move on. No one will associate you with this in another year. You've always been so high-spirited, so ambitious. I'm not worried about you. Go back to putting that energy to achieving great things and I promise you, you'll land back where you want to."

We say our goodbyes after that and I continue packing, letting his words wash over me. How am I supposed to put my energy into something else when I have all this time alone with my mind? I sigh, stuffing clothes into an empty duffel I found in the back of a closet.

I'd been good about not going back on Odilie's Instagram the past couple of days. Instead, I'd been on LinkedIn, emailing old industry connections with my résumé. I was okay with a pay cut. I was okay with a demotion, even, if it meant I could work again. But so far, crickets.

Huda seems to have a particular stronghold in the industry right now. It makes sense, given how explosive her growth has been, that no one wants to be disloyal to her, or get on her bad side, by offering me an interview. And of course, my name doesn't help. The fact that Magdelena's investment loss was my fault isn't exactly a secret, either. It doesn't matter how much experience you have if the moment someone googles you, you're associated with horrific crimes, whatever my dad says.

In the wake of these rejections, Odilie's Instagram is beckoning me again, enticing me to lose hours to scrolling. And there's the itch to know what happened to her face, to figure out why her looks changed so dramatically. So much to know about a woman to whom I'm so intrinsically tied, whom I never even met.

So that evening, after I'm done packing and have left my

suitcases by the door, I don't sleep right away. Instead, I bring up a bottle of wine, a glass and log on, darkening the room, so the only light is from my Mac.

The tab is still open, right where I left off on that picture of her with her contoured nose, her sparrow-like bones. Maybe it's futile to try to find a sign, something in earlier photos or comments that I missed before, but I'm too curious. So I scroll back a few posts and inch up the screen, much more slowly than I did before. And I start reading the comments more closely.

And then, under a filtered picture of the beach, I see it. A comment I must have missed from a woman named Thelma Kay. "Loved our chat and drinks. Can't wait to do it again soon! xx." I click on her profile, but there's almost no information; her profile picture is a silhouette of a woman. The account is set to private.

I switch back to Odilie's profile and scroll back up to the initial photo, the one with her new face. There are fewer likes and comments on this photo, I realize, than most of Odilie's previous posts. Fewer of her friends are impressed, showing their love.

It's so, so late. And I want to get out of this house as soon as possible tomorrow morning. So I close the laptop, plunging my room into darkness, and slip under my mother's ugly comforter for, I hope, the last time.

One year ago

QUINN COMMENTED ON my glow as soon as he saw me that evening, back from my daylong date. "I made extra toast this morning and lo and behold you weren't even in your bed!" He sat in front of our TV, balancing a container of Pad See Ew on his knees when I shuffled in. Tom and I had stayed in bed for a while, until I eventually fell back asleep, awakening to dusky light filtering through the bedroom's large windows. He was propped up in bed reading.

"I can't remember the last time I stayed in bed this long," he said, kissing me as I stretched. "It's nice."

"This isn't my usual routine, either. But you're right. It was nice." I languidly got out of bed, started putting on my clothes. It *had* been nice. A little too nice. I was afraid of how late I'd stayed there, of how long I'd lain there asleep, inhabiting this bed that wasn't mine. I told him I needed to get some work done for Huda, that I hadn't realized how long I'd slept.

He walked me downstairs, retrieved my jacket from the closet by the front door. "Next Wednesday? I'm not letting you leave until we have a third date planned. I know you want to slip away." And for a quiet moment his eyes glistened so coldly, flashing with an emotion I couldn't quite place, maybe hunger. Ruthless and insatiable.

And then it was gone. He was warm again, a playful smile curving his lips. "So Wednesday?" he repeated, and I said yes, Wednesday. Before rushing out into the evening, down the steps and onto the sidewalk.

It had been fun. I hadn't even been aware of how comfortable I'd been until getting on the subway, my mind playing the past twenty-four hours in a loop.

"Do you like him? Daddy?" Quinn twirled a noodle with his chopstick. I rolled my eyes.

"We're not calling him that."

"That's what he is though, right? A literal daddy. But don't dodge the question. Do you like him?"

I sighed, took off my shoes and got comfortable on the couch next to him. "It was nice. He's kind of sweet. I don't really think he knows how to date yet. It's a little weird but kind of endearing. Do I like him, though? I'll let you know on the third date. He demanded it to be on Wednesday."

Quinn arched an eyebrow. "Demanded?"

"I'm telling you, I don't think he really knows how to date. He was with his wife for a while." I crossed my legs on the couch and tried to steal a bit of food, which Quinn swiftly moved out of my reach.

"I've never heard you be so soft on someone before. Especially a man. He still can't demand you see him around *his* schedule. You know that, right?"

I grunted. "Of course I know that. I'm just kind of touched, you know? That he remembered how much I like Ryden, that he was so vulnerable with me. It gives me a high, having access to that kind of male vulnerability." The last part dropped out of my mouth before I even registered it. But it was true. It had always been true. And in the past maybe I would have used it to my advantage. Maybe in the present, too.

It was unseasonably warm on Wednesday, almost summer-like. I had sweat through my work clothes as I descended into the subway, my cotton Magdelena T-shirt sticking to my back, my long hair tied up and twisted on top of my head. I'd felt guilty leaving Huda as the rest of the team cleared out of the office. She had to go over the expense reports tonight, her least favorite activity. Attention to detail, budgeting for the next month, that was my job, to guide her in the right direction. But she waved me away. "I know you have a date tonight. I'll be fine. You can fix my mistakes in the morning, anyway." I acquiesced, told her I'd be back in the office as early as possible.

I was excited for the date. It had been so long since I'd been genuinely excited for a date, instead of ambivalent, almost forgetful that it was happening at all. I examined my thoughts about this, tried to analyze them into rationality. He was definitely occupying brain space that was usually filled with a laundry list of other things: buyers I needed to contact for work, trade shows and events I had to organize, what food I needed from the store for that week. Instead, his face kept coming to mind, chiseled and handsome, almost stoically so, his imperfections becoming more and more idealized in my head, as if the chemicals in my brain were erasing his flaws.

He was taking me to Selena, a restaurant by the Brooklyn Bridge on the water. The obvious course of the night would be a walk back to his brownstone. I tucked a toothbrush into my purse. I almost brought a change of clothes but decided against it. I would just come home before leaving for the office. Or, worst case, I'm sure I had some clothes stashed in my desk somewhere.

I chose a white eyelet baby doll dress with piping, its edges frayed the tiniest bit, an intentional deconstructed touch. I'd found it at an Upper East Side Housing Works. It made me feel young and innocent, like I was playing dress-up. I put on too much blush, bright pink lipstick. I kept my hair knotted on top of my head, put on tiny silver hoops.

Now that it had cooled down, it was gorgeous outside, the sky so many variegated, orangey hues. By the time I got up to Brooklyn Heights, the sun was officially setting, but still the sky was a molten pink, the colors mirrored in the water.

He had an outdoor table, with a direct view of the sinking sun. He was on his phone when I approached, his brow furrowed, typing away at something. He didn't even sense me near. I had to reach out, touch his shoulder, before settling in the chair across from him. Even when he looked up from the phone, his gaze was still confused for a moment, like he didn't expect me to show up.

"Vera. I haven't ordered drinks yet," he said, his eyes darting away from mine, over to the water.

"That's okay. I'm capable of choosing my own libations." I opened the wine menu lying in front of me, perused it, deciding on a vodka martini. I expected him to chuckle, but he was shifty, tapping his fingers on his phone case. I found that, without his inquiries, I didn't have much to say to him at all. I wasn't certain how to begin the conversation.

"I'm not sure why I chose outdoors. It's going to get cold when the sun goes down. We should try to go inside." A waiter came to take our orders. He asked for a vodka martini, too, without looking at the menu.

"I like it. I want to stay out here," I said, taking a sip of water.

"There are too many people, too much going on. We're right by the park." He pinched his nose, ran a hand through his hair.

"What, are you embarrassed to be seen with me?" I meant it as a quip, a joke. I'd never spent time with anyone who would be embarrassed to be seen with me. If anything, it was quite the opposite.

But he paused before smiling. And for a vicious, mocking moment I felt something I hadn't in a long time: insecurity, a deep-dwelling shadow of a feeling, one that I couldn't quite define until he plastered a benign look back on his face, pretended I hadn't ruffled any feathers.

"Of course not. You look beautiful." But it wasn't the answer I wanted.

The martinis came. I gulped mine down. "Who is here, Tom? Who do you not want to spot me? And why?"

He took a sip of his own martini, eyed me, sighed. "I shouldn't have made reservations here. My ex and I used to come a lot. For anniversaries and birthdays, that kind of thing. I keep thinking she'll pop up. Or one of her friends." It was the first time he'd mentioned his ex so explicitly and I realized I didn't even know if she still lived in this neighborhood, what her life was like.

"But who cares, right?" He chuckled at that, took a long, smooth sip of his martini. The olives looked like eyeballs at the bottom of a jar full of formaldehyde.

"She has her friends, you know. Who keep tabs." He jerkily reached out his hand to me, grasped my fingers. "But let's forget about that, okay? I want to focus on you." I didn't grasp his fingers back. Instead, I felt my gaze hover over all the other diners, trying to decide who had been the trigger, the one who had made him anxious.

The rest of the dinner went fine, if not a little stilted. We discussed work mostly, a recent acquisition he had made that I'd seen a headline about in the news. Dry stuff. We ordered steaks and they were dry, too. I watched him raise his voice at the waiter, imperiously ask him to serve us rarer meat. It made me sour seeing that; I cast my eyes to the ground, sat on my hands. He was right. It was cooler now that the sun was down.

We left the restaurant both visibly agitated. He tried to take my hand as we walked out, toward the promenade, and I didn't oblige. We walked in silence, sidestepping dog walkers and late-night runners. On the grassy enclaves dotting the promenade, people sat and picnicked, even as it grew later. I was jealous of them, suddenly, laughing with their friends, cuddling their dogs, pouring wine into Solo cups. I rarely wanted to be with people my age, but at that moment I did, desperately.

And then his phone went off, shattering our silence. He looked at the caller ID and groaned, pocketed it. But as we continued south, it rang again and again and he didn't silence it. Until eventually, I touched his elbow and said, "Please get that. For my own sanity." And he did, walking away, leaving me stranded in the middle of the walkway. I wasn't quite sure where we were headed, even. I just wanted to go home.

I could hear the tone of his voice even from several feet away. Seething with vitriol, almost tangible in its righteous anger. He wasn't even speaking too loudly; it was the body language, his clenched fist, the way his jaw moved. I could see it all from the lights lining the promenade. Whoever had called him wasn't letting him off the phone, either. And after about ten minutes I started walking away, out of the park, taking out my phone and studying Google Maps to figure out where the nearest subway station was.

I was walking toward Court Street when I heard my name. He was a block behind me, jogging toward me, in too good shape, too close to evade. I stood by the subway entrance and waited. He didn't even have to catch his breath once he stopped short in front of me.

"I'm so sorry about that, Vera. It was my ex-wife. Penelope

has the sniffles. She wanted me to check the name of some kid medication back at the house, so she could buy it. But I shouldn't have picked up. I was spending time with you. Come back to my place? I'll make it up to you."

I felt my lobe. One of my hoops had fallen out. "I hope she feels better. But I think I want to go home tonight." I started making my way down the stairs, but he grabbed my arm.

"Please, Vera? I fucked up, I said I shouldn't have picked up. Forgive me?" His eyes were wide and moist, almost manic in the light filtering out from the subway station.

"How long ago did you separate from your wife?" I asked before I could think.

He stepped up a stair, away from me, but still holding my arm, his grip tense, reddening my skin. "About a year ago. We'd taken breaks before that, though." In the light I could see his razor burn.

"Well, she doesn't deserve to be talked to like that, especially if she's saddled with your sick kid." I shook his hand off my arm and continued down to the station.

He walked behind me, his shoes scuffing the backs of my feet. "Come on, Vera, don't be like this. It's one fight you overheard. You have no idea what she was saying on the other end."

I turned to face him before going through the turnstiles onto the platform. "Can you leave me alone? I just want to go home for the night. I've had a long day." His face tautened, his lips twisting into a grimace. I backed farther away, the ghost of his hand still gripping my arm, tapped my debit card at the turnstile and pushed my way toward the other end of the station.

I wondered if he'd follow me. But when I looked back there was no one there, only the dingy walls of the station, someone using quarters to purchase a new MetroCard. I sighed and stepped onto the arriving train, leaving the night behind me.

14

Present day

I FIND HAMANO'S hair everywhere. On my vanity, in the corners of my bedroom, silky strands in even stranger places, like my windowsill. I vacuum it all up, sage the apartment— at the end of the day, I *am* my mother's daughter. Quinn yells at me to open a window. The woman downstairs with the loudest dog stops in her tracks when she sees me, as if I'm an apparition. I move past her, a swift ghost haunting her.

I missed this apartment. The sunny windows in the living room, the way one flame on the stove never comes on. The ugly light fixtures and the dust collecting on the spines of the books on our giant shelf. I missed Quinn and the way he whistles in the shower and the smell of his organic laundry detergent and the coasters he uses on the already protected living room table.

It's good to be home. And after one day of it, we're going to the West Village for the ceremony, and I wake up drenched in sweat, moisture slicking the backs of my knees, the nape of my neck, panting out a few breaths. Tom was in my dream. He was there, at the ceremony, and he came up to me, he kissed me, loud and smacking, and the sound, it echoed across the room. And then he devoured me whole, bits of my flesh spitting out of his wet lips as he chomped down. It hurt. It hurt in the dream, even though you're not supposed to feel pain in them. And maybe I wanted to hurt, like she did, venom choking her into unconsciousness, into death.

I take time in the shower, conditioning the ends of my hair, staring at the water spiraling down the drain, imagining blood making the water red, her blood. And then there *is* blood and I realize I have my period, that it's come early, and it dawns on me, not for the first time, that Odilie will never have bodily fluids again, that adolescent Penelope will never know if her mother would influence her to love or to hate what she sees in the mirror.

I wear a billowy, unassuming sponge crepe dress, nude pumps, a long, loose eggshell-white spring coat that grazes my ankles. I put on only a dab of makeup, something to hide the blueish tinge under my eyes. I chopped my hair off when my longer locks were in the news. Now it's shoulder length, ratty and split since I haven't had a proper cut in six months. I twist it up, attempt to put it into a bun. Look in the mirror and wish, wish so hard that I'll like what I see. The way I always used to.

Quinn meets me in our living room. He grabs my hand, kisses it, gives me a long look. "You know I'm not pressuring you to go to this thing. I'm the one who shoved it in your face, who suggested it. But we can back out whenever you want. We can leave as soon as we get there. We can go get brunch instead."

I take a breath, close my eyes, think of young Odilie with her overplucked eyebrows and shy resignation. I want to go. I want to go and see her people. I want to know her as a living, human thing. Not as my foil, not as my tragedy. "Let's go," I say, and he holds my hand as we descend the stairs.

It's in the courtyard of an apartment building, ornate and sunny. I wonder who is hosting. It must be a friend. Do they know that I was invited? I keep my sunglasses on as we cross the large mosaic-tiled lobby. We're stopped by a mustachioed guard from the security detail. No press. He makes us drop our phones into a bucket, checks us for cameras, other devices. We meet his standards and are ushered in.

Quinn takes my hand again. I take a breath and hold it. We walk down a mirrored hallway, past an elevator bank. Until finally, finally, we're at the courtyard, one windowed door propped open. And all I can see for a moment are prismatic hues, the helix of colors and sweaters and plants and sun blinding me.

And then we're outside in the fresh air, claiming a pair of seats at the very back, the last line of chairs arranged pew-style.

No one has given me a second look. Not yet.

Up front, there's a microphone, two large photos of Odilie. Someone is passing out programs. Quinn takes one. I don't. My chair is at the end of the row, so fortunately, no one can sit beside me. But a distinguished-looking older couple takes seats next to Quinn. And I know immediately they'll start chatting to him because he has that effect on anyone above the age of sixty.

"I'm glad they're doing this now," chirps the old woman. "It's more decent this way. None of those vultures trying to get a look inside the town house. I'm Paula Edwards, by the way. This is my husband, Hank. We own 159 next door. I remember when they moved in. Seemed like a perfectly happy couple to me." Quinn nods along, keeping his fingers entwined with mine.

"You know, I always say to Hank that I never trusted him.

We had adjoining gardens and he would always lie about what new construction they were going to do. But she seemed nice. She really did. Her poor soul. What a thing to happen on our quiet street. No one's made an offer on it yet, though I'm sure it'll be snatched up within the year. I've heard, though, that there are a lot of legalities tying up the property. Shady stuff, if you ask me. He was such a dog, that man." She clucks her tongue. "Anyway, how did you know them?"

Quinn is saved from answering. A tall, blonde woman in a turquoise caftan has approached the mic. She's welcoming everyone. She introduces herself as Louisa Bennington. She thanks someone called Shirley for her hospitality, for allowing this event to be hosted here. She reminds us that we're celebrating a life, not mourning a death. That she encourages everyone to donate to an organization fighting intimate partner violence. That there will be Aperol spritzes, Odilie's favorite, and some light hors d'oeuvres after the speeches, the performances.

I feel dizzy. The scent of lavender washes over me, planted in this garden, this courtyard. I'd smelled it on her, not on her, related to her. The perfume on her vanity that I spritzed onto my wrists. How naive was I? Her stuff was just lying around and I believed his bald-faced lies, never questioning.

I close my eyes, squeeze Quinn's hand as hard as I can. Panic, cold and dark and seeping, is erupting inside me. I keep my eyes closed, my alarm preventing me from standing up, from leaving, from moving an inch. From hearing whatever is going on toward the front. Instead, there's just a dark buzz threatening to erode my consciousness.

And then.

Quinn is lifting me up out of the chair and leading me toward the edge of the courtyard. Everyone is getting up. The ceremony is over and I somehow blocked out the whole thing. "Are you okay?" he whispers.

"No. I think I need to leave." It was a bad idea coming here today, with the wafting flowery fragrance, the people, too many people in one space who knew her, who loved her. And who am I? Some fraud, some harbinger of unsettling, horrific harm. What was I doing? What had I thought I was going to glean from this? This wasn't only bad for me, it was bad for them, too. All I could possibly bring these people was misery.

I step back into the building, into the cool marbled lobby, away from those hordes, when I feel a tap on my shoulder. Quinn shields me, tries to hustle me away. But I turn, out of instinct, or some rusty part of me that used to know how to act at parties.

When I turn, I see Odilie as she was ten years ago, that face peeping out of caked-on makeup, poorly dyed hair. "Vera! I wanted to say hi before you left. I'm really glad you came. It means a lot to us." I gape at her for a moment, her smile kind, even as her eyes are red-tinged, her mascara and liner smudged by tears. "I'm Page. Odilie's sister."

She must have spoken at the ceremony. It must have been obvious that I would have known who she was. And yes, Page, of course, Page. Odilie's little sister; she'd posted one photo of them together. And now she'd morphed into a woman a little younger than me, so hauntingly like Odilie that it was like seeing a ghost.

"Page," I say and she leans in for a hug, long and tight. "Good to meet you."

"My parents, my family, they'd love to meet you. I know you were on your way out, but if you could just stay one more minute?" And I'm being coaxed back into the courtyard, toward her family huddled at a table, strangely segregated from the rest of the group, as if they're the outsiders here, at the anniversary of their own daughter's death.

And for the first time since I got here, I can feel the thrum of murmurs. Out in the open, in the sun, people are recognizing me. No roar. Only a quiet rush of whispers, eyes on my outfit, my shorter hair. But Page is pulling me forward into the thick of her kin and I can't turn away now; I can't get lost again in the crowd when she seems to be pulling me inside something.

We reach the table. And then I'm thrust into outstretched arms, my nose buried deep into a blue cotton sweater. It isn't until I step back, away from the embrace, that I realize who is holding me so tightly. Odilie's mother, small and round, hair short and blond and curly. Pink lipstick. Earnestness radiating from her like dust motes when you beat an old rug. I can feel the stickiness of her lipstick stain on my cheek.

"Vera," she breathes, her eyes dewy with unshed tears. "So good to finally meet you." She clasps my hands, her carefully filed nails digging into my skin.

"Likewise," I mumble. The sun suddenly seems too hot, the glare penetrating my sunglasses, forcing me to squint behind them.

Odilie's mother, whose name I still haven't caught, gestures at the small knot of people. "Here we have Audrey and Laura, Odilie's cousins. My husband, Richard. Dorothy and Eugene, Odilie's aunt and uncle. Penelope is staying in Michigan, with our neighbors." The relatives wave at me and I forget all their names immediately, my hand still hanging limply in hers. They're all clustered around this table, looking bemused, grieved, uncomfortable.

"We're so very happy to meet you," says Odilie's dad, the one who was sick, whom she was taking care of while Tom was with me. Her dad looks frail. He's white-haired, his skin nearly translucent, veins purple and gnarled. His eyes are blue, but almost filmy, like so much moisture has collected there the past few months that he seems to be perpetually crying.

I smile tentatively. Odilie's mother drops my hand but continues to beam at me, her daughter and husband looking at me with matching smiles. Behind me, I can sense the titters, the whispers, and I inadvertently move myself closer into the trio, as if they can save me from those wandering eyes and wagging tongues. Quinn begins chatting with a cousin, leaving me stranded with them. They bring me into the shadows of a tree.

It occurs to me, again, that no one is coming near us. I would blame it on myself, but even before I entered this part of the courtyard, no one was nearing them. It's like all of us, the ones who were so acutely touched by this situation, are plagued. I wonder how used to it they are, the pointed glances and murmurs.

"We really are glad you got our invite. We wanted to meet you so badly. Page was the one who actually suggested we send you one." She looks over to Page, who gives me a meaningful look, lips pursed, eyes soft.

"I wanted to meet you. It's just been horrible for you. Horrible for all of us, of course. I think that now that things have quieted down a bit... I thought it would be good to get to know one another a little." I'm itching for one of those Aperol spritzes, something to dull the surreality of this conversation, their even tones, the sun.

"That's what my friend Quinn said, who I came here with. He thought we should meet, too." I try a tight grin, wring my hands. "Did you fly over from Michigan?" The sun moves again, the heat prickling my skin once more.

"Mom and Dad did," Page says, answering for them. "I'm living here now for the time being, to take care of a few things. I'm staying at Louisa's daughter's." She blinks a few times, as if to ward off more tears. "You know what, let me grab a couple of those Aperol spritzes, okay?" I thank her as she tiptoes off, circumventing the crowd like she's a stranger at her own sister's death party.

"It's hard for us," Odilie's mother says suddenly. "Hard for us here, I mean. You can see it. We can all see it. They avoid us, these friends of Odilie's. They're very generous, of course. They've put us up in a great hotel. Page is staying in some beautiful house, rent-free. But they don't care about getting to know us, you know? They're a little scared of us. Or maybe we're not classy enough for them? I'm not sure. But they don't talk to us. They won't engage with us." Her husband pats her absentmindedly on the shoulder.

"Mandy, they just don't know what to say." He turns to me. "No one ever knows what to say. Do you get that, too?" His voice is so gentle, with such calming undulations, that I almost begin to tear up, too, from the sheer kindness of it all.

"I do." I'm saved from saying any more by Page, who comes back up to us and hands me a glass of the orange liquid. Immediately, without thinking, I've chugged half of the glass.

"They're good, right?" Page says brightly, primly sipping her own. "I never knew the Odilie who claimed this was her favorite drink. But I believe it." It's an odd, throwaway thing to say, and I'm about to interrogate her further about it, when Quinn comes up to us, his own drink resting decorously in his hand. He introduces himself, looks at me inquiringly to see if I'm okay. I nod, almost imperceptibly.

"This is a really beautiful event. You must be so pleased to be celebrating Odilie's life like this. The eulogies were so lovely, too." Quinn raises his glass, as if to signal a toast.

"We didn't have a hand in planning anything," says Page. "We basically got an invite list and some cards to send out amongst family, and that was it." She takes a deep, long swig of her spritz, mimicking my own quick chug. "But I guess Odilie would have liked it. I wouldn't really know."

Mandy gives her daughter a pointed glance. "She liked flowers. She liked pretty things. She would have liked this, even if we had no hand in planning it."

"Especially because we had no hand," Page murmurs. She

turns to me. "Want to leave? I could go for something a little stronger." She widens her eyes, her lash extensions rising up toward her brow. My first instinct is to say no. It's too weird. I did enough by coming here and chatting with them, validating Quinn's very astute point that they actually did want to group-grieve with me.

But she's looking at me so candidly, so sincerely, that I can't help but blurt a "Sure," spunkier and more forthright than I'm used to being with anyone, at least for a very long time.

"Yay! I saw a bar on the corner that looks good. Mom, Dad—I'll check in with you tonight?" They nod, their acquiescence spooking me just a tad. It seems so genial and so odd. They're not foisting Page on me. If anything, she's foisting herself. But now they'll be here, in this place where they feel so excluded, without her.

"I'll see you back at the apartment?" Quinn calls to me as Page leads me away. I answer affirmatively, look back and watch my only support system fade into the background of the party. We go into the lobby to grab our phones and then, instead of exiting out the front door, she leads me in another loop around the event, keeping close to the spear-topped iron fencing surrounding the enclosure. Somehow, no one is looking at us; no one is staring. It's like Page is a shield blocking me. Or maybe no one cares anymore, the spectacle of the family and the other woman coming together dulled by the alcohol, by more distracting topics of conversation.

We slip out a side gate that leads into an alley and then onto the street. I wonder how Page knew about this spot, whether she had planned out escape routes the moment she entered the courtyard. We're immediately accosted by the blaring sounds of cars and trucks whizzing past on the way to the Westside Highway, noise that was somehow muffled by the shrubbery.

Page confidently leads us to the corner. She has placed her hand in mine, in a vise, and when a truck comes hurtling along, almost jumping the curb, I have to pull her back, as if we're tethered to each other. As she promised, a bar with blond wood paneling and funky tiles awaits. She plops herself down at an outdoor table and waits for me to do the same.

She asks about me, where I live, what I've been doing. I answer in the best way I can, stilted, but honest. I say I'm looking for another job. But am I? No one has asked me these questions in so long; they've only been transmitted by my mother, by Quinn. Page nods, doesn't push, which I appreciate.

She tells me where she's staying, that she's not sure how long she'll be in New York, but it's already been a couple of weeks. She says she lives outside Detroit, near her parents, that she's between jobs, but doesn't elaborate so I don't ask. She says she's lonely here, that she hasn't had the chance to really explore the city yet.

She pauses.

"I know this is weird of me. I mean it must be absolutely surreal to you, right?" She gazes at me, forcing me to expel a response.

"Which part?" I say lightly, my mouth twitching into a grin.

"You know, it was so shitty what the media did to you. And even shittier to pit us against each other, like we were supposed to hate you for something you seemingly had no control over. Or didn't have the full story about. My mom, well, she just felt bad for you from the beginning. I mean, after the initial horror and trauma wasn't plaguing her day and night. It still is, of course, but you know what I mean." A waiter comes to take our order and Page orders a gin and tonic, like it's 9:00 p.m. and not three in the afternoon. I order a glass of sauvignon blanc.

"I know what you mean."

Page sighs. "She's wanted to tell you for so long that she doesn't blame you for anything. None of us do. But Mom especially." The waiter comes with our drinks and she takes a sip of hers. "We didn't really know Tom, is the issue. We didn't really know Odilie. Except Mom denies that, of course. We only met Penelope when she came to Michigan right before the deaths. No one was invited to her birth, anything having to do with their little family. But no one likes reporting that. It doesn't fit well with the tale of the saintly woman who doted on her father, only to be ripped away from the earth by her sociopathic, philandering husband." Page clinks the ice in her glass. At a table behind us a small dachshund starts whining for its owners' food.

I sit there, hand shaking as I sip the crisp wine. Page is right. That is not what I had envisioned at all. In all my dark, lost spirals into which my own worst feelings about myself had plummeted, not once had I suspected that Odilie's family didn't know their own daughter, their own granddaughter. "Did she just move away and stop keeping in touch?"

Page fishes the lime from her glass, sucks on it like a teething baby. "She met Tom when she was super young and then she basically vanished from our lives. She wasn't exactly estranged. She would call us out of the blue sometimes. We were all friends on socials. Once or twice she and Tom visited us. But otherwise, there was this strange barrier between us and them. It wasn't breakable. And God, my mom tried. But Odilie and Tom were very quiet with her, and quiet about each other." She drinks the melted ice. "And now my folks are suddenly parenting a toddler again, which is a whole other type of weird. Penelope won't remember her own parents. She's too young. She stopped asking where 'Mama' was months ago. I think my mom didn't want to bring her here because she was afraid she'd recognize something, be traumatized or whatever."

I want to ask about Odilie, about the transformation on her Instagram, but I stop myself. Page seems to be on a ramble, and maybe this is a long-delayed, much-needed speech for her. And I'm not ready yet to admit to being such a stalker, to spending so many hours perusing her dead sister's old life.

"Were you actually a huge bitch in high school? In your work life?" Page says suddenly, her words tinctured by the smallest slur. "That's what they all said about you. I mean the lowliest of the press. On Twitter, too. That you were mean, conniving, always expecting to get what you want. But you don't seem that way to me at all. Of course, this past year has changed you, I'm sure."

I finish off my wine before answering. I'm not taken aback by her comment. I like Page's direct, almost aggressive, approach to this question. She's not trying to force me to admit that I was the bad guy, which many others had tried to do. She's simply asking, point-blank. "I was popular. I've always known my worth. I've always wanted to get ahead, and I'll do anything to get there. Then I worked in fashion for years, which is famously cutthroat and bitchy. I don't like mediocrity. I'm not going to hand out favors or have interest in people whose ideas I don't think are worth my time. So, sure, I can be harsh. But say that to a man and see how he responds."

Page nods, as if this settles her question. "I never understood that angle of all of this. Why should your actions at seventeen, even your actions in your work life, mean anything in the context of my sister?" The waiter comes back, saving us from answering. Page orders another gin and tonic and I follow her lead, get a cranberry-vodka with a dash of lime for myself. Fuck it. This conversation requires it.

"I ask myself that question a lot. Once everything happened, it was like a deluge of malice. I hadn't experienced that before." My tongue feels heavy in my mouth, the spritz and glass of wine already dulling my senses, any inhibitions that I would have had even in a typical drunken scenario slackened by the bizarreness of the situation. "I'm a woman, I guess. Isn't that enough? I'm a bitch and I'm a woman. Or I'm a bitch *because*

I'm a woman. Odilie, she seemed so wholesome. They needed me to be her foil, I guess. There wasn't *too* much to use against me from my adulthood. I'm a hard worker. I stayed mostly behind the scenes at Magdelena, which of course didn't stop people from saying that I was a nightmare to work with. It's not like I'm famously a villain in any kind of a public sector. But I guess more people than I realized had a vendetta against me in high school, harbored resentments. Old classmates reached back to my childhood, to my earlier days, when I was a bit of a classic mean girl. And then other people whom I'd presumably rubbed the wrong way as an adult piled on." I shrug, as if saying all this aloud nonchalantly was routine for me. The day, its meaning, is growing hazy around the edges. Page and her familiar face bobbing along with the rest of it, a landscape of a dream whose peripheries I know, but whose subject is still a mystery, forcing me to fumble through it until I jerk awake.

The waiter comes and brings our drinks. I twist my lime into the red juice.

"It's odd that they didn't do the same with Odilie. But I guess it wasn't needed, right? She was pregnant and then dead. She was already a martyr," Page says. There's the slightest tinge to her voice, a hardness that I can't quite place, that maybe my filmy mind is creating out of nothing. "You know his lawyers are still obstructing anyone from doing an investigative documentary or a podcast." She knocks back her drink with the ease that she drank the others, the ice clinking against her glass as she sets it back down on the table. "What was he like? In the brief period you knew him?"

I start. Take a sip of my drink. I can't taste the vodka at all, but I can feel its warmth in the very center of my belly. The words, they're wobbly in my mouth before I speak. Because I'm not sure what she wants to hear. No one has asked me this; no one except that macho detective I was forced to speak to, with the overgrown nose hairs. Who was put off by the way

I enunciated my words, the posture with which I held myself as I answered his questions. I could tell by the way he spoke down to me, even as he was asking me about my potential part in a homicide. A suicide.

He had slipped me his number to call, if I could think of anything else. But he had also scrawled his personal one, in spidery black lettering. I wonder, when I didn't call, if he was one of the men who began 4chan threads in my name, dedicated hours to hurling as many insults about my appearance as possible.

I blink back to the present, Page's brown eyes gazing at me under her feathery false lashes. "He was rich. Generous, I guess. Sorry, that sounds bad coming from me." I close my eyes for a moment. "He was kind of a cardstock of a man, if I'm going to be completely honest. He went through all the motions, but I couldn't get a read on him at all. At the time I don't think I knew that. He…he played me. I was attracted to this kind of fumbling vulnerability he showed to me, handsome but hapless. The more time moves on, the more I realize that that was bait, to reel me in." I'm about to say the last part. *And we all know what happened when I wriggled away.* But I don't. We all know much too well.

Page's eyes shift to the sidewalk, watching the passersby with their dogs and children. I hadn't been aware of the noise at all, but now that I am it's jarring. The undulations of all those voices, the tires reverberating off the asphalt as the cars whoosh by. It all suddenly seems so overwhelming to me.

"No one in my family is German," Page says abruptly. "My parents went on this trip to Berlin. Their only trip out of the country, to visit my dad's friend at the army base. On the night they conceived her, their waitress was called Odilie. They remembered the name. I was always so jealous of it. I mean who wouldn't be, with a name like mine? I'm named after my grandmother, no whimsical backstory for me. But a name like Odilie, you're meant for more than Wyneck or Novi, right?

I used to blame my name for the fact that I stayed out down there while she was living this glamorous life in New York." She finishes her drink, so I do the same.

"I should get going. Go and meet up with my parents. They're a little shell-shocked, as you can imagine. But I like you, Vera. Can I see you again?" Her words are steadier than mine are, buoyed up by the liquor, her cheeks rosy but not as heated as mine, her eyes roving my face like she's looking for a nook in which to nestle herself.

Do I want to see her again? My tired, drunken brain scrambles for an answer to that question. Before I can dwell on it, I feel myself nodding. "Yes, yes, of course. Let me give you my number." We pay and get up, the sun slowly waning. I'm foggy brained, confused about the time, the spring air choking me with its freshness. My head needs to be buried in the dark, no filtration, no light. It's all too much. I want the murk of a dark, dank bedroom.

She hugs me, cradles my neck, holds me so tight that for a claustrophobic moment I think maybe I am buried in the ground. She kisses my cheek, her boozy breath chafing my ear, her saliva wet and welcoming on my flushed skin. "See you soon, Vera. I'm sure we'll have lots more to talk about." She squeezes my hand, saunters off, her walk so even-keeled and sober that it's obvious what she's doing all those evenings alone in the city, in the yawning caverns of the brownstone she described. But can I blame her?

I make my way to the subway station, shaky, weak. Drunk. But I manage to get on a train, find my way home.

Later, when I'm sequestered under my duvet, three Tylenols thrown back just like all that empty-stomach alcohol, the curtains drawn and the lights dimmed, I take out my laptop, and, like a zealot perusing a sacred screed, I pull up Odilie's Instagram, right where I had left off.

It's summer now. Odilie is posting less, only photos of her seemingly alone out at restaurants. But she couldn't be alone. Because they're not selfies; someone must be taking her photo. She is demure, tiny, elegant even. She dines at places with cloth napkins. She's still in Wyneck, but it's a different kind of Wyneck, the chichi part, maybe. Whiter sands, better maintained Jack Rogers sandals, a shot of her on a yacht.

Always alone, her face devoid of meaning, of any expression at all, really. She's perfected the distant, mysterious but somewhat affable curve of a lip that I associate with women of a certain economic class. There are fewer likes, fewer comments. But that one name keeps showing back up, Thelma Kay. Was she there today? This new friend of Odilie's who somehow collided with her during this sudden shift in character?

And then a jolt, a shallow inhale of breath, because there he is. For a moment I want to avert my eyes, bludgeon the tiny, pixilated part of my computer screen showing his smug, handsome, sadistic face. I can't even see the full photo at first, my brain zeroing in on him and him only. His hair fuller, jaw sharper, skin deeply tanned, his shirt unbuttoned just so. It's different from the video of him rocking Penelope, where I could barely see his features. This photo lays it all bare.

I cross my eyes the tiniest bit, so his face glazes over in my vision, so that I'm incapable of focusing on it. And I gaze at the picture as a whole, refusing to let my eyes travel over to his image again.

It's a picture of five people, and I scan my eyes from left to right, starting with Odilie, in a cream-colored dress, fingers grazing the stem of a wineglass, the golden liquid frosty. She is wearing pearl studs, her hair swept behind her ears, collarbones peeping out coquettishly from her exposed neckline. Her smile is wide and toothy. It's evening. The group is at a table near the beach, at some kind of party, but with enough lighting to make the photo show up pretty clearly without the need for flash. Next to Odilie is another man, blond and portly and red, wearing expensive chinos, his blue eyes lacquered with the sheen of a frequent drinker. Hanging on his arm is a woman, also blonde, her head too large for her small shoulders, one eye squinting, making her face look lopsided.

And then there he is and there's a long, tanned arm hanging loosely over his shoulder, the slim wrist encircled by a golden bracelet in the form of a snake. It takes me a moment to put two and two together, that this arm doesn't belong to Odilie. Of course, because Odilie is at the other end of the table.

This woman, she's gorgeous. Her hair is curly and dark, her eyes sharp, intelligent, staring directly at the camera, almost waging a battle with it, daring the photographer to try to get more out of her. She's wearing an emerald green dress, her breasts supple in the cupped bodice. Her nails are magenta, and even at the end of the table, the worst spot in a group photo, she makes herself known, present. As I shift my gaze to take in the whole group, she outshines them all, so magnificently and with such intent that I'm shocked my gaze had flitted directly to him at first, instead of to her.

She's with Tom, that much is certain, her body language almost comical in its blatant ownership. She owns him and knows it. He's almost diminutive in her embrace, in the way that she's wrapped herself around him. Like the bracelet coiling around her wrist. If I zoom in, on the casual crook of her hand on his shoulder, I can see that her fingers are rigid with tension, her nails digging into his shirt.

I hover over her, to see if she's tagged, if I can identify her. And I startle again. Because it's her. It's Thelma Kay. She's commented, too, with a wide grin emoticon, resembling Odilie's toothy smile and "Teeth=secrets." What could *that* mean, I wonder?

15

One year ago

I WASN'T ENTIRELY sure why I reacted the way I did. Of course, any woman *should* be turned off by a man yelling at his ex. But I had my own temper issues, my own simmering rage. I wasn't known to be polite and cordial with exes, either.

But something about the way Tom seethed, the way he chased after me, it made my skin crawl. Like I'd accidentally ripped away a shroud he was using to cover his basest, most animal reflexes. That shy, timorous vulnerability he'd exposed, it seemed like a farce. And the fact that he didn't even seem concerned about his child, it reminded me of my mother, grumbling because she had to miss a vacation to Punta Cana with her sorority sisters to take care of me when I had a weeklong flu as a little girl.

He sent me a flurry of texts, of course, all of which I ignored. Each of them more desperate than the last, apologizing profusely. Saying that what I saw wasn't his typical behavior, that he'd had a rough week and had taken it out on his ex and kid, on me. Eventually, by the following morning, the texts stopped.

Quinn rolled his eyes at the depravity of it all and told me to follow my intuition. Huda was more forgiving of him. When she sashayed into the office the next morning, an hour after me, she asked me about the date before we even went over the expense reports. She sucked on her yogurt spoon thoughtfully. "It might be a blip, you know. At least he knows he did something wrong. Some men would still be confused."

I made a minor correction to the report and looked over at her. "I'm not looking to settle for some guy who just barely gets it. Let's not give accolades where they're not deserved."

She swallowed more yogurt. "I just think everyone should have a second chance. Get back to him, at least. You shouldn't ghost this one, especially when he's so hell-bent on getting in touch with you." I sighed and didn't answer, pushed over the laptop and attempted to get her to focus on the spreadsheet I was working on.

At noon, a bouquet of roses was sent to the office. Everyone oohed and aahed. I moved them to the kitchen area, sent an office-wide email that anyone could take them home if they wanted. Huda plucked one and smelled it, a sensuous grin enveloping her face. "You are so cold, Vera. They're pink! How sweet. He admires you. Please get back to him."

But I didn't. The gesture itself rubbed me the wrong way. It was too grandiose, too public, too reliant on external valida-tion. It reminded me of men who propose in front of a crowd, giving their partner no way to reject them, lest they embar-rass their girlfriend and themselves in front of so many people.

Quinn agreed with me, later that night when he got home

from some Thursday night shenanigans. I was on our couch smoking a bowl in my underwear, watching *Married at First Sight* when he strolled in and started digging through the fridge for a snack.

"Yeah, that's too much. After a third date, too? It's a little manipulative. And kind of an insult to you. Like shouldn't he know you're not the type of woman to be bowled over by some flowers?"

I continued to leave his texts unanswered, but I didn't want to ghost. I'd rather just let him down easy. Not necessarily because I cared, but because I had a prick of fear, a nagging instinct clawing at the back of my head. Well, maybe I did care, just a little. I'd been excited to see him after all. I'd had such a long, languid, nearly hedonistic second date with him. But some of that longing had ebbed away, no matter how good the sex was; once he stopped being soft and vulnerable this wasn't fun anymore. I wanted out.

I finally composed a text Friday morning.

> Hey. I've had fun with you, but to be quite honest I don't think I can date a man with familial responsibilities right now. As clichéd as it sounds, it's not you, it's me. I wish you the best.

On Saturday night he started texting me again, incessantly, so I blocked his number. And I swear to God, I forgot about him for days.

I went out Saturday night with Quinn and our friends from college, Claudia and Evan. I hadn't seen them in a while and they were a little cool toward me, but as we drank, everyone loosened up. We did some coke, smoked a lot of cigarettes. Went to three different Bushwick bars.

The next morning I vomited for a solid hour, drank some

Pedialyte. Slept it off, ate some runny eggs that Quinn made for me. We got stoned and watched *Midsommar*. We Face-Timed Sam, even though he and Quinn were technically still on a break. I didn't even touch work and Huda was barely in contact with me, except to ask about where we should go to dinner on Wednesday night with the owner of a popular Los Angeles boutique.

Tuesday was another bright, unseasonably warm day. I grabbed a chocolate croissant for breakfast, let myself bask in the sunshine on a bench in Union Square before heading into the office. The day filed along as normal; there was a supply chain mishap that we had to run a fire drill for. A brief concern that an Instagram influencer turned designer may be knocking off one of our designs.

It wasn't until midday that I heard anyone jabbering about what had happened. "OMG, Katie, this is so sick," our social media manager Todd said to our content creation freelancer. "This Brooklyn tech bro totally just annihilated his pregnant wife."

I heard her squeal. "OMG he is hot!"

"I know, right? The psychopaths always are. Check out Richard Ramirez. Those cheekbones! This one offed himself, sadly, so no chance to be his prison pen pal," Todd sighed.

I thought nothing of it. I didn't even ask to see what they were talking about. I had too much on my plate.

It wasn't until Huda, sitting in her office, called me on my cell. "Dude, I'm like thirty feet away from you. Just text me." I could see her on the phone with me through the glass door of her office, her face sickeningly pale, like a ghoul. I could read her lips through the clear glass as I heard her speak to me on the phone.

"No, Vera. You have to come in here. Now." Her voice was rough and guttural, a scraggly alley cat's rumble.

I closed her office door behind me, so no one could hear our conversation. "What is it with the theatrics? I'm telling you, we'll get legal on the knockoff stuff. It'll be okay."

But she just shook her head, turned her laptop toward me, so I could see the screen.

THOMAS NEWBURN, MILLIONAIRE CO-FOUNDER OF LOGISTICS START-UP, KILLS PREGNANT WIFE AND SELF

And then everything in me shattered.

Huda sent me home in an Uber, told me to take the rest of the day off. In those first few moments, the hours when all of it seemed like a garish cartoon, the veracity of it refusing to sink in, I almost laughed. I texted Quinn something along the lines of *He's dead. And he killed his (ex?!!!) wife?! What the hell is happening?*

I howled into my pillow, giddy with the nonsense of it all.

When did the horror sink in? When the paparazzi showed up the next day, their noise like an insect's hum? I asked Quinn what was happening outside and he checked for me and they got him, too. They knew who he was somehow, from their collective claw, intent on snatching any morsel of info they deemed themselves worthy of. Quinn shoved his way back up the stairs, his face vacant and chalky like the outline of a body's head at a crime scene, and told me they were there for me.

I got information in spurts. At first, I glued myself to my phone, refreshing Google every few seconds for new information. Then, when it started rolling in more, it paralyzed me, my brain barely able to communicate with the rest of me, shock waves coursing through my body like squiggling worms.

The housekeeper, Anna, the person who took care of those

gleaming white walls, was the one who alerted the police. The moment she stepped inside, she smelled sulfur. And immediately, she ran to Penelope's room, on the third floor, letting out a wail of relief when she spotted the small girl in bed, sound asleep, her chest rising and falling, heartbeat steady. Her head already feeling dizzy, muzzy and muted, Anna picked the toddler up and ran out the front door, dialed 911 as she breathed in the outside air.

They're in his office. I know it. Mr. Newburn's office. There's an old gas fireplace in there. No windows! The lock on the door is broken. It does not open from the inside. It broke when she was away and he said he would get it fixed before she came home but I don't think he did! Anna screamed and panted to the 911 operator, frantic nonsense, her words punctuated by sobs, according to the reports in the papers.

She was right. Tom had coaxed Odilie into the room with the broken door, certain that Odilie would guilelessly walk in with no knowledge that they would be trapped inside.

The police stormed in with gas masks. When they entered the home office, where the bodies lay, they found deep scratches striating the door, clawed cries of hope and wretchedness from her nails. For long minutes before her death, she had futilely been trying to escape him, escape that room. She died knowing his fatal goals for both of them.

The gas fireplace had been adjusted to emit carbon monoxide from the moment it was turned on; to turn the gas off, Odilie would have had to adjust the combustion shroud, which sat in the middle of the flame, if she even knew enough about gas fireplaces to begin with. She could have turned off the flame and adjusted the very hot combustion shroud, and *possibly* saved herself. But the police investigator reasoned that as wooziness descended, logic departed, and an animalistic instinct for survival had overtaken instead, thus the grooved marks on the door.

They also found trace amounts of Ambien in a glass of wine sitting atop the desk. Later, toxicology reports suggested that Tom had slipped the pill into Odilie's drink, a weekly doctor-approved treat for her during her pregnancy. The Ambien, on top of an antihistamine she had taken to sleep, dulled her faculties before the poisonous gas put her in a final sleep.

Even if she *had* managed to turn off the gas, merely being trapped in that windowless room would probably have killed her, considering the amount of carbon monoxide released. The brownstone, with all its shiny objects, wasn't properly renovated and didn't have a stopcock. Not the first time the investigator had seen shoddy work from an expensive contractor.

Days prior, SNAPea had removed all technology from the home office, no computer to use for help. Tom had also left both their phones in the kitchen. Aside from his suicide note, there was another paper left with crude markings, some kind of blueprint for an animal enclosure that Tom had been working on, perhaps for horses.

The detectives were the ones who found the note, slipped into a desk drawer, that was later leaked to the press:

To Whom It May Concern:
I have been left with no choice. Vera MacDonald has left me with no choice. These past few days I've realized how much her cold rejection of me has carved a hole in my heart so painful and so enormous that I cannot go on living. I'm sorry, Penelope. But this is the best decision for all of us. Your mother deserves everlasting peace, free from my transgressions. Vera, even as I write this, I still love you.

There was no evidence of prior abuse, physical or verbal. Sure, I'd heard him yell at her over the phone. Sure, there were rumors that he could be absentee, that even when giving his child a bath, he was prone to neglect, to forgo instructions or supervision. But the police didn't care about that. To anyone who knew them, they were a content couple, with normal rifts, normal make ups. Nothing to see here.

Huda told me to take more time off. And I thought, I thought that it was an act of grace, as Twitter was flooded with death threats, Facetuned images of me sucking penis, my high school yearbook photo with darts through my eyes, semen on my face, a deepfake of my face blasted through with a rifle on a video, bone-chillingly real. *Child Killer.*

Child killer. Because to so many, Tom—and I, by association—had killed not only a mother, but a child, too. An unborn child.

I tried to go back to work. Huda said no, no, take more time off. I stayed inside the apartment. Quinn brought me food. I didn't eat it. I wasted away. I had had the foresight to delete Instagram even before the paparazzi showed up, but I still searched my name. I marveled at all the creative ways you can hate a person, especially a person you don't know. It was my unwholesome oxygen, no choice but to breathe it in, this malice from phalanxes of people who wanted me dead for a murder I didn't commit.

But if I didn't commit it, it was still my fault they were dead. That last text conversation was leaked, too, the one in which I told him his family was the reason I didn't want to date him. All my pals, the ones who wanted me murdered, too, raped with AK-47s and then shot through my uterus, they were right. I, with my excuses, my flimsy attempt at asserting boundaries with a man I'd only gone on three dates with, had caused all of this. It was like being given a power I couldn't contain, a magic spell gone horribly awry with fatal consequences.

Of course, logical people and decent media outlets didn't

blame me. But giving grace doesn't equal clicks. And the people most fascinated by the story were the ones who wanted to assign me the role of villainess, who needed a living scapegoat.

My friends, my colleagues, sent apologetic, perfunctory texts. I reached out to the ones whom I'd known for years, saying how broken and lost I felt. There were a few short exchanges, but no one wanted to touch me; no one wanted to be associated with me. No one knew how to handle me, the mess I'd made. My deliberate avoidance of meaningful relationships ricocheted right back at me.

Finally, finally, while I was showering long and hard for the first time in a week, Quinn installed something on my computer, on my phone, preventing me from searching for myself. Some kind of parental control. And I screamed at him. *This is all I have left.* And he took me by the shoulders and said. *Vera. Vee. You have me.*

I showed up to work sometime later, who knows how long it had been, really. Huda had been avoiding me, telling me to take more time. And when I got to the office, early as usual, my key didn't work. Huda was in the building; she knew I was there. I called her, texted her. She ignored me. Twenty-three minutes later there was an email. Cursory. I'd been terminated. Ostensibly for some mistake I'd made on an expense report. They would send my things to me.

I went into the bathroom in the lobby of the building, turned on all the hand-drying vents and screamed.

Later, I would learn that Huda had lost a round of investing from Apax. Because of me. Because of the way I had tarnished the brand. The investors were willing to renegotiate if I were scrubbed clean from the company. It was timing's fault, in my opinion. If the investment meeting had been even a month later, I think she would have been in the clear. It hadn't even occurred to me to ask her how it went, even while I was off, because it was a given that it would go well. But no. I, my face, my name, had fucked everything up.

Then I packed my things, bid farewell to the apartment and fled to my mother, who had only checked in on me once during this whole deadly mess of a mistake.

One survivor, said all those papers, referring to Penelope. But sometimes, sometimes I feel like I was in that home with them that fatal evening, the *second* survivor of Tom's violent, nefarious final act.

PART
TWO

1

ODILIE

Ten years ago

THE WOMAN CAME in for a whitening. But her teeth were already white, bone white.

Odilie Patterson didn't take much of a glance when she was called in, briefly, to help out Dr. Forsyth; Elena, the hygienist, was out sick that day and a tiny office like theirs required the receptionist to help out from time to time.

So she stood holding a tray of tools for the dentist, the woman's mouth stretched by the rubber mouth guards, her teeth painted brown for the laser whitening. There was nothing really to take notice of. Even in her front office role, Odilie was already used to staring down people's throats, watching the dentist scrape tongues, hearing the loud complaints as her boss began to drill. It had become such background noise to her that sometimes, when a patient yelped in agitation, it took several attempts to break Odilie from a reverie, to pull her back to reality, to watch as Elena motioned for a patient to *spit out the blood.*

This woman, Odilie remembered, never once complained of pain. Though the laser could sting if patients had sensitive teeth, the only sign of any perceived discomfort was a tightened fist, delicate and birdlike, a fist that could do no damage.

The teeth whitening was her last appointment for the day, so shortly after that woman left, Odilie did, too, waving goodbye to Dr. Forsyth before he disappeared into the bathroom to change out of his scrubs. Once Odilie was outside, the air thick, almost like the humidity itself was sulking, she stuck a piece of gum into her mouth, felt the way it pulled at her molars. It was May. It shouldn't have been that hot out.

She took a moment, savoring that piece of gum, before she walked to the parking lot, where her Camry would be sitting. Tonight she was supposed to go over to her parents' for dinner, which she rarely enjoyed. She had moved out for a reason, though her parents also lived in Wyneck only a few short miles from her.

She stuck another piece of gum into her mouth, chewing viciously at the thought of seeing her family, having to withstand their indifference. Maybe she wouldn't go over until later. Maybe she'd have a drink all by herself at home before driving herself over.

She was so deep in thought that she almost didn't notice the teeth-whitening woman standing by her own car, a red Alfa Romeo Guilia, smoking a cigarette, her richly tanned arms leaning against the hood. It was such an obviously sexy pose, her fingers coiled around the filter, her tight jeans showing off her toned buttocks aimed toward the sky. The pose itself wasn't even natural. Why not lean against a window instead? Stand more upright?

It was obvious she was a summer resident, here a few weekends early, before Memorial Day. No one who lived here year-round could afford that car or those Pilates-toned arms.

Odilie paused by her own car, lifted a hand in a wave. "You know you shouldn't be smoking right after the whitening. It can reverse the effects." It was a cloying, prudish thing to say. But there was something about this woman, the way in which she carried herself, that provoked Odilie, made her want to engage. She couldn't put her finger on why.

The woman rose up from her awkward position, her black tank top rising with her, offering a sliver of toned stomach. She took another drag of the cigarette, exhaling the fumes in Odilie's direction. "Thanks, hon. You *would* know best." She smiled then, her eyes squinting ever so slightly with the effort. Odilie saw the crinkle even from two cars away. "Have you ever smoked? Or do they bar you from working at a dental office if you have?"

"Maybe once or twice in my heyday," Odilie answered, surprised by her own quip.

"You're barely twenty years old," she said, not unkindly. "Well, how about thrice for good measure? It's a whole lot more relaxing than that gum you're chewing." Odilie paused her rotating jaw and spit the gum into a wrapper. Was it that obvious? She really should be getting home, especially if she wanted to have that drink before heading to her parents'. But maybe a cigarette would suffice, would ease the blooming tension she already felt in her chest at the evening ahead.

She circled her car and joined the woman by the Alfa Romeo, its bumper gleaming in the setting sun. "Peri," the woman said as she stuck out her hand, long nails digging into Odilie's flesh as they shook. "But you should know that already. Since you were just looking inside my mouth." Peri plucked out a cigarette and handed it to Odilie, lighting it for her as Odilie brought it to her lips.

"I love the dentist. It's so relaxing." She flicked some ash by Odilie's foot. Odilie tried for a scoff. "You think I'm kidding? That's why I made this appointment out here in the first place. I missed the dentist. All I want to do is lie back in a chair and have people make me prettier. The pain is worth the gain. That's a cliché, but it's a true one. Especially for women. What's your name?"

Odilie told her.

"Wow, fancy. You don't hear names like that in these parts." She eyed Odilie's burning cigarette, the ash sticking to the filter. Odilie self-consciously flicked it. She didn't want to inhale again, afraid she would cough.

Then Peri reached out, grazed one nail gently down Odilie's cheek, the gesture so quick, so light, that when Peri took her hand away Odilie felt, for a moment, like she'd imagined it. She shivered, despite the heat, her gaze dropping to the corner, to the car's tire.

"You have it all there, Odilie. You have the makings of someone." Peri's hand lingered, outstretched in the air like the painting of Adam and God's fingers touching, the only proof that it had grazed Odilie's skin, had made her flesh tingle.

"The makings of what?" Odilie heard herself say, a feathery whisper. She wanted Peri's nail back on her skin, on her spine, counting the knobs.

Peri smiled, those teeth like white shiny pebbles, sanded and polished by the beach's waves. "You have gumption. That's all. That's all I mean." And with that she opened her car door, stretched herself in, like a cat in the sun. "Babe, you're about to burn yourself," she said, cigarette dangling out of the window. And then reversed out of the parking lot, a plume of smoke disappearing behind her.

And Odilie felt the hot prick of the ember dying down on her fingers, the cigarette burnt down to its filter. She enjoyed it, the searing pain, for a moment, before she let it drop on the asphalt. Before she walked back to her own car, her index and middle fingers blistered on the inside. She sat for a second, her hands on the wheel, staring into the sky darkening into a hazy blue, clouds wispy like the smoke, her teeth aching, quivering with need. But for what, she did not know.

Gumption.

The word danced around her as she sat at dinner. For once in her life, Page was in trouble. She had gotten a B+ on a math test. Page was a genius. The one her parents cherished. The one who, though she was five years younger, had shown more promise at age five than Odilie had in all of her twenty years. A wunderkind. That was what some crotchety elementary school teacher had called her. Could read at three years old. Knew her multiplication tables before she graduated from kindergarten. Had won the science fair, the spelling bee, the poetry contest, the girls' soccer championships year after year after year. She would go on to win homecoming queen, prom queen, in a few years' time; Odilie could sense it.

Page was the Pattersons' prize. Page was *Wyneck's* prize.

No one had expected Odilie to go to a four-year college. When she announced she had matriculated at Wyneck Comm, there had been a thirty-five-second pause at dinner—Odilie had counted. "Well, that will be a good way to spend your days for now," her dad had responded, his voice devoid of enthusiasm.

Which was perhaps why her parents were so desperate for her to meet someone, to start a life with children and diapers and nap times and routines. If she wasn't going to excel in school, she had to excel at being a mother, right?

But Odilie didn't want that. She wasn't entirely sure what

she wanted. She had her small joys. She liked the ephemeral joy of eating a good meal, drinking a good drink. The way that almost felt like love. She liked the clean, sterile feeling of the dental office. She liked the dental hygienist, Elena, who worked there with her. She sort of liked her tiny apartment, which she shared with her friend from high school, Kitty. She enjoyed being alone in it, watching Dr. Phil on the afternoons when she wasn't in class or working at the dental office. She liked the way her sheets felt when she would fall asleep, cool against her skin that always ran hot.

She liked sex when she had it, though her assignations had been few and far between. Most of the time, though, it was never worth more than a handful of hours. It was never worth wrapping herself in another person's sheets.

Odilie had simply accepted her mundane, uncluttered life. The way she could fade, ever so gently, into the walls of any room she was in, her voice too mousy for large groups, her looks too plain for any sort of wayward glances.

Gumption.

After dinner, while Page was still arguing with their parents, telling them that she *had* to go to Misty's slumber party this weekend, despite her grades, because if she didn't, she wouldn't be invited to Misty's *birthday* party, which was next month, and Misty was going to be a junior so this would set her up for next year, Odilie went into her parents' bedroom and pulled out the blue, green, and red covered Oxford English Dictionary.

Gumption.

"shrewd or spirited initiative and resourcefulness"

Odilie sat on the bed, marking the page with one burnt finger. This wasn't her. This woman, Peri, she was seeing something that wasn't there, an aspirational Odilie that didn't exist.

Odilie traced her finger on her cheek, the same pattern, the same spot that Peri had. What had she seen? What had she seen that Odilie couldn't see in herself?

The next morning at work Odilie lingered by the front desk, listening to Elena rant about her baby daddy, sharing a Danish. "He dropped off Cayla two hours late last weekend, no text, nothing, then explodes at me when I take fifteen minutes to respond to *his* text. Every single time. I'm this close to telling him he can't have weekends anymore." She prattled on. Usually, Odilie was attentive, a good listener. She was great at being a vessel into which people dropped their secrets. And she liked Elena, her spunkiness, her curly hair that she never straightened. But this morning Odilie's attention wavered.

"What do you know about the last patient we had yesterday when you were out? Peri? Came in for a teeth whitening. Obviously not a local."

Elena thought for a moment. "Oh yeah. You have trouble getting her records up or something?"

Odilie shook her head. "No. We were just chatting in the parking lot. She was friendly."

Elena flicked a crumb into her mouth. "Oh funny. She's new. I've never dealt with her before. She's definitely loaded, though. Forsyth said she was coming in again in three weeks. For no damn reason."

Odilie nodded and thanked Elena, threw out the wax paper the Danish had come in and went behind her desk to check the calendar; Elena was right. Peri *was* due back in three weeks.

Gumption. Three weeks from now, she'd have the gumption to ask what Peri meant. That was a promise to herself.

VERA

Present day

THE DAYS ARE somehow lonelier in the city than they were at my mom's. It's strange how that works, maybe because of the juxtaposition of my idleness with Quinn's waking up every morning and getting ready for work, leaving the apartment for the day. It occurred to me that in my old life, I barely spent time here. I mean I *did*, to eat and sleep and watch TV, but the walls and corners, the little crevices where the light and shadow play, I never knew them as intimately as I do now.

I itch to text old friends, those people who didn't know how to handle my sudden notoriety. But it's like time has created too much of a rift; I was barely around before, and now, when I need companionship the most, I'm both too prideful and too afraid to reach out for it. I don't want to expose my desperation, and at the same time I don't want to be rejected.

I leave the apartment, occasionally, to take walks in Prospect Park, to wend my way through my neighborhood, Prospect Heights, Park Slope. I apply for jobs. I get a couple of interviews at apparel-adjacent companies, a marketing position for a beauty-supply brand, a sales position at a retail tech start-up. They all go fine, but no one calls me back.

Sometimes, after Quinn leaves, I sit in our living room underneath the green blanket on the couch and pull down the shades, engulf myself in darkness, like I'm in a cocoon. Fortunately, that activity grows old quickly, late spring's sunshine always seeping through the windows to remind me that I shouldn't self-isolate, that pitying myself was never a good option, anyway.

Quinn notices my aloneness, in the way I jump at him when he comes home after work, asking him how his day was, if he has evening plans, if there's any DIY project he wants done around the apartment. It's the first time in my life I've felt needy. "You should get a hobby," Quinn finally says one day when he comes home after happy hour drinks with his coworkers and finds me watching the eighteenth season of *Keeping Up with the Kardashians*, when I'd only been on the first a week ago.

He's right. I should have some constructive pastime, aside from intermittently reaching out to old work contacts, scouring LinkedIn. I wonder, in one moment of tumultuous self-reflection, if I should have been applying all along, from the moment Huda officially fired me. If this gap in employment is actually making matters worse for me, apart from my name.

I've abandoned Odilie's Instagram for the time being, the browser window with the picture of her, Tom and Thelma Kay lingering, hidden, on my laptop screen. It's like my own bizarre process of revisiting her life froze when I entered it physically. I try to look up Thelma Kay. I google her. I google her in combination with Tom, against my better judgment. Nothing comes up. It's like she vanished. Unless, of course, Thelma is a fake name, used only for social media.

Then one day, about two weeks after my move back to the city, I get a text from Page.

> Hi Vera! Been thinking about you. Was wondering if you wanted to come over sometime this week? Super casual, just to chill. Maybe we can order in pizza? ☺

I follow Quinn like a puppy when he comes home, waving my phone in his face as he tries to make a stir-fry for himself. "What do I do? Do I go see her? This is so weird, right?"

Quinn sighs, begins to chop an onion. "She's obviously lonely. You did your due diligence, though, by going to the ceremony. You don't really owe her anything else."

"That's not an answer," I say as he dumps the onions into the pan to sauté.

"Okay, then go! Unless you think it'll make you spiral or something." He turns to me as the onions sizzle. "Look. I can't really tell you what to do here. I'm not in your shoes. I'm not in her shoes. Everything I say might be a misstep. Any advice I give could be bad or incorrect. But what have you got to lose at this point?"

I blanch slightly at those last words. Even though I know what he means. He adds some spices to the onions. "If it's too strange, you never have to see her again." But he's wrong about that. She has my entire reputation in her hands. If she wanted to, she could start up a new bit of online trolling, tell everyone I'm as callous as they all think I am. Not that that would really be a huge part of the news cycle these days, but it could instigate some online hate on Twitter. Which wouldn't be great if I'm trying to get a job.

It's that trepidation that compels me to text her back.

In my old life, Page would have been someone I ignored, if not disdained. I would have easily discarded her, her name, and any defining attributes soon after meeting her. She's almost tacky, but not in a camp, fun way. It's more like she is trying *so* hard, doing *too* much, with her hair, her makeup, all of it flashy and unbecoming, gel stuck to strands of hair and foundation a shade too dark, sponged on top of an orange-y spray tan.

But I don't have a lot of choices for company right now. She asks me to come over the following evening, as if she knows that I won't have any plans. And she's right, I don't, but I wonder if I should feel a little bit slighted. I push that aside, though, and try to dress in the least intimidating, most welcoming, way possible. I can't look like I want to upstage her, like I want to throw her Midwestern-ness in her face. Baggy blue jeans, a baby blue T-shirt, Adidas sneakers. I apply minimal makeup, put my hair up in a little ponytail. I don't want to be *noticed*, or perhaps noticed for what I used to be.

Page is staying in the house of one of Odilie's friends, Louisa Bennington, the blonde with the turquoise caftan who spoke at the ceremony. The house was actually bought for Louisa's adult daughter, who now lives in LA, Page had told me over drinks, so she has the entire place to herself, a Cobble Hill brownstone. "I'm a huge real estate junkie. I mean, my dad's in the business. The place could be in *Architectural Digest* if that daughter had finished decorating it and hadn't moved." I decide to walk there, even though it's over an hour away, hoping that the air might make me feel less insane, less buzzy with anxiety.

As I walk, it dawns on me that Page's reasons for being here are vague. She said she was handling Odilie's legal matters, the house, all of that. But she didn't explain what that meant exactly or why she would be the one qualified to do it. Not that it's any of my business. But maybe it is, maybe a little bit. I'd googled her name, too, to try to find out more about her career, her aspirations, and there was not much, aside from her relation to her sister. Her LinkedIn said she had worked for a realty developer outside Detroit.

Brooklyn is humming with activity. It's a beautiful May evening, the weather hovering at around seventy degrees. People are seated at tables scattered outside restaurants, drinking and chatting. There's a positive charge in the air, a casualness that is so inherent to New York in the springtime. Anything could happen; the evening could blur into a party; two strangers could meet while ordering at the same bar; acquaintanceships could be forged.

This sense of contentment gives me a surge of optimism as I walk toward Cobble Hill. It was this sense of wonder, of anticipation, I realize, that made last spring, before everything happened, feel so full of possibilities. Why I so easily agreed to those dates with Tom, fell so quickly for his overbearing charm. I was seeking sensation, growth and novel experiences after a long, dreary winter.

I finally reach the brownstone, three stories tall with a Black Lives Matter sign in the window, well-maintained flower boxes. It's friendlier than Tom's was, aside from the blatant virtue signaling of its white proprietors. I approach the doorbell, pearly white, somehow completely impervious to the city grime.

Page answers quickly, as if she's been waiting inside the door for my arrival. "Vera! Welcome!" She embraces me tightly, a choke hold. She wears a simple V-neck T-shirt, the cups of a poorly fitted bra's underwire visible under the translucent cotton, and denim cutoffs, the cheap fabric unspooling in long white threads at the cuffs.

"Come in, come in. I bought some wine and I already know where to order pizza from." She leads me into a modern-looking, open-plan living area with floor-to-ceiling windows. It's almost loftlike in its design, the ceilings rising so high I'd have to crane my neck to see the recessed lighting there. Page has kept the curtains drawn, drowning the room in artificial darkness. When she moves into the kitchen, she is in shadow for a moment, blending into the dim corners of the room, forcing me to fumble my way after her.

As promised, Page has put out a frosty bottle of Reisling with two glasses, an ironstone plate with cheese and crackers and charcuterie artfully arranged in a pinwheel, on a large kitchen table with a bouquet of spider chrysanthemums bristling in the middle. Page pours me a glass.

"I have to water the plants. That's basically it. She still has the housekeeper come once a week, so I don't even really need to clean. It's obscene. I took a bunch of photos when I first moved in. But I don't feel like I can post them anywhere without betraying Louisa's trust. The downstairs is mostly done, but the Bennington daughter sort of stopped caring once it came to the second floor." She plucks a piece of cheese and chews it thoughtfully, and I follow her eyes as they sweep over the black-and-white-checkerboard marble floor, the handmade intarsia tabletop. "You know, I always wondered about the kind of life Odilie had living in New York. She gave us money every now and then. Not that we were strapped for cash or anything. My parents are pretty soundly old-school American middle class with their 401ks. But this shit, it's kind of dazzling." She looks up at the ceiling as if she's gazing at heaven. "Anyway, how have you been?"

I tell her about my job-hunting process, take a sip of my

wine, the chill hurting my teeth. "Ugh, it all sucks," she says. "Companies really only care about their bottom lines, not their employees, huh?"

We continue drinking. At some point Page pulls out another bottle of wine, finishes more than half of it herself, orders the pizza on her phone. She doesn't touch on anything Odilie related again, as if she actually just wants to get to know me. She asks me about growing up and going to NYU. About my family, my old job. She knows Magdelena by name, says that she once bought a pair of their pants during a sale and loves them. She asks about navigating New York, all the expenses, whether I want to stay here. Whether I ever want to settle down. What my relationship with my parents is like.

I find myself answering honestly, whether it's the wine or Page's open face, the encouraging smile she gives me, nudging me to go on, tell her more. "I can't imagine leaving the city. Even with how irrationally expensive it is to live here, I can't be anywhere else. It's almost cosmic. I can't explain it. Like I spent my entire childhood waiting to come here and now I have been for a decade and I'm steeped in it, the rhythms of life here. That sounds cheesy, I know, but there's no other way to describe it. I think the only thing that would pull me out would be a family. But I don't even think I want that, either." The pizza comes and Page doesn't offer us plates, so we grab from the box, hot cheese oozing to the table as I take a slice.

"Odilie never talked about New York," Page says suddenly, showering her pizza with red pepper flakes. "She just told my parents and me one day that she wanted to move. Then she started dating Tom. But again, we knew close to nothing about him. The move was completely out of the blue. We weren't even sure if she was still working. It was all very bizarre." She takes a bite of her pizza, a murmur of ecstasy tumbling out of her mouth as she chews and swallows.

I pour myself more wine. "You all really knew nothing about him? Even SNAPea?"

Page shakes her head midchew. "We knew he was rich. He had rich friends and that's how they met, I guess, through her new set of friends." The wine goes to my head, a vertiginous feeling of risk, that maybe inspires what I say next.

"She changed herself, didn't she? Lost weight, got some minor retouches."

Page places her wineglass down with a bit more force. "So you've been looking at her social media."

I feel myself redden, straighten up, try to channel whatever self-possession I need to answer her. "Yes. I looked at her Instagram. I guess I wanted to know more about her." I play with the stem of my wineglass.

"You mean her past. You and everyone else. That change you're talking about was like, the hook for the documentary they wanted to do on her," Page says nonchalantly, and I flinch, taking another slice of pizza, her face haloed nicely by the dim lighting.

"It was?" Of course it was. I'm not the only person who has done an Odilie deep dive, not in the age when all audiences want to do is guzzle down the new true crime story du jour. And they've probably learned far more than I, especially with no connection to her, to that scrawny, decomposing body.

"Yup. I can't explain it. My parents can't. We're not even sure how she paid for it. All I know is that, during the first big transformation we didn't see her for a few months. She said she was really busy at work. Her roommate at the time moved away that fall, so we lost touch with her, too. I don't even remember her name." Without a word, she pads across the kitchen and takes some good Espadin mezcal from the liquor cabinet, pours it into two shot glasses and brings one over to me. "Tastes like you're on a private jet, I swear. You're supposed to sip, but whatever," and she quaffs it before I even have my first taste.

"Anyway, like I said before, Tom's friends and colleagues refuse to do interviews, divulge any sort of information. Something to do with his company. I don't think any producer wants to touch that, from a legal standpoint. And of course, there's always the possibility of doing something just about the crime, but the intrigue won't be there. Everyone wants to know all about Odilie's and Tom's inner lives. How they met, what his childhood was really like. But no one can answer any of it. It's like Odilie stopped confiding in anyone once she met him."

I take a sip of the mezcal. It is good, earthy and tart on the tongue, the heat of it a balm down my throat. "How about her friends? The ones who planned the ceremony?"

Page reaches for the mezcal, stops herself, her hand flickering away from the long-necked, agave-adorned bottle. "If they know anything, no one will say." She finally fingers the bottle, pours herself a shot. "I had to empty out their house. And I kept looking for something—a diary, an album of photographs, anything that would give a hint of what Odilie was doing, was thinking. But there was nothing." She sips the mezcal this time, offers me more and I refuse.

"Has anyone tried reaching out to Tom's family?" I say, staring through the bottom of my glass, to the marble floor tiles below.

"Everyone's dead. Well, he has a brother, but he's off somewhere, down in Central America doing God knows what. I'm not even sure there was a funeral held for him." She shrugs. "I mean, maybe there was, organized by his friends or company or something, but of course I wouldn't know." She sighs, takes another sip of her drink, stares at me, the room dimly lit, her eyes reflecting the flickering candle she's set between us. Eyes on fire.

"But I want to know about Odilie." Her voice, it's suddenly solid, a glass pane without any fissures, like she hasn't drunk a single ounce of alcohol. "I want to know about her life here, who she was, what she did, where she went." She reaches out to me, her fingers dancing toward my arm, not quite grazing the skin, square-cut nails, flecks of old polish creasing the cuticles. "I barely knew my sister while she was alive and now she's not and I don't know who I missed. I want to know who she *was*. I want to know what's been left unsaid." She pauses, stops her fingers' dance. "You can help me."

I startle, the liquor flooding to the tip of my throat. "Help you?"

Page nods, still leaning forward, her breasts balanced on the table. "Her friends feel bad for me all alone in this house. They keep inviting me to things, but I don't want to embarrass myself. I know I don't know how to act here. But you, you're so confident, so well put together. So New York. You know how all these people operate. You've worked in luxury fashion. You've spent time with people like them. You saw how they treated us at the ceremony, like they didn't even know how to engage with us—like my family and I are from another planet. I want you to tell me how to fit in." She pouts, ever so slightly, her brows drawing together in a look of consternation.

I lean back, cross my arms, stare Page down. "I'll think about it," I answer finally, after a beat of silence. "But only because, maybe, I owe you." An admission, a confession, grounded in reality or not: I owe you for inadvertently killing your sister.

3

ODILIE

Ten years ago

ODILIE COUNTED THE days until Peri's next appointment; she highlighted it in the antiquated office calendar system as close to magenta as she could get on the ten-year-old computer, to match Peri's nails. The color, it glowed from the screen like a treasure.

Finally, the day arrived and Peri was late, gliding in without a second glance at Odilie. Odilie felt her chest deflate, like her actual beating heart was flat as a pancake.

But she knew exactly when Peri would exit the squat, stucco office and vanish with the setting sun. After checking out Mr. Elphonso, an aging man with leery eyes and a leathery hide, Odilie turned off her computer and hustled out of the practice a few minutes early, making her way to her car.

Peri had paid in advance. There was no credit card to be

processed, no insurance to be checked. Odilie had gotten permission to leave a few minutes early that evening.

She got into the car, unfolded the mirror and brushed her hair, redid her eyeliner, swiped Chapstick across her thin lips. She could have done all of it in the employee bathroom with its garish artificial lights, the white tiles like cleaned teeth. But the car gave her more space, more breathing room. A chance to position herself and her next move, to spot Peri before she even entered the parking lot.

Odilie had never loved the way she'd looked. But she hadn't hated it, either. She kind of accepted it as her lot in life. She saw her mother's eyes, her father's nose and lips, all the little makings of one whole face that was her own, nothing more, nothing less. She knew she wasn't ugly by any means. But she was also fairly realistic about herself. Her looks weren't going to stop traffic. If anything, they'd quicken it, like her magic power consisted of blending in with the roads, the streetlights, the trees lining the interstate.

Her body served its function. She didn't think about it much, except how to occasionally decorate it, what colors to paint her nails, that sort of thing. Like every other woman on the planet, she had bad body image days. But for the most part, she didn't think about any of it. She existed in space and that was the extent of it.

Peri had been the first person, the first woman, Odilie had seen who really owned herself, who was aware and had intention behind every movement, every slight bend of a finger, every tilt of her head. When Peri occupied space, she possessed it, like the air itself would leave an outline when she exited a room.

When Odilie knew that Peri would walk out in exactly two minutes, with the little goody bag of toothbrush and floss they gave away after every cleaning, Odilie stepped out of the car.

Then, as if this were her evening routine, she plucked a cigarette from the freshly unwrapped pack she'd grabbed from the gas station on her way to work today, and lit it, leaning against her car, her rear touching the driver's side door handle.

She didn't inhale. She let the embers eat at the tobacco. Until, finally, she saw a figure head out of the glass-paned doors, the dentistry office's name etched in white, and walk toward the parking lot. Peri's hair had so much bounce, even from here, a glossy brown buoy in a sea of cars and offices and asphalt.

Odilie held her breath. She inhaled the nicotine. She exhaled. And then Peri was walking toward her, toward her own car. And Odilie waved slightly, using her hand holding the cigarette, the way she'd practiced in front of the mirror. A casual, almost nonchalant movement.

And Peri caught her eye. She smiled. "I'm a bad influence, aren't I?" she called, making her way slowly but assuredly to Odilie.

"You were right. It's more relaxing than the gum. And better on the teeth."

Peri laughed, wind through bare-limbed trees at night. "Can I bum one?" She stood, now, right by Odilie. She smelled like hyacinths, and Odilie fumbled through the box, almost dropping the cigarette before handing it to Peri. "I liked you better than the girl I had in there with me today. You're more efficient. This one, she was so *gentle*, so worried that every little prick would send me into a spasm." Odilie chuckled back quietly.

"When it's painful, you know it counts," Peri said. "I want my gums to bleed." They stood in silence, gazing at the short row of cars, listening to the sounds of the highway on the other side of the hedgerow planted around the dentist's building. "What are you doing right now?" Peri asked, ashing the cigarette.

Odilie's chest thrummed. "Just going to go home and watch TV with my roommate, I guess." She kept her voice steady, even as her hands shook. She didn't quite know then why she was so nervous, what about Peri made her want to grovel, want to impress her, want to be her. She just knew that this person excited her in a way nothing else in her life really had before. Not in an erotic, passionate way, really. It was like Peri was a chasm with an unknown bottom and if Odilie jumped, she'd know something about the world that others didn't. The feeling was intoxicating.

"Want to get a drink?" But it wasn't a question. They both knew it wasn't. So Odilie found herself, not a moment later, following Peri's car as it wound out of the parking lot and into the evening. As her eyes lingered on the vehicle, she had the sudden worry that it would vanish, taking Peri along with it.

Wyneck was a summer destination, a coastal town that attracted Northeastern tourists all season long. Like many other seasonal villages, there was a divide between the local and tourist haunts, the neighborhoods, the types of food they ate. Odilie had grown up watching people come and go all her life, watched houses open on Memorial Day then shutter in September, after Labor Day. Every May she watched her sleepy little town transform overnight, shop windows smudged with debris suddenly gleaming when the first tourist family walked down Main Street. It was oddly discordant to grow up alongside the wealth that the summer dwellers brought, the Jaguars, the yachts, the specialty stores that kept popping up all throughout her childhood with fifty-dollar candles and sweater sets with a used car's price tag.

The town's economy catered to tourists. Odilie's dad worked at the one real estate company, Charter Sails. He'd worked there since he was in high school, a generational local. Her mother was a schoolteacher and ran the day camp the public school held during the summer months for the WASPy mothers who yearned to relinquish their children from 9:00 a.m.-3:00 p.m. every day, too used to school-day schedules.

The fabric of Wyneck depended on a particular kind of obscenity: palatial houses steps from the ocean with high insurance costs and property taxes, but no central AC, landscaped with hydrangeas in hues not typically found in nature, and lawns the color of Astroturf. One stretch of beach was subdivided into multiple private ones but few public ones, sand the same sun-bleached blond as the young children who built sandcastles on the shores and learned to swim in the gray waters, very occasionally drowning in their murky depths.

When fall came upon Wyneck, the town let out a communal breath, a sigh of relief commingled with anxiety about what the slowness could do to people, the fraught winter months that lay ahead that made the locals think too much, shoot deer or, accidentally, each other after several rounds of scotch, dare each other to jump into the ocean right when the first snow was about to hit.

Odilie wondered what bar Peri would choose as she idly followed her. They were driving toward the water, so she guessed The Crab Shack, the tourist haunt that turned into a dance party every weekend at midnight. Odilie knew that they doubled their prices after midnight, too, but that hardly anyone noticed, the lights too dim, the summer people too sweaty and soused to ever care to look at their tabs.

She was surprised when Peri pulled into The Fools, the townie joint that deliberately didn't paint its facade, clean its windows, try to mask the odor of fish from the dock not five yards away. Usually, this intentional negligence worked to keep the summer dwellers out. Not Peri, it seemed.

Peri grabbed a table outside on the back deck, overlooking the dock where fishmongers' boats floated idly beside small yachts. It was such a good representation of the town, this view, that it made Odilie smile.

Peri flagged down a waiter and immediately ordered both of them an Aperol spritz. "You'll like it, I promise. Now, tell me all about yourself," Peri said, leaning forward. She was wearing a T-shirt dress covered in sequined mouths, tongues lolling out of every glittering cherry-red lip.

Odilie cocked her head. She felt underdressed in her jeans that somehow felt style-less, her cotton H&M T-shirt, her Keds. She felt like a child playing grown-up. Even though Peri couldn't be that much older than she was. That was another thing about her; Odilie couldn't really guess her age at all.

"I'm not sure there's much to tell. I've lived here all of my life." The words made her tongue sting, a bad taste searing her molars. Why was there nothing else to say? And she wasn't lying, either. She didn't have a story to tell. Why did Peri expect anything more of her? And why was this simple, uncomplicated life story not enough?

"That's something. I moved to New York from Florida. This whole summer house thing, it's fairly new to me." The waiter brought over their drinks. "Cheers to you." They both took a sip.

Odilie fiddled with the beaded bracelet on her arm. "You said I had gumption. When we first met. But I'm not sure what you meant." Peri leaned back, looked over Odilie's head to the few people steadying themselves as they disembarked from a sailboat, barefoot, back onto the dock.

She looked back at Odilie. "You have this look to you, like you want something different. That you're already doing things a little differently than your friends, your parents. That if we dug into you too deep there might be a steel trap. That you'd bite." Peri eyed her over her glass, her gaze traveling up and down Odilie's face, poring over it like she was studying something, a scientific experiment.

Odilie swallowed more spritz. She wanted to know more about this woman who had occupied her thoughts so heavily, who said all these fantastical things about her like they were fact. Who seemed to suggest that Odilie didn't know herself as well as she thought she did. "Do you have that bite?"

And Peri danced her fingers on the tabletop. "Isn't it obvious? It's more of a claw." And then she began to speak and Odilie hung on to it, every word of Peri's life story like it was scripture, like she would repeat it back to herself at bedtime, a nightly prayer.

Peri was born in Saint Petersburg, Florida. At age six she and her family moved to Miami. Her father worked in construction, her mother as a housekeeper. When she was eleven, her father died. She and her mother and siblings were out at an aunt's birthday party. Peri came home early; she was having bad period cramps. When she walked into their apartment, it was the smell that hit her first, shit wafting through the house. She thought it was a dirty diaper that someone had forgotten to throw away. She headed to the bathroom to grab some Advil and lie down. But she couldn't find it in the medicine cabinet. So she went into her parents' room to dig through her mother's bedside table, a forbidden act but she was in a lot of pain. That was when she found her father, hanging from his own belt, dead. He had defecated himself, a common occurrence in people who die by hanging, something about how the sphincter muscles release.

Odilie brought her hand to her mouth. She had never heard someone talk about death so openly, so defiantly, as Peri. It was frightening; it was intoxicating. Peri's lips puckered over the straw in her drink, leaving it rimmed with red lipstick. She was a good storyteller, her eyes fervent as she continued, her face becoming even more vibrant and expressive, her eyes widening with every twist and turn.

After this incident she was burdened with looking after her three younger siblings while her mother worked. She hated it, she said. She hated handling those kids that weren't her own, who didn't appreciate the fact that she was sacrificing her own childhood to be their mother. Peri said that when she was feeling particularly annoyed and vengeful, she'd lock them in their shared room, give them some snacks and toys and go off into the evening. Sometimes she'd come back and someone would have soiled themselves. She would spank them, force them to clean themselves up.

Where was Peri going? Odilie asked, on those nights she left her siblings behind. "Everywhere. Nowhere. Friends' houses. Just walking by myself for hours at a time. I wanted to be alone, away from them. They reminded me of how sad my little life was. But out there, in the city, it smelled different. Like I had choices. My father's shit clung to everything, the smell of it. Even after we left that apartment, it was all around me, suffocating me."

When Peri was fifteen, she did what she always did with the kids. By that point, her brother was eleven himself, fully capable in her mind of looking after the younger ones. So she went out, went to the beach, empty that day because of the wind, and sat by the waves, looked out into the ocean and thought about her life in five years, ten years, when she'd be far away from her family and all their traumas. She sat on the shore for hours. She decided that the next year, when she was sixteen, she would leave home. She was already aware of her beauty. It wasn't a subtle thing, the way that men gawked at her, the glances she got in even the plainest of clothes. She knew she could use it all to her advantage, that her looks would get her ahead in life.

But she didn't have to wait a year, it turned out. When she

got home, everyone was gone. They were at the hospital. Her youngest brother, seven years old, had fallen out a window. It was a miracle he was alive. But his little body was broken. His little brain bleeding. Peri should have been watching him. From that point on, she was exiled from the family. Her mother asked her to pack up and leave that night.

So she did.

Peri glossed over the rest. She said that she started sleeping on friends' couches, that eventually she got scouted for modeling, as she always knew she would. That she began to inhabit other worlds, quickly and eagerly. That she hadn't seen any member of her family since her mother pushed her out, and she preferred it that way, that family is ultimately a poison holding you back, manipulating you into a loyalty that isn't owed or earned. And now she was here, in Wyneck, with a rich boyfriend, incredible views of the ocean. The shit, it didn't follow her here. She made sure of it.

"Wow," Odilie finally said, swizzling her drink, the ice melting slowly despite the heat. "That's quite a story. See, that takes gumption. You *do* have the bite, the claw, whatever you want to call it." She was confusing these metaphors; Peri's words so deliberate and pretty on her tongue, even as she spoke about such detestation. Odilie could watch her talk for hours. "I haven't been through anything, really. My life, it's sort of small."

Peri smacked her lips, leaned forward, whispered, "Your life, it's just begun." They drank more. Peri asked Odilie about her family, her sister, her childhood dreams. Odilie answered, said that she couldn't even remember if she'd had any outlandish goals, like to be a princess or an astronaut. That she was never pushed in the way Page was, and that that made her sad, like her parents expected so little of her that they didn't even try. "I try to be a good person," Odilie slurred. "A good citizen. I don't ask for much else." Peri had nodded at that, no judgment.

"Do the locals and tourists mix often?" Peri asked, dipping a cracker in the pimento cheese a waiter had set out.

Odilie shook her head. "We're fairly divided. Different locales, different beaches. I grew up around you all, can recognize faces and names, hung out with some of you. But it wasn't very cool to be interested in your lives. We have a lot of small-town pride."

"It's cool to disdain us, I imagine," Peri surmised and Odilie nodded her head before she could stop herself. Peri was right, though Odilie had never thought about it that way. It came down to jealousy, she imagined, like the ability to leave this town was only for those who stayed three months; that an invisible barrier was erected the moment the last tourist left.

Peri paid for all those drinks. She put her black Amex down and the waiter took it away before Odilie even had the time to protest. After it was returned, Peri took her hand and they walked to the beach, away from their cars, their movements synchronized, their arms swinging.

When they got to the beach, Peri collapsed onto the damp sand, her back to the ocean, the waves tickling the ends of her hair. Odilie joined her. It was dusky. The moon was new. The only lights were from the houses higher up on the beach, windows glowing.

After a long quiet moment, during which they listened to the waves behind them, hands still clasped, Peri rolled over. "Tell me a secret. Something you've told no one." Her breath was hot on Odilie's cheek, but it sent quakes up and down her spine. The spot on her face that Peri had traced, all those weeks ago, it seemed to burn with the memory.

A secret? Did she have one to tell? Everyone has secrets. That they shoplifted something from a mom-and-pop shop once; that they had cheated on a test; let their sister take the blame when something was broken in the house. But a secret she had told no one else? Odilie bit her lip. She thought about her conversation with Peri, what Peri seemed to see in her. She was still confused as to why Peri had even asked to have drinks with her. Weren't there a thousand other things a woman like Peri wanted to do aside from spending time with an invisible girl from a tiny town? Odilie didn't have the *gumption* to ask. And maybe that was her problem, she was beginning to realize. That she thought so little of herself that her instinct was to question why someone would even want to hear what she had to say, be interested in her thoughts and opinions.

She swallowed. Turned to her side to look at Peri. Even in the night, the whites of Peri's eyes shone bright, like little moons themselves. "I think that I've felt so constrained by my expectations for life, that it's never even occurred to me to ask for more, to want more. I feel...unseen, and I thought that was my lot in life. Average looks. Average smarts. Average life." She breathed, put her hand on her stomach and traced her naval through her T-shirt. "But somehow, meeting you, more seems possible. I don't feel so...stifled."

Peri reached out and touched Odilie's face, in the same spot as the time they'd first met, caressed Odilie's cheek with her entire palm. "I see you."

Odilie's face burned bright and hot and red. She wondered if Peri could feel it.

4

VERA

Present day

I WAKE UP hungover and smell bacon frying, cinnamon bread warming in the toaster, but I lie still, trying to detangle the rest of the night.

I'd left Page's soon after she asked me that impossible thing, my head already beginning to throb from the mezcal and wine. She'd tried to get me to stay longer, to watch a movie, drink more, maybe even go out. But the longer I sat there, the glasses sweating, the more I began to question why I was there to begin with, with Page and her familiar face and her unanswerable questions.

I understood why she wanted my help worming her way into Odilie's snooty New York social scene. Her hair had the texture of straw and was too blond, her lash extensions too long, her makeup heavy-handed, and the color of her spray tan, if she insisted on having one at all, should have been two shades lighter.

But how could I immerse myself even more deeply in this tragedy? It was like running into freeway traffic, hurling myself onto the tracks in front of an oncoming train. How the hell could the end justify the means here? And what exactly *was* Page's endgame?

When I finally put on a sweatshirt and roll out of bed it's past noon, and through the wall of my bedroom I can hear muffled voices from the kitchen, the smells I woke to waning but still present in the apartment. Quinn must have someone over. Did a date spend the night? I pull on a pair of soft cotton shorts under my sweatshirt, just in case there's a stranger in the house, and open my door softly, walking down the narrow hallway leading to the kitchen and living room.

Quinn is sitting there, at the drop leaf table we extend to accommodate guests, but not with a stranger. It's Sam, Quinn's on and off again partner. I guess they're on again. Sam was one of the friends whom I'd texted, asking for help, hoping for some kind of lifeline when my world was imploding, but they'd barely responded.

Quinn and Sam are midconversation, sipping mimosas, the light streaming beatifically on the table, pink tulips in a blue vase the centerpiece of the drop leaf. They're both in tasteful sweats, Sam's shirt cropped, Quinn's hoodie flatteringly framing his face. Their dishes seem scraped clean, only a few specks of syrup left clinging to the pastel-colored plates Quinn insisted on buying. I feel like I'm walking in on something, third-wheeling where I'm not wanted.

Sam glances at me over their drink, smiles at me, raises their hand in a small wave. "Quinn thought you'd be locked in there for the rest of the day. But you have emerged! Come, sit. Have a drink." Why is everyone suddenly asking me to drink with them, I wonder? And before I can protest, Sam is pouring far too much prosecco into a glass, topping it off with a drop of overpriced fresh-squeezed orange juice. I take an extra chair, pull it over and sit with both of them, sliding my legs underneath my butt.

"There are extra eggs and stuff if you want to grab anything," Quinn says but I stay put for a moment. I'd barely socialized for a year and having two back-to-back engagements was proving to be too taxing.

"You look good, Vera," Sam says, leaning in to take stock of my morning breath, smeared eyeliner and rat's-nest hair, barely combed before drunkenly passing out last night.

"Ha ha," I say. "Quinn failed to mention you'd be coming over. But it's good to see you. Really." Is it? I take in Sam, the diffused light like an aura. Their hair is cut into a shorter afro than I remember it, their large brown eyes incandescent, even more visible. "Wish you had hit me up earlier, though. Didn't expect to get iced out by you, of all people." The words are out of my mouth before I can stuff them back in. But honestly, it feels good to scold someone.

They're so unfazed, they don't even blink. "Friendship is a two-way street. I was sick of your shit. I invited you to all my photo shows for months and you never even bothered to RSVP no. Then, last year when I told you my mom was sick, you didn't even check in. You expect everyone to drop their shit when, what, you lose your job? Miss me with that." They're not saying it with any bitterness, just so matter-of-factly that I can't even build a retort. I never even went to their artists' residency in Hudson, so close to my mom's place.

I pinch the bridge of my nose. I'm tempted to yell out that God, it was more than a *job loss*. But Sam is right, even if they're being snarky about it. Before my whole mess, I really did let my career dictate how I treated everyone else. And I miss that, that all-encompassing activity that lit up every part of my brain. But I need allies right now. "You're right. You're right, okay? I'm… I'm sorry."

They nod in my direction. "Normally, I would ask for a better apology than that, but you *have* been put through a bit of a wringer, so I'll take it. Wanna hear what I've been up to or what?" I nod and they tell me, stretching their legs out, ankles crossed, getting themself comfortable like they'll be around for a while. They have an exhibition coming up at Rubber Factory, photographs of the Black community in Woodlawn, Chicago, where their dad is from, a community that's slowly getting displaced, and they're still freelancing, doing graphic design stuff for various small companies, right now a Black-owned gardening company. The residency was good for them, they say; a good respite from the city.

"Did you feel the same way? When you left?" they ask. It's a pointed, almost mean question, and it startles me a little because it's a welcome reminder of why I got along with them all those years ago when we met in college. I knew Sam was going to be my friend the moment I saw them, so confident and tall and long limbed, snarky like Quinn was, but edgier. I wouldn't have called them mean or callous, but there was a hardness to them that called to me, that made me want to bum a cigarette off them after a Steinhardt class one night.

I stutter out a laugh, keeping my cool. "Yes, it was such a good break from my boring, uneventful, mundane life. Nature is really the balm that soothes all sores." Quinn emits a chuckle and I give him a grateful glance, a silent thank-you.

"How was last night, by the way?" Quinn asks. And I know I could easily say something like "fine," leave it at that, wipe the evening from my memory or conversation. But something about having Sam there, this familiar face, a good ghost of my past, makes me barrel through that instinct. I like Sam.

Maybe I should try liking people more, start giving more of them the benefit of the doubt. "It was kind of a mess. She's kind of a mess. The whole thing, her whole situation, it's dark in how unanswerable and dismal it is. I'm not sure I want to see her again. I don't think I can give her what she wants, not in the way you originally thought I could, all the healing shit." I finish off the mimosa, traces of pulp swimming at the bottom of the glass.

"Don't blame me. I told you to do what you wanted."

I sigh. "I'm not. I promise. This is just my sad little life now."

Sam leans in, plants their chin in their hands. "Okay, I know you two have your own weird language, but I'm your guest and you seem to be intentionally excluding me. Hello! I exist! Who is *she*?"

I begin to tell them, starting with the situation at the ceremony, the strange comfort Odilie's family had found in me, the way Page seemed so lonely, desperate for company in the city. How the more I spoke to her, the more she wanted information from me that I couldn't exactly give her, that her family's pain was deeper than I could have known because of how little they actually knew about Odilie. How she wanted to learn about her sister, the life she led up to her death. Page's goal to associate with these wealthy Brooklynites; the favor she was asking of me.

I even tell them about Odilie's Instagram, and Quinn's eyes widen because I hadn't shared one word with him about my midnight sessions on her account. "I guess Page wants resolution. She wants to know who this dead person was, and I can't tell her that story. And part of me wishes I could. And then the other part is like, fuck this, get me as far away from Page, her demons, as I can get. But of course, that's also impossible." There's a stretch of silence when I finish. Outside there's the rumbling of an argument, something about parking, and I focus on that, waiting for Sam, for anyone, to say something.

"You're right. There's not much else to find on Odilie's Instagram," Sam says so factually that it almost sounds like an echo of my own thought. Quinn gives them a confused look, brow wrinkling in bemusement. Sam holds up their hands in an "I surrender" pose. "I did it, too, okay? You're right, Vera. There are a lot of cyber sleuths who were as interested in Odilie's personal life as you and her family are. I looked at her Instagram. I know all about the makeover scene out of *Clueless*. There's nothing too interesting after that shift, by the way. Odilie's Instagram gets boring again. Though, she does move to New York." Sam starts clearing the plates, bringing them to the kitchen, dumping them in the sink.

"What the fuck?" Quinn mumbles in a voice I'm clearly not meant to hear. "You're friends with a person whose life has been completely blown apart by this, yet you were stalking a dead lady like she was some past hookup? What is wrong with you?" Quinn's voice is quiet, restrained, a sure sign that there's anger simmering. Indignation.

Sam shrugs. "I was curious. I felt weird sharing info with Vera. I did my own detective work. You know I've always been interested in this shit. I was literally the first person you knew to begin listening to *My Favorite Murder*. But anyway, she's here now." Sam turns his head toward me. "Vera, are you mad at me for looking into this stuff instead of talking to you about it?"

I'm suddenly so immensely hungry that it's all I can think about, as if the clink of tableware landing in the sink sparked a Pavlovian response in me. I get up without a word, and serve myself some cold eggs and bacon, sit down and practically finish the plate before answering. Quinn and Sam wait in their positions, Sam by the kitchen's entryway, Quinn still seated, as if we're in a painting, the moment suspended.

"No, I'm not," I finally say, wiping bacon grease from my mouth. "It's a fucking car wreck. Of course you couldn't look away. And it's even more tantalizing because you knew one of the key players." The room itself seems to exhale with relief. Quinn pours himself the last of the prosecco, no orange juice. Sam sits back down.

"Well, do you want to hear my advice, then? You've probably thought about this yourself," Sam says.

I shrug. "Yeah, sure. Whatever."

They rub their hands together, like a cartoon villain. "Use her. Use Page for your redemption arc. How amazing would that story be? The mistress and the mourning sister brought together by their need for connection. 'Anyone can learn to love one another, even two people the opposite ends of a murder.' It would be fantastic for you. And you said she's lonely, anyway, so what's the loss? You'll be doing her a favor." Their eyes bulge in anticipation. "But here's the clincher." They turn to Quinn. "*You're* going to write it."

Quinn knocks back his prosecco. "*Me?* Are you out of your mind?"

"A little." They shoot me a wry glance. "Everyone and their mother knows you're tired of shuffling papers. You pretend that this is the way it goes, that you're so *grateful* to be working for such media *legends*." Quinn looks like he's going to throttle Sam, but Sam holds up a palm to silence him. "Don't deny it. No one blames you for it. We all know how talented you are. This is what you do. Vera, you get to know Page super well, do whatever she wants you to do. Then, when the timing is right, you spring the idea of Quinn, your Journalist Friend, writing a story about your friendship. It'll be very respectful, Quinn has known you for years, he only has your best interests at heart, you'll be able to control your narratives, blah blah blah." They pause for dramatic effect. "And the best part is? What if something else comes out? Another affair Tom had? Some kind of clue that he had a propensity for violence? Quinn, you'll have exclusive access to the inside story behind the biggest murder to hit rich white New Yorkers since the Killer Nanny. Your career will skyrocket! Vera, everyone will pity you! It's a win-win. All I ask is that when the time comes, I take the photos." They rap the wall as if to say *fin*.

We stare at them, dumbfounded.

Until finally, to our shock, Quinn says, "You are insane. But I guess the craziest ideas are sometimes the ones worth pursuing. But only if Vera consents."

I feel a burp, cover my mouth with my hand. This *is* insane. But Sam is right. If there was some public proclamation of my friendly relationship with the Pattersons, then I might be able to get a job again. I wouldn't be such a fucking leper. I could help Page do whatever she needed to do to move through this whole quagmire. And from the looks of it, that didn't seem to be much except drinking, giving her pointers on how to fit in with Odilie's buddies and making sure she doesn't look like a mall rat from the boonies.

"Okay, okay. But I need support with this. I'm not getting myself twisted up in this girl's crazy unless I know we have a game plan." Quinn and Sam nod in response.

"Whatever you're most comfortable with," Quinn says solemnly.

Sam's eyes are gleaming. "Text Page. Say you want to hang out. The sooner, the better." I grab my phone, but there's already a text from her, no greeting just a simple missive:

Odilie's neighbor, Ruthie Carroll, invited me to dinner with her and some of Odilie's book club friends. Help?

5

ODILIE

Ten years ago

ODILIE DIDN'T HEAR from Peri for days.

Every moment she was alone, she checked her phone, cradled it, threw it on her bed and watched it bounce to the floor. She hid it underneath couch cushions so she wouldn't check it, powered it down and watched TV for hours so she wouldn't look at it.

And every time, when she checked, there was no new message.

Her roommate, Kitty, didn't seem to notice Odilie's silence. She prattled on as they watched *The Bachelor* together, their weekly tradition, pointing out the girls she thought were desperate, the ones she thought were slutty, the ones she thought had a fighting chance. Odilie had known Kitty all of her life; they were supposedly best friends. They'd both waded through school together, on the outskirts of the social scene, occasionally invited to parties, never creating waves, their names easily forgotten by their other peers whom they'd known all their lives.

Kitty was also taking classes at the community college and working for her father, who owned the convenience store in town. Up until this point, Odilie thought she liked Kitty. She knew everything about her, her favorite movies and the odor her feet gave off if she skipped a day of showering. But hearing Kitty now, her voice whining in Odilie's ear, Odilie wished to swat her, crush her so her blood burst, like an engorged mosquito.

From the other side of the couch, she told Kitty, "You're just jealous of all of them. You would *love* to be as desperate and slutty as any of them. You'd love to do anything but sit on this brown couch and grind your teeth and pick at your toenails and work for your father. Anything. You're just too slow and sad to do anything about it." And then Odilie got up, leaving Kitty's jaw hanging open.

Odilie went to her room to think about Peri.

She knew this feeling, of course. It was like a crush, waiting for a boy to text her after a date. She wasn't exactly attracted to Peri. It was more than that, more powerful, more all consuming. She wanted to be in Peri's presence. She wanted to bask in her halo. She wanted her attention, to see the curve of her lips when she smiled. She wanted to feel Peri's innate confidence swathing her like a quilt around her shoulders.

On day four Odilie began to worry. She gnashed on her gum, began to bite at her cuticles. She replayed the entire night, all the way through to their time on the beach, their confessions, Peri's tale about her childhood. Had Odilie said something wrong? Had she made some kind of slight that Peri took as judgmental? Did Peri wake up the next morning and wonder why she had wasted her time on someone like Odilie?

She was distracted at work. She called in the wrong medication for a patient. She mixed up schedules, overbooking and underbooking. She'd stopped listening to the hygienist, Elena; zoned out during their morning chats. "What is up with you?" Elena asked as they shared a Krispy Kreme doughnut.

"Nothing. Just a bad period," Odilie answered. She wasn't hungry. And every time she gazed at the doughnut's crumbs she thought about Peri, her rail-thin arms, the way her waist and hips and thighs could fit between two cars parked bumper to bumper.

Life seemed gray suddenly, as much of a cliché as that was. Kitty wasn't talking to her, resorting to passive-aggressive jabs like leaving one bowl in the sink unwashed. Odilie didn't care about that, though.

The small joys of the sun on her back, the feel of her sheets after a day of work, they were all tinged with the memory of Peri, of her silence. Peri had suddenly become everything fun and adventurous and bright in Odilie's small, small world.

And then, on the seventh day, Odilie's phone pinged and she saw that name, the name she had been dreaming about seeing on her phone for what felt like years.

Let's get together again soon! Xx.

And a comment on one of her Instagram posts.

They met up again. They had dinner. They went shopping. They went to the movies. They lay on the beach one Saturday morning and drank mimosas, waded into the water and felt the buzz of the alcohol mix deliciously with the salt of the sea spray.

They lay on Odilie's couch and watched TV, having to pause and rewind constantly because they would make comments, start another conversation, forget what had just happened on the screen and start over.

Peri, even with her shadowy vulnerabilities, was bewitching. She would tail Odilie, her toes nipping Odilie's heels, like a hawk preying on a mouse, into the bedroom, the bathroom, the aisles of the grocery store. Or like a child, a child who knew exactly what she wanted and that she would get it with little protestations. It was menacing; it was moving.

What did they talk about? A lot of it was Peri telling long, languid tales about her life. "I met my current boyfriend at a club in the city. I was seeing someone else, someone much older. It was the first night in a while he let me out, to have some fun. I saw my current boyfriend right away, this little puppy dog with overwhelmed eyes. I wanted him for myself, wanted to take him home from the pound. We've been together three years." Odilie couldn't imagine anyone dictating to Peri when she could go out and she said as much.

Peri shrugged. "It was part of our relationship rules. I mean, no young girl dates a man upwards of fifty without knowing what they're getting into, if you catch what I'm saying. He took care of me, taught me things. I wouldn't be where I am today without him." Odilie tried not to gape at this admission. Peri seemed to have lived sixty lives before she turned twenty-five.

"I wish I had someone to tell me who to be," Odilie said. "I'm not even sure what I like in life, besides the basics. I took early-education classes this past school year, but that's only because my mom is a teacher. I don't think I want to be one. I'm not sure what I want to be. My imagination has only stretched as far as this town, this county. And I'm not sure why." She thought about lying, about making herself seem more introspective, more interesting. But there was something about Peri's penetrative gaze that demanded the truth, that extracted it from Odilie like a wriggling worm from the soil.

Peri asked Odilie about her dating history, her boyfriends. "Are you straight?" she asked pointedly, one evening as they walked along Wyneck's edge, on the rocky beach that hugged this side of the coast, jagged rocks scraping the undersides of their feet, holding hands to steady themselves, like Odilie had held Page's when they were so, so young.

"I'm straight," Odilie answered without having to think too much about it. She had never had sexual feelings toward women, had never felt lust. Sure, she envied a girl for her looks, her grace, but that had never translated to wanting to derive pleasure from her.

Odilie didn't mind the question, though she thought she would have if it had tumbled out of anyone else's mouth.

Peri always came over to Odilie's, saying she didn't want to have to deal with her boyfriend, that he always had colleagues over, his work strewn all over the place. That was why they were in Wyneck in the first place; Peri's boyfriend was some businessman whose biggest investor summered here, too. Odilie accepted this without question.

"I feel comfy here," she said to Odilie on more than one occasion. "Comfy with you, like I can be myself, spread out. Sometimes it just feels so suffocating over there, like I only exist as a mirror, an object that can reflect those men's worth."

Kitty, of course, did question Peri's presence, especially on the mornings when Peri appeared in the kitchen, fisting handfuls of blueberries that Kitty had bought specifically for a batch of pancakes. "Is she paying rent?" Kitty asked Odilie icily, cornering her in the living room.

Odilie rolled her eyes. "She's my guest. Have some respect, please. I had to unclog the shower for her to use it last night and all the hair was yours." Kitty gasped at Odilie's tone, the cruel, spiteful way she spoke back.

"What has gotten into you?" she huffed, marching into

her own bedroom and slamming the door in Odilie's face. In a different life, when Odilie had been a doormat, she would have cared. She would have groveled for Kitty's forgiveness. Now, she couldn't even *try* to care.

One day Odilie and Peri stood in front of Odilie's bathroom mirror naked after a swim. Peri's skin glistened from the sun, her breasts high and taut, her legs toned, the calves slender and defined. With not a drop of makeup on, Peri looked exquisite, edible almost, her skin so smooth and clear that it reminded Odilie of frosting.

It was hard not to compare herself, to stand next to this woman who seemed so self-possessed in her own nudity. Peri didn't even seem to be aware that she was standing in front of a mirror, her crotch waxed, her ass curved and high and supple. She was simply drying her hair with the towel, rubbing it fiercely through her long brunette mane, her eyes shielded by the terry cloth.

When she swooped up, her eyes landed on Odilie, who was now busy staring at her own reflection in the mirror, her eyes averted from Peri's. Odilie used to see a lot of function in her body, the way it took her from place to place, how it allowed her to see and smell and *be* in the world.

But standing next to Peri, she felt more than naked, like her skin was being stripped away, like her bones were wrong, in the incorrect places, like her face was wide and featureless, haphazardly stretched over her skull in a misshapen, formless blob of flesh. She felt uneven somehow, wobbly in her own disjointed body. She leaned into the mirror, touched the bump of her crooked nose, took her cheeks in her hands and rubbed them, as if that would produce collagen. She wanted to melt it all away, to take her nail scissors and cut away all the extra skin on her face, her thighs, her arms, her stomach. Next to Peri, she hated the way she looked in space, the *amount* of space she took up, like she was an extra chair at a table that only seated four.

She noticed Peri watching her watch herself in the mirror and immediately backed away, grabbed a towel and wrapped herself in it. "You know you can get anything fixed these days, if something bothers you a lot. People are such naysayers about plastic surgery but if it'll make you feel more confident, then why not?" Peri said, stepping into the bedroom to slide on some underwear, a flimsy lilac thong that only accentuated her tanned, toned, buttery buttocks.

"Have you?" Odilie asked. The thought hadn't even occurred to her until that moment, that Peri's physique could be anything but natural. She stared at Peri's chest as she asked it, her brown nipples small and hairless, little chocolate morsels nestled into the large, firm, upright breasts. Everything about Peri seemed drawn, sculpted, no mole out of place. The symmetry of her was astounding.

Peri shrugged. "Here and there. Just some tweaks. I have a friend who's a cosmetic surgeon. He gives me discounts. I wouldn't worry about it unless you're serious. You're cute as you are, obviously." And Peri slipped into her sundress, a diaphanous aqua number, and let the subject drop as Odilie stared at her friend's silhouette in the dress, the sun filtering through it from the open window, her breasts nearly visible.

Of course, the conversation clung to Odilie, stuck to her like gum on her molars. The more time she spent with Peri, the more she allowed Peri to direct their conversation, to give her style advice, to pick the movie or TV show they would watch; the more she internalized the fact that she let Peri do all these things because of the persuasiveness of her presence. And Odilie was wise enough to know that this kind of presence couldn't be store-bought, couldn't be molded from scratch out of plastic. But maybe changing her exterior would help Odilie manifest that *gumption* that Peri had spoken about, that was lying within Odilie somewhere deep inside.

Because the truth was, the more time she spent with Peri, the less full of gumption she felt. It was impossible to compare herself to someone who got everything she wanted all the time, who was so full of life and knowledge and had overcome such obstacles. Of course, Odilie wanted some of that light, a halo of her own, and she knew, down to the marrow in her bones, that spending time with Peri would yield those results, that her personality would eventually rub off onto Odilie. It was just a matter of time.

You're cute as you are. The words crept their way in when she was about to fall asleep, making her jerk fully awake. Cute. A word for dogs or kittens, babies. Not a word for a woman with *gumption*. Peri must not have meant it that way, would never have deliberately tried to erode Odilie's confidence like that. But she had.

One evening, after Odilie had finished work, Peri picked her up in her Alfa Romeo. "We're going to a party tonight," she said the moment Odilie slipped in, luxuriating in the car's aromatic, cool, perforated-leather interior.

"Whose party?" Peri said the name and Odilie's mouth twitched. The Sanders family. They were infamous; wildly rich, with reckless party habits that echoed their spending ones. The kids, all three of them, had grown up in Odilie's periphery. She'd watched them every summer from a distance. Their extravagant birthday parties, a whole petting zoo filling up the backyard. The Audis they all got when they turned sixteen that they'd zoom around in with only a learner's permit until one of them inevitably got too wasted and crashed it in some bushes.

And their cruelty, the way they got servers fired when they wouldn't give the kids alcohol. The snark with which they heckled opponents during tennis games, sailboat races. The jeers as they pushed people off their yacht, fully clothed, called it hazing, said it was all in good fun.

The middle child, Annabella Sanders, had done something terrible to Odilie once when they inexplicably ended up at the same pool together. Annabella claimed Odilie's father had given them a bad price for a second summer home—a cottage, they called it right near their first. Odilie was prime prey; the moment that Odilie surfaced after leaping from the diving board, she realized her bikini top had floated away, that Annabella had grabbed it, was playing catch with it among her other siblings. Odilie hadn't worn a two piece since then.

"I can't go to that," she said quietly.

"Yes, you can. You'll be with me. It'll be fun, I promise." Peri turned into Odilie's small parking lot.

"Then you have to change my face, make me someone I'm not." It was supposed to be a joke. But Peri, her face lit up like she'd been waiting for Odilie to say something like that all this time.

"I can do that. Easily. Come on." And she rushed out of the car up the stairs to the apartment.

6

VERA

Present day

I SHOW UP at the Cobble Hill brownstone with garment bags.

It's like a seed, the tiniest blossom of the old me coming back, my arms sore from the heaviness of the bags, my feet wedged into pumps, cropped black pants showing off my ankles. Page answers the door in sweats. Her eyes shine at the clothes, all from my closet, dug out after a year of disuse. My brain feels heady, the high of being back in business, directing something, making an outfit happen, assembling all the pieces so an endeavor can go smoothly.

Page shows me to her room. She's taken over the master bedroom, windows cloaked with golden curtains, a make-shift ancient bedstead, a Moroccan rug relieving the bareness of the floor. Other than that, it's scarcely furnished, as she'd mentioned earlier. I ask her to give me a rundown of the guest list, whom she wants to talk to, what drinks she thinks they'll serve. She looks at me intently, her eyes roving over all the clothes I pull out, the bag of makeup I fling into the adjoining bathroom. The bedroom already has her touches, a stickered laptop perched precariously on the bed next to a large, icy glass of something that smells like a cocktail. Her clothes piled on a partially upholstered chaise longue in the corner, dirty underwear peeking out from what looks like an old container of Pad Thai. Her clothes are so mass-market. They tell tales of tiny children's fingers plucking away at threads; of disintegration after too many tumbles in the washer. I make a mask of my face, hope my look of disdain fades away.

"These women, you said they're a mixed age group?" Page nods docilely. "Well, if it's a Brooklyn-based book club, they *may* have actually read the book. But they'll also be talking about husbands, wives, kids, schools, politics. Politics is a big one.

"Ten years ago? Their eyes would have glazed over if you brought that shit up. Now it's *all* about performative activism, no matter if their husbands are literally running a fossil fuel company. They want to seem 'woke.' The wealthier they are, the less they'll show it off. Think of what Mark Zuckerberg and his wife look like when they're shot by the paps. They're in sloppy sweats.

"And they all have the same political stance, I assure you— progressives, left on all social issues, with too much cognitive dissonance to recognize how they, and their partners, are contributing to vast income inequality. They will happily criticize Obama but will unabashedly lust after him, if they're straight. They hate Trump, obviously, but secretly love the tax breaks they got because of him. Do not mention the latter. Most of them will have voted for Warren in the 2020 primaries. They're very into #girlboss energy, but the more adept ones will know how to critique it. Their kids, if they have them, will probably only eat organic whatever, though one of them will espouse mindful eating without actually practicing it. They love 'natural' wine. They love clothing they can brag was locally sourced. They love *food* they can brag is locally sourced. They love to brag about their Bail Fund donations and the time they almost got arrested at an anti-police protest, while hiring security detail for their more lavish parties and telling you not to take the subway at night to *those* areas, meaning predominantly Black and Brown neighborhoods. Most of them will be white, but there might be a light-skinned Black woman thrown in the mix, maybe someone of South Asian descent. You cannot, under any circumstances, suggest that they don't work, even if they literally do not make their own income. Or mention their hired help, except if it's the nanny and only if she's 'part of the family.' Also, if you try to sound too intelligent, they can sniff you out as a noob and *will* patronize you. Let the hostess take the lead, too, even if she's a bore. Compliment her, follow her conversation topics, let her be your guide. I've made the mistake of upsetting one too many women in their own home in my day, so don't make my mistake." I pause, take a breath. Page is on her phone. When I step closer, I see she's taking notes and I smile in spite of myself.

"How did you figure all this out?" she asks, her voice earnest. "It's not like you're from here."

I pause, take a moment to genuinely think about that answer. "Trial and error. Lots of time helping VIP clients at Magdelena." Having a clear-eyed vision of what I want, I say silently to myself.

"The best way to fit in, to get people to like you? Especially uber-rich, powerful ones?" Page looks up expectantly from her phone, eyes me studiously. "Ask them about themselves. Pretend like they're the most interesting person in the world. Listen more, speak less. You can't go in there talking about Odilie, asking direct questions about her. Let her come up organically. My roommate taught me that. He's a journalist." Page types this up on her phone and I straighten my spine. My little pupil.

"Now, let's do your makeup." I guide her into the bathroom, which is cavernous. Two sinks, a new shower, a Jacuzzi. They really gutted whatever charming interior was here before they made it into this nouveau riche monstrosity.

I pull the stool from the vanity and Page sits down obediently as I perch on the bathroom's decorative chair. "The key here is to be as simple as possible. You'll be a laughingstock if you look like you tried. We're going for the natural look, so wipe everything off you have on now." And Page does so without protest, smearing a face towel black and beige and red, a mottled bruise of a color.

I start on her. Her brows are a mess—overly shaped and far too long, but I can work with all of it. We sit there in silence as I draw on her. She's actually kind of pretty, once you take away all the bad makeup. She has good, round eyes, cute freckles, nice cheekbones.

"I wonder if Odilie did this," she says quietly as I even out the fawn-colored eye shadow I've picked for her. "I mean, I know she did. She had that whole makeover that you already know about." She opens her eyes, meets my gaze, her pupils latching on to mine, brown eyes so like her sister's, ones I saw pixelated over and over again, that for the briefest moment her face materializes in her irises, like Odilie is coming to life behind her sister's eyes, grasping for me, for my neck.

I startle and blink and when I open my eyes, Page's are closed again. I use a Q-tip to wipe away some powder at the top of her lid. "Let's call this a make-under," I say. I don't want to think about Odilie. Even though she's everywhere, watching from all the little bathroom crannies, haunting the face into which I'm looking, so, so alike.

I pinch my skin. *Not right now,* brain.

A half hour later I have Page dressed in a linen shift dress, unembellished tan sandals on her feet, her baby chick–colored hair combed back into a loose ponytail. She's wearing concealer, a dusting of the fawn eye shadow and a red lip, nothing else. I've taken all the bracelets off her arms, unclasped the rhinestone cross from her neck. I've given her a small saddle bag to keep her phone and wallet in, removed the cheap pearl studs from her ears. She looks good, I think. Natural.

"There you go!" I say brightly. "Do you need help finding the subway? I can walk you to it before I head home."

She looks at me quizzically. "But you're coming with me, Vera."

I pause, scoff unintentionally. "No, I'm not."

But Page doesn't laugh back and she doesn't make a move out of her bedroom doorway, either. "I need you there. To hold my hand." Her eyes, they widen, a quiver on her lips like she might cry, and I back away, farther into the room and she follows, her face so close to mine I can taste her exhale.

"You think *I* can spend time with Odilie's friends? They hate me. I'm part of the reason she's dead." I feel dizzy. I want to lay my forehead down. I wonder, for a tiny shimmer of a moment, if Page has drugged me somehow, like her mere presence has shot poison through my bloodstream.

"I've already mentioned inviting you. No one thinks that way. No one who actually *knew* Odilie and Tom. Trust me." The last part a shiver of a phrase.

I'm about to protest again when I hear Sam's voice in my ear, *Do whatever she wants.* So I let out a sigh. "Okay, let's go for it." And I force myself to smile, my mouth aching from the effort.

I take off my own pumps and opt for the Thom Browne

loafers I got on the RealReal, hope that my blousy top isn't revealing my cleavage too much, that my naturally pouty lips and sharp cheekbones that cast me so easily as the evil mistress have been neutralized by the lack of makeup, the under-eye circles I'm not covering up.

Once we're heading out the door to Brooklyn Heights, only a short walk away, I turn to Page. "They know I'm coming, right?"

Page gives me an obstinate look. "Of course they do."

And we're off.

Ruthie Carroll's home is not like Tom's or the Benningtons'. In fact, it's shabbier. I only get a quick glance at it as we're ushered into the back garden by another woman, Shirley, who had hosted the remembrance ceremony at her apartment building. Shirley's ample chested with silky hair and looks to be in her midthirties. The kitchen appliances are old, the stairs leading up to the second floor worn and mottled, the paintings on the wall dingy and boring, stuff you'd find in the bathroom of a kooky Ridgewood bar but without the irony. Page almost looks disappointed, her shoulders slumping the tiniest bit when she takes in her surroundings.

Ruthie greets us in the garden. "*So* glad you could make it!" she squeals, giving us both a hug. She's petite, with springy brass curls, wears a white linen shirt and pants, and is barefoot. She can't be more than thirty.

She guides us to a picnic table, a pitcher of sangria and many citronella candles dotting its surface. The other women are here, all three of them, and they introduce themselves. "Come, sit, sit. We all read *A Little Life* for this month, but since we have you all over, we'll avoid that whole discussion." Ruthie beams at us like we're the hot fudge on her sundae, pours us some glasses and starts chattering about her Core Club class this morning.

I study these women, the ones with whom Odilie chose

to spend her time. And I can feel them studying me, looks of confusion and contempt crossing their faces as Ruthie tries to talk her way out of the awkwardness. They're suspicious of me and I don't blame them. I resist the urge to stare them down, ignore them, make them feel insignificant and power-less. Instead, I try to fade into the background, sitting back in my chair, hunching my back a little, making myself smaller.

I learn that this is Ruthie's parents' house. That they now live full-time in Accord, New York, where they have a second home. That the whole place is hers now. She wants to remodel it, but just can't find the time between work and dating. And she just can't find the right decorator, the one who can make her granny-chic fantasies come to life. Shirley, the one who let us in, nods in commiseration.

"How did everyone meet?" Page butts in and I'm surprised by her forcefulness with these women, her ability to insert herself into the conversation. She's been sneaking glances at me the entire time, so furtive and quick that they leave me unsteady. I can't tell if she's trying to make sure that I'm okay or if she wants reassurance about her own behavior.

Ruthie giggles. "This isn't, like, something we're proud of. But all our boyfriends and husbands work together or have worked together! And Shirley's wife. You know, a lot of the big tech companies are headquartered out in California. But we're here, instead! It facilitates friendship among the fami-lies," she adds. Then these women all knew Tom intimately, or their partners did. The thought leaves a bad taste in my mouth, a gurgling in my stomach.

"And Joanie and I are on the board at Tree of Life. So we spend a lot of time together," a woman who introduced her-self as Clarissa says. She's Black, the only nonwhite person here, just as I predicted. Her head is shaved, and she's older than the other women, closer to early forties, wearing a pink cotton jumpsuit.

"Tree of Life is a nonprofit focused on creating more parks and natural landscapes in low-income communities," explains Joanie. She's spry, prim and pregnant, hair chopped into a pixie cut, dyed blue, wearing a denim maternity dress. She's the most ageless of them all.

"Odilie was on their board, too," Shirley says, dropping her name like an extra ice cube in an overfilled glass of water, a sudden frosty splash. I hear the silence, the beat of it, as everyone looks nervously at each other, every lip trembling like a robin's tiny ruddy chest.

"Yes, she was!" Ruthie finally says and there's a collective swallow as we all drink a large draft of the sangria. "It has rum, red wine, pears, apple and orange slices!" Ruthie says for the second time that night. And I can, thankfully, feel it.

The night moves along and I relegate myself to silence, only speaking when I'm spoken to, keeping an easy, breezy smile on my face and listen to Page, fulfill my duty of watching her, making sure she doesn't slip up. She's doing a pretty good job. She follows my rule to an impressive degree, continually asking questions. The one mistake she makes is when she outwardly acknowledges that she's never donated to a politician in her life, and I save her by saying that as long as she votes, that's all that counts.

Clarissa, I learn, lives in Williamsburg, Joanie in Tribeca and Shirley in the West Village, of course. Clarissa's looking to buy property in Mustique and Page inquires about that avidly. Joanie is thinking of bottle-feeding the third kid, her boobs have had enough, thank you very much. Shirley and her wife, Layla, may move out of Manhattan and live year-round in the Hamptons, but she says that all the time and it never happens, especially since their kids are loving their school. "Though I'm trying to convince them to have a running track on the roof, on Layla's dime of course. Bea loves sprinting and the school *needs* to support her dream!" Ruthie's boyfriend's company, some VC firm, is going into the cannabis industry.

At some point Ruthie procures a joint and that's passed around. Everyone seems to have, thankfully, forgotten about me and I go inside to use the restroom, taking my time on the toilet, swiping through my phone. I'm pretty drunk, I realize, as I stand up and look in the mirror. A little cross-faded. I wish Ruthie had put out snacks. As I wash my hands, I wonder idly if I could go to the bodega and come back with something. I'm sure no one would miss me.

When I exit the bathroom, I'm confronted by Shirley.

She's leaning on the granite kitchen counter that extends nearly to the bathroom, her arms crossed, like she's been waiting for me. I give her a little wave, try to decide if I should feign ignorance and make my way back out.

"I was kind of weirded out when Page was like, 'Can I bring Vera?' I mean, it's strange you two are hanging out in general, not gonna lie. But you're actually pretty cool. Not domineering at all. You know your place. Good for you for spending time with Page. I know she needs friends." She takes a drag from her vape pen. "Page has *really* been wanting to get to know us. It's kind of sweet. She emailed me the moment she got to the city and was like, 'Can you introduce me to all of your and Odilie's friends? I've heard so much about you guys.' It was so earnest. People aren't earnest enough these days." She takes another puff.

My head is swimming. Didn't Page say that Odilie's friends were pursuing *her*?

I try a smile for Shirley. "I just want to do right by Page," I say. My mouth feels sticky.

"You really got a bad rap, didn't you? Let me tell you this."

She gestures to my face with the vape pen. "Odilie was super reserved. I don't think she dug female friendships. Everything was always surface-level with her. But she did not give *two shits* that Tom was having an affair. She was over that bastard. She was totally going to leave him. She didn't say that *exactly*, but I could tell. And the media spun it like she was some devoted wife. Always pitting women against each other.

"My friends and I, even their husbands, we never held anything against you, not personally, anyway. You were in the wrong place at the wrong time. It was those creep wannabes who cleave to drama who really seemed to hate your guts. Not the people on the inside." She shakes her head, her sand-cast chandelier earrings tinkling with the movement. "Anyway, I wanted to catch you before we went back outside. You're cool." She eases herself out of her position at the counter.

"Odilie knew he was having an affair?" I say quietly, the words like glue on my dehydrated tongue.

"Oh, yeah, it was obvious. All euphemistic. But I saw her the day he did what he did, and she *knew* he wasn't happy about something. I'm a good read of people. I mean, I probably shouldn't be such a blabbermouth, considering what my wife does and all. But I feel like everyone did you dirty." Shirley drawls the last part. "Enough of that, though. Come back out and party!" And she saunters her way back outside, vape smoke trailing after her.

Leaving me standing there, dumbstruck, my hunger vanished, gaping at her retreating back.

7

ODILIE

Ten years ago

WHEN PERI WAS done, Odilie could barely recognize herself. She was not a beauty. No one would call her a beauty. But Peri had fixed her up as much as anyone would be able to with the limited material Odilie provided.

She overlined Odilie's lips, to give her a small pout; she magically highlighted Odilie's cheekbones, usually hidden under baby fat. She gave Odilie false lashes, fluffed her limp, mousy-brown hair into beachy waves, hid the freckles dotting her nose, filled in her brows to give them a lush arch. Odilie felt like Anne Hathaway in *The Princess Diaries*.

"I got you a dress, too!" Peri called from the bedroom. Odilie heard the harsh knock on the door—Kitty, trying to use the bathroom where Peri and Odilie had been sequestered for hours. Odilie opened the door without giving Kitty a second glance and ran into her room, where Peri had laid out a shimmering pink satin dress.

"I can't accept this," Odilie said breathlessly, her fingers rubbing the material.

"Of course you can! Now, put it on, because I want to take some pictures before we head out." Peri looked stunning in a baby blue dress that hit high up on the thigh, her perfect breasts jutting out of the square neckline, defying gravity.

They drank good champagne on the floor of the bedroom, forgoing glasses, swallowing huge sips out of the bottle instead, the bubbles making Odilie sneeze, laughing at the silly photos they took on Peri's phone, their heads touching, Peri leaning hers on Odilie's shoulder, Peri and Odilie pecking each other on the lips, Peri cupping Odilie's face.

"How do you even know the Sanderses?" Odilie hiccuped.

"My boyfriend is trying to get the dad to invest in his company. And I've seen the kids around. You know, New York party scene and whatnot." Odilie did not know, but she nodded along like she did. Peri must have sensed Odilie's unease. "You fake it until you make it, like me. Everyone just loves to talk about themselves. Nod along, compliment them. And soon, you'll know all the same people, be invited to all the same parties."

"Will your boyfriend be there?" Peri didn't talk much about him, the elusive man who was the reason she was summering in Wyneck in the first place. All Odilie knew was that he was a workaholic. Odilie had the feeling that Peri held the reins in their relationship; she couldn't see it any other way.

"Nope. He's in the city tonight." Peri took one last swig from the bottle before getting up, pulling Odilie up with her. "Let's go. If we stay here any longer, we won't leave."

They walked there, arms linked, using their phones as flashlights. Odilie knew a shortcut, down all the beaches, essentially people's backyards. The ocean was quiet for now, its waves incongruously peaceful for what seemed like such an exciting night.

"God, you're so easy to get along with," Peri sighed, her feet brushing against Odilie's as they padded through the sand, their steps in sync.

"Why?" Odilie giggled. She was feeling amazing, her chest blooming with anticipation of what everyone would say when they noticed her with her painted face, her beautiful dress. They had left Kitty in front of the TV, Cheez-It crumbs dusting her chest. Odilie couldn't believe that only a few short weeks ago that was what she'd have been doing on a Friday night, too.

"You're just so…easygoing. Hanging out with you is effortless," Peri answered and for a second Odilie's heart deflated. She wanted to be adventurous, fun, amazing. Not easygoing. But if easygoing was why Peri had chosen her as a companion, then so be it.

They smelled the bonfire before they saw it lighting up the sky, flecks of charred wood flying toward them even before they rounded a corner, smoke filling up the sky like a pagan sacrifice was underway. Surrounding the bonfire was a semicircular white cloth-draped bar, numerous stacks of logs, music blasting from an unseen speaker. It was like this was the Sanderses' idea of something casual.

People were milling around the fire, hair and outfits aglow in the light, embers shooting out of the pyre into the heavy night air. Peri squeezed Odilie's hand, her long nails pinching Odilie's lifeline. Then they entered the light, shadows dancing on the sand.

Odilie recognized some people right off the bat, people who were Wyneck summer regulars, whose houses her dad helped rent out, helped them buy, sometimes, but rarely, helped them sell. She wavered about saying hi; these were people she'd spied on for years, from the corners of beaches, from across the street in town. They definitely didn't know she existed, or if they had noticed her in passing once upon a time, Odilie was sure that her face could easily be mistaken for someone else's, that she was just as replaceable in these people's memories as one grain of sand is for another.

She watched Peri decide on her next move. Her eyes were roving over the crowd, possibly trying to find Annabella Sanders. To Odilie's surprise, it wasn't a Sanders who came up to them first, but another summer resident with bright red hair. Caroline Perkins. The name came to Odilie in a flash.

The old Odilie would have slunk off toward the edges of the party, social anxiety getting the better of her. The new Odilie, however, well, she had the *gumption* to introduce herself.

She was about to extend her hand, when Caroline embraced Peri, her elbow unintentionally untangling Odilie's and Peri's linked arms. "Per! Thank God you're here. I was getting so *bored* without you." The women started chatting, dropping names and places Odilie didn't know, a language Odilie wasn't fluent in. Gossip about who had a drinking problem, whose bachelor party was happening when. A few people's promotions, someone's boyfriend's stock portfolio. A house someone had recently bought in Lyford Cay.

She stood patiently by Peri's side, waiting to be introduced, trying to cut in during any pause. But there weren't many. A few other women joined, all of them hugging Peri like she was a long-lost friend, pecking her on the cheek, telling her how gorgeous she looked. Odilie felt herself slowly but surely being edged out of the conversation, succumbing to the shadows, to the parts of the beach from which they'd come, that weren't lit.

"Peri, come up to the house. We got the good stuff up there.

Only for you, though," Annabella Sanders said, putting a finger to her lips, her irises dilated, teeth grinding along with the music's beat. She noticed Odilie, but didn't seem to recognize her, eyeing her up and down, before grabbing Peri's wrist and pulling her toward the brightly lit pathway that led to the house.

"I won't be long," Peri called back as if Odilie were an afterthought, giggling at something Annabella said as Caroline and the other girls followed their hostess. Soon their figures were only silhouettes, then one big coagulated lump of young women. And Odilie stood there, alone in the sand among a crowd of people, as if adrift in the wide, wide sea. When she touched her face, a strip of false lashes landed on the pad of her finger, its individual spikes splaying out like tiny knives.

8

VERA

Present day

QUINN WANTS TO spend time with Page, get to know her so when we eventually spring Sam's wild idea on her she'll be more likely to accept it. I'm still reeling from Shirley's revelation, the knowledge she imparted to me, that Odilie was at least somewhat aware of Tom's infidelity.

I had mentioned it to Page as delicately as I could. She told me it was strange, thanked me for the information, said she would try to inquire about it further with Shirley. But as far as I know, she hasn't yet.

The moment I got home that night, I'd scoured the internet for a quote from Shirley. The conceit so many of those media stories ran with, as Shirley said herself, was that Odilie was in the dark. That she died ignorant and naive about her husband's transgressions, that I had cantered in, on a shadowy horse of the apocalypse, and caused this mayhem that Odilie had no hand in or knowledge of.

But no. Odilie had most likely *known*. And not only that, but possibly hadn't cared? It didn't make a difference, not really. She was still dead. But if she was forgiving of me before she died, maybe I could forgive myself. Maybe the public could forgive me.

I finally find it, on the third Google page, a line tossed into an early general news story about the case. "Odilie's friend Shirley Cassat alleges that the affair wasn't a secret, that in fact, the deceased woman had shared with her confidante some grievances about her husband's mood upon her return from Michigan." It's buried in there, a throwaway line so crowded out by dozens of others that it makes my brain itch, like something about the lack of visibility isn't quite right.

But pursuing *that* apparent obfuscation of the facts would be going down a conspiracy theory rabbit hole.

Page wants to meet us at the Brooklyn Museum, so Quinn and I walk there. He prattles on about workplace shenanigans, the stories on his roster about some new TikTok House scandal, the latest canceled celebrity, a short profile on some wellness guru's latest skin-care line. Even if Quinn won't admit it, he definitely wants to report on more important stories, just as Sam had said. There's a bitterness there, overly steeped tea, that I hadn't noticed before.

"We'll make this story happen," I say as we approach the steps to the museum. "I promise you." And he stops, gives me a look, and it occurs to me that I, unaware of my own misconduct, have probably broken numerous promises to Quinn when work ate up my life. But this one I'm intent on keeping. For both of our futures.

Page is already there, back in her old wardrobe, a cheap-looking Lilly Pulitzer knockoff and scuffed Jack Rogers. But her makeup's minimal; the only hint of her old cosmetics is her lip gloss, pink and shiny as a Barbie jeep.

But she's dyed her hair and cut it to her shoulders.

And it takes me a moment to realize that it's my color, espresso brown. That if we simultaneously shed, no one would be able to tell the difference. The color doesn't really suit her. It makes her tan look even more orange and her brow color doesn't match. But at least it's better than the baby-chick blond.

"Nice haircut," Quinn says by way of greeting and Page smiles, showing teeth, and I'm swept back for a moment to that photo on Odilie's Instagram, the first one of her new look, the way she had grinned.

We make our way through the permanent collection, pausing at Gilbert Stuart's painting of George Washington, *The Peaceable Kingdom* by Edward Hicks with all those weird animal faces transfixing their gazes at the viewer. It's not such a peaceful painting, I decide. Every beast looks afraid, scared to run, stuck in place, in an eternal fight or flight mode.

And Page talks, her voice rising several decibels too high for a museum. I'm so close to wanting to tell her to shut up, but I can't offend her. Not this early on. "I want to go to Ruthie's parents' place in Accord. I hear they have American quarter horses. One of them won the AQHA World Champion Show last year, in the reining category, so it seems like some kind of side hustle for them? Though that horse upkeep definitely *exceeds* whatever money you get in prizes. I didn't know you people in New York rode Western like they do in Texas. And did you see Clarissa's Etsy shop? It is *so* cool. She makes this, like, welded jewelry. I'm trying to get her to gift me a piece. I wonder if she wholesales the jewelry or if it's all direct to consumer. Oh, and Joanie's having some kind of party in a few weeks. She wrote a book! It's something about parenting." And on and on and on.

Quinn turns to her as we enter the small Decorative Arts wing, a puzzled smile plastered on his face. "Are you in a group chat with them or something?"

Page nods. "I'm also chatting a lot with Louisa, you know, whose house I'm staying in. She's *so* nice." And she launches into a story about Louisa giving her a list of restaurants to try in Cobble Hill, the best dry cleaner and shoe repairman.

I think back to that *other* tidbit Shirley let loose, about Page's earnestness, her yearning to meet all of Odilie's friends, which goes completely against what she told me.

I wander away to an exhibition of Hannah Hoch's work, get lost in a wall of her Dada collages, defying the Weimar German government, the clutter and creepiness of them, the unsettling feeling I have that I'm being watched again and again by the photomontages of heads plastered on legs, by the eyes detached completely from a face.

On our walk back, Quinn is quiet, like he's fumbling with something, a stone he's about to skip on the surface of the sea to see if it sinks or glides. Finally, "There's something weird about Page." We pass the doorman-staffed buildings lining Prospect Park and Eastern Parkway, a woman talking loudly on the phone about her ex-husband, a group of kids with a soccer ball running toward the park. "It's like she's putting on an act." He takes a puff from his Juul.

"What do you mean?" I say absently, my mind still on Hannah Hoch's work.

"It's like she's intent on making us see her one way, making Odilie's friends see her another way. I can't quite put my finger on it. She seems too eager?" He lets the question float between us and I shrug.

I had asked her whether she'd spoken to Shirley about Odilie's potential knowledge of the affair, and she said she hadn't, that she wanted to follow my own advice and ease her way in. I couldn't blame her.

"As long as I can use her to exonerate myself, who cares if she's eager." Quinn doesn't have a retort to that, but he's silent again until we reach our stoop, his keys flashing out of his pocket.

"She has her own game plan, Vera. She's smarter than she looks." And he lets it drop as we enter the apartment, then makes a beeline for his bedroom, so I do the same for mine.

9

ODILIE

Ten years ago

ODILIE WALKED HOME from the Sanderses' party alone. She had waited for Peri, texted her, called out her name in the wind, as if Peri could hear it all the way up there in the house on the hill. Ricky Sanders had approached her. She noticed his knuckles, still hairy as ever, remembered spotting them long before other children their age had developed any kind of body hair.

"You! Do you know where she went?" He slopped beer on the sand, wetting Odilie's bare toes. Odilie stared at him blankly, stepping back out of the light of the fire. He sighed in frustration. "Peri. Where did she go?"

Odilie was mute all of a sudden. What did this idiot want to do with Peri? He studied her for a moment, his eyes glassy with drink, roving. "Was it you? Did she want me to meet you?" Odilie stepped away, farther out onto the darkened part of the beach, Ricky backlit by the fire behind him. "Be careful. She's a real mean son of a bitch," she heard him call after her. And she ran down the beach into the night, until the noise of the revelers was masked by the sound of the waves and she could walk again, across the rocks, back toward her apartment, her face flushed with the effort, with shame.

Odilie cried, dampening her pillowcase. She scrolled through her phone, waiting for Peri to text back. She went to Facebook and Instagram and swiped through Peri's photos. She traced Peri's face on her small screen, her symmetrical features, her eyes so discerning and sharp, even in the pictures that were blurry, taken in clubs and bar bathrooms. Lying in her bed, Odilie mimicked Peri's expressions in the dark, the way she worked for the camera, her bottom lip puffing out, her eyes never crinkled, always widened.

Fitting in with these people, regardless of her past, was easy for Peri because she was so beautiful. Because she was confident and unapologetic.

Odilie could never be that way.

She clicked out of the app, put her phone down and closed her eyes, summoning Peri to her, like she could astral-project her way into the room. She put her hands on either side of her face and in the dark, tried to rearrange it, pulled at her lips, pinched her cheeks, rammed her fist against the bridge of her nose.

Soon, when the lightest pink was streaming through the curtains, she fell asleep. Peri still hadn't responded.

Odilie woke up to a tickle, a hot breath in her nostrils that almost made her sneeze. There was a weight in the bed next to her; she could feel the mattress's imbalance even before she opened her eyes. When she did, she saw wisps of shiny brown hair on the pillow next to her, lips parted, blowing currents of air her way. She blinked, dreaming, knowing the vision would dissipate.

But it didn't.

"Morning, sunshine." A lock of her own hair curled by a magenta-red nail, the bedroom bulbous, warped, like she was looking at it through the wrong end of a telescope. "You left me there, all alone." A pout, dewy as grass at dawn.

Odilie blinked, her voice arching out like a hissing cat, rough from having slept. "You left *me*." She rolled over, petulantly, like a child, clutching the comforter to her.

She felt a hand on her spine, tracing little invisible rings on her skin, the shift in the bed as Peri moved closer, cupped Odilie's ear. "You weren't talking to the other girls, Odie. I need them, you see. Their boyfriends and their fathers, they're all potential investors for my boyfriend's company. I was only up at the house a moment and when I came down to the beach you were gone. I thought you could handle things without me there." Her voice, so soft in Odilie's ear, oozed dismay, the low notes like vanilla extract splashed into sweet batter.

Odilie turned back over, nose to nose with Peri. She felt the glisten of tears, the telltale tug in her nasal cavity that she was about to cry. "Why are you hanging out with me? *I* don't have a boyfriend who can invest in your boyfriend's company. Why waste your time with me?"

Peri raised a finger, the pad of it at Odilie's lid even before she felt the first tear. She caught it, licked it. "Because I see something in you. Those people, they're so *boring*. They aren't excited about anything. They're so jaded by their wealth, by their excesses, that they aren't curious anymore. You— You, I can have fun with. You, I can be myself with. All the goofy, weird, stupid parts of myself." She smiled slowly. There was a lipstick smear on her teeth, the same fire-engine color she'd worn last night. She was wearing the same clothes, in fact, like she'd never gone to sleep at all.

"How did you get in here, anyway?" Odilie asked, taking in Peri's face, the makeup washed out and leaking like she'd been swimming. She probably had been. And yet, on her it looked glamorous, a woman caught in the rain.

"I banged on your door until your roommate woke up and let me in," Peri giggled. "She was not happy. What a curmudgeon that girl is. She has such a stick up her ass." Odilie didn't disagree.

"I want to be less like her," Odilie said softly. She wondered what time it was, how long Peri had been stretched beside her. How long Peri had watched her sleep.

Peri licked her tooth, the one with the lipstick stain. She'd known it was there. "You know what we could do? What could be quite fun, actually?" She raised her eyebrows, a silent salute. "Let's treat you to a fresh new look. Then, next time I take you to a party, you'll have the gumption to talk to people, to know your worth." She clicked her tongue in anticipation. "I know the right people around here. We can even get you some fillers, too. On my dime. Well, my boyfriend's, of course, but you know what I mean. It'll be fun!"

Odilie squinted, had to stop herself from stretching her face out the way she did last night. "Okay," she whispered without thinking, because thinking too hard about this would be something the old Odilie would do.

Peri leaped out of bed at that moment, jostling Odilie. "Anything you want fixed, we can make it happen. I promise." She smiled that bone-white smile.

Peri held Odilie's hand as the needle went into her lips, plumping and shaping them, even though Odilie's mouth was numb so she couldn't feel the pricks. Back at home, she sat with Odilie and applied ice packs to her swollen lips on the couch in the apartment, periodically getting up to crack open a fresh instant cold pack.

"What happened?" gasped Kitty when she came through the door, took a look at Odilie's face.

"She's getting prettier, honey," Peri called back, smiling menacingly until Kitty retreated to her room. She rolled her eyes at Odilie and Odilie rolled them back. "None of her beeswax."

When Odilie got some light Botox on her forehead, Peri did it with her, to show her that she needn't be afraid. They slept together in Odilie's bed, ensuring that they didn't crease their faces too much twenty-four hours afterward.

Peri helped Odilie decide on a new hairstyle, new blond highlights. She flinched with Odilie when the stylist chopped off five inches, giving Odilie a sharp bob. "But God, we can see your angles already," Peri murmured, running her fingers through the wet hair.

They went shopping at the mall in Springwood, two towns over, the luxury one with the Neiman Marcus. They bought pricey makeup from the counters, clothes from designers Odilie had never heard of. Peri told Odilie to get a size smaller than she normally would, to fit her goal weight, to give her motivation.

"There is no way I'm fitting into any of this. Ever," Odilie countered, tugging up the three hundred dollar jeans that barely went over her thighs. Afterward, when they were in Peri's Alfa Romeo, she handed Odilie the Trifecta, as she called them: a pack of cigarettes, sugar-free Red Bull and an orange bottle of Ritalin. "How do you think I can stand any of this?" she said, waving her hand in the air, at what Odilie wasn't even sure. "We all need artificial pick-me-ups. Thank me later, babe," Peri murmured, zooming out of the parking lot, one hand on the steering wheel, lighting a cigarette with the other.

Later, when they were back at Odilie's apartment, sprawled on her bed, Odilie drinking, and gagging, on the Red Bull, she turned to Peri. "Why is your boyfriend letting us spend so much of his money?"

Peri walked to the window, opened it, poked her head out and lit another cigarette, blowing smoke into the summer sky. She waited one more exhale before she turned around, answered Odilie. "It'll benefit him in the long run. Don't worry about that." And before Odilie could question what that meant, Peri lunged back into the bed, cigarette high in the air and grabbed the can of Red Bull, splashed some vodka from the handle on the bedside table into it, took a swig from the can and handed it back. "Cheers! You look incredible."

And Odilie, she felt incredible, too.

10

VERA

Present day

PREGNANT JOANIE HAS written a book, some kind of self-help tome, and she wants me at the party.

She texted me herself, and it strikes me that she may want a crowd of rubberneckers there, that the residual scandal around my name might draw more attendees. At first, I wasn't going to go, not until Page asked me to get ready with her and I resigned myself to my new fate as her stylist and BFF.

I've spent some more time with Page between the museum visit and now. We've hung out in Prospect Park, gotten drinks in her neighborhood, spent some time in Manhattan, too. I wanted to screech when she responded to someone trying to sell her a watch, almost pulled my hair out when she visibly became frightened by a panhandler on the subway. She has an irritating habit of trying to peer into people's ground-level brownstone windows, trying to steal a voyeuristic glimpse into their shuttered lives.

Otherwise, it's fine. She's annoying, but kind of smart in her own way, and seems harmless. I catch myself wondering what her life was like back in Michigan; she says she worked in real estate, but hopes to try something else once she settles things here. She talks openly about her friend group back home, telling me all about the drama behind her best friend's bachelorette party, how she was supposed to plan it, but she's decided to stay in New York longer. How all those girls aren't speaking to her right now because of that. She shows me a picture of them and I grimace without meaning to, their hair and skin all like Page's when she first arrived here, sorority girls aged five years. They all have *Live, Laugh, Love* and *First, Coffee* decor in their houses.

"How did you do it? Get used to living here?" she asked again as we ate Shake Shack in Madison Square Park, the original location, upon her request.

I shrugged. "You just do. I grew up coming here once a month. When I was in high school my friends and I would go out on the Lower East Side, too, and stay with people we knew who lived in the city. It's much easier if you actually grow up here, though. All that grime is in your bones."

I've been recommending books and movies to Page, places to shop and eccentric people to follow on Instagram that I think would offer her more conversation topics.

She tells me that she wants to move here. That once the Benningtons eventually kick her out she wants me to help her find an apartment.

I ask her if she has learned more about Odilie, if any of this is helping. "Yes, knowing who her friends were has definitely helped. It's brought me some closure," she responds as we meander through Central Park one day, toward the Upper West Side.

"Do you have an end goal? Something specific you want to find out?" I finally ask as we round the Great Lawn.

She squints, doesn't slow her pace. "I guess I want to know that there was nothing I could have done to stop it." I nod, let the subject drop. I know that burden.

When Page answers the door the evening of the book party, I'm struck again by her hair, her clean face, the freckles standing out on her nose, no longer covered by layers of foundation. It's when I look down at her feet that I notice the same Thom Browne penny loafers I was wearing the night of the book club.

She notices me looking. "I got them from Vestiaire Collective. I wanted to break them in!" She smiles and I smile unsteadily back, feeling a pinch between my eyes.

We head up to her bedroom and bathroom and start doing our makeup, all of our products the same expensive labels, mine tumbling out of my makeup bag and scattering across the bathroom counter. I make sure that they don't get mixed, pulling my stuff closer as I rub concealer under my eyes.

"I'm excited!" Page murmurs as she looks at the eye shadow palette, trying to decide which color to use. "I feel like we're going to meet so many cool people."

I start on my eyes, too. "They'd better not ask me too many questions."

Page scoffs. "You're still worried about that? Come on, it'll be fun." She jostles my hip with hers in a way that bothers me and I have to bite my lip to keep from saying something scathing. "It's not like you're drowning in invitations these days, anyway."

I place my small eye shadow brush down and try to find her eyes in the mirror. But it's like she hasn't even realized it's a snarky thing to say. She just continues doing her makeup, content as can be.

It's something I would have quipped back at back in the day, especially if I was annoyed with someone.

She finishes her makeup and it's subtle, my own signature swipe of eyeliner at the corners of her eyes. "Want me to get you a drink?" It takes me a moment to say yes, I would love a drink. I watch her flit out of the bedroom with her phone tucked into the back pocket of her jeans.

When she comes back, she has two wineglasses filled with what smells like gin and tonic, mostly gin, a wedge of lime floating in each glass like a congealing body part. "I like Joanie. Her husband started that FinTech company all the celebrities use. He's met Jay-Z and Beyoncé. Joanie said they had dinner with them in the Hamptons." I'd researched all the women at the book club party's partners. Clarissa's husband works for the investment firm that backs SNAPea, and Shirley's wife recently sold her company to SNAPea. It all seems so incestuous.

I lay out Page's clothes for this evening, all nude colors, The Row slacks and a knit top that shows a sliver of her stomach, Suzanne Rae mules for her feet. She takes a long sip of her gin and tonic before setting it down and getting dressed. "Did you actually sleep with that person's husband like that Twitter thread said?"

The question startles me so much that I almost drop my glass. I hadn't thought about that Twitter thread in a while, blissfully blocking it from my mind after spending too much time reading and rereading it, trapped by my own shame.

I pause for a moment before I answer, trying to decide how honest I should be. "It only happened once. I didn't make a habit of it." This was true. It had been a sole one-night stand that I regretted deeply with an anonymous man whom I met at a bar, without a ring on his left hand, if I want to strip myself of the guilt; one night when I had gone out alone, longing for the rush of sex with a stranger. The evening had ended abruptly when I saw his wife's name flash on the screen of his phone as we lay in a hotel room postcoital. If I wanted to drown myself in guilt, the hotel room would have been clue number one. "And I swear. I didn't know Odilie was still with Tom."

Page waves her hand. "Oh, I don't care about that anymore. I was wondering more how you reel them in. Men, I mean. You seem good at it."

I take a long sip of my drink, gin glazing my throat, almost making me gag. "Exude confidence." I shrug. "You're the hottest bitch in the room. Harness your power. But don't be too intimidating. Men don't like that. Smile, approach them." All stupid clichés but they work.

Page nods like she's mentally taking notes. "Easier for you, though, since you're gorgeous." I don't disagree with her.

The place where Joanie's hosting her book party is scene-y, with an adjoining bar that I'd seen countless times on Instagram in the days before my fiasco. The bookstore itself is arty, with splashy stippled walls and shelves lined with trendy reading: everything from social justice-adjacent "readers" to obscure poetry to coffee-table monographs. The room in which Joanie is speaking is so crowded that I can barely see her at the front when we arrive.

She's making some joke about birthing a baby and a book at the same time and then starts to read a passage. I scan the room, seeing if I recognize anyone, if anyone recognizes me. Thankfully, all eyes seem be focused forward, so I haven't been spotted. There are the book club ladies dispersed in the crowd with their various spouses, a lot of parent-aged people in expensive-looking natural-fiber outfits, husbands in shorts and sockless loafers, sipping on artisanal beer. A couple of kids who begin to cry and have to be shushed by their parents, or nannies, who knows which.

Joanie reads a passage about homeschooling toddlers, how her three-year-old, now five, had endless tantrums day in and day out, interrupting the lesson plan. How Joanie ended up renouncing any kind of screen-time preschool and doing it all herself, reading one book on early childhood education, and setting up her own "home office" in her apartment where she created lesson plans, usually on a whim. That now, two years later, back in regular school, little Kaya was number one in her class at reading, which Joanie is *certain* was because of her time being homeschooled, which, she drops in quickly, almost as an afterthought, only lasted two months before she hired an in-home tutor.

Page isn't listening. Her eyes are scoping out the room instead, looking for someone. I follow her gaze, notice the curve of her lip when she spots what she wants to see. A sandy-blond guy, alone, with scruff and visible ankles.

Joanie drones on, so I tell Page I'm getting a drink and wander off toward the bar, a darkened, wood-paneled alcove with funky stained glass lamps and vintage book covers papering the wall, things like pickled eggs and brined oxtail on the menu. I take a seat, still within earshot of the reading, and order myself a gin drink infused with lavender. Then I find out that this whole event is open bar and order a second before I'm finished with my first.

A man joins me, wiry and slight, thinning hair and thick glasses. But I know that at these types of events, the diminutive men are usually the ones you can't underestimate. He tilts his glass at me. Water. "Vera MacDonald," he says, a fact on his tongue not a question. "My wife said you'd be here tonight. She's the one reading right now." He finishes his water.

So I was right. It's FinTech-Beyoncé-Bro, the man who is currently paying for my drink. I tilt my glass back at him. "Colin Mallard."

"Like the duck," he replies. I edge away from him, toward the corner of the rough-hewn countertop.

"Why aren't you listening to your wife speak?"

He curls his hand over the bar and helps himself to some

cherries, in full view of the bartender who does nothing to stop him. "I've listened to her practice this maybe ten times. I've also read the book ten times. She doesn't care that I'm back here, I assure you."

I stiffen my stance, put an arm defensively in front of myself, swivel my body away from Colin. The last thing I need is for someone to see me talking to another woman's husband.

"We're not all bad, I promise you." He knows what I'm doing, or what I'm trying to prevent, and that makes me queasy, a shiver in my legs.

"Tom was my friend, a hard worker and an ass. And absolutely psychotic, it turns out. But we're not all like him. I'm not. I'm a pretty good husband. I've never cheated, I do childcare, I listen to my wife practice her passage ten times. I believe women." He tugs a cherry from its stem.

"Why are you telling me this?" I say, inching away, back toward the crowd of people.

"You're so young. So beautiful. I don't want you to write off men forever because of your experience." *And what a presumption to make*, I want to say back, *that I need your assurance*. "Tom was a bad, weird egg. He only went after you to piss off Odilie. He told me that himself, that he was annoyed by her and wanted to play some mind games. I'm not sure what happened in the interim, what spell you cast on him, but his only goal, at first, was to get back at his wife." He takes another cherry and I can see him prod it with his tongue, the way his mouth moves, his canines, inexplicably biting into the stem, too, this time.

The room warps, narrows. "I'm going to go back out now," I say cheerfully, forcefully, taking my drink with me as I round my way out. He shrugs, doesn't stop me.

All I see is red.

11

ODILIE

Ten years ago

JULY WAS SMOKE and haze. The cherry taste of calorie-free energy drinks, nicotine-stained hands, cocaine bumps at three in the morning. Laughter ricocheting off the walls of Odilie's bedroom, the room dark except for the glare of the laptop, showing old reality shows, sitcoms from the sixties, soft-core porn. Anything Peri was in the mood to watch. They'd been kicked out of the living room, from the TV, because they'd ashed cigarettes on the carpet out there and didn't clean it up, left rings from their condensing glasses of vodka, little happy trails of Ritalin dust on the wooden table Kitty said was her grandmother's.

Odilie went to work bleary-eyed each day, clutching a large iced coffee, black. No more sharing Danishes with Elena. "You look amazing," the hygienist cooed as Odilie shrank, her lips ballooning from her hollowed-out face, her skin taut and pore-free. Not allowing herself to feel anything but amazing was a happy, easy existence. Any moment she felt herself dipping, she'd pop another Ritalin, crunch a cube from her iced coffee, take a smoke break. It turned out that life was so much less gray this way, on so many stimulants, like Odilie was gazing down from the sky at everything below through a mist of glee, of ecstasy.

She had never had a friend like Peri. She had never had a close friend like this, period. What did they even do? What did they even talk about? In her fleeting moments of sobriety, Odilie wasn't sure. From the moment Odilie got off work, they spent most of their time holed up in the apartment, chain-smoking and watching TV on the laptop, their legs entangled. Peri said she slept all day, arose when Odilie clocked out. Odilie found her a few times curled up in her bed, her gorgeous, finely chiseled face so angelic in slumber that Odilie wanted to squeeze it.

At night they went to the beach and walked the shores, collapsing with their backs to it, letting unseen waves crash into them, knock them down. Sometimes they went to town and Odilie watched Peri walk into one of the touristy housewares stores, sniff the candles and come out with six different ones she didn't need. Peri always needed to be doing something with her hands, smoking, spending, gesticulating wildly. In the moments of quiet they shared, she would grip Odilie's own hands until the bones cracked, the pressure leaving red imprints on Odilie's skin.

"I worry sometimes, that if I stop moving, everything else will stop, too, this world I've built for myself," she would confess quietly, cigarette quivering in her fingers. Odilie began to notice that even when Peri appeared relaxed, at ease, when she was with groups of people, she would be tensing her fingers, bending them and stretching as if to check if they still worked.

Sometimes they did cocaine and went driving, the windows down, cigarette smoke flying past them like Isadora Duncan's scarf. They'd drive with no purpose, in the little red Alfa Romeo, and Odilie would show Peri Wyneck's back roads and she'd zoom down them going a hundred miles per hour, their hearts in their throats, their screams intermingling with the dusty sand, the stars.

On occasion, they almost seemed like one person. Odilie would lift her hand and expect to see Peri's long magenta nails. And sometimes she did, because she'd taken to painting hers the same color. Peri's mouth would twitch and Odilie would raise a finger to her lips and see if hers moved, too. Their limbs would become octopus tentacles entwined in the sheets, their musky sweat commingling into one odor, one stench, that the bedroom was steeped in.

"Doesn't your boyfriend miss you?" Odilie asked Peri one evening as they lay together in bed, Peri's fourth night in a row sleeping over, her body cuddling against Odilie's even when she was in the deepest sleep. Peri shrugged. "We're not out here for leisure. He has shit going on every day, in meetings, on calls. I'll see him when we get back to the city."

The city. Odilie didn't want to think about that, Peri's inevitable return to New York, to her real life. *This is just a dream to Peri.* That thought wormed its way into Odilie's head more than once and she would have to go to great lengths to suppress it, to disable it, to knock it out of her skull.

And was Odilie real without Peri? That was another thought. Sometimes she felt like she was part of Peri's fever dream, a figment of Peri's imagination, magicked up by Peri's sheer willpower.

"This isn't my real life," Peri had murmured more than once, on the third night of a bender, puffing anxiously on a cigarette. "What do you want to do, Odie? When you're out of this town? Who do you want to be?"

Peri had asked this question before, of course, but still Odilie had no solid answer. "I want to be more important than I am now," she'd squeak out and this was when their differences shone through because Peri, in moments like this, she liked to remind Odilie how far she'd come.

"I grew up poor, was living on people's couches. Now I'm summering in Wyneck." And in one rare, sharp-tongued moment Odilie almost barked back, "Well, you're still basically living on people's couches," but she didn't. She didn't because she loved Peri, loved how being friends with her made her feel.

One late morning Peri told Odilie they were going to a party again. "I haven't been out and about since the Sanderses'. I need to show my face." They were going on the Flickermans' father's yacht for lunch. Odilie, of course, knew the Flickermans, had been enrolled in camp with them as a child. There would be others there, but not many. It wouldn't be as intimidating as the Sanderses' party, Peri promised.

Still, Odilie took a shot of vodka, chased with a Ritalin, pocketed a Xanax just in case. Peri picked a bikini for her to wear, and an embroidered cover-up to slide on over it, a giant hat and sunglasses, almost like Odilie was going in disguise. It was her first time wearing a bikini since the incident all those years ago with Annabella Sanders.

They boarded the yacht, the *Marigold*, at one of the docks, Odilie following steadfastly behind Peri as they greeted their hosts. Peri air-kissed everyone, the two Flickermans and their other two guests whom Odilie vaguely recognized even with their sunglasses on. "You look gorgeous," she murmured to one of the women, imitating Peri's low tenor.

They sat around a white-clothed table, champagne buckets decorating either side, heaped fruit platters, gravlax and a row of bagels only two people touched. Caviar in silver scalloped bowls on ice, which everyone *did* seem to devour. "So how do you know Peri?" Sarah Flickerman asked, a blank smile on her face. She didn't know who Odilie was and in this moment Odilie relished that.

"We met at the dentist," she answered simply, taking a sip of the champagne.

"What a strange place to meet," Sarah said, popping a strawberry into her mouth. "Do you see Dr. Armstrong, too? He was so amazing with my veneers." Sarah flashed them, all of her teeth filed down and burnished to the same size.

The conversation sped along, about people everyone knew in common, names that Odilie only occasionally recognized. But she was able to nod, to smile, to laugh at all the appropriate points, her head tilted back, champagne flowing down her throat. She was being slightly ignored, she knew that, even by Peri. But with the alcohol, with the excess adrenaline from an empty stomach, Odilie didn't mind. The sun was hot, the yacht was beautiful, the ocean was lovely. She felt like she belonged, albeit marginally.

When lunch was cleared away by the white-coated staff, their jackets embroidered with the boat's name, everyone went to the deck to tan. Someone, a friend of Sarah's from her job at a music label, spread out some MDMA crystals on the edge of the boat, hoovering them up in one snort. Everyone else did a line, so Odilie did as well, the crystals burning harsher than the coke Peri had recently introduced her to.

Soon, they were all jumping into the ocean, lapping up the salt like dogs. The water, it felt like satin against Odilie's skin, like the most luscious, transcendent bathwater she'd ever experienced.

She lay down when she stepped back onto the deck without even drying off, the sun baking her skin. She felt a wet, warm tickle in her navel and giggled, her eyes squinting open at Peri licking the salt water off her stomach, the group laughing at her antics. Odilie smiled. She was part of the joke.

"I'm going to go pee," Peri announced, beckoning Odilie to come with her.

"Go in the ocean!" one of the guys said, but Peri ignored him and took Odilie's hand, guiding them to the bathroom below deck. She squatted down on the toilet as Odilie gazed at herself in the mirror. Her mouth felt stretchy, gooey and her teeth kept clacking together, rocks sliding, crumbling away, turning to sand in her mouth. She bent over the sink faucet then, gulping down water. She'd never been so thirsty in her life.

"Give me your hand," Peri said suddenly from behind her, and Odilie took one last gulp of water before acquiescing, thrusting her palm toward Peri, their bodies pressed so tightly together in the tiny niche of a bathroom. Peri's eyes glowed white light, it seemed, as her fist tightened around Odilie's hand.

Odilie didn't realize what was happening at first, her high so buzzingly perfect, that when she saw the stream of blood she thought she was dreaming. She gazed at it, mesmerized, looking at the little rivulets pooling in her palm.

And then, delayed, a smarting pain. She yelped, looked up at Peri, who had a tiny pair of sewing scissors in her hand, to cut off loose threads, the ones Odilie knew she always kept in her purse. Odilie felt her mouth gawping, her own blood like slick salon polish on the scissors' blades.

"Lick it. Lick your wound," Peri said, a low mumble. And Odilie took up her hand and obeyed, her tongue smearing the blood, her saliva numbing the sting. "Good girl," Peri said gently, her eyes dilated, her teeth hard at work sucking on her lower lip.

And she grabbed Odilie's chin and thrust a kiss on her cheek.

When they went back outside, into the sunlight, the scissors were tucked away, Odilie's hand licked clean, a minuscule stain on the edge of her bikini bottom the only proof that she had bled at all.

12

VERA

Present day

I'VE STARTED COLLECTING magazines and newspapers. Every backdated print edition I can get my hands on from when the news first began covering the murders, from *People*, the *New York Post*, the *Daily News*, the *Daily Mail*. Every day a new package comes filled with papers, bulky with them, and I sit in my room and leaf through and clip. Clip away at headlines and images of Tom and Odilie and Penelope and me, those words and pictures once so hurtful now reduced to a dull throb. I clip and I clip and I paste onto creamy, deckle-edge paper, collages of my head conjoined with Odilie's, eating fruit from the ad next to a story defaming my name.

I lose myself in it, this manic collaging. Quinn thinks I've lost the plot. He mutters to himself when he comes home, knocks on my door and finds me tucked away in my room,

X-Acto knife on paper, more and more ideas coming to me the longer I stay up. The more the project grows, the more news stories and new images I find.

This is the action, the activity, the brain distraction I'd been craving for over a year now. The plotting and planning and executing skills that I'd honed so well as I was building my career had floundered, grown dusty from disuse. But now, now it feels like I have something to do. A purpose again.

And the more I concentrate on the collaging, the more I can see something forming. An inkling of an idea, called forth from the past, when my college professors all told me that I had an eye, when I spent my time experimenting with shapes, colors and textures in art classes. There's something happening here, a manipulated vision that I think could help me in the end. I am certain I can turn this manic art therapy of mine to my advantage.

Something had flickered in me after seeing Hannah Hoch's work, reading articles about famously defamed women who took the fall for men's transgressions. How Monica Lewinsky, Yoko Ono, had finally gotten some apologies from the masses. I hadn't practiced fine art in ages, but I could, I would. This wasn't going to be some one-off tacky tribute collection; I could monetize this, somehow, some way. I just wasn't sure how yet.

This constant motion, the disembodied act of continually slicing myself and the others off the page, I need it. I need it because I'm suddenly on a rampage against Thomas Newburn.

I was set off that night at Joanie's book party, an inescapable rage that I don't think I'd let myself feel, ever, in the totality of time since the murder/suicide. Sure, I'd been angry. I'd pitied myself for the hatred flung my way. I'd hidden from the world, made myself small, did everything I could to stop that disdain, and had harbored resentment about it.

But this anger, it was something different, bubbling and poisonous and on the verge of boiling over, scalding anything that was in its proximity.

Joanie's husband had told me that Tom had sought out an affair as a ploy. I was a pawn in a marriage with a woman who probably didn't even *care* whether he'd had an affair. My life ruined just because this fucking *idiot* wanted to make his wife antsy. Not because he, misguidedly, wanted to find love in the wrong place, not like every other cheating man out there who was *bored* of domesticity. No. This psychopath wanted to gaslight his wife, instead accidentally fell for *me* and then killed her and himself.

I'd reentered the book party with a smile plastered on my face, my hands shaking, the ice clinking in my glass. I couldn't help myself; I'd pulled Page aside and told her what Colin had said. She'd given me a pointed glance. "His motivations don't really help me right now, do they?" then melted back into the crowd ready to have Joanie sign her book.

So while Page is ostensibly trying to get to know her dead sister, *I* want to get as much information I can about who the hell Tom was, what kind of sick fuck would ruin so many lives. It won't bring Odilie back. But it could help *me*. It could help Quinn's story, to fully reveal what Tom's game plan had been, what his history was, whether there were other women out there who had been charmed and cheated and physically hurt by him, who might be afraid to talk.

Which is why I've been calling every day, all day, for an appointment to speak with Tom's brother. He's an anthropology professor in Connecticut, a former college baseball star turned academic. Page was right; he had been in Central America, on sabbatical in Nicaragua, had avoided the entire shitstorm in the States. But he was back now and was entirely unwilling to connect with me. One morning, with all the time I have, I hop on the train and go to confront him in person.

The college he works at is small and lush, one of those campuses out of a brochure with a quad, picturesque dorms, an arboretum and a small lake. I take a map from the admissions office and find the anthropology department easily. It's finals season and the air is tense; students chain-smoking in front of the library, a stern quiet canopying the school.

I looked up Professor Newburn's open-door office hours, and in my jeans and sweatshirt I blend in well with the other students going in and out of the academic building, a baseball cap on my head in case anyone is a true crime junkie.

He's with a student when I get to his office, so I wait patiently in a chair, its vinyl upholstery worn thin. Tom had told me about his brother, Brandon, how growing up he felt so inferior to him, and I wonder if anything had changed once Tom got rich, if *Brandon* started harboring resentment toward Tom, whether their dynamic had changed later in life. I want to know Tom's psychology, what made him commit such atrocities. Anything I could glean about his childhood. Next, I would force myself to talk to more of Tom's friends, try to wring information out of them, put all the pieces of the puzzle together. Anything to squash him even further and more messily into the ground.

Brandon, I knew, had refused to make a public statement, aside from saying how sorry he was for the Patterson family. I hoped that I could wriggle something out of him, a little morsel that could help Quinn, could help his story, help me. Something he would feel guilted into saying when confronted with a survivor of his own brother's brutality, especially one as pretty and pitiable as I.

Once the student slips out, I slip in, closing the office door behind me. The walls are covered in maps, colorful low relief ones, peeling from the walls. He's behind a large dented metal desk, papers scattered in folders in no organized fashion that I'm aware of. It takes Brandon a moment to look up; he's in the middle of underlining something in red, presumably a student's paper.

"Hello! Um…forgive me, what's your name again?" He gazes at me, trying to figure out where to place my face. He's shorter than Tom with a crooked nose, graying hair, five o'clock shadow on his puffy jowls. They have the same eyes, though, and it takes me a moment to compose myself.

"It's Vera. Vera MacDonald. I knew your brother."

He startles. I can see him trying to gauge how he can get out of this, how quickly he can run to the door. I sit down across from him, just as a student would.

"I'm not asking for anything except information. Your brother ruined my life and I want to know why." I say it simply, softly, nonthreateningly. I add a tremor like I'm holding back tears. "I'm not the press. I'm not a journalist. I'm only a girl who wants answers." I pout, blink, make myself as small as possible in the chair. I tell him that I've lost my job, all of my friends, that my family won't speak to me. That I'm all alone in the world.

He pinches the bridge of his nose. "There is nothing to say. The man who killed his pregnant wife is not the one I knew." He closes his eyes, briefly, as if to erase me from his sight.

"Then who was he?" I grip the chair, whiten my knuckles. "Please, I'm out of answers. I lost my career, my reputation, because of this man. I just want to make peace with the whole thing, to know that it wasn't my fault." I'm laying it on thick, but it seems to be working. It's hard to resist a sad, gorgeous girl.

And he launches into a story about his little brother, who was spindly and weird all throughout their childhood, who was behind in reading and math, had to get extra help after school for it all. The last guy picked for sports teams, the one with barely one friend all the way through high school.

"He went to college, though, and I guess something clicked. He got very interested in economics. He worked his ass off in a way that my parents and I found surprising. He suddenly had all this motivation. He was still a weird kid, but he was suddenly accepted into MBA programs, prestigious ones, too. He ended up at Columbia, as you know, and graduated from there at, like, twenty-four. He became this fiercely competitive dude, too. If you made a joke to him, like, 'You're no good at chess.' Or 'I'd like to see *you* wrestle,' he would immediately challenge you to a game of chess, try to wrestle you in your front yard." He paused, shuffled some papers. "To be honest, we were estranged. After our parents died, there were some issues with the will and we parted ways. But I do remember him saying, when he began to date Odilie, that he liked how she could relate to having a larger-than-life sibling. It was supposed to be some kind of jab at me, I suppose."

Page? I think. Insecure, lonely Page the larger-than-life sibling? I'd have to examine that later.

"You know, he changed a lot in business school. Became much more socially adept, if that makes sense. Learned how to schmooze. This was a kid who couldn't string two words together if he was forced to make small talk. And suddenly, he was playing golf with men whose assets are about twenty times as much as mine. He toned up, got a better haircut. I guess you could say he grew into himself." He thrummed his fingers on the desk, thinking. "It had something to do with his girlfriend at the time. I can't remember her name—I think it was the name of some Greek goddess. But she helped him with all that. Helped him build up his company, too."

I find his eyes. "You have no idea what her name is?"

He shakes his head, gives a helpless shrug and pauses again, as if deciding whether to voice anything else, and I lean forward, patiently, coaxing him onward. He sighs, relenting. "There were rumors, things I heard here and there. Oddness in him, in that relationship. I think he liked bringing in a third, that sort of thing." He stutters the last phrase out like it's a crumb stuck at the back of his throat. "But at the end of the day, I don't know anything. The shy, weird Tom I knew was certainly not the one who would have annihilated his wife and unborn child. It's scary to me, scary to know I grew up alongside a monster. That we could turn out so differently with the exact same genes."

We hear a knock on the door. "That would be my next student."

I thank him, start to make my way out. "Vera?" I turn toward him. "Nothing Tom did was your fault. I feel guilty, too, sometimes. Wonder whether I should have been in his life again. Maybe if I'd reached out, if I'd been present, none of this would have happened. But it's not worth it to live in the *maybes*. It really isn't. I hope you find some closure." He raises his hand to say goodbye and I do, too, watching his eyes, Tom's eyes, as I back out of his office, into the afternoon.

13

ODILIE

Ten years ago

AUGUST.

The heat in Odilie's bedroom was sticky, suffocating, the blades of the ceiling fan lazy, too, like the blades couldn't quite stretch far enough to make a breeze. Odilie and Peri relocated to the beach, an eroded patch of shore near the east end of town, a place that the water always threatened to swallow up. When the tide was high, the patch disappeared altogether and the girls were taken with it, human buoys on gray waves.

Out in the sea, bobbing with whitecaps, things got deeper, a swollen tomb of lost secrets buried in the brine. "My parents didn't want me," Odilie told Peri. "I came too soon. My mother, she wanted to get her Masters of Education, do more than just teach in a small-town school. They constantly re-

minded me of the ways in which they tried to forget me."
Accidentally left at home for an hour when she was five, like
the *Home Alone* kid but without all the siblings, while Page
was strapped to her mother's chest.

A dance recital, age nine, Odilie looking out in the audi-
ence and seeing everyone's parents but hers, cameras held high.
Afterward, when she was brought home by another parent,
her mother lying in bed with a stomach bug, her father out
somewhere with colleagues. "Sweetie, your teacher knew we
weren't coming. She should have told you," her mother said,
swallowing another dose of Pepto Bismol.

The words Odilie heard when she was fifteen, sneaking
down to the kitchen at night for leftovers from dinner, her
parents sitting in the adjoining room with friends. "We don't
really get her. Page is so happy and talented and motivated.
Odilie, I couldn't tell you one passion she has, one thing that
makes her tick. She's a totally blank canvas." Her father, four
beers in.

"Well, she's a teenager. Isn't that their whole thing, to be
as disenchanted as possible?" This from one of her parents'
friends.

"It's not her age. She's always been this way. I almost didn't
know she was my baby in the hospital nursery except for the
hair. That gorgeous first name's wasted on her." An admission by her mother, followed by a sip of something. "She'll be
fine, though. Being passive and invisible like that can actually
help you in life. There are fewer expectations."

Peri danced in the sea like a siren, seaweed snaked around
her neck, her arms, splashing Odilie, who now knelt in the
shallow water, trying to cup tiny fish, to bring them to the
surface, to watch them struggle to breathe.

Peri told Odilie about the pictures she kept in the big book
by her night table, naughty pictures she called them, photos

she took with her boyfriend on a self-timing camera. How she would look at them before she went to sleep some nights, when she wasn't at Odilie's, and touch herself.

"Sometimes I think I'm meant to be bad," Peri whispered once to Odilie, the bottom half of her face sinking under water, her lips burbling bubbles just at the surface of the sea.

"There's nothing wrong with pleasuring yourself," Odilie answered. It wasn't like Peri to admonish herself like this. It threw Odilie off-kilter, made her want to dunk herself to the very bottom of the ocean and stay there, eat the sand, gnaw at a scuttling hermit crab.

But Peri grabbed her, in that viselike grip, shared other withering, starless secrets. "My mother would beat my father, throw things at him. Like glasses, picture frames. We would all hear it. Once, she made us watch as she scorched his fingers with a candle, grabbed his hand and told him he had to teach his kids how to withstand pain. He didn't flinch. I almost thought he enjoyed it, all the agony. He loved her. She never touched us. Once I saw him in the bathroom and he had welts on his back the size of nickels. Pain, it can be white light and make you greedy, for both the giver and receiver." She pulled out a green tendril from the water, a sea plant, bit into one of the bulbous ends, her teeth crunching on it before she spit it out. "But then he killed himself. To this day I don't know if the two are related, this propensity for pain, his depression." She dove back under, swam away from Odilie, her hair like a shimmer of a shark in the newly placid waves.

Peri had to leave for a few days, go back to the city. Doctors' appointments, a meeting with her agent about a campaign he was angling to land. She hadn't been working much recently, she'd confided to Odilie, just the occasional gig. She was getting too old. "Don't miss me too much," Peri called as she reversed out of the parking lot of Odilie's apartment building.

Take me with you, Odilie wanted to call back. She wanted to throw herself in front of the sports car, let it mow her down. She would welcome the crunch of bone, her innards splattered on the asphalt, if it meant she wouldn't have to go back to a Peri-free life.

Those days were bleak, Odilie sequestered in her bedroom, a lone plume of cigarette smoke dancing along with the ceiling fan. She didn't know what to do with herself, what her life had been like prior to Peri. What had she done to pass the time? Work, sleep, eat? She barely did any of those now, anyway.

Without Peri, she had the glint of an idea that she didn't exist at all.

At work, there were always cursory greetings and chitchat, but she could be anyone, a faceless person, a stock image of a human. She felt herself taking up less space, too, her body more air than flesh, newly formed gaps and voids that hadn't existed before.

When she got home, she lay down in bed again and her weight felt insufficient, an entire side of the queen-size mattress empty where she was used to the heat of another person. She went to the beach, alone, let the water sting her open eyes as she looked at the bottom, at the granules of rock and sea debris. When she came up for air, she was startled to find no one else around, no one yanking her by the hair back into the water, no one dangling hermit crabs dug out from their shells, their little claws dancing, naked and helpless, in the air.

Back in bed, her comforter smelling like the sea, she thought of the people she used to spend time with. Kitty. Other people from high school, childhood, that she thought she'd been friends with, whom she thought she liked. But no, she was merely existing alongside them, thrust with them because of their proximity. What were they all doing now? Drinking pilfered Four Loko beverages on a beach somewhere, fucking men with slimy hands, indifferent to each other, conversing about nothing? Overplucking their eyebrows, seething at the tourists, the summer people and their bikini waxes, healthy nails, flawless skin?

Something strange had happened earlier that day. Kitty, who hadn't spoken to Odilie in months at that point, cornered her in their parking lot with Calypso Rogers, a girl they both knew from high school, who had been prettier than them, hair blond and silky, tummy flat and pierced. "Calypso says your new BFF is bad news," Kitty stated haughtily, as Odilie tried to get to the front entrance of the low, brick-faced building. "Tell her, Callie."

Calypso looked down to the asphalt, wrung her hands. "She was really horrible to me," was the mumble that slipped out.

Odilie had rolled her eyes. "Okay?" And she sauntered into the building, even as Calypso called out, "Wait." But Odilie wasn't waiting for anyone, especially not jealous townies.

Odilie turned to her side and she slept, slept longer and heavier than she had all summer since she'd met Peri. When she woke up some twelve hours later, her bedroom was still gray, her brain still a swampland of inexplicable grief, Peri still away, hiding in the shadows of Odilie's mind.

She closed her eyes again, willed it to be Tuesday when Peri would return.

14

VERA

Present day

SAM COMES OVER to the apartment for dinner this week and quickly withdraws into our tiny kitchen, cooking an entire roast duck a l'orange, the greasy scent and smoke so pungent that we have to open all the windows and take the battery out of the smoke detector because it keeps on beeping. While the duck is cooking, they come into my bedroom to see my collection of clippings, a total fire hazard. But when they start actually looking at the collages, their face softens.

"These are actually pretty good, Vee. Very good sense of composition and color. You have a great eye. It's good to see you making art again." They leaf through the images.

"I've made a dozen so far and I can't stop myself, can't stop my hands. It's a fixation at this point."

"You should make a website, put these on T-shirts or something. Try to sell them."

"That's exactly the idea," I say quietly and they nod.

"Let me know if you need my help."

Quinn unlatches the drop leaf table and sets it as Sam serves us the duck with rice and green beans. We haven't been digging in for long when they ask how our little journalism project is going.

"Vera is on a Tom Newburn *manhunt*," Quinn says. "I'd say she's mad that he's already dead so she can't murder him herself."

Sam raises their eyebrow at me and I spear some duck, moist and pink. "I keep learning these things. I go to two events with Page and everyone is babbling to me." I tell them what Shirley and Colin said, about my visit to Brandon Newburn. Their eyes shine.

"OMG you are such a Sherlock. You need to find out more about these alleged threesomes! One of the wild things about this story, so far, is that no one can get *any* info on Tom, his business practices, his life. You could crack that right open! These people obviously don't mind having you around if they're tolerating you at events."

"Except Vera isn't spending time with Page anymore," Quinn says, shaking some salt onto his green beans.

"She hasn't invited me anywhere since we went to the book party together. And neither have any of Odilie's friends," I explain to Sam.

They shake their head. "You have to invite yourself. Insert yourself. You're supposed to be becoming besties with her, remember? And the cherry on top is that the more you spend time with her, the more inside access you may have to Tom. I bet you these friends of his are guilty of something. Like it's making them itch and they *know* you don't want the media attention, so they'll just babble to you."

"Easy there," Quinn says. "This is Vera's life, not your HBO Adrian Lyne and Wine."

Sam cuts into their duck. "Please. Vera doesn't need any coddling. So next step is to hang out with Page again. I know you're used to being *invited* to things and making zero effort in any kind of relationship, but what you're going to do is ask Page for a movie night. At her place, not this zoo with your dark art filled with her sister's face. Then you'll tell Page you'll accompany her wherever she wants to go with Odilie's friends." They take a bite and chew happily.

"That was my plan. But the thing is, I don't think Page needs me anymore. I think she's learning how to assimilate on her own, getting whatever info she needs about her sister," I say and Sam gives me a stare like I'm stupid.

"That's why you have to nudge her. Have you ever in your life had to work an ounce to keep a relationship alive?" I pause, think. "Yeah, I didn't think so." They grab my phone sitting next to me on the table, ask for my passcode, which I reluctantly give.

They pass the phone back to me.

Hey Page! Hope you're well! ☺ Want to do a movie night this week?! I would invite you over to mine, but it's a MESS. LMK when you're free! Xx.

"This is not how I text," I say, annoyed by the excessive exclamation points.

"Exactly," Sam retorts, serving themself more rice.

Page is a lot cooler toward me than usual when she invites me in, like she's doing me a favor by having me over, barely even looking at me as she concocts a couple of margaritas. I make a decision early on not to mention my visit to Brandon Newburn—I'm not sure how Page would react, if at all.

But I can see I've made an impact. She looks very Cobble Hill with understated makeup and a subtly expensive gray athleisure outfit. Her hair is cut into a better style and there's something about her hands, too, that tugs at my brain, a twitch in my memory.

We sit in front of the giant TV with our drinks and popcorn and I'm grateful for the movie, *The Devil Wears Prada*, because she's being uncharacteristically quiet. She's been on her phone all night, very clearly texting someone.

When the credits start to roll, I'm two margaritas in and feeling bold. "Who's the lucky person?" I ask, gesturing to her phone.

She finally looks at me, blushes, slides the phone onto the table, screen down. "You're going to judge me," she says, almost darkly, like whatever's coming is about to throw me off course.

"No, I won't." And I smile welcomingly, even though yes, it's very possible I will judge her.

She shifts her eyes away, then back to me. "I'm dating Jackson Ledecky."

I think I've heard her wrong, but I need to keep the contempt out of my voice. "You're dating Jackson Ledecky?" I say stupidly.

She nods. "I know how it sounds, but he's been *so* nice. He's been taking me out for all these insanely expensive dinners and sending me flowers and taking me to parties and introducing me to people. And the sex is unbelievable." She lets out a hiccup of a giggle while I try not to choke.

Jackson Ledecky was Tom's COO at SNAPea, surely the tall, lithe blond guy whom I'd spotted her scoping out at the book party. I hadn't known what he looked like, but I certainly knew his name.

Jackson Ledecky was one of the best friends of the man who had murdered Page's pregnant sister.

I try to stifle my reaction to this insanity. "Well, I hope he continues to be nice to you!" I say lightly. So this is why Page hasn't reached out in weeks, why I had so keenly felt she didn't need my help anymore. "Did he know Odilie well?"

I must have done a good job disguising my disgust because she seems to relax. "Yeah, he's great. I think he was weirded out at first by his connection to my sister, but now that we've gotten to know each other he doesn't seem to care. He's taking me to some huge party at the Benningtons' place out in Wyneck this weekend actually, where I used to live, so I guess it'll be nice to visit." She completely ignores my question about her sister, inching her hand back toward her phone and that's when it comes to me: her nails are painted the same burgundy, shaped into coffins, just like mine always used to be before my life fell apart, over a year ago. When I still cared about that.

"Wow!" I plaster on my biggest smile. "Could I tag along? I've always wanted to visit Wyneck!" I can tell Page is making the calculations, deciding whether it's worth it to invite me. "I know where we can get you the best outfit on sale. And I have an in at the Carlyle Hotel's salon, if you want to get your hair and makeup done!"

That hooks her.

15

ODILIE

Ten years ago

ODILIE GOT A CALL from Page Sunday afternoon. "We're doing family dinner. Six o'clock." Odilie heard the crack of a peanut shell over the line, the chomp of the nut inside, Page's current favorite.

Something to do. Odilie wondered if her parents had thought to invite her or if it was Page's idea. They hadn't seen her in months and she hadn't run into them, either. She wondered if they had heard whisperings of her, if it had traveled to them who her new companion was, whether her parents would approve of Peri as a friend. They, like all the locals, harbored sharp suspicions about the summer dwellers. But they liked their money.

Odilie put on one of her new pairs of jeans. Peri had been

right; two months later and Odilie could slip them on easily. She did her makeup, highlighting her newly formed cheekbones, whipping the mascara wand over her lashes. She smoked a cigarette in her bathroom, ashed it in the sink. She smoothed out her brows, plucking the stray hairs just the way Peri had taught her.

When she stepped into her parents' house, all the lights were on, the table set, the smell of a steaming tuna casserole making its way into Odilie's arched nostrils. The scent made her want to gag, nicotine and stimulants sloshing together in her shrunken stomach. She sat in her spot at the table, waited for them to join her.

Her father shuffled in first, squinted at her. "You look nice," he said shortly before making himself comfortable at the head of the table. He was silent after that, his eyes on the newspaper. Soon, her mother came in, too, with the food. She asked Odilie to get the salad from the kitchen. It was only when they were alone together back there, her mother filling up the water pitcher, that she studied Odilie, her new shadows and hollows.

"It's different. You look different. Don't forget the dressing." And Odilie went to grab it, her fingers worrying the label on the bottle.

Soon, they were all seated at the table, Page bounding down the stairs at the last moment, her hair shiny and twisted on top of her head, her brown eyes alive and glistening. "Nice jeans," she said to Odilie before diving into the casserole. No one questioned Page serving herself first.

"We have some news," her mom beamed, passing the salad to Odilie's dad. She had that quake in her voice, the proud one that reverberated while she gleefully kept others in suspense. Odilie sank lower in her chair, took a sip of her water.

No one had noticed her empty plate, that she hadn't bothered to serve herself.

"I got into Schermerhorn Academy! Full scholarship, too, starting in the winter semester for sophomore year," Page yelped, stabbing a piece of her casserole. Schermerhorn Academy was the best boarding school on the East Coast, with an alumni association of presidents and artists and scientists. Their acceptance rate was reportedly lower than Harvard's. A spot at Schermerhorn meant astronomical opportunities, a ticket to an Ivy League college, a job wherever you pleased, a network of people who could make your life a dream with one whisper in some other powerful person's ear.

"We didn't even know she applied. She got the acceptance yesterday!" Odilie's dad exclaimed, raising his water glass as if in a toast. "We are so proud of you, honey. How you got through that application process with no help from us isn't too surprising, but gosh I couldn't even fill out my own doctor's form when I was your age!" And the three of them started chattering about the day Page would move, the textbooks she would need, the clubs and teams she'd want to join.

Page sat with her dinner devoured, her head cocked in her hands, smiling, the perfect teenage dream. She would be the first Wyneck local to be accepted at Schermerhorn. The high school was holding a party in her honor in the fall. She would do one more semester there while also balancing a few online courses at Schermerhorn to get ahead. "Are you going to miss Ryan?" mused their mom, salting her casserole. Ryan was Page's boyfriend, a moppy blond boy who played soccer.

Page scrunched her nose. "I'll find someone else. I like Ryan, but he's so *ordinary*. I want someone who challenges me." Her dad grunted in approval. Odilie sat there, her plate clean, her water glass empty, watching both of her parents' heads turned, preening over their younger daughter. It was like there was a crick in their necks; they hadn't turned over to Odilie's side of the table once.

Before she could think too hard, Odilie picked up her fork, held it high and dropped it back on her plate, the noise shattering the self-congratulatory mood of the room. Her parents, Page, they finally turned to her, confusion etched on their faces like they'd forgotten she was there.

Odilie laced her fingers together. "I have news, too," she said primly, watching their expressions, the way their eyes screwed up with impatience, waiting for Odilie to finish what she was saying so they could turn back to Page. Odilie smiled, put her shoulders back. "I'm moving to New York, to the city." And once it was out of her mouth, she was. She had to. There was no change of plans to be made.

16

VERA

Present day

IT OCCURS TO me, as I sit in the plush backseat of the limo Jackson Ledecky hired to drive us from the city to Wyneck and back, that it makes sense, in its own twisted way, that Odilie's group would be so nonchalant about my presence, even though I was so closely associated with her death.

Because these people, they're used to twisted and sick. They're good at forgetting, at hiding it underneath mounds of money, of burying decaying skeletons beneath pore-less skin, their rot like fertilizer, sprouting more and more green-eyed trees. It isn't a new thought, but I'm enraptured by it as I gaze at Jackson and Page. She's flung herself on top of him, across the limo from me, her legs dangling over his, nibbling at his jawbone. And he's gnawing at her, too, his little teeth snagging on her earlobe, a tiny rodent in her flesh.

I'd looked Jackson up last night. Before he joined SNAPea, he'd worked for another logistics company that had eventually folded. Folded because of constant and numerous human rights violations, from warehouse workers fired for taking pee breaks to docked pay if a shipment went out even thirty minutes late. Human rights violations that Jackson Ledecky, at the nimble age of twenty-five, had been responsible for implementing and then exonerated of.

God, how this world turns. At least Page and I look good.

I'm wearing a black Bec + Bridge dress, short with mesh bands, low heels, my hair down, minimal makeup. I need to look understated tonight, to avoid too much attention, to work my magic and try to find more info on Tom. If I seem too intimidating, too sexy, I know this won't work.

Page, on the other hand, has gone all out. She's wearing a white gown, corseted and strapless, that hits right above the ankle and chunky sneakers, her hair high up on her head in a loose bun, a Bea Bongiasca necklace grazing her collarbone. Her eyes are smoky, her lips a pleasant pink; there's no garish makeup in sight. I texted my old contact at The Carlyle and was able to slip her in. I hadn't been there in well over a year obviously, but they snipped off my split ends, gave me a blowout. No one complained about my presence.

The car winds its way, finally, through Wyneck, Jackson and Page spilling champagne all over each other like kids going to prom and I look out the window, trying to size up this town, the one where Odilie grew up. But it's night, too early in the summer for it to be boisterous. All I see is a main strip with darkened windows, a few people loitering outside one bar, otherwise a snug silence. And the sound of waves crashing in the distance, a noise so constant that at first, I don't notice it, that it takes me a moment to place it.

We're here, the front gate open, presumably allowing any

odd person to walk in off the street. But then I see the security detail, shrouded by the night, standing inside the clipped boxwood walling off the front of the property as if to trick the poor uninvited souls into thinking they can easily crash.

I'm underwhelmed by the house. It's more of a cottage, actually. The Benningtons are supposed to be billionaires and this is the kind of place a rich kid might refer to as his "starter house." I follow Jackson and Page forward, stumbling as they hold on to each other. "This is their guesthouse." Jackson turns his head over his shoulder and explains. "They've been using this one because the main one is under renovation. But you'll see, it's deceptive, because it stretches way back to the beach."

We enter and I'm immediately accosted by the throngs of people, the thumping bass, the art on the walls so lubricious that the prude in me wants to look away, image upon image of tits and ass and vulvas, a teenage boy's fantasy of a woman, splayed out ad nauseam on every damn inch of wall. I pucker my lips to keep from frowning.

Louisa Bennington, whom I recognize from the remembrance ceremony, comes up to us, kisses Jackson on both cheeks, hugs Page. She's ageless due to the work she has had done, wearing a Rick Owens playsuit, her hair now lilac-colored instead of blond, falling down to her waist, her eyes so bright blue I wonder if she's wearing contacts. "Louisa Bennington," she says, offering her hand, cupping our shake with her other palm. "Pleasure to have you all here." Her gaze is so blank that I'm positive she doesn't recognize me. Before I can introduce myself, she's gone, trailing into a swarm of newly arrived guests.

The crowd is eclectic, very Elon Musk and Grimes. Many suits with hair transplants, a lot of lithe women with tiny tattoos covering their arms. There are people occupying every inch of every surface, atop mirrored tables, meant to hold unread coffee table books, on the laps of other people's husbands. As we head farther inside, I spot the book club crew sitting in a corner on giant yellow floor cushions that could be called beanbags if they weren't made of upholstered ostrich hide.

I feel eyes on me, a few titters from people who have recognized me. So I slink away and go to the beanbags, Jackson and Page having made a beeline for the bar. "Hi!" Ruthie says and leans over to greet me, dressed in some pseudo-bohemian pants and top ensemble, stacked heels, her voice so chipper it makes my teeth ache. "My boyfriend couldn't make it, so I wanted to go with Joanie and Colin, but then *they* couldn't make it since she's pregnant and all. Thankfully, I found Shirley and Layla." She gestures to Shirley, who is deep in conversation with another guest. "Clarissa and her husband are outside smoking with Layla, Shirley's wife, but they'll be coming back in soon. There are a lot of cool people here. At last year's party, my friend hooked up with this dude who owns five Hockney pool paintings, and so he commissioned Hockney to paint the bottom of his pool! Everyone has a story like that. Apparently, that acquisition of Tiffany by LVMH happened because of a conversation at this party. And you know about all the sexcapades, I'm sure." She prattles on and I survey the scene.

"The sexcapades. Can you explain that to me?" I say, even though Ruthie is three topics ahead. I wonder if that has anything to do with what Brandon Newburn mentioned, about Tom's sexual predilections.

Ruthie bites her lips, looks off to the side and then moves closer to me. "Well, I've never partaken in anything. But the rumor is that the Benningtons were quite busy back in the day. I mean, lots of upstairs shenanigans. It's calmed down in the last few years, as they've gotten older. But you still see people heading home together, sometimes spouse swapping."

I'm about to ask further, see if I can somehow finagle a Tom anecdote out of her, but she's quickly distracted by another woman, a tall redhead in vintage McQueen, who yanks her out of the ostrich beanbag and into the heart of the party.

If I were of sound mind, I would be using this opportunity to network, to try to pin myself to some heiress with a burgeoning shoe line. And I should be, I know I should be, but my brain is so far away from that right now that I can't even imagine switching to professional mode in order to extract a business card from someone, let alone schmoozing long enough with an influencer to wriggle my way into her business.

The plan, once I establish that I'm not a threat, is to get a drink and stand alone, wait for one of the men who worked closely with Tom to intersect my line of vision, introduce myself and slowly go in for the kill, try to glean information about what Tom's brother called *oddness*. I've got my hit list and they're bound to be here tonight. The greatest prize, the meaty zebra, would be Mr. Bennington himself, whom I spotted near Louisa, a large man with a full head of what looks like real hair. But he and Louisa will probably be too busy hosting to talk long enough with me.

Jackson and Page return to my side, handing me a drink, which I throw back easily without paying much attention to what it is. I put my hand on Page's shoulder and smile at her. "I'm going to wander around a bit. Be back soon!" And I get up before she can offer to come with me.

I begin winding my way around the clumps of revelers, get myself another drink just so I have something to hold. A lot of people, I realize, are staring at me, pretending not to, going back to their conversations while their eyes hover over their conversation partners' shoulders. It's more curiosity than anything; I don't feel coldness, meanness, more like I'm a small spectacle, a trapeze artist at a party filled with people who are used to inventive distractions.

I wander outside to get some air. Clarissa, her husband and Layla are there; he's a stocky guy with a shaved head to match his wife's and Layla is tiny, five feet and no heels, with short hair gelled into spikes. Clarissa is chain-smoking. Layla is, inexplicably, knitting, her fingers clicking the needles rapid-fire. I decide to say hi to them before I move on with my quest.

"I'm trying to quit smoking," Layla says by way of explanation, showing me the pattern she's making. "This is the only thing that helps. And smelling it." Clarissa, however, is much drunker, waving her cigarette in my face.

"You! You're here!" She raises her palm in greeting. "You know how weird it is that you're suddenly hanging out, that I'm suddenly seeing you everywhere?" I watch an ember die on the ground. "I mean, it wasn't like Odilie was the most effusive person. I barely knew the woman even though we were 'friends.' She was so quiet, kind of weird? I wonder if there's more to that story. I really do. Such a fucking tragedy. But better to let dead dogs lie. Or is it sleeping dogs?" She laughs, a honk.

Her husband grabs her hand. "Leave it alone, Riss." But there's a glint of delight in his eyes, like he's turned on by his wife having words with me. I put him on my list of potential information sources and smile lightly.

"It's totally okay. I'm used to it," I say and move on, making my way back indoors, attempting to insert myself into other groups, the collective vibe getting more raucous, more debauched, my face staring back at me, again and again, from every mirrored surface.

Two hours later and my feet hurt, my hair is limp, my mascara pooling at the corners of my eyes. I'm sitting outside in a freshly vacated lawn chair, imbibing my fifth drink of the night, staring out into the darkness. This has been a total bust. I've spoken to so many people that my cheeks hurt from stretching my face into a smile, my mouth dry from the exertion. I've talked to almost everyone on my list and each one—no matter how drunk, or how much I batted my eyes, touched their thighs—refused to talk about Tom in any meaningful way.

I think back to Colin at the book party, offering me unsolicited information, and wonder if I've overestimated myself, if the real key is to *not* want it and then the details will come. I look up at the moon, the same one shining anywhere for everyone, whether you're a murderer or a survivor, a billionaire or unhoused.

I've been trying to expend all this energy to absolve myself, when maybe I should just let it go, let the tides turn and see where they take me. Maybe I'm not *supposed* to live a big life. Maybe this whole horrific situation was supposed to teach me to be quieter, less myself.

And maybe there really is nothing else to know. Maybe Tom was a normal guy who snapped one day because of me, the oft repeated tagline of my narrative.

Someone sits in the chair beside me, letting out a sigh. Most of the party is now on the beach, where the DJ is playing a late-night set. "Car isn't coming for two hours," the voice says, and I turn to see Jackson sprawled out, hair mussed, what looks like a hickey on his neck.

"Where's Page?" I ask.

He takes a sip of the frosty beer he's holding. "Passed out in one of the bedrooms upstairs. I used to be able to rage until at *least* three. Now it's one and my goddamn head is already beginning to hurt." He puts down his beer, puts his head in his hands. "God, Tom and I would get up to no good around here back in the day. He could be such a wacky guy. He loved the beach at night, loved night swimming. We would get plastered and see who could go out farther into the waves. He could never say no to a challenge, but I always chickened out and let him win. Have this childhood fear of drowning, you know?" He picked up his beer, swallowed some more, his voice trembling.

"Do you miss him?" I say quietly, perking up ever so slightly.

Jackson looks out in the direction of the beach, concealed by more shrubs. "Yeah, yeah, I do. I know I shouldn't say that, but he was like my brother, you know? Being here just brings me back to the summer he stayed here, the summer he met Odilie, actually."

I sit up. "Tom stayed here?"

Jackson nods. "Yeah. Back when he first launched SNAPea."

I pause, trying to figure out the best way to segue into my next question. "Were you close to Odilie?"

He takes another sip of his beer, letting out a satisfying sigh. "Not really. She was kind of reserved. He became that way, too. I mean, he was always a workhorse, super focused, but after that summer he was really closed off."

I take a breath, finessing my next words, parsing them out in my head before I open my mouth. "I keep hearing that about Odilie. That she wasn't a very forthright person. Was Tom attracted to shyer girls?"

Jackson shakes his head. "When I met him, he was dating someone who was the total opposite." He doesn't say anything else, so I prod him.

"How so?" I keep my voice light, delicate, like it could easily blow away into the waves.

"She was so crazy. But gorgeous. Had Tom wrapped around her little finger. He used to tell me that he and Peri, that was her name, kept, like, secret pictures near their bed. Kinky stuff, sometimes with a third. He had a weird name for the photos, his 'pearly whites.'" He licks his lips. "The whole end of that summer was a mess, though. Mr. Bennington kept grumbling about how much shit Peri left here."

He blinks suddenly, his eyes focusing on me. "Fuck, you don't want to hear any of this, do you?" He puts a hand through his hair, his eyes suddenly wide, almost fearful. "Forget I said anything? Page will kill me if she knows I'm talking to you about her sister."

I get up, new energy and a new mission on my mind. "It's okay. I'm going to go pee, though. Find me back here when the car comes, 'kay?" And I bolt, back into the house.

There is no way the pictures are still there, I tell myself. It's been a decade. But it's like an invisible hand, the ghost of Odilie, is guiding me up the stairs, toward the master bedroom, which I'd heard from a partygoer was the first room on the left of the second floor, a bright pink monstrosity with animal print rugs, flowers that look like genitalia, but not in a tasteful Georgia O'Keeffe way.

There's a hum at the back of my head, an itch I'm trying to scratch at. Jackson said, *his pearly whites.* I think back to Thelma Kay's comment on the group photo of Tom, Odilie, that other couple, Odilie's stretched out grin. *Teeth=secrets.*

There are two enormous night tables next to the California king-size bed, neon pickled lime green with one deep drawer apiece. Nothing sits on their surfaces except a pair of gold-flecked Murano glass lamps, so I pull out the first drawer. It's empty except for some ZzzQuil, a pair of tweezers, a couple of old magazines.

I move to the other side, to the other giant ugly nightstand and its enormous drawer. This one is much fuller, a hoarder's paradise: everything from Q-tips, to rash cream, to dried plants to a bunch of loose silverware, a tape measure, some fabric swatches. And a stack of books.

I remove each one, shaking them for loose contents. *To Kill a Mockingbird*, a cookbook, *The Rules*, a book on the geography of Wyneck, an old local Yellow Pages. And a hefty tome on teeth, slick color photos of the fangs of wildcats, of carnivorous plants and human babies. Of sharks. And my brain trembles, lights sparking.

I open it, feel for something, turning the pages rapidly, check inside the spine's end band until finally, finally, I feel something come loose and I carefully slip it out, nestled in a page about the red fangs of the triggerfish.

When I turn it over, I want to yell, the sound catching in my throat, behind my tonsils, the contents as deadly and carnal and hideous as the mouth of the cannibalistic tiger salamander gaping at me from the cover of the book, its fangs dripping with the blood of its own kind.

17

ODILIE

Ten years ago

PERI RETURNED FROM the city. Odilie came home from work and could smell her before she saw her, the tobacco and hyacinth, and another scent, the pungency of acetone, wafting through the walls of the apartment. When Odilie opened her bedroom door, Peri was on the bed painting her toes, wiping at the polish bleeding into the corners of her cuticles with a damp cotton swab.

"Can you do this for me?" she asked, waving the polish wand at Odilie. "My fingers are too clumsy." Odilie obediently sat down, swiped the blue polish onto the remaining toes, her hands and fingers working meticulously to stay in the lines. "My nail salon was closed today. Something about a toxic gas leakage. As if all those polishes aren't toxic enough." She flexed her toes in Odilie's face, the ligaments in the high arch of her foot rippling.

She started talking about the appointments she went to, her agent, who told her she needed to quit smoking, that her eyes were going to turn yellow. She admitted, in a moment of fragility, how when she was younger she had wanted to be cast in higher fashion editorial spreads, to walk the runway, be taken more seriously as a model. But her agent hadn't thought she possessed the right look for it.

"But otherwise, I look great. Perfect. He called me perfect, because I am." She bent down, carefully, so she wouldn't smear the polish, cupped Odilie's face and kissed her nose. "Thank you. Thank you for doing my nails." Odilie smiled back, stood up and plucked the cigarette out of Peri's hand and dumped it in a glass of water.

"Agent's orders," she said as she dug around for her own pack, lit up.

"You love me, don't you?" Peri whispered from the floor, studying the shimmering navy blue on her toes. Even her toenails were perfect, little half-moons, not too long, not too short. Not like Odilie's that never seemed to grow; raggedy bits that took up only half of her chunky toes.

"Of course I do," Odilie replied. Of course she did. She thought about sharing with Peri her declaration, about how she was going back to the city with her, how she refused to be left behind. But that could wait; that could wait until Odilie had figured out a plan for how to get there. A plan that took *gumption*, that forced autonomy, that made Peri respect Odilie.

Because that was the reason, right? Odilie didn't have to dig too deeply; she wanted Peri to shine that smile on her and know that she had launched this person into the stratosphere, had made her brave enough to move from her hometown, to want something in life that had always seemed out of reach. To know that thanks to Peri, she was heading for the city, straight to the erratic, beating heart of it.

Peri leaned over, cupped Odilie's cheeks, squeezing her lips into a pout. "Do you love me the most of all?" Her eyes narrowed, her clench tightening so much on her flesh that Odilie felt her tongue slipping out from between her lips. She nodded rapidly and Peri's eyes glistened for the tiniest flicker of a moment with unshed tears, before releasing Odilie's face.

"We're going to a party tonight, by the way," she said, standing up, stretching, her white T-shirt rising to show her tanned, taut stomach. "It'll be different. More suits. You know, older people. But I promise, you'll have fun. We'll both have fun." She rubbed the fleshy spot between her thumb and the back of her hand. "You'll meet my boyfriend finally, by the way. He's excited to see you." And she flounced over to the bathroom, to take it over before Kitty could. *To see you.* As if he knew Odilie, as if he had met her before. She followed Peri into the bathroom.

He was still a mysterious figure, someone who seemed to be constantly at the edges of Peri's existence, extending an arm or exerting his presence in quiet, unobtrusive ways. Odilie had seen pictures of him, on Peri's phone, on her Facebook, on her Instagram. He was handsome in a classic way, a little too smooth and polished, but that was to be expected.

Once, when Odilie and Peri were walking home from their strip of shore, hair salty and wet, Odilie had asked Peri, "When did you know you were in love?" Odilie herself had been in love once, with a boy she dated the summer after junior year of high school, whom she met at a party. He had been sweet, good to her, she'd felt happy and relaxed in his presence, their conversation never stilted or forced. He was only in Wyneck for a year. He ended up transferring schools for senior year, going up north to Maine. She hadn't spoken to him since, but she kept up with him on socials, noticed his new girlfriend. It used to give her a pang, of what might have been. But it didn't anymore. When she thought of him all she recollected was empty space.

Peri had turned to her. "You know, I don't think it's all about love. Sure, I love him. I've gotten the little butterflies, the mooning, maybe in the very beginning. But now, now it's more like a partnership. We just work well together. We have our own lives and we collide when we need to." *Collide*, Odilie had thought. What a strange way to put it. But she thought she understood what Peri was saying, that if their relationship wasn't exactly one of convenience, then it was something similar to that. And maybe that was normal in Peri's world of general exuberance. Not in Odilie's where the women she'd grown up with craved love, craved affection.

They stood in Odilie's bathroom now, the sink and counter covered with makeup. Cream, powder and paint smudged the edges of the mirror, clouding the corners of their reflections. Odilie had it all down now, the primer and light foundation, the highlighting and contouring, the way she could fill out her brows to look more alive, the slow and steady lining of her lips. "You'll need to get new injections soon," Peri commented, glancing over at Odilie as she curled her lashes, so thick and voluminous that she never needed falsies or extensions.

They finished their makeup, exited the bathroom to Kitty holding her crotch. "You could have left the door unlocked," she growled, planting herself over the toilet bowl without even closing the door.

"Do it in the kitchen sink next time, sweetie," Peri sang out, grabbing a bottle of Chablis that had been chilling in the fridge.

"She's scared of you, you know," Odilie said as they pulled on their dresses, hooked each other, took swigs from the mouth of the wine bottle, redoing their lipstick and littering their purses with pills, Kleenex, keys. Odilie hadn't seen the scissors in a while, the sewing ones, and she imagined she'd dreamt all of it, the nick Peri had given her while she was high, the blood a delusion brought on by the satin sun that had made her head swirl.

"I know she is. And that's her own fault. I can't cater to everyone." Peri shrugged, spritzed on perfume, her shoulders shimmering with its fragrant dewiness. She stepped back, took a good look at Odilie. "God, you're beautiful. I'm so jealous of you, I could push you out this window. But then who would my best friend be? Everyone else is so fake, so horribly vain. But us, we get each other, you know?"

Odilie gazed back at her best friend, the two-piece outfit she wore, lacy black-and-white flowers on a matching crop top and skirt, her hair pulled up into a sleek ponytail, hoops hovering so wide they grazed her cheeks. "You're not jealous of me," she answered softly, grabbing the bottle of Chablis from Peri's hands, guzzling down the last dregs of it herself.

"I could be, one day. But where would that leave us?" Peri reached out to untwist a strap of Odilie's dress, black and billowy, short, her feet shod in five-inch heels, spindly legs for miles. It was a Peri outfit, one she would never have dreamt to wear herself. But here she was, in it, maybe a vision, her lips overlined, her hair straightened into the sleekest version of her bob, cat eyes. An entirely different person from three months ago. She relished it.

Peri rounded her car up the gated driveway, dropping it off with the valet in front of the lacquered front door, tendrils of hothouse ivy clinging to the Spanish colonial-revival facade. Odilie didn't know these people. The house she had never set foot in, though she knew of it as a cavern.

It was dimly lit inside, a whole staff of uniformed servers handing out flutes of champagne immediately upon entry. In the center of the foyer table sat a vase with flowers of such exotic hues and so luscious, they seemed to have been plucked from the wilds of some foreign land, shipped overseas specifically for this event. And for all Odilie knew, they were.

This was someone's birthday, Odilie realized. At the bar lining the right wall, in the beamed-ceiling room just past the entryway, a server was mixing a specialty drink, something called "The Birthday Bonanza," essentially an Aperol spritz, just like the drink Peri had made her try the first night they became friends.

Odilie continued to follow Peri into the house, idling behind her, checking out the many artworks, the gilded finish on the banister leading up to the second floor. Odilie had grown used to, if not jaded by, this kind of opulence. But this was somehow *more*, richer, as if whoever owned the property had come into their wealth so hastily that they'd thrown a vast fortune into the house with no consideration for what was tasteful or en vogue.

There was zebra, cheetah, and tiger patterned rugs, an entire aquarium built into the middle of the bathroom Odilie ducked into, slippery, unusable scented soap the shape of seashells; an oil painting of the beach, oversize and engulfing, hung at the entrance to another room. So many rooms into which Odilie was trailing Peri.

Peri guided them outdoors toward a backyard, where more people were milling about around a giant aquamarine pool, miniature lanterns twinkling in the trees and on the pool's surface. The flora bordering the lawn here was fantastic, too, oranges and pinks that Odilie had never even seen in a sunset. In the distance she swore she spotted large animals, ponies maybe, prancing about, their tails flicking. Their nocturnal presence just another showy display of economic supremacy.

How far back does the property reach? Odilie wondered. It

seemed to stretch for miles, the horizon receding into infinity. It must be a trick of the light, she thought, something to do with how the grounds were laid out. She was about to ask Peri about the perimeters of the property, but Peri quickly became engaged in a conversation with a tiny blonde, her teeth too big for her face, her sunken, speckled chest giving away her age more truthfully than her face did. "Louisa, this is my friend, Odilie Patterson. Louisa is our host for the evening!" she heard Peri say, and as Odilie extended her arm to shake this woman's hand she felt Louisa's gaze hover over Odilie's shoulder, as if she were so uninteresting, she didn't even merit a moment of eye contact.

"You have such a lovely home," Odilie tried. Louisa murmured something in response and took Peri by the arm, guiding her away.

"There are some people I want you to meet. I introduced Tom to them earlier, but they're thrilled by the idea of meeting the beauty behind his brains..." And the two of them wandered off, leaving Odilie standing there with her flute of champagne, conspicuously alone. Just like the evening at the Sanderses' party.

Odilie knew Peri wanted her to try, to go up to people and speak with them, make her presence known. That was what people with *gumption* did, anyway. But Odilie knew that no one was interested in speaking with her without Peri there, especially in an older crowd like this, less likely to get wasted or coked up and spill their secrets to anyone or anything, including drying plaster.

So Odilie began to walk in the direction of the ponies, through the boundless expanse that was this lawn. She took off her heels so she could walk on the grass, feeling the lush greenery on the soles of her feet. It almost didn't seem real, the texture of the blades between her toes.

She walked on, away from the swarming partygoers, their sounds becoming more and more muted, the lights from the pool and the house diminishing as she kept advancing forward. Maybe it was the expensive champagne, but her body, it felt different, lighter, like her feet were now barely touching the ground. All the speed and cigarettes, Odilie had found that she'd grown too used to them, that her body was beginning to reject them, that after months she could now feel the swell of hunger again.

The pangs, they came in succession, but even those, that pain, was a reminder of something better, something she hadn't known she yearned for until it was staring her in the face. Elena at work, who had first been so in awe of the transformation, now seemed distrustful, saw the way Odilie went out for a cigarette instead of sharing their morning pastries like they used to. But Odilie knew she wouldn't say anything, knew that she was safe from any real critique by her colleague. She looked too good now for that.

And besides, Peri never forced her into it, never told her she needed to be more angular, that she looked better with visible bones. This was all Odilie's doing, all of her *will* and *discipline* and *gumption*. Letting her body rot with nicotine and drugs to welcome concavities between her ribs.

Finally, after what felt like an hour of walking, Odilie reached the pen where the ponies were roaming. From far away, it had seemed like they were freely trotting about, but this made more sense: there was metal fencing enclosing them, a little barn off to the side to house them.

They were so beautiful up close in the moonlight, blond and shiny like a child's toy, some of their tails and manes braided or adorned with bows. She reached out her hand to one and it moved gracefully forward, nuzzling her fingers. She wondered how they were so nocturnal, if their wakefulness at this hour was just for the party or if night ponies existed, solely for show, who could be dutifully awakened at any hour of the evening.

"They're for his kids," said a voice to her right as she continued to stroke the silky nose of the animal, her shoes and champagne flute still clutched in her left hand. She whipped her head around and a saw a man in the shadows, around the other side of the fencing, forearms flush against the enclosure.

"His little girls wanted ponies. I think they've outgrown that stage, but he keeps them around to show off. They're some rare breed, I guess. I'm not really up-to-date on my pony knowledge, unfortunately." Silhouetted by the moonlight, he stepped closer to her.

"You're Peri's boyfriend," Odilie stuttered out. She recognized him instantly, the classically handsome face and chiseled jaw, the ease with which he carried himself, so like Peri. What was he doing out here, away from the party?

"That I am," he said in response and extended his arm. "Tom. Tom Newburn." And before she could say her own name, "You're Odilie." He studied her, a puzzling expression on his face, not unlike a smirk, but softer. "I've heard a lot about you."

"Good things, I hope," Odilie found herself saying, almost coquettishly.

"Only good things. Peri thinks very highly of you and trust me, that is a great compliment." He crinkled his face into a smile, the moon casting an almost ethereal glow on his exposed teeth.

Odilie took a long sip of her champagne, finishing it in a great gulp, suppressing a burp.

"I can refill that for you," Tom said, edging closer. He was so near her now that she could smell his cologne, subtle and musky. She remembered Peri saying she had gotten it custommade for him from some boutique-scent brand. "I was getting bored over there. I wanted to go for a walk. Saw a pretty lady tiptoe her way out here and decided to follow." He took the champagne flute from her, his hand gently brushing hers as he hoisted the glass.

He plucked something from the ground, a Mokara orchid blossom, from one of those mystical plants that seemed to grow all over the property. "Don't tell," he whispered, placing it behind Odilie's ear, its petals tickling her temple. "They'll kill me if they knew I pulled it up." His hand, it stayed there behind Odilie's ear, his fingers on her tragus. And it was like the world was ringing.

"Tom, you need to come back. They're about to bring out the cake for you." Peri's voice shattering the silence, the whimsical grunts of the ponies, the moment between the two of them like a flower disintegrating in Odilie's belly. "Oh good, you two met." She grabbed Tom's arm, gave him a quick peck on the lips.

"Wait, this is *your* birthday party?" Odilie asked, shifting her shoes to her other hand, her fingers touching the flower self-consciously.

"Guilty as charged," Tom answered, snaking his arm around Peri. "And I guess I need to get back there before they realize I'm missing." The couple began walking toward the house, Odilie following a step behind them.

And then Peri's hand slithered out, grabbed hold of Odilie's and now it was the three of them, bound together, reentering the world, the light, humanity.

Peri's nails left a streak on Odilie's arm, red like a sunburn.

18

VERA

Present day

THE COLLAGES. FOCUS on the collages.

That's been my manic mantra the past few days since I saw the photo, snatched it without thinking, almost forgetting to put everything back in the drawer how I'd found it.

It's now in Quinn's room. I'd shoved it over to him the second I got back to Brooklyn, knocking on his door at 5:00 a.m. when the limo had finally dropped me off. I'd been silent during the car ride back with Page and Jackson, the picture stuffed into my handbag, a noxious bomb ready to burst.

Quinn had come out of his room bleary-eyed, glasses askew. Had studied the image with an investigative eye, poker-faced even in the presence of such gruesome imagery.

"We need to find the women in the picture," he finally said. I told him that I recognized one, that her name was Peri, Thelma Kay on Instagram. "Which one is she?" he asked solemnly.

"The one holding the other down," I replied, squeezing my eyes shut.

Later in the day Quinn had knocked on my door. I was still awake, hours and hours after arriving home from the Benningtons'. He said he was looking into Peri, Thelma, whoever she was. He sat on the edge of the bed. "There's something very wrong here," he said gently, almost soothingly. "There is no way in hell the NYPD missed this. There's especially no way in hell all the media frenzy surrounding the case missed this." He paused, running his hand along my comforter. "The photo was just tucked into a book, you say?" I nodded and he sighed, sinking his fingers deeper into my bedding.

"SNAPea is hiding some dark shit if this photo is in the chairman of the board's bedroom. Some dark shit on Tom, too. Maybe this is why the media sicced everything on you, because someone was paid off." He wove a hand through his hair. "I'm going to try to find Peri, see if she'll talk. Then we can get this dead motherfucker and his entire cohort. I promise you that, Vera." His eyes blazing, a fervor in them I'd rarely seen in our entire friendship, like he'd found a purpose, a mission.

I continue to focus on my collages, putting all my mind matter into them, and as I'm leafing past an article about Instagram updates in one of my back copies of US Weekly, it hits me. I can use my old self. I can put my old self in all these little collages, in the corners, hidden somewhere, big or small. That's the missing ingredient that would bring these works to the next level.

The problem is that I don't *have* any photos of myself anymore. When I changed my number, I chose not to have access to my old Cloud. The best shot of getting personal photos, photos of me that weren't printed in any news outlets, is to redownload Instagram, find all those selfies and photos Huda forced me to post on my grid, in my Story archives.

Of course, that means opening the sluice gates on an entirely new flood of hate messages. But maybe people *have* forgotten. Maybe if I just lurk on the app and don't post anything new, no one will even notice that I'm on there. I can just collect the photos I need and disable my account again. It shouldn't take more than a few hours.

So I do it and suddenly find myself scrolling through a life that seems to belong to another woman altogether, like I'm cyberstalking a stranger who just happens to look like me.

My Instagram is captivating. Almost in the same way Odilie's was, like I'm looking at a facsimile of someone I almost know. Right down to my body language, I can gauge something so existentially different from who I am now. I even hold my arms at a different angle; the way my face creases when I take a selfie is now archaic, from a different era.

I could get lost in myself, in all my different outfits and poses. All the different photographs I took of the city, of strange, aesthetically interesting things I saw. A dead fish washed up on a beach. A close-up of an orange rind. Photos that made me happy in the moment. Now that I'm looking at them with fresh eyes, I can see the artistic merit in them.

I remember Huda chiding me to post more pictures of myself, which is how all the fun outfit photos start accumulating. I hated doing those, not because I hated how I looked or how I dressed, but because it felt too compliment seeking, like asking the world for validation I didn't need. But I played the game and well. My photos, out to dinner, at galleries, in the park, are all well lit, well staged. I look mysterious and enticing, but also approachable enough to sell Magdelena, a brand whose messaging is inclusivity.

Huda should have paid me for this shit on top of my salary, I think.

Or maybe I should have realized my own abilities when I had the chance.

I start downloading all the images I want for the collages, ones where my outfits are on full display, where my form is distinct and noticeable, where my old signature burgundy coffin-shaped nails pop.

Since I'd disabled my Instagram right when I heard the news last year, everything really is like an untouched archive, from the Before Times. There aren't any comments connecting me in any way to the murders. And for a second I wonder why I hadn't reactivated earlier.

Looking at these photos, I feel that itch again, that tingle that I may be missing something. I stare at a photo of myself in front of a mirror at Violet, a boutique hotel in the East Village, my hair done up in a twist, my lips painted red, wearing a navy sheath dress. The mirror is ornate, gold and rococo, and the room behind me is vast.

And without thinking about it, without *allowing* myself to think too much about it, I open a new Instagram tab on my laptop and go to Odilie's page, start looking at her grid, studying the photos that I'd flown past last time I looked.

And there she is, staring into the mirror at the Violet, wearing the same dress, her hair done up in a twist, wearing a red lip, her nails burgundy and coffin shaped. In another, she's sitting outside at a restaurant, sunglasses on, smile wide, the picture taker out of view. She's drinking a bellini, the pink bubbles of the drink contrasting with the white linens of the table. A pasta dish with seafood sits in front of her, untouched, waiting for the photo to be over.

And this, this resonates somehow, too.

My mind can't keep up with my hand. I'm onto the next solo shot. And the next. All of them at different restaurants, galleries, bars, in various well-crafted outfits. All of them achingly familiar. Too familiar. Like I'm looking in a mirror that's been punched and warped, the glass about to shatter onto someone's head, cut it wide-open.

I close my laptop with a start. Shut my eyes. Breathe. But I have to know. I have to know for sure. So I open it back up again.

I click on my profile and start stalking myself again. And there I am at brunch, smiling with some coworkers at Pastel's in Greenpoint where I ordered the seafood pasta, my bellini raised high and proud, a week before she went, before she sat at that table and ordered what I ordered and ate what I ate and posed like I posed, her stomach, her eyes, getting their fill of me.

But is it me? Is it Odilie? As I toggle between the two tabs, the images, I'm not sure anymore. And after a while I can't tell us apart, our faces, hair, anything that would make us distinct washed away in the images, blown up on my computer screen. Our matching smiles and pouts and manicured hands holding our phones for selfies in our matching outfits and meals and geotagged locations and lives.

I throw my computer, watch it bounce and land with a sickening crack on the hardwood floor. But I can't look anymore, at this parallel life, this uncanny valley of a woman who is dead, who can't explain herself, who for months seemingly wanted to impersonate me, to be me.

I feel the wetness on my cheeks before I realize I'm crying, shaking. I'm afraid. For the first time, I'm really afraid.

19

ODILIE

Ten years ago

TOM TOOK HER breath away.

It didn't matter how cheesy that sounded. Whenever Odilie thought of him, it was like a punch to the gut. Her body, it buzzed with the memories, washing through her like a warm bubbling bath, the faucet turned on a little too hot. He enveloped her every thought, clinging to them like film, no matter what she was doing, where she was, whom she was with.

She found herself making excuses to go into town, to dawdle in stores she had never stepped foot into before. She searched for his face on every sidewalk, on every beach, peering below baseball caps, looking for that jawline, the insightful eyes. She went to the grocery store for the first time all summer, circled the aisles, prayed that he'd come in at just that moment, that he would accidentally bump her with his cart, leave a bruise that she could press on for days.

At the party he had included her, made an effort to introduce her to people, called her a friend, acknowledged her existence wholly and entirely. He explained to her the gaps of information that she was missing when he was in conversation about people she'd never heard of, topics she didn't understand, places she'd never been. He filled up her champagne glass over and over again even though he was the birthday boy, and this was his party.

After the cake was sliced and handed out, when the music got wilder and shoes were discarded, swimsuits donned, the older guests finally leaving, he gave her a slice of cake, put his hand on the small of her back. "Thank you for being such a good friend to Peri."

My *God*, that stare, so penetrative like he could fuck her with his eyes, the spot where his hand had laid, hot from the touch of his skin, even after he took his palm away.

It was crazy, nonsensical. They had barely exchanged more than a few words with each other. She didn't know him, his likes or dislikes, his secrets, his favorite color or animal. He was in a relationship.

He was in a relationship with her best friend.

She found herself lying to Peri, telling her that she had to do some after-hours administrative work for Dr. Forsyth. She told her that Kitty was away, that there was no one to let her into the apartment if she wasn't there. Thankfully, she had never asked for a key.

Just to give herself space to think about Tom fully and completely without distraction, lying in bed, staring at the whirring blades of her ceiling fan. She didn't even have to touch herself to feel the dampness creep out down there. Just summoning his image in her head turned her on, standing in the moonlight with those damn ponies, his teeth as white and shiny as Forsyth's best dental patients.

Later, a couple of days after the party, the only time they'd spent together since, Peri asked her what she thought of him as they sat on the beach at night. Odilie bit the inside of her cheek until it bled. "He's nice. If he makes you happy, I'm happy." Peri nodded, launched into a story about him, how on their first date he'd gotten concussed; they'd played tennis and she'd swatted the ball right into his temple.

Odilie found herself laughing along. But it wasn't funny, not really. She wanted to be beautiful enough, confident enough to hit Tom Newburn in the head and still get a second date. Peri, the way she talked about herself, her pore-less skin and honk of a laugh began to irk Odilie, prickle at her. When Peri touched her, she began to flinch.

She played and replayed her meeting with Tom in her head. What the hell was it that made him so enticing? Or was it the context, the gorgeous night and the ethereal landscape?

The fact that he was forbidden?

She could still feel each brush of his hand, the way his eyes looked pooling into hers. Was he even that handsome? She couldn't exactly recall the distinct features of his face. If she tried to remember all the parts and reassemble them into a whole, it didn't work, either. Everything was based on these feelings she had, on this invitation he seemed to be sending her to get to know herself, get to know him.

One evening, four days after meeting Tom, she did something she never normally would. She texted a guy from her high school. She ended up on his mattress with no sheets or a bed frame in an apartment filled with other men, her insides split open by unlubricated sex. But she liked the pain in that instant. It made her forget, for a moment, about Peri's boyfriend.

Odilie called out of work, ignored Peri's messages the following day, wallowed in her apartment with the sheen of a hangover. She drank a lot. Chain-smoked and didn't make her bed. She hated herself. Hated herself for falling for a guy she couldn't have. Falling for a guy for no good reason other than he gave her attention for ten minutes. She was supposed to have *gumption*, right? People with gumption didn't lie around so listless. They made changes to themselves, to their lives, to avoid feeling like this.

On the second day of her slovenly depression, Odilie finally messaged Peri back.

So sorry. Bad seafood. Been vomiting for hours.

Peri said it was fine, that she figured Odilie was sick. But that they were having a last-minute party tonight, she and Tom, and Odilie *had* to be there. It was going to be wild, a going-away party for one of Tom's work partners who was leaving for the summer.

She had been friends with Peri for four months and had yet to see her house. *I have a dress I want you to wear. The maid will bring it. I'd bring it myself but I have to organize this thing*, Peri wrote and for whatever reason Odilie expected a burlap sack, a nun's habit, as if Peri could sense from Odilie's short, polite exchanges with Tom that she was instantly and completely obsessed with him.

But what came was cream colored, spaghetti strapped, practically sheer, skimming over Odilie's bony frame so nicely that she got ready early to wear it, the feel of it so tantalizing on her skin, a gossamer dessert of a dress.

It was odd to get ready without Peri, the air quiet, the space palpably bigger. Odilie was surprised by the silence, that not a single word fell from her mouth. But it was nice, somehow, not to have the chatter, to have the whole mirror to herself, not to have the interstices of the rooms be taken up by Peri, her breaths, her scent, the clatter of her teeth.

On the drive over, Odilie tried to control her thoughts. Whenever the erupting excitement of seeing *him* again threatened to break the surface of her subconscious, she pinched her arm so hard that she left little welts all across her skin. She was so busy attempting this masochism that she didn't even realize she had already arrived when she pulled up at the house, another estate with tall shrubbery masking the facade.

Odilie parked on the street, stepped out and pushed the front gate in, walking up the stone path to the front door, wide open and letting anyone inside. She knew about this property somewhat, that it had recently been acquired and that the house was built on spec up by a developer. It wasn't that grand; it was expensive-looking, sure, a Stanford White–inspired shingled beach house. But it was slightly smaller than Odilie was expecting, an ordinary two-car garage, the front of the house almost shrunken, like it was scaled down from the original architectural plan and constructed in a hurry.

But when Odilie entered she understood. All the money was poured into the art, canvases hanging on the walls of nude women, photographs, paintings, sketches. Crotches splayed, breasts augmented to Anime-style proportions. Peri had mentioned they were renting it from investors in Tom's company, that she hadn't had a hand in decorating the place. But still, Odilie couldn't help but suddenly associate these images, the women with their fingers fondling their vulvas, eyes downcast, big billows of yellow hair shielding their faces, with Tom. With what he could do to her.

She pinched herself so hard she began to bleed.

The party was already at a dull roar, much looser and more untamed than the one she'd been to previously. The music was contemporary, the people young and supple. Odilie raised her hand to say hello to Caroline Perkins, the redhead from the beach party, but the woman looked right through her, going for the mounds of coke dumped on the mirrored table in the corner of what Odilie believed to be the living room. There were so many reflective surfaces she caught her new face in. Mirrored walls, mirrored tables, mirrored cabinets smoked and scratched to simulate age.

She joined the group, sitting on the edge of the sofa as they snorted up the white powder. There were two guys with gelled hair and shaved faces, leaning back on the sofa, hands clutching drinks, watching with amusement as Caroline motored up the drug. "Do I know you?" asked one of them, his forehead already shiny, eyes bulging.

Odilie shrugged. "Do you want to?" she challenged him, realizing that she didn't have a drink, nothing to do with her hands.

"Yeah, yeah, I think I do." He introduced himself as Jackson. "You're Peri's little sidekick, right? The one she brings around because none of the other chicks will give her the time of day." He laughed at his own joke, swilled his beer.

"Easy. Be nice. Offer her some blow," said his friend, his voice a low drawl, his face housing too-small eyes, a nose that didn't quite fit. She recognized him from a few summers back. He'd concussed himself at the public pool. His father had tried to sue. He leaned over and cut Odilie a line. Caroline was gone, off making a beeline for a new adventure.

Odilie went on her knees, the table too low to properly sniff sitting down, the nasal drip hitting so soon that she almost gagged on it.

"Atta girl! Look at her go. So tell me how you got here, Peri's Sidekick?" Jackson asked while the other guy went to get her a drink. And when he came back, she found herself telling them, these men, every little detail of what landed her here in this space at this time, her jaw clenching with the effort. She realized she couldn't stop talking, that her entire history with Peri was just spilling out of her, like she was making up for the quiet at her apartment, and she was only taking breaks by sipping the drink that the other guy had brought her, something bitter and tangy and green that she was sure she'd never tried before.

And were they even listening to her? She didn't know; she didn't care. "I love her. She's done so much for me, but part of me sort of wants to *be* her, too, you know what I mean? That ferocity. I want that. I'm jealous of her but I shouldn't be because she has only been kind to me, but at the same time where the fuck *is* she? I haven't seen her yet and she *knows* I hardly know anyone here. Can you help me find her? Have *you* seen her? God, it's so like her to leave me stranded like this. But maybe it's good for me. Do you think it's good for me? I should go try to find her."

But she couldn't get up. She was twitching in her seat, like her thumping heart would burst out of her chest if she made any sudden movement. And they were laughing at her now, exchanging glances like she was some kind of show, only invited for their own amusement. And in a sudden burst of distress she worried that she was; that the only reason Peri had wanted to spend time with her, to befriend her, was to laugh at her and her middle-class amicability, her doglike loyalty and infatuation. How could she be so stupid?

And then a hand on her back, warm and enticing. A voice in her ear, "Let's get you away from these clowns." And one of them, the one who wasn't Jackson called to *be careful*, and she wasn't sure who the missive was for. But she was with Him now. She was with him and he was touching her and all would be okay.

He brought her out to the beach, steadying her as they

walked down the narrow pathway through the private entrance. Out here, with the cool breeze, she felt better, saner. She cocked her head at him. "You're leaving your own party again."

He smiled at her. She could see the curve of his lips from the light of the house. There was no moon this time. "It was getting stuffy in there. I like the ocean at night." Odilie took off her heels, felt the sand between her toes.

"Like Peri. She loves the beach at night." It came out more bitterly than she meant it to, and she covered her mouth like she had said something obscene.

"Yeah. Like Peri. Only Peri got that from me. Even though she grew up around the beach, I was the only who would take her out past sunset. It wasn't in her nature otherwise." That was a weird way of putting it, Odilie thought, like Peri was an animal, commanded by certain seasons and times.

"Where is she? I haven't seen her yet."

He shrugged, sat down on the sand. "I'm not sure. I lost her earlier on in the evening." He ran his fingers through some grains and she suddenly felt awkward standing over him. So she sat down, too, and he inched his hand closer to hers. "I think she wanted us to find each other," he said slowly, breathlessly, the sound of the waves almost capturing, and losing, his words.

She didn't know what he meant. But she leaned into him, her head humming with the drugs and alcohol and lightness of starvation and exhaustion from the past few days. And he didn't back away. Instead, instead, she could feel his lips on hers and it didn't occur to her until a moment later that it was her doing, that she had leaned in first, had found his face and kissed it.

Gumption, she thought. That took more gumption than anything else ever had in her short, boring, listless, useless life.

PART THREE

1

TOM

1.5 years ago

IT WAS HARDER than he thought to enthrall her. To lure her in.

He found himself, at first, checking her Instagram, seeing the places she frequented, where she enjoyed having a drink after work. She would often geo-tag the location; he would race over before he thought she'd leave, would sit at the bar and nurse a beer, willing her to come over, to ask for her tab, so he could offer to cover it.

There were easier ways of doing this, of course. Countless ways he could pay to have her information hacked, to utilize his vast network to his advantage, to insert himself in her life without physically having to be where she was. But at first, he wanted the challenge. He *missed* the challenge. Everything these days was too easy. Accumulated wealth and power made everything seem so boring.

And then finally, one night, it happened. She was out to drinks with her team from work. She was drinking a dirty martini, her hair long down her back, parted in the middle like his wife seemed to favor these days. She got up, smiling back to the group, rolling her eyes at a joke someone threw at her. She walked with purpose, her back straight. Poised. She was poised, that was the word for it, her gaze intent and focused on the task at hand.

When she arrived at the glass-top bar, she didn't have to call the waiter, waving her finger to get his attention. No, her mere presence commanded that he serve her, the languid, comfortable way she arched her back over the bar implying such an ease with herself that she didn't just acknowledge special treatment; she expected it.

Kind of like me, he thought as he sipped his scotch on the rocks.

She asked for more olives, a little plate full of them. And the bartender did it, grasping the green little eyeballs out of their square black hideaway behind the bar and arranging them gently on a glass plate. He watched her watch the placement, her eyes raking over the rest of the garnishes, the cherries, the lemon and orange slices. Once she received the olive dish, he watched her pop one into her mouth immediately, her eyes closing for the briefest moment in delight, her lips parting furtively to spit out the pit into a napkin before she carried her olives back to the table. This was his move, his time.

"What's your martini order?" he asked her. Of course, he knew it by now, but she couldn't know that.

She glanced at him, squinting her eyes as if to see more clearly in the dimly lit bar. "It's a secret recipe. I don't tell anyone, much less strange men at bars." And she turned on her heel, back to her friends, her coworkers. The bartender gave him a pitying glance when he turned back toward the bar, stinging like he'd been slapped.

That night he found himself staring into his wife's magnifying makeup mirror, a spurt of uneasiness flowing through him that he wasn't even sure he could name, that he hadn't felt in years. Was he losing his touch? It *had* been years since he last sought attention like this. Attention usually came to him, in heaps, bulldozers full of it. Was he graying too much at his temples? Had the baby's nightly screams caused more creases to form on his forehead? Was the PRP for his male-pattern baldness not as effective as he believed?

He wasn't used to this, this sinking sense of self, not since adolescence. And brought on by nothing, too. A throwaway comment by a woman he thought he could more easily lure in. Who *was* she, exactly? How did she have the capability to make him feel this way? She reminded him of someone he'd known years ago, an ex-girlfriend, that astute, awesome sense of self-worth. It scared him. And a part of him delighted in his fear.

The following day he went into HQ and pulled over Sy Masters, a twenty-year-old tech wizard whom the CTO had hired. It was obvious Sy was shell-shocked to be alone in a conference room with the CEO, as he scratched nervously at his pimply, pockmarked face.

Tom didn't spend much time in the office, and he didn't plan to stay beyond getting what he wanted. He liked to be heard, but not seen, especially these past few years. He spent most of his time in his home office, windowless, soundproof, his private little dungeon.

"You need to access the back end of these apps. We have legal safeguards in place. It'll be discreet. You won't get in trouble. I want you to find this name." He showed Sy the list of apps, the name. Sy studied all of it for a moment on his monitor, looked back up at Tom quizzically.

"You want me to scrounge around dating apps?" And then he remembered whom he was speaking to and he quickly tilted his head back down, licking his lips and tapping his fingers on the desk table.

"You signed an NDA when you started working here. Remember that. Email me the results by tonight." He left the door open, so Sy would have to eventually get up and close it himself. And he walked out of the offices as quickly as he could, before anyone else tried to catch him and begin conversing, tried to rope him into staying any longer. When he stepped outside it was snowing.

2

VERA

Present day

THE CITY IS slick with heat, sticky with it, summer suddenly, cruelly, pushing spring out of the way though it's only mid-June. As I walk, it's like I'm moving through a dense fog, the humidity clouding over me in sagging plumes. Sweat trickles down the nape of my neck. I wonder, passively, if I should have lathered sunscreen on, gobs of it, like my parents used to put on me when I was a child. You could fry an egg on the sidewalk, as they say.

I like it, though, the heat, the unrelenting nature of it. It feels like a gritty balm somehow, like I'm exfoliating the truth I had just learned, scrubbing its ugly surfaces. I step back into the sunlight after walking in the shade of some buildings for a few blocks, feel the sun beat down on my shoulders. There's not a cloud in the sky.

I had checked what I'd found, what I thought I'd discovered, once, twice, three times. For a sustained moment I'd believed that what I was experiencing was some kind of narcissistic transference, that I had become so indistinguishably intertwined with Odilie that I was suddenly seeing myself in her.

But there was no doubt now. She knew me. At first, I wondered if she had been trying to signal to him, to let him know she knew he was cheating on her by posting these passive-aggressive pictures that mimicked mine so precisely. But it went further than that, much further. Months before I had even started talking to Tom, she had been looking at my images, following my every move. And for what? Why? None of this could be a coincidence. But he had found me on that app. He hadn't been following me himself. Right?

Why the hell had they chosen me to be the center of their domestic mess? Their deaths may not reveal any answers, either. But there's one person whom I can think of to ask, even though she may have no answers herself.

When I walk up the stoop, I don't even bother to ring the bell or knock on the door, because I know that hidden in the soil of the window box is a spare key, which I'm sure the Benningtons would prefer Page kept on her. But at least it's buried deep in the mulch. When I push the door open, I'm engulfed in dark and chilly shadows. The central air, blessedly, is turned on, but my eyes have to adjust to the dim light. It feels subterranean, a respite from the blazing sun outside. It's the kind of overfunctioning AC that will soon make the house *too* cold. That will have you grabbing for a sweater, despite the sweltering weather.

I start calling out Page's name, trying to figure out where she is. She really has made the place into a tomb of sorts, probably anticipating the extreme heat. I had warned her; there's nothing like a New York City heat wave. You can suffer through all kinds of summers but there's something uniquely gruesome about the humidity here, the stink of garbage and people, the air so polluted that it seems to collude with the humidity to make the outdoors as uncomfortable as possible.

I find her, finally, still in bed, fast asleep, two blankets wrapped around herself. Next to her, the remnants of a drink, what I suspect were ice cubes long ago melted to water. She's not an elegant sleeper. Her mouth hangs open, hair sticking to the corner of her lip. She's so stationary that for a second her stillness is corpse-like, her slack jaw like a stiffened hinge. Then she lets out a light snore. Thankfully, Jackson is nowhere to be found.

"Page," I say too quietly.

"Page!" I say again, my voice near her exposed ear. She jolts awake right away, alarmed by the noise, a look of panic crossing her face before her eyes adjust and she sees me.

"Oh hey. What's up?" She fishes around with her hand on the bedside table, finally finding a half-filled Poland Spring bottle and guzzling the rest down. Once she's hydrated, she seems clearer-eyed, more alert. "Sorry about passing out at the Benningtons' the other night. To be honest I barely remember our ride home." She hiccups.

I sit on the edge of the bed, figuring out my next words. I'm suddenly uncharacteristically shy. It hadn't occurred to me that I may have trouble presenting this information, that it would be hard to do so without inevitably disrespecting Odilie, her memory. I hadn't planned a speech, or any sensitive way of explaining the situation. I guess I just have to show her. "Can I have your laptop?"

Page nods slowly, steps out of bed, the downy hair on her legs rising slightly as her skin makes contact with the synthetic cold. Once she gives me the laptop, I get to work logging in to my Instagram account, pulling up my profile, pulling up

Odilie's. I watch Page's face as I do so. But she doesn't bat an eye. She's most likely spent time recently on Odilie's page, in her strange attempt to emulate her life.

Then I show her. Toggling between the two tabs without a word, trying to make Page understand without explaining. It's bizarre to be sitting in this room that feels like evening, with so little light filtering in, the laptop's blue glare turned on low. After I'm done flickering through the photos—there are ten in total—I take a long glance at Page, trying to gauge her expression.

"Your sister, she knew me. Which means Tom, he probably knew who I was, too. I'm not sure what this means. I don't think it changes anything. But it's weirding me out." And then I'm scrambling around for more words, because Page is still silent. "I'm sure this, this mimicry was totally benign on Odilie's part. We both know who the real culprit, the villain, was. But I mean, this is your *sister*. Do you have any idea what was going on in her head to do this?"

I'm beginning to feel cold, icy even, from the AC, the whirring of its central coolant suddenly so acutely audible. Page sighs, a long, resigned sound, and it feels like she's been holding it in for months. Her eyes shoot up to meet mine, her legs crossed on the edge of her bed. "I knew, Vera. I knew. That's why I wanted to meet you."

We sit at the dining room table, a large glass-and-onyx showpiece, and she tells me.

Not before pouring herself a Bloody Mary. She starts off simply. "I've been lying to you, Vera, about my motivations here. But let me back up. Odilie, I think she sort of hated me."

And then Page confirms what Tom's brother had hinted at, that Page had been the bright star in the family from the moment she was born, a happily planned birth. That as she grew up, she excelled at everything while Odilie disappeared into the shadows. "I think the final straw for Odilie was that I got into Schermerhorn Academy on scholarship. She left for the city shortly after I was accepted." Page looks down at her drink, stirs it with a long piece of celery. "But I only lasted one semester there. I got kicked out for smoking weed and then I was shipped back to Wyneck so fucking embarrassed. Shortly afterward, my dad got a job in Michigan and moved us there. I think he was embarrassed, too. To have had this fledgling star of a daughter suddenly fuck up so royally. He never would have left his hometown otherwise." She chomps on the celery, little thready pieces of it stuck between her teeth, as I try to figure out what any of this has to do with me, with Odilie's imitation game.

"Back in Michigan, I still did well in school. I got a bunch of money to go to U of M. Right out of college I started working in real estate, like my dad, but in Bloomfield Hills. Luxury real estate. I was good at my job. I had spent my entire childhood in Wyneck on the periphery of the lives of people with second homes. Third homes. I wanted in on that life, but I knew I'd have to start thinking bigger to get there. So I came up with a business plan. What if all these multi-millionaires with their ski houses and lake houses and ranch houses and beach houses and off-shore-account houses and investment-property houses, what if they were all part of an exclusive club that allowed them to use each other's homes when they were vacant, which is most of the time? Kind of like an ultra-exclusive Airbnb." Her eyes grow wide, a tiny smile edging at the corner of her lip. She is relishing telling me this, I realize. Pitching it to me like I'm some kind of backer.

"I broke my ass trying to get a meeting with this investor I knew, who'd had some success with a fitness app. He said to me, 'This is a good concept, but if you're selling a luxury product you want to *look* luxury, know how these people operate, and I'm not sure you can do that. If you can land a big-time series A investor, maybe in New York or San Francisco, I would put money in the second round.'" She stirs her half-eaten celery in the drink absently as she continues her tale.

"It was kind of a shitty thing to hear, for sure, but it didn't discourage me. I understood what he meant. I called up Odilie for advice, because you know, she *knew* people. We weren't close but I thought she'd at least go to bat for me. She said, 'Go ahead and tweak the business plan and then I can pass it on to Tom and his people.' So I did exactly that. Spent the next few months making more connections, speaking to mentors, studying other start-ups, rewriting the business plan.

"Then Odilie comes to visit my parents in Novi and I think, *this is the perfect opportunity to show her what I've been working on.*" She fishes out the celery again, chomping on it with such force this time that there's a spray of spittle in my direction, her eyes blazing.

"And do you know what happens? She doesn't even look at it. After telling me she would send it to Tom, do you know what she says?" Her eyes narrow now, the muscles around her jaw taut. "'Page, no one is going to listen to you. The investor you spoke to was right. You're just not the right fit for that world. You don't dress right, you don't have the right life experience, you're just not sophisticated enough. Your best bet is to sleep your way in.'" She spits out the last part, a grimace threading her lips. "That was it. All those months of hard work spat back in my face. I begged her, pleaded with her. I knew *I* couldn't just email Tom a proposal. I barely knew the guy. But she dismissed me. 'I don't want to deal with Tom right now, anyway.' Like it was such an inconvenience to reach out to her *husband*.

"I was pissed, so I found a way to get what I wanted without her help." She shivers, an involuntary reaction from the story, the AC, the drink, who knows.

Page had watched Odilie unlock her phone again and again, stealthily. She watched her fingers dance over the keypad, and it wasn't so hard to deduce her passcode, but Odilie didn't go anywhere without that phone. Then one day Page found an opportunity.

Odilie was taking a nap on a Sunday afternoon, stretched out on the guest bed, her phone propped up next to her on her pillow. Silently as possible, she slipped it off the bed and typed in the password.

She sent an email to Tom with the business proposal, pretending to be Odilie. But the urge to snoop was too strong, so then Page started going through her apps. She clicked on Instagram and went into Odilie's direct messages. There was nothing too wild there. But then she went into the Saved posts, where she found a gold mine of images, dating back months and months, all from the same account. Pictures that were almost identical to the ones that Odilie herself was posting on her grid.

At the time, Page didn't think much of it: an aspirational account that her sister was mimicking, weird but not alarming. I had enough followers to call myself a micro-influencer.

It wasn't until later, until she saw my name, my picture associated with her sister's death, that she remembered. And she told the detectives straightaway—that her sister knew the woman her husband was having an affair with, had been obsessed with me for months, that maybe there was more to the case. She didn't tell anyone else, though, not her parents or her friends. She knew it must be delicately handled information.

In another case, one where there were multiple living suspects, where there had to be a strong defense, they may have dug deeper. But they didn't. This was an open-and-shut case. They wanted to move on.

"He sought me out," I mumble mostly to myself, Colin Mallard's words echoing in my ear, about how Tom started having an affair to deliberately piss off Odilie, the tipping point for my rage. I put my fingers to my temples, rub them. "Page, why the hell didn't you tell me any of this? Do any of her friends know about her obsession with me?"

Her eyes harden and I have the strangest urge to arm myself, that I've brought a knife to a gun fight.

"No one else knows. Or if they do, they haven't mentioned it. And I think they would." She gulps back some of her drink, smearing red along her mouth. "Tom died a week after I sent that email to him. I don't know if he even read it. And now it's been another year with no progress. Odilie had every opportunity at her disposal without lifting a finger, but I've been working my ass off and getting nowhere. Until I realized I could use you. If Odilie thought you were sophisticated enough to emulate, surely you could be my way into this world. And I had everything I needed to guilt you into helping me."

I unclench my jaw. "You could have just *told* me. I would have helped you."

Page looks at me long and hard. "You said so yourself, when we first met. You don't *like* helping people. You and I both know that playing on your obvious guilt was my best bet.

"We're not that different, you and I. We're both ambitious. We both grew up a hair's breadth from this world. You were a good study. Are a good study." She wipes at her mouth with the back of her hand nonchalantly, as though this revelation that she never even cared about her sister's death, that she's just been working a *business* angle the whole time, shouldn't surprise me. And on some level, I guess it doesn't.

"This was never about Odilie. Ten years ago Odilie went off and lived the life I'd always imagined for myself. I *want* that life. I *deserve* that life. And I'm going to get it. Jackson is introducing me to an investor next week. And a lot of that is because of you, Vera. So thank you." Her shoulders relax, her fingers stop fidgeting, as if she is *so* happy and proud of herself for giving me this information, for unburdening herself.

I want to scream. My hair, her hair. My clothes, her clothes. My fingers, her fingers. Mimicked, stolen by both of these deranged sisters.

My arms wrap around each other, a self-inflicted hug. This is all too much, so many overlapping false pretenses, from her, from me. From Tom and Odilie. My head is throbbing and the Bloody Mary smells like menses, dark and putrid, barren.

But before I can leave, I need Page, who is far more insidious, far more calculating, than I ever realized, to tell me something. I whip out the photo of Peri, Tom and the nameless girl. I watch Page's face as she takes in the horrific image, see her flinch, put a hand to her mouth. "Do you know who that girl is?" I ask, pointing to the one being forced down by Peri.

She nods. "Why do you have this? Where did you get it?" But I ignore her questions.

"Who is it?" And she gives me a name.

I put the photo away, make my way toward the door. "Not a word about that photo to anyone. Unless you want your precious new life to come crumbling down." She nods solemnly.

And then, as I'm one foot out the door, something occurs to me. "Tom found me on a dating app, though. It was supposed to be totally random, but it must have been deliberate. How did that happen?"

Page looks at me almost condescendingly, like I'm asking a stupid question. "It's Tom Newburn. He invented SNAPea. He could easily have hacked into the app and engineered a match with you."

3

TOM

1.5 years ago

HE'D ORDERED POACHED salmon for both of them, but Odilie barely touched hers. It was their first meal without the baby in months. *You have to stop calling her* the baby. *She's nearly three years old*, she would whine to him. He hadn't wanted kids. That had been an agreement when they got married, along with many other concessions, his and hers.

And now she had revealed that she was pregnant with a second.

Back then, when they had made that initial agreement, she was besotted with him. All he had to do was touch her lightly, on the arm, on the back, and she would instantly swoon. The idea of bringing anyone else into their little dyad had seemed foreign, a disturbance to their already carefully controlled relationship. He was beginning to learn, though, that things change. That as eager and easy a woman can seem in the beginning of a relationship, that isn't the bare-bones reality. His wife wanted a kid. She got her kid. His wife wanted *another* kid. She got another kid. Through no fault of his own. Sometimes he suspected she had intentionally stopped taking her birth control.

"Don't you like me this way, starved and weak, like a little fawn? Even pregnant?" She reflexively touched her stomach, where she wasn't even showing yet, taking a sip of sparkling water. It was the first thing he'd heard her say; she'd been talking, those pillowy lips of hers opening and shutting like a ventriloquist's doll. But this was the only phrase of hers that wormed its way into his ear, as if the rest of her speech were a hiss, lost in the burble of their fellow diners.

"Sure. I wouldn't want you regressing to a plump little townie. But you're becoming emaciated. That's not exactly in vogue right now, is it?" He hadn't noticed any weight loss, if he were to be honest. But these days he liked needling her, reminding her what his money had turned her into. What she used to be. How she would still be toiling in some small-town dreary office if it weren't for him. It was ugly behavior; he knew that. But after what he'd discovered, he couldn't help himself.

"I can't keep up with the trends," she muttered, taking a sip of water, eyeing his champagne greedily. She had already had her doctor-approved glass of wine that week. Did she hate him now? He often wondered that, whether it was truly hate or only ambivalence. How she would feel if he disappeared, if he cut her off, if he called up his private wealth manager and cut her, and the baby, and now the second baby, out of the will entirely, liquidated trusts, clawed back her shares of the company. Would she mutter so bitterly then? Would she grovel at his feet? Or, and these were in his lowest moments, would she enjoy it, being away from him, severed from him? Would she revel in her freedom?

And then, as if she were reading his mind, she glanced up at him, speared some salmon while maintaining eye contact, and chewed the pink flesh thoughtfully. "I want to go away for a little while. I need to see my family." She sat back in her chair, challenging him to disagree, to prevent her from going.

He knew where this was coming from, this punishment of sorts.

He had almost drowned the baby. While bathing her, he'd been distracted by his phone. Odilie came into the bathroom not five minutes later, and the baby was under, her husband's eyes still glued to his phone screen.

There was screaming, the phone swatted out of his hands as she dove in, grabbed the sinking child, who, now that she could breathe, was sobbing, loud, soggy, guttural sounds. "What the fuck is wrong with you?" his wife had growled, snatching her child and leaving him in the bathroom with his broken phone.

He'd felt terrible, afraid of himself, too. Terrified that this was what he was capable of when he wasn't watching himself. Since then, he'd remained even more distant from Penelope. If he couldn't handle a simple bath-time routine, how could he handle anything bigger? How could he handle fatherhood? He needed to do better; but figuring out what better meant proved too taxing right now.

Which was why he nonchalantly said what he did next. "Okay." He stabbed his own fish, swallowed it with the bubbles of his champagne. Making a fuss, telling her she couldn't, admitting how afraid of himself he was, it would only cause more disturbance to his meticulously laid-out life.

"That's it?" she answered dully. "You don't even know how

long. I'm going to be taking Penelope, too, you know." She
still thought she could use the baby against him.

He shrugged in response. "Do what you want to do. It's
not my problem." He felt this nasty urge to bother her, to really push her buttons. To see that scowl that would mar her
face whenever she was disappointed in something, whenever
something upset her, puzzled her, didn't add up.

"It *was* your problem for years. And anyway, I'm not asking for permission." She dabbed at her lip with her napkin.
But she *was* asking for permission. He knew she was. It was
one of the things they'd agreed upon when they got together,
that their life would be private. That because of his past, they
would both have to carefully consider whom they allowed into
their fold. Of course, back then, she didn't know the extent
of his peccadilloes; she was too enamored with him to think
over what she was giving up.

They sat in silence, her eyes narrowing on the food she was
pushing around her plate. "I know you don't *care*." She spat out
the last part. "But I already bought the tickets. We're leaving
in March. I haven't booked a return yet. I'm just going to be
staying at my parents'. It shouldn't be too hard to find me if
you want to track me down." She glared at him again, brown
eyes reproachful, then turned away, eyed the rest of the diners.
Her profile was pinched, vacant. She looked tired, like the air
had been pumped out of her. How long had she been like that?

They'd gotten a good table, tucked in a corner away from
the madding crowd toward the front. He could tell she felt
isolated. And he *had* isolated her, in the general sense, away
from her family, her hometown. He knew this. But she had
also wanted estrangement; she wanted to purge herself of her
old life, her old face. Nothing he had done to her had been
by force.

He paid the check, walked her out of the restaurant, called

an Uber. He had a driver for the mornings, but he enjoyed the anonymity of his evenings, not having anyone, not even someone on his payroll, know his whereabouts. His wife complained about that, of course. Said that it made her feel unsafe to wait around for a cab or car service. She'd never really gotten used to the city, even after years here, still used Google Maps to navigate some streets, still gave homeless people change. Still refused to take the subway. He would smirk at all of that, his little small-town girl.

He could pinpoint the moment that the light sort of dimmed from her eyes, when she realized that this life she had lusted after wasn't exactly to her liking, that his obsession with work had excluded her. It was when she was pregnant the first time, when she expected him to dote on her, before she knew better. They'd been sitting in the house watching TV, her stomach sweaty, veined and swollen, unclean and grotesque to him, like an uninvited, unkempt guest. Which he supposed the baby was.

She had her feet up on the table. Of course, those were swollen, too, malodorous and sticky, unpolished. Her feet had always weirded him out, made him think of sinewy sides of ham, hanging at the butcher's, ready to be sliced. She was scratching a spot on her ankle, using the nubby nail of her left toe. "Can you get your feet off the table?" he had finally said, waves of disgust rippling through him. She was used to his commands, of course, had initially loved the way he loved her, molding her into the kind of woman he wanted her to be. But at that point his commands hadn't been laced with such revulsion. She'd glanced at him, her eyes softening, turning into puddles of liquid before he could even rephrase the request, maybe explain to her in more precise, cautious words.

She'd left the sofa, her and her belly, and gone upstairs. Didn't speak to him for days after that. And when she finally did, it was with halting trepidation, contrition, self-doubt. He had made her this way. He knew that.

On the ride home in the Uber, she faced her window, silent. He slipped out his phone and checked on the research conducted by Sy, the twenty-year-old hacker. The woman he was after now was only on two apps, one that was exclusive, for people with a so-called high profile. The other app was one on which the women made the first move. That one wouldn't work.

So as his wife sat beside him, he tapped out a profile, setting a trap, a frisson of excitement running through him. God, his wife would hate him for this; it would make her boil over. And that was exactly what he wanted.

She deserved it for her betrayal.

4

VERA

Present day

IT'S TOO MUCH. All of it is too much. I'm drowning again, but instead of hiding upstate, I'm cutting my image, slicing and dicing myself, little paper strips of my skin and hair and eyes cluttering my floor, getting trapped between the floorboards. Day in and day out, inserting myself into my collages where I hadn't thought I was needed. Valencia filter, Hudson, Jakarta, peeping out from grainy newsprint. My bed has become a mausoleum of tiny me's, earlier me's, saner me's. When I sleep, I sleep on the couch.

"Is this what they wanted to do to me?" I trill at Quinn, pointing at the photo I'd purloined from the Benningtons' nightstand. The camera is set at the end of a bed, almost giving a bird's-eye view. Peri smiling so wide her gums are showing. I've looked at the photo a thousand times at this point, the unmistakable glee in Peri's eyes, the terror on the face of Calypso Rogers, the girl Page recognized from Wyneck. And the absolute blankness on Tom's. All their bodies lissome, Peri's breasts like hardened cookie dough, so succulent, Tom's chest lean and depilated, sprawled on top of this girl on a bed, their prized sacrificial lamb. Peri almost laughing as she carves a little triangle in the flesh near the girl's mons pubis, a fang, a pair of small scissors glinting white light. Calypso's head over the edge of the bed, upside down in the photo, her teeth gritted, her eyes glazed over with panic so primal, it seems to climb out of the photo and grip me in its claws, her mouth in a silent *o*. Tom mounted over her, about to thrust inside her as she lies on her back.

We thought for a moment that there was a fourth person in the room, capturing the photo, but if you look in a corner, you can see a tripod's legs reflected in a mirror.

"Is this what they wanted to do to me? Odilie and Tom? Am I Calypso here?" I repeat and of course, Quinn can't answer that. All he can do is try to explain the picture for us, get as much info as he can to create a narrative, a story that will exhume Tom from the grave, bring down anyone else who was in charge of keeping him safe.

There was a moment, a short-lived one after I'd spoken to Page, when we thought about going to the police. But Quinn, as he said, suspects something far more sinister is going on here, that the police could be implicated in some kind of a cover-up. He wants to get to the bottom of it alone.

I've never seen him so single-minded, all the work, all the research. He knows everything about SNAPea, about their IPO plans, the name of every founding member and investor. He knows the kinds of socks Mr. Bennington prefers, the dorm he lived in at Harvard. He plans to submit a draft of the piece to his boss soon. We're both crazed, he with his research and I with my insane, derelict art.

We haven't told Sam anything about the photo. Quinn says we can't tell anyone else about it, that it was already risky enough showing Page. Page, whom I refuse to see, whose cunning is a reminder of how stupidly, easily, flattered I am, how I'd missed wielding power so much that I was led to believe her intentions were pure, that she was some poor, lonely girl missing her sister.

Yet, she was using me for her own personal advancement while I was using her. It would be laughable if it didn't bother me so much, if her pulling a fast one on me wasn't such a move from my own playbook.

It doesn't matter. We've stumbled on something much bigger than a human interest story on my and Page's supposed unlikely friendship.

It's not like she's texting me or anything, either. She's too busy with Jackson, with her alleged investor meetings, insinuating herself deeper and deeper into the world she so craved, single white female-ing her sister like her sister single white female-d me.

I'm adding that, I've decided. My little doppelgänger twin, to the collages, little paper dolls of Odilie and me holding hands, a little happy, joyous, deadly circle dance, pasted among a sea of headlines, alongside other bits I've started to incorporate—bones picked clean from meat I've cooked, scraps of Saran wrap over our tiny heads like we're being asphyxiated again and again, by Tom, by the media, by each other.

"This is really sick," Quinn murmurs one day when he spots me applying my finishing, mixed-media touches.

"Then it's doing its job," I reply, smoothing out the plastic over my smiling sepia mouth, reddened lips that I've X-Acto-knifed and turned upside down into a sinister frown.

My fingers, this movement, it directs my attention away from everything that is roiling in my head: What is it about me that compelled these people to become so obsessed?

All I want, all I crave, is to restore my equanimity, find a trajectory out of this mess. I want to make myself into a martyr, so I can convert that martyrdom into money, into power. And I'm figuring out how, one collage at a time.

I think of my mother, her criticisms, her obscene self-involvement. The standards to which she held me, this endless need to be perfect. The fact that my major woman role model for the first years of my life was someone so focused on her own self, the universe so casually and unquestioningly revolving around her.

Some girls, some daughters, they would have rebelled. They would have made themselves ugly, average creatures, would have forced themselves to fade into the background. But not I. I was instilled with a need to be special, to have all eyes on me. Because my mother showed me that was the only way to live. But look where that got me, Mom. Look where that got me.

I prick a stigmata-size hole in my head, watch my flesh ruffle around the knifepoint.

5

TOM

1.5 years ago

VERA'S DATING APP profile was one of the better ones he'd seen; her answers were witty, her pictures elegant and sexy, giving just enough information about her body, her sexual energy, while still leaving you wanting more. He suspected, somehow, that not too many of the men she met "got" her, aside from her obvious beauty, and that she had a long line of dating dolts who weren't on her intellectual level, who couldn't keep up with her references and quips.

Good thing he was up to standard.

This was better, he thought, than stalking those bars looking for her, putting himself out on a limb that way. Women these days, they didn't trust meeting men in person; it was better to lay all the cards on the table that dating was what they both wanted, that they were both available. He wanted her to come to him easily, with no qualms about who, in the strange, unfamiliar darkness of a bar, he might be. Better to put his profession, his age, his pictures, up, to be completely transparent about who he was. Or who he wanted her to think he was.

He'd chosen photos he knew were attractive, soft, not too intimidating. He'd done his research. He had spent ample time on her profile, on the articles in which she was quoted for that fashion brand. He knew how, in the way Peri had trained him to, to subtly decipher what this woman would be attracted to, what she'd be looking for. She was confident in a way that made him uneasy; if her security came from male attention, she was good at hiding it.

But there was also something lonely about her, a vague veil of protectiveness that emanated from her photos. In many of them she was surrounded by people, but upon further investigation, he would find that they were mostly coworkers, not friends; people with whom she was thrust together because of her industry, her rising importance in the New York fashion world.

Loneliness was perhaps not the right word. Yes, she seemed to hold her guard up, but she didn't seem lonely, not really. There was nothing very try-hard about her online presence; her photos were sumptuous, sure, but nothing seemed too deliberate, too studied. She seemed to be literally showing off snapshots of her life. It was nothing like his wife's social media presence, earnest and aching with plaintive falsities, pastel and planned.

He could tell that a man in her life had to be a tad subservient to get her prolonged attention, that she was not one to depend on a partner for personal endorsement, that if she wasn't the alpha she wouldn't be interested. She needed to feel in control, to feel like she could hurt him, wound him, if she really wanted to.

It was something about her posing, her nonchalance, the intrinsically chic way she lived her life, that gave this weakness away, this need for power in her romantic life. This was not someone who would easily be used. He would have to keep that in mind, tamp down his own urges for authority.

How had he learned to be so discerning? He asked himself this question a lot. For someone who, admittedly, didn't much *care* for people or their habits, his emotional intelligence was quite high. It had to do, of course, with Peri. The one who taught him everything he needed to know.

His wife was leaving for Michigan with the baby. Their house smelled like lotion, for a bitter Midwestern March, even though she had stowed away all her toiletries so carefully in labeled Ziploc bags, inside their suitcases. "You can have the maid do that, you know," he told her as she folded her clothes, put them in airtight bags to save room. It seemed like she was leaving for a while. How long did she expect to be gone? He hadn't bothered to ask. She rolled her eyes at him.

"I want to do this myself. I want to do something for myself. My mom knows a good prenatal doctor over there, by the way, not that you care." With a huff she coiled her hair dryer's cord around its handle, took items from her vanity and placed them in a bag embroidered with her initials. "I don't feel like I exist, Tom. Don't you get it? I don't feel like I exist here. I don't feel like Penelope exists, either. Maybe if I go away, this new baby will have a better chance at existing." She rose up from packing the suitcase, looked him straight in the eyes with that newly defiant gaze he'd somehow grown used to. "You don't help those feelings, you know. You don't help them at all."

He heard her go into the baby's room, heard her cooing to her, probably about her big bad father who diminished her mommy. He had given her this life on a silver platter and this…this *iciness* was how she was repaying him? It seemed obscene to him if he thought too hard about it, which, yes, he'd been doing as of late. That was what inspired his whole pursuit of the other woman, of course.

A few months back, when his wife was asleep, he'd slipped her phone out from its charger and had gone downstairs to his home office. He knew her passcode; she thought he didn't. He knew she changed it every month to prevent him from snooping. But he was agile. He could tell from her fingers dancing on the keypad exactly which digits to type in. When you get used to someone's finger movements, how they navigate space, reveal thoughts and feelings, deciphering these types of gestures become far easier.

This numerical code seemed like a birthday, though he didn't recognize whose. She cycled through birthdays a lot: her mother's, her current best friend's, the baby's. At some long-ago point, his. Usually, when he breached her phone, he would spend a while in her iMessages, see whom she was communicating with. Maybe a short foray into her emails, too, her web searches. Most of the time, he came up short. His wife, it turned out, was boring, to an almost maddening degree. Once, he'd found a link to pegging porn in her search history, but that was as spicy as she got. Even her texts to her friends were mind-numbingly dull, logistics about wine nights, questions about childcare.

But he still felt like he needed to keep tabs, even if all the information didn't amount to anything useful. He'd learned that, too, from his ex. She'd taught him that if you let someone in, you can never be too careful, that you always need to stay one step ahead of them, to always check over your shoulder.

This one time, however, when he'd opened her phone, he found a new app downloaded. Upon first glance, it seemed like a meditation app; the little icon was a figure looking upward at a peaceful sky. But instinct told him to open it, anyway. Not everything was as it seemed, of course. Even an iPhone app with poor user experience.

He'd been right; it was a meditation app, with different guided exercises for varied times of the day. But there was also a journal segment, a place for sad, diffident people to chronicle their supposed changed feelings after a week, a month, of daily guided meditations. What a bunch of bullshit. He clicked on the journal icon, aware then that he was sitting in total darkness. It hadn't occurred to him to turn on a light.

Every entry was filled, days out. He scrolled down to the first one input and settled into his wingback chair to read, expecting some cheesy, insipid bullshit about how much better she had slept the previous night after meditating for thirty minutes over a turmeric latté in the morning. But it wasn't that. It wasn't that at all.

Ugh, I hope Tom doesn't find this. He checks my phone, but I'm crossing my fingers that he won't discover any of this, trapped in this app. He almost never speaks to me, but when he does, I feel like I'm talking to an automated machine, like I don't exist, except when it suits him, when he wants something from me. I can't believe I ever saw something in him aside from his greed. You know, back in the day, I loved how decisive he was, the way he craved supremacy over me. It was sexy. But he also saw me, noticed me. That doesn't happen anymore.

And the thing is, he knows what to say, the right words to woo just about anyone. That's what I hate most about him, this slickness. It feels like a disease. Like I'm covered in oil. Sometimes when he's home working in that stupid man cave of an office, I want to wring his neck. Come up from behind him and garrote him.

It didn't used to be so bad. It was good at one point, wasn't it? I saw Joanie with Colin on Monday after that silly thing at the art gallery; they were fighting, a real argument because Colin had booked some vacation during her grandmother's birthday. It was refreshing to see, actually. To see real emotion in both their faces as they went at each other. Of course, Joanie apologized to me afterward. She was so embarrassed. She said she'd forgotten I was even in the house, that her emotions just leaked out of her. I said it was fine, that we all have our little marital disputes, that I of course was privy to the worst of them myself.

But am I? He doesn't show the least bit of interest in me anymore, aside from making sure I don't talk to anyone outside his approved sphere or to neg me. He's never shown the slightest interest in Penelope so what else is new there. God, I feel like he's taken everything from me at this point, like I'm this floating flesh sac with no personality, nothing to lose or gain. When I gave up everything to be with him, including the best friend I've ever had, I thought I was giving it all up for something real. But now I know he was never any more real than anything else in this fabricated city. I wish he'd disappear. Even his presence makes me inescapably annoyed, all those weird grunts he makes when he sleeps, the sniffle of his nose. I can't stand any of it. He's absolutely insufferable.

And on and on and on it went, picking him apart until he was slaughtered and disemboweled on a table, a pig with its intestines hanging open like an old-fashioned telephone cord. Oddly, as he'd sat there reading, he hadn't felt a thing. He'd been strangely detached from all of it, as if these slanderous phrases were about another husband in another marriage, one who had nothing to do with him.

It got worse, though.

I did it. I reached out to Peri. Or I tried to, at least. I think she's changed her number. I'm not sure what came over me. I just feel so…lonely? I know who she is, what she did, but I miss her. No one has ever made me feel the way I felt when I was with her. Sometimes I don't think I've really felt anything in ages.

That was what did it, the ultimate betrayal. That was what made him want to tear his wife to pieces, to gnaw at her soul until she disintegrated.

Ten years ago Tom and Peri had reveled in doing depraved, violent things to other women during sex. It had started early on. About six months into their relationship, they'd started to bring in other women, random girls they met at bars. But soon those easy conquests became stale, vanilla.

Then one day, when the couple was alone, Peri brought a pair of tiny, nonthreatening scissors into bed. "Carve me, baby." He had laughed, taken the scissors from her, so small that they looked like they were from a child's toy chest, and cut the air with them.

"I'm serious," she said, reaching for them with a sinewy arm. "Prick me." But he laughed at her, dangling them from his pinky, the blades so minuscule next to his fingers.

Her eyes darkened and she lunged for the instrument, grabbed them so roughly from his finger that he felt the joint snap. And she plunged the scissors into his thigh, leaving a dime-size slash. Before he could realize what was happening, she began to lap up the blood with her warm tongue, leaned over to kiss him, her lips dabbed red. And this obscenity, not the cut itself, turned him on like nothing else had before. He wanted more of it.

Soon, Tom began fantasizing about incorporating more pain, others' pain, into their bedroom routines. "I can make it happen for you, for us," she whispered one night. And he didn't believe her at first. But then she did it, his fantasies coming to life right before his eyes.

There was something about Peri, the way she thrust herself forward so unabashedly, making him a partner in her domination, that made him want to *own* that domination. He'd always fantasized about controlling them, all those girls who had rejected him in middle school, high school, their tiny mouths twisting in disgust at the mere *thought* of going out with Tom Newburn. And with Peri, he had the power to actually do it.

She procured girls for other men sometimes, too. Powerful men. Plucking the discards from her own sexual conquests and handing them off to a network of suits salivating at the idea of sex with lithe, beautiful young women who weren't professional sex workers, merely girls Peri had found and delivered. Tom, these other men, they wanted to fornicate with the kind of girls they could meet in real life. They wanted docile, homebody types, not the Peris of the world. Or, rather, not the type of woman Peri was, self-possessed and strong-willed.

Tom and the other men would pay the girls off so they wouldn't say a word. And for a while, it all went swimmingly, mostly because Tom loved Peri. He loved how she made him feel, all the potential she saw in him. How powerful he'd become since she came into his life. He never mentioned that, in some ways, Peri also scared him. How would that look, to be so fearful of a woman?

He had met her at a club during his last year of business school, out with his colleagues from the venture capital firm he'd soon start working for, trying to make friends.

Tom had only recently grown into himself. It wasn't until an economics class in college that everything clicked, that he learned, fully absorbed, that he didn't have to be a big, bulky guy who could knock other men down to be successful. That if he worked hard, harder than anyone else, he could be ahead of everyone, ahead of his brother and his father. Ahead of all the bullies of his childhood.

At the club, he'd done a bunch of blow with his coworkers, a few too many tequila shots. But none of it had helped. He still felt like running through the exit door to escape the pounding bass, the scratch of people's voices as they sang along to the inane lyrics.

She seemed to sense this from the get-go, gorgeous and slinky, all over him, inviting him to get up and *dance*, her movements like his heartbeat on the cocaine, rapid and hard, pulling him onto the club's floor from the safety of the booze-lined table his friend had bought. The moment she thrust herself onto him, he felt a bulge like he was thirteen again, watching his father's pornos, taped over the WWE matches his mother despised, on the VCR in the basement.

"Relaxxxxx," she breathed into his ear, licking it, her tongue quivering over the lobe, slithering into his actual eardrum. And he had. He relaxed right then and there into her arms, closing his eyes and enjoying the music, the gyrations of her body.

They started dating soon after. She gave him the tools he needed to bring SNAPea to investors. Taught him how to talk to people—how to get what he wanted. She believed in him, believed in his tenacity.

After a while Peri grew bored, even amid the wild, sadistic sex, the fleeting one-night stands the two would have with girls who were too intimidated, too disconcerted, didn't *understand* Peri and Tom and what they wanted. Who consented, but barely, their voices merely tremors. She wanted a third, a real third, someone whom she could dominate, but who wouldn't feel confined by them.

Then she found Odilie.

"There's something about her," she had said to him. "Something in her. She'll be good for us, bring us closer." She was a perfect fit for what Peri liked, docile and mild mannered, a *nice*, malleable girl who could be tweaked to her liking. Peri had to groom her first, gain her trust, make Odilie dependent on her.

But then Tom had met Odilie, and Peri lost her power over both of them.

It had happened suddenly, a quake of desire Tom hadn't experienced in years, that he hadn't even experienced with Peri. After the night at the beach where they shared their kiss, they began sneaking around, meeting up during Odilie's lunch hour, having cramped, teenage sex in her car, navigating around Peri's loose schedule. Odilie was everything that Peri was not: soft and naive and submissive. It was the first time a woman had looked at him like she did. Like he had dominion. There was an eagerness about her, a puppy dog's need for attention. With Odilie, Tom had recognized what he could be capable of without Peri's grip on him. He didn't need her anymore.

Yes, for a while, he had relished Peri's domination of him. It had been his deepest, darkest fantasy. But the excitement of it, the thrilling, titillating novelty of it had worn off. He craved something more normal, more domestic, now that he was making headway professionally. The cruel, dangerous sadism wasn't stimulating him like it used to. And surely, the crowd that had accepted Peri because of what she could procure for them would be tired of her soon, too.

One afternoon, parked in a shady back lot where Odilie knew they would be undetectable, Tom told her the whole sordid truth. She was sitting on top of him in the passenger seat, both their pants off, breathing heavily into each other's mouths, when he reclined the seat, tilting his head away from her.

"She wants us to do this, you know. We don't have to sneak around," he said softly, eyes flitting away from her. Odilie had blinked rapidly, confusion settling between her brows.

"What are you talking about?"

He looked up to the car's ceiling, gazing at the gray fibers. "This was all part of Peri's plan. The only thing missing is her, here. Peri had this whole idea to groom you and make you into someone we could dominate together." Odilie scrambled out of his lap, to the driver's seat, her nude bottom planted on the leather, face hardened, her hands gripping the wheel of the car like she wanted to drive them right into the ocean just beyond the brush where they were parked.

"But I don't want to do that anymore," he finished, twisting his body so it faced hers. "I want you all for myself."

She was silent, her eyes still over the dashboard, staring into the distance. Until she pressed the palm of her hand into the center of the wheel and the car wailed long and loud, flushing the birds out of their branches. Eyes still trained forward, she murmured it. "The bitch was using me." And. "She's using you. You're better than that, Tom. She made you this way. I—I can make you better." It was a resolute statement. She pivoted toward him, suddenly. "Do you want to be with me?" Her voice regaining its docility, an imploring edge to it, like she was afraid of his answer.

And looking at her, fastening his eyes on hers, he nodded. "Yes."

"Then we both dump her."

And they did. The way they did it was, in retrospect, brutal and callous, out on the beach behind the Benningtons' guesthouse, both of them confronting her at once. The sky was gray, a rare rainy day that summer. "I made you both," Peri spat. Tom thought she'd throw a rock at them, one of the big ones that littered the edge of the shore. But she didn't. She stayed still, chillingly so, given the wind and the impending rain, stoic and taut, her hair the only lively part of her. "I thought you both loved me." Her voice a hiss against the waves.

After, she disappeared from their lives, from New York, too. It was understood by Odilie that Peri had conned her, given her a symbiotic friendship that she'd been convinced was love, but was in truth a Machiavellian trick. Odilie now understood her to be an evil, evil person who would be banished from their lives forever, even though she had been the one to bring them together. She didn't know that Tom had paid Peri to stay away. Turned her into just another girl who'd been used to serve a purpose.

Tom, in his quietest moments, was ashamed. Ashamed of what he had wanted with Peri, angry at Peri for making him feel this shame, for daring to unearth his darkest desires and get him to act on them.

One of the cardinal rules when Tom and Odilie got married, along with leading a private life so that Tom's transgressions would never be revealed, was that they would never speak of Peri again, that they never talk to her or try to contact her.

And Odilie had broken it.

VERA

Present day

QUINN HAS FOUND Calypso Rogers.

It wasn't hard. How could it be, with a name like Calypso Rogers? But he's been blocked. He tried every avenue to get to her and each time, Calypso has found a way to prevent access. One day, though, an email drops into his inbox.

> Dear Mr. Sun,
> Stop. Stop all of this. I guarantee you that no one will speak to you. No one will know what you're talking about. I want to live my life. If you continue to harass me like this, I will have no choice but to call the police and report you for stalking.

"Why will no one speak to me if they don't know what I'm inquiring about?" Quinn muses.

I check out Calypso's socials. She's pretty and well-off. She has a Maserati, a McMansion, twin girls, a husband with a mustache. She lives in Colorado. She doesn't work. Her husband does something in healthcare. Her parents are working class, from Wyneck. Her husband's parents own what looks like a gas station in South Carolina.

How can she afford the Maserati, the four-car garage? we wonder. But everything is conjecture when she won't speak to us.

One evening in late June, Quinn asks me, "Are you still angry at Tom?" Much to his chagrin, I've moved my collaging out of the bedroom and into the living room, our carpet speckled now with paper and glue, eyes and ears.

"I am. I'm madder than ever. I'm mad at Odilie, too. I'm mad at this ruthless Big Tech fraternity that protects men like Tom. I'm mad that I did nothing wrong and I'm still jobless because of the way our society treats women who dare to have possession over their own sexuality. I have so much rage that I could go light a fire with it, extinguish this entire city with one exhaled breath."

Quinn kneels beside me. "So you think I'm doing the right thing, pursuing this story?"

I drop my tools, look him in the eye. "The only thing stopping me from creating a crater in this earth is this demented snipping. Of course I want you to continue. Anything to help me move on." And he nods obediently, goes back to his room to do more research, I presume.

It's all true, this rage, this anger. And I'm happy that Quinn has this fire lit under him. But as I spiral deeper into myself, into my art, it occurs to me that the end result should be about *me*, not SNAPea. That at the end of the day, whatever Quinn finds, my redemption should be top priority, the theme of the piece. I should be the one to reap the most benefit from the article. I'm the one who found the photo, who led him on this journey after all. In a way, he owes me.

He's looking for Peri now. But she's nowhere, not as Thelma, either. I remember Brandon Newburn saying she had a name like a Greek goddess, if that was even the same girlfriend he was talking about, but Quinn can't find anything on that lead, either. It's like she dated Tom and disappeared, like he made her disappear.

Out of desperation, I text Page and ask her to ask Jackson what Peri's last name was. She tells me he doesn't know who I'm talking about and I want to slap myself for not asking him at the time. If I were to ask him myself now, I'm sure I'd get the same answer. He's protecting her, and Quinn and I are following a map that's already been torn to bits. Quinn hasn't given up, though. He says he's going to track her down, and I believe him.

In the meantime, I've slowly, very slowly, been uploading my collages to Instagram, the ones not so overtly about me, about Odilie. I've started a new account without my full name. But there's been traction. As Sam anticipated, people are asking for T-shirts and mugs and tote bags with my prints on them.

But I have bigger plans.

One day, as I'm working on uploading new pieces, my laptop propped up on my stomach, Quinn rushes in without knocking. I didn't even know he was home. His face is red and slicked with sweat, like he ran all the way here from his office.

"I found her," he says between labored breaths, not helped by his Juul lung. "Persephone Thelma Kay Barnes, Peri for short. Now Persephone Tanner, wife of the heir of Tanner Industries." He blinks rapidly, almost manically. "Tanner Industries, as in, munitions. They're mentioned during every school shooting and direct action by the US Military. She's worth billions, Vera. That photo, it's a gold mine." He wipes his face with his shirt.

I raise my brows. "A gold mine about to explode."

7

TOM

1.5 years ago

HE'D STAYED MAD at Odilie for a few days. It didn't sound
like she was *actually* back in touch with Peri. But even the fact
that she'd tried it pulled something loose in him, a screw that
had been holding his sanity together all these years. How dare
she hurt him like that, break the foundation of their partnership. Make him feel, even for a moment, like the shameful
little boy he'd sometimes felt like in Peri's presence. How dare
she diminish him like that. Did his feelings, his buried weaknesses, mean so little to her that she dismissed them without
a second thought? How dare she defy him.

Biting his knuckles, sitting in his home office, he decided
he would get back at Odilie for all this newly illuminated pain
he was feeling, the stir in his gut and clench in his chest. He
would find a way to make her pay.

The vitriol, the anger she had revealed in her diary entries, that didn't matter to him if she had remained loyal to him, loyal to their pact. And Odilie hadn't. She absolutely hadn't.

So on another night, before she left for Michigan, he took her phone again to check her journal.

He scrolled through until he hit something that was a tad more interesting, almost fascinating. Because it didn't start with the kind of hardness as the rest of the entries, full of complaints about him, did. This one was softer, lovelier. The woman he'd met all those years ago resurfaced, the earnest, hopeful one.

At first, I was just curious. I swear! I was at that yoga retreat up in the Hudson Valley this past weekend to clear my head and this woman, God she was annoying. Such a Chatty Cathy! I used to love the company of women like that, who I could kind of nod along and listen to.

Anyway, point is this woman could not stop talking about herself the entire retreat. And she mentioned a daughter who lives in the city. She said she's running a fashion brand, that she's becoming a big deal, that if you google her name, it shows up on the first page of Google. Those were her words. She kept bragging and bragging about this daughter of hers, so finally, I asked for a name and she was all too eager to give me it. She kept right on chatting away, almost looking through me. I swear if she saw me again, she wouldn't know who I was. That's how self-involved this woman is.

I got bored that night and technically we weren't even allowed to have our phones, because this is a tech-free kind of place, but who the heck listens to those rules, anyway? I mean, the place has Wi-Fi for God's sake. I looked up the daughter on Instagram, and I swear to God three hours went by and I was still scrolling. She's everything. Everything I aspire to be. It's like she's wormed her way into my head and I can't stop thinking about her. How, I don't know, polished, *she seems. With her perfect outfits and perfect face and perfect poise. And her feed, it doesn't seem curated at all. It's like she has this well-oiled confidence to know exactly how to post and when.*

Looking at it, I don't know, she makes me feel alive again. Like there's something out there to aspire to, like maybe if I try hard enough, I can be just like her. It's a tantalizing feeling, isn't it? I want to be her. I want to be her so badly it's scaring me a little. I won't even follow her from my personal account because I don't want her to notice me, to notice how small and sad my basic little life is. Not that she would notice me; she has enough followers that one more wouldn't even alert her. But the idea of her coming across me, of looking through her follower list and judging me with disdain, is too much to handle. So I just check her profile every day and see what she's up to. She's public, so it's easy. And she needs to be public for her job, so that setting won't go away anytime soon.

She reminds me of Peri, that unabashed confidence that seems to ooze out of those tiny pictures into the palm of my hand as I hold my phone. But I can't think about those similarities. I can't think about her, *especially since I never heard back.*

But Vera, Vera MacDonald, she's the second most self-assured person I've come across since her. *I wish it were contagious. God, I wish I could skin her and wear her, Vera. I want to meet her. I want us to be friends. But not yet, not now. I need to play a long game. I have to learn how to be her. Be more like that. God knows I tried all those years ago. But this time I won't fuck up and get distracted. This time I'll get what I want. I'll have the gumption to infiltrate Vera's world. By the time I offer my friendship to her, I'll be an entirely different person. She'll be enthralled. That's my promise to myself.*

8

VERA

QUINN HAD TRIED every tool in his kit. He'd attempted every journalistic trick up his sleeve in his quest for more info about Thelma. Peri. Whoever she is. He'd engaged a private investigator, a professional hacker, barely legal maneuvers. She wasn't on Google. She'd had her name basically wiped from everywhere, any remnants of her past erased like she'd never existed at all.

There had been a point, Quinn said, where he thought he was truly losing it, when he had looked at that despicable picture so many times, he thought he'd merged with it, his face showing up in corners of it. He began to wonder if Peri existed at all anymore, if she'd died somehow along with Tom and Odilie.

But he'd found her. Nothing much. Just that she was married to Darius Tanner, that they lived somewhere near Atlanta. No mention of children or images of sprawling estates. She was private, Persephone. Darius, the Tanner heir, was private, too.

But Quinn, he was giddy. A picture of a billionaire with a dead rich person, brutally inflicting sexual pain on a third? It was too good, the story too juicy. This would *make* Quinn's career. This would establish a sordid pattern of abuse from Tom, exonerate me, show him for the psychopath he truly was.

I'd had the flicker of a thought, that I didn't voice to Quinn, that we should extort her instead. Get some money out of this instead of an article. Use the financial gain to somehow bolster both of our careers, our reputations. But Quinn, he is a better person than I am. He wants SNAPea and that whole cohort to fall, to really expose the obscenity beneath the shine. To make certain that all these powerful, rich men keeping each other's secrets would have their lives ripped out from under them. Like mine had been.

Quinn's plan was to finally show the picture, what he'd found out about Persephone, to his boss, who would—he hoped—pull his weight to get additional sources, to really beef up the article Quinn had already started to write.

But it's the weekend and I'm at my mom's house and Quinn's big reveal could happen on Monday.

I hadn't spoken to her in months, since we'd had our giant fight, but she'd invited me up to the Hudson Valley via text saying she missed me, that she knew there was a heat wave coming to the city and that I could cool off up there with her. I'd ignored her, but then my AC broke and the mugginess descended on the city, so I texted her back and said I'd be there.

She welcomes me like nothing has happened and I go back to sequestering myself in that horrible bedroom with the cherry-print wallpaper, the one-eyed swan lamp, the AC

turned to sixty degrees, a portable fan oscillating lazily to and
fro as well, but none of it is able to penetrate the oppressive
heat. I lie on the bed, too hot to move. I feel a fly on me, but
it takes too much effort to swat it, so I let it creep on me like
I'm a living dead girl.

This time, though, I do accompany my mom out. I go to
her morning yoga class with her, try her disgusting smoothies, let her make me a Reiki appointment. During lunch at
one of her favorite vegan spots, cashew-cheese that looks like
bird shit smeared on a piece of bread, I ask her why she built
me the way she did.

"You were born that way, Vera," she says, taking a long sip
of her black tea. "But sure, I wanted you to plant your feet on
this earth so you would not be easily swayed. I wanted you to
leave your mark, because try as I may have when I was your
age, I never did. I never thought you would do it the way you
did, though."

"How did you try?" I ask, pushing away my plate of mi-
crogreens.

"Oh, you know. I worked in PR until I got pregnant with
your brother. I was good at it, too. But then, I'm not sure,
motherhood kind of made me feel like I had to shy away from
that kind of life, like I had no reason to take up that much
space anymore. But I resented that feeling later, and I wanted
differently for you. I wanted you to be the kind of woman
who *took* the space, who *dictated* the space, not just existed in
it. I wanted you to be cunning and strategic in every facet of
your life, to get out on top. Kindness, it's overrated. Kind people don't get shit done because they're too worried what other
people will think. And I wanted you to get shit done. And
obviously, the more successful you were, the better I would
look. So it was a win-win in my eyes." She stirs her tea, looks
out the window at the sunbaked sidewalk.

"There's someone I want you to meet. I met her in yoga. She's a fixer."

I roll my eyes. "Mom, God, stop right there."

But Mom is on a roll. "She fixes public scandals. Every celebrity or politician or businessman who's been canceled? She's the one behind getting their career back on track." She fidgets with her bracelets, moves them up her arms.

"I don't need anyone like that. I thought you said so yourself, that I can take care of myself."

She flits her eyes down, into her tea. "I know, I know. But do this for me, okay? She knows your whole story. And she's coming over this afternoon to chat with you."

I resist rolling my eyes again. "Fine. *Fine*. But if she's some New Age freak who says she's going to spirit all my problems away, I swear I won't visit again."

We go back to the house and Mom leaves to run some errands, probably to see her new boyfriend. She tells me to wait around for the "fixer" to show up, so I go and lie in bed, waiting for the doorbell to ring. If only I could tell my mom that hopefully in a few short days my life will change again, for good.

Finally, I hear a car pull up and park in the small driveway and I get up, anticipating the doorbell. I go downstairs and open the door before it rings, peek out.

And there, her hair cropped short, dressed blindingly in white, is Persephone Tanner, leaning against her car and smoking, one finger waving at me, nails magenta like tongues.

Persephone Tanner sits at my mother's kitchen table, smoking inside, all windows open, and tells me a story.

When I first saw her, I had backed away, into the house. Locked the door, had the wild urge to call the cops. But she wasn't fazed. She knocked softly. "Vera, I'm not going to hurt you. I promise." Her voice so silky smooth, a ribbon of a sound, like an old-time movie actress beckoning a man forward. And wasn't that how they all spoke, before they knifed you, burglarized you, set your house on fire? I'd refused to open the door, palming my phone, ready to ask Quinn for help or dial 911.

"I just want to clarify a few things," she called out again, in that beguiling tone. "I want to help you. I think you're quite brilliant, Vera. I've seen your art. I bought one of your tote bags. You have an indescribable eye." She waited a beat, waited for me to fall for her flattery. "You're smart to be cautious. But I promise I'm coming in peace."

And I opened the door a crack, asked her to lift her hands, empty her pockets, her purse, like I was some kind of TSA agent. But she wasn't armed, except with sunglasses and cigarettes, a lighter. She didn't even have her phone on her.

Unsurprisingly, Persephone is not a fixer. Persephone got a call a few weeks back from Mr. Bennington, who said an illicit picture had been taken from his home and he hadn't been sure by whom; she asked what picture and he sheepishly answered, *The picture you told me to burn.*

"Obviously, he was still looking at the thing nightly or something. He always was a pervert."

She tells me that ten years ago she and Tom stayed in that house, just as Jackson had told me. She tells me that they were into some kinky group sex together, everything consensual, she swears, though she knows how it looks. That they would sometimes take photos. That she left the house in a hurry at the tail end of summer, that in her haste she forgot one picture. She called Mr. Bennington and told him to destroy it, that it would destroy the company he was helping to build if the public knew Tom was a weird sex fiend. He didn't hesitate, said he would in a minute.

Obviously, he never did.

She tells me, ashing her cigarette in the swooping stomach of one of my mother's New Age hand-thrown pottery tchotchkes, that she started to freak out. She had a *real* life now, a kid, a husband who was obsessed with privacy. The last thing she wanted was to have that picture leaked anywhere. She'd already done such a good job of distancing herself from Tom that she was never linked to him when the murders occurred.

"Someone is trying to extort you," Mr. Bennington had said grimly. And then her cybersecurity detail noticed that somebody called Quinn Sun was poking around, trying to find information. After that, after learning Quinn was a journalist, after learning who I was, it wasn't too difficult to see what our plans were.

"You got the short end of the stick, I get it. I would be pissed, too, if I got blamed for some lame guy's crimes and he was dead, so you couldn't even kill him yourself. I would also want to dig up any skeletons I could find on him." She stabs the cigarette into the makeshift ashtray, wriggles her hands, deciding whether to light another. "To be honest, I'm sure that was intentional. I am *certain* that there's a lot of dirty shit behind the scenes at SNAPea that none of those board members want getting out. It would not surprise me if Bennington or one of the other buffoons paid off the NYPD not to dig too deep, had their PR team construct a narrative that put you front and center of the crime and sold that to the media. Those guys have a finger in every pie. And I would know because I'm married to one of them."

Her features, they're so symmetrical, like a sculpture carved from marble, that it's hard to look away. She's mesmerizing, incandescent, even the way her lips move is so precise. I can't help but pay attention to what she's saying, like she's hypnotizing me, almost, like I'm cast under her incantations.

"But I don't have *that* much empathy for you. Initially, I wanted to blackmail *you* to get my picture back." She laughs. "That's why I came here. I tracked down your mom, joined her yoga class, hoped that she would talk. And God, did she *talk*. About how powerful you are, how you'll do anything to get ahead, how proud she is of herself for raising you, even though she's not supposed to be, given your circumstances." She taps her nails on the table, *clack clack clack*, like a machine gun.

"But then something else occurred to me. Something far better than my blackmailing you into handing off the photo. Or giving away any of my husband's precious money in order to have it back. Because we're not that different, you and I. I see myself in you, in your gumption." She pauses, grabs my hand, interlaces my fingers with hers and tells me what I'm going to do. What we're going to do.

9

TOM

1.5 years ago

HE WATCHED VERA circle the gallery, her movements so delicate, but purposeful. Like with every step, she knew exactly where she was going. Her deliberateness, he knew about that, had expected it, based on his perusal of her online presence. But in person, it almost took his breath away, a punch in the gut.

He wasn't used to being with someone who met him where he was at, whose sheer presence almost made him second-guess himself, to quake like he was ten years old again, picked last for softball. It wasn't just her beauty, though that was certainly part of it. She was so deliciously assembled, her facial features absolutely aligned, her skin lush and warm. But her power rested in her certainty, the decisive way she talked, walked, ate. She knew what she wanted and grabbed it, no matter what it took, no matter whom she walked over along the way.

The idea was to begin dating Vera, to use the charm he hadn't oiled in years to entice her, make her fall for him, and then show off the conquest to his wife. *Look at my power. Look who I was able to steal right from under your nose. You think you can bring Peri back into the mix without a second thought? Look what I can do to* you. What happened to Vera herself after his little game was over? Well, he hadn't thought that far.

But now all of that seemed so petty, such a clearly childish reaction to a marriage that was already built on the backs of something shaky and disturbed. Vera here, in the flesh, was intoxicating. He understood his wife's obsession now, the desperate way she wanted to emulate her. Now, now he wasn't sure he wanted to let her go at all. And he'd trapped himself, too, in the lies he was telling her about his morals, his ethics. Initially, he had been acting as the man he believed she would fall for. And now he wanted to *be* that man for her, the kind, gentle one who was a little unsteady on his feet, a little awkward, powerful but powerless.

He wanted to impress her; that was part of the issue. He felt an urgent need to make her see the good in him, to convince her that he wasn't a bad guy. He'd known the tickets to the art gallery show were a bit too flashy for her taste, an obvious try-hard move. But he *wanted* her to experience something different, something only a person like him could provide. That was the crux of it, the difference. Her feelings, her thoughts, mattered.

The next morning he watched her sleep in the bed he shared with his wife, her lips opened partway, drool escaping through them as she breathed in, out. He wanted to stick his finger into that little wedge of an opening, have her suck it, make his fingertips dewy with her saliva. But he stopped himself, heaved himself out of bed as quietly as he could. He would do what kind, attentive men on overnight dates do and get her food; he'd done it himself once upon a time. Before Peri, before Odilie.

When he returned, they lay back in bed together nude, egg yolk sliding onto the sheets between them, everything bagel seasoning getting caught in the pillowcases. He nibbled at her lip, licked the smear of avocado by the side of her nose and she made a noise, a small tickle at the back of her throat, nestled herself closer to him and he couldn't help but kiss her, on her eyelids, her nose, her lips. He felt himself swooning over her, getting buried under her presence, slowly but surely. It was like Peri all over again. Intoxicated until he wasn't. Until he found Odilie and she seemed like exactly what he needed: sturdy, docile, predictable.

"What scares you?" she asked suddenly, peering up at him, staring at him with unblinking eyes.

He shifted his arm, so it was wrapped around her torso, snaking its way to the small of her back. "Nothing. I'm scared of nothing." He let it roll out without thinking, and he knew by the way she tensed, so very slightly arched her back, that he had said the wrong thing. That the Tom he had only recently decided to conceal was rearing its ugly head.

"I mean, I'm scared of my loved ones getting hurt. My daughter." And he checked himself, that instinctive, primal part of himself. There was a pang at the thought of losing Penelope, dull and throbbing buried deep in his bone marrow, some kind of biological vestige. This child he hadn't wanted, this child whom he barely knew, whom he hadn't taken the time *to* get to know. Made especially apparent by the unfortunate bathtub incident.

But Vera, she pushed his chest a little, giving herself room to cock her head and look at him. "You're lying, aren't you? And that's okay. I asked for a reason." She settled back down, her cheek resting on a pillowcase, gazing up at him. "You know what I'm afraid of?" She entangled her fingers in his chest hair. "I'm afraid of losing my power, what I've built myself into. My career. Of being so powerless, so awfully *debased* that I lose belief in myself. That I lose myself."

If he put his face any closer to her, her features would blur, melting together. "That could never happen. As long as you're smart about everything, of course. Don't make any bad judgment calls." He gave her a sheepish grin. But she didn't reciprocate.

"So what are you really afraid of?" she asked again, more forcefully this time, louder, like their heads weren't mere inches apart.

He sat back, put his arms behind his head on the pillow, her face meeting his armpit. "I guess in some ways I'm the same as you. I need power. And if that's usurped, then I'm all gone. I'm not sure who I would be."

And in a moment, he felt her lips on his.

When he got the text from her ending things, he couldn't process it at first. He felt his body weaken as he stood at the entranceway of the Core Club, ready to join a meeting about the new acquisition. He felt on the verge of collapse, his heart dropping to his knees and plummeting to his feet. It wasn't until he read it a second, a third time that he understood it, that he could comprehend the words.

He knew it was coming. He wasn't an idiot. She'd been avoiding him, dodging every message, every abject apology. The other evening he had taken his anger about the situation out on his home office door, twisting the knob so roughly that the handle's mechanism broke, requiring him to use its wobbly bar lock when shutting himself in there.

But to actually receive the text, this rejection. It hurt. A sharp jab in the stomach, a foreign flutter of a feeling that he wasn't sure he'd felt since he was a boy, since he was thrown around by those other kids, his name scrawled in chalk on the playground calling him the f word, the note penned in red ink by a girl in seventh grade telling him she would rather die than go to the school dance with him, would rather see her mother die, too. Since his brother had taken up all the space at family dinners, talked over him, his parents' eyes glowing in Brandon's direction as Tom sat there, small and scrawny hunched over his meatloaf, making lines in his mashed potatoes with the tines of his fork.

When he walked into the meeting, Darren Bennington looked up. "You look like the devil visited," he chuckled, igniting a rise of laughter from the rest of the group. Tom mechanically smiled back, forcing his lips into a rigid smile. He was frustrated with Darren. The board wanted Tom back at HQ full-time. With the addition of the D2C marketplace, they needed him around the other employees. They would be moving his home office equipment, with all its software and data, to HQ as soon as possible.

He sat in the meeting, his fist clenched on the table, stuttering out responses as it progressed, his mind elsewhere, reconciling, grasping, maneuvering in his head her text to him. Replaying each word. This was not supposed to happen. He had been certain of it. Once he fell for her, things were supposed to develop exactly the way he fantasized they would, escalating under his watch into something truly meaningful and exquisite. He hadn't originally been planning for that, necessarily, but now that he was faced with this rejection, he realized that that was exactly what he'd wanted.

As Darren was jabbering on, Tom immersed himself in the moment he believed her tune had changed. Maybe at dinner, his and his wife's old haunt? He hadn't meant to be so rash with that decision; it was only when they sat down that he realized that any number of her friends could spot them. He only brought it up as an effect of his anxiety about it. And now, now he wished more than anything that he'd kept his mouth shut.

She had seemed cold to him, too, when he'd been on the phone with his wife about Penelope. But that was a domestic tiff; Vera had no idea what his wife was saying on the other end, and he couldn't imagine that a woman like Vera, whom he was sure was used to putting people in their place, would be turned off by a slight show of frustration on his part. After all, he had only raised his voice a little to turn her on. Show off that he, too, was steeped in authority, no matter if it were family or work. But she'd run away, hadn't she? She'd told him she hadn't liked it, that Odilie didn't *deserve* that.

"Tom?" Someone had been asking him something. And they'd had to repeat themselves. He cracked his neck, turning his head from side to side, forcing the room to hear his bones squelch.

"Sorry. What did you say?" Tom asked and Darren looked like he wanted to walk out, maybe punch Tom in the nose. But he remained vigilant, disciplined enough to keep his composure. Everyone else in the meeting shifted in place, visibly uncomfortable. Did he care? No, even as Darren spoke again, Tom's mind inadvertently wandered to her text. He itched to look at his phone, to stare at it again, to read it like it was scripture, a holy text, to parse out meaning from the gray-and-black bubble.

When he arrived back home hours later, after taking himself to a bland-looking bar, the kind of place he hadn't set foot in since college, he almost tripped over the suitcase flung open in the front hall, the contents spilling out like pus from an infected wound.

His wife was home. And she was angry about something.

He found her in the kitchen, her stomach bigger than it had

been the previous month, an excrescence on her frail frame. The remodeling had been done last year, with louvered cabinets, the island corbeled, the fridge upgraded to the latest Subzero model. The stove was always having issues. It had been a stupid, superfluous expense; they hardly used the kitchen unless they had a private chef cooking there. But there she was, whipping something in a bowl, the wire whisk's thrust so aggressive it looked like she would pull a muscle.

"Penelope is asleep. You should go say hi to her. She should be reminded what her father looks like." She didn't look up from the bowl. He approached her, was suddenly assaulted by the odor of onions. She didn't look up, even as he came nearer, tried to draw her into him. She was whipping so hard she was creating peaks in the egg whites, tiny castles for the fluffiest frittata in the world.

He took her chin, tilted her head up and planted a soft kiss on her lips. She didn't reciprocate, keeping her mouth firmly shut. "Get the fuck away from me," she growled, shoving him with the rim of the bowl. And he did. He walked backward toward the edge of the kitchen as she stared at him from the island, her arm almost mechanical with its whirring movements, still beating away at the eggs.

"I've been seeing someone," he said softly, the weight of the words dripping out of him without warning. He said it louder, more lasciviously. "I've been seeing someone."

She finally stopped whisking, the bowl still clutched to her chest. "Of course you have been." She rolled her eyes. "I heard you the first time, by the way." She put the bowl down, turned on the stove, the blue flame dancing as she heated the nonstick pan, adding oil to it, anyway.

He clenched his fist. "Don't you want to know who it is?"

She tossed in the onions. "Not particularly. You're so *boring*, Tom. God, it's probably your personal trainer or something. Some cliché. Sorry to say, but you're just not interesting enough to be having an affair with someone outside the immediate realm of possibility." The onions sizzled.

He clenched his other fist. "You don't know me at all." And she rolled her eyes again.

"I know how weak you are. You let Peri bring your weakest impulses to light. You're a petulant, powerless, selfish little man, Tom. And I feel bad for whoever you've charmed this time. And I'm grateful it's not me. I'm grateful that I finally have the balls to say that, too." She took out a large knife, a pepper. De-seeded it, began chopping. "Anyway, aren't you going to ask me about my trip?"

He opened his mouth, closed it again, his jaw tightening with her every barb. "It's Vera. I'm seeing Vera. Vera Mac-Donald. You didn't have the wherewithal to actually meet her, to get to know her. So *I* did."

The knife, it clattered down onto the island, nearly falling off the edge. When she looked up at him, he felt for a moment that he should reach for it, grab the weapon and make a run for it. Her eyes blazed, reflecting the dim light from the stove. *She could kill me now, this moment.* That was how angry she looked, her face on the verge of a scream, mouth puckered so venomously, a snake about to bite.

The fire alarm went off, smoke billowing off the hot oiled onion pan. And she began to cry.

ODILIE

1.5 years ago

SHE HAD A PLAN.

At first, it had been a wish. A dream, something she clung to as she lay in the guest bed in Novi, her lower back aching as her abdomen blossomed into a fuller, rounder protrusion, Penelope resting beside her, sucking a wet thumb with her rosebud lips. Odilie gazed at the clouds painted on the blue ceiling of that bedroom and was at once whisked away to so many mornings and nights spent in the same position in her childhood home, hoping, yearning, aching, to be someone else.

And it struck her, as she lost herself in the whites of those stenciled clouds, that she was right where she'd begun, settled back into the familiar comfort of her own boredom, her own static ways. Though everything had changed, nothing had.

She nestled Penelope closer, sniffing the top of her head. She had hoped that coming to Michigan, that sinking back into her familial roots, would force her to be grateful for the life she led now, the glamour, the wealth, the friends in high places. But Odilie still felt two-dimensional, flimsy, very likely to be swept up by the wind, walked all over, tracked with muddy footprints.

The only way she felt even a modicum of self-respect, of pleasure, of control, was through her mothering. And that was why she had so casually, so easily and remorselessly, gone into her OB-GYN's office one day nearly four years ago and had her IUD taken out. She wanted someone, something, to mold, to create into the person she so desperately wanted to be.

Parents always complain about everything going by too fast, of childhood being so fleeting and so pure that it was impossible to hold on to, to capture properly. For Odilie, however, Penelope's childhood, her babyhood rather, was a slow slog in the mud. Odilie yearned for the day when she would have to enact some actual parenting skills, would have to teach her daughter life lessons rather than basic words. She yearned to have a little girl, not a toddler, to shape into someone far different from herself. Because the truth was, even at nearly three years old, Penelope was already too sweet, too docile. The other mothers would ooh and aah at how *easy* she was to manage. But Odilie craved defiance; she wanted somehow, in some way, to feel more seen, to be forced to lead, to be given control. To not live such a placid existence, to not be taken for granted by Tom, who made her feel like she could disappear at any moment.

She hoped her second child would wail all night long for her.

She had been feeling stuck, ignored by Tom, a wallflower once more, a mere inconvenience whom he had to greet when he wasn't in his tomb of an office. And now more recently, a punching bag, whom he liked to taunt, to psychologically pummel, whenever he noticed its presence.

When they had first gotten together, she relished him, the way he noticed her and included her, how worldly he'd seemed. A bit later, after she'd moved to New York with him, she'd even delighted in the way she was his paper doll, allowing him to dress her, trim her, shape her into the woman he wanted to overpower. She trusted him, loved how he perceived her and wanted her to be *better*.

Somewhere down the line, though, she'd grown tired of it; she wanted autonomy. She wanted to make her own choices. She had forgotten her obsession with gumption, with emulating Peri's self-possession. Now, now a decade later, she yearned for it again. At this juncture in their marriage, Tom either ignored her or harbored disdain. Yet, she did nothing, said nothing.

But then the incident happened with Penelope and the bathtub and her rage, it burst to the surface, became boiling hot. Because it was one thing to be disinterested in *her*, his wife, but it was a whole other problem to be indifferent to their child. Especially because after that wake-up call any husband with a soul would have stopped working so much, would have loved and appreciated his family a little more.

Not Tom.

Odilie had told her friends—women she drank with and read books with, who were mostly the wives of her husband's business partners, foisted on her because of Tom's insistence on insularity—that she was visiting her father who had recently undergone surgery, which wasn't a lie. But her dad was doing just fine. It was Odilie who seemed in need of some kind of medical intervention; that was what her mother said in so many words. "Something's not right," a dismissive mutter, because even grown-up Odilie was still only worthy of a murmur.

Odilie spent her days in Novi talking to Vera MacDonald.

Or, rather, her inner Vera. *You really need to change your life, Odilie. Get rid of that husband. Be your own woman; foster that independence. Tom is only holding you back. You have so much to live for, Odilie. So much you can do with yourself. Tom, he never wanted a wife who could be herself. You need to rise to your own occasion and be your own person.*

She would argue with Vera, tell her how that wasn't possible. How any which way she looked at it, she felt like she lost. Getting out from under Tom's thumb was an insurmountable task. She was too weak. She had no spine. No economic independence.

Remember that meeting you had with the lawyers back when you were getting married.

Odilie answered that yes, she did.

Remember that clause: in untimely death, you and any children would receive all of Tom's assets.

Odilie froze in bed, her hands gripping the covers. *No, no, I don't remember that clause.*

Sure you do, Vera answered. *Tom is indifferent. He's a snoop. He's a greedy pig who will only ever care about his business. He has no attachment to his own daughter, for God's sake. Why should he deserve to keep on breathing when he's not making this world or your home a better place?*

Odilie shifted away from Penelope in the bed, heard a little moan escape her mouth as she didn't feel the warmth of her mother beside her. *He's a person. A living, breathing person. He's the father of my child. No one deserves to die.*

Vera was silent in Odilie's head before speaking again. *Take some power back. It'll be easy. No one will ever accuse you of wrongdoing. Make it look like a suicide, like he couldn't get his new proj-*

ect off the ground, that he'd been wallowing in some severe depressive episode, which he'd been too afraid to tell anyone about. A man like that? They'll say he has everything, so he was probably too scared to ask for help. Too ashamed.

It'll be easy, I promise. A simple solution. He'll be dead, he'll be out of your way and you can start afresh.

Could it be that easy? Odilie continued watching the clouds on the guest bedroom's ceiling. She could swear they were floating, moving like real clouds in a real sky. She turned to Penelope and watched her breathe in and out. Her heart alive and beating. Like Tom's, like her own.

She wasn't actually going to *do* it. Of course not. It was just a happy little film that played on repeat in her brain at all times. When she closed her eyes, she could feel herself getting into the rhythm of it, embodying the *other* Odilie, the one who would so tactfully kill her husband, inherit his money, mourn with crocodile tears. It made her smile, this movie. Smile so hard that it brought her outside, into the sunlight, for one of the first times since she arrived in Michigan.

She didn't want it to be bloody. She resented Tom; she maybe even hated him. But she didn't abhor him enough to wish a painful death on him. No, she would do something simple, something that would lull him into a deep, dreamless forever sleep. Carbon monoxide poisoning. *A simple solution*, as Vera had said.

Before she even got back to Brooklyn, she had it all planned out. He spent every evening in his home office, that dungeon of a room that she never even went near. Sometimes he even slept there. Windowless. Soundproof. With a gas fireplace to make him feel like he was some medieval king with roaring, royal flames that she knew he kept on every night until May. Before he went in there for the night, she would finagle that fireplace so that once it was turned on, carbon monoxide would filter out. He would be trapped in there, while she and Penelope would sleep peacefully on the other side of the house, none the wiser. He wouldn't even realize what was happening to him until maybe the last moment before he lost consciousness.

Still, it was just a movie in her head. It wasn't until Tom, so casually cruel, had said that thing about Vera MacDonald that a fissure seemed to crack wide open in Odilie's head, that she felt a tremor of herself floating away, a dust mote in the sunlight. She was sane, she had always been sane, steady, sad and a little lonely, but with a firm grip on reality. She knew the Vera voice in her head was her own, for example. But after that admission, God, she wanted him to die. Harder than she'd wanted almost anything, than even Tom himself, when she had first seen him and fell so stupidly in love.

The Vera voice in her head, it vanished then, expelled by Odilie's wrath toward her husband. She wasn't angry about the cheating, the affair. No. Tom had taken something that was so rightfully Odilie's, so cherished, a friend however imaginary. He had tainted the only embodiment of perfection Odilie had in her otherwise discordant, unhappy life. He had soiled something precious.

At first, she thought he was lying, trying to get a rise out of her. After he'd gone to bed, on the couch, she'd taken his phone, looked at his text messages. She read through their conversation, noted that Tom *had* been lying about one thing: Vera had dumped him that day. Odilie called the number, to eliminate any doubt that this was Vera, that Tom hadn't just saved his side piece's number under her name to fuck with Odilie. She prayed that no one would pick up and no one did. And then there was the click of a voice mail, Vera, her voice lower and huskier than Odilie had imagined, saying her own name, that she wasn't there at the moment and whoever was calling should text her.

Odilie had an idea.

She took Tom's phone into bed with her. He wouldn't wake up; she'd seen him swallow an Ambien before he went to sleep on the couch. Under her covers, her face peeking out of her blanket, she called Vera's number a few more times. No answer. She texted Vera a few more times, long, drawn-out, painful essays about how much Tom liked her, that she had to give him a second chance. The more she sent, the more deranged they got. That he was in love with her. That he didn't know how he could live without her. After about two hours of this, Vera had blocked her, or Tom—she could tell from the messages, which went from blue to green on iMessage and Odilie deleted the entire conversation, slipped back downstairs and tucked the phone next to Tom, right in the place where he'd left it, his little teddy bear.

Now the note. It would be difficult to feign Tom's handwriting and she knew if she tried and even one letter seemed off, it could be her downfall. She paused, tried to get herself in Tom's head. It couldn't be long. Tom was known for his terseness. She had opted for typed; who *handwrote* their suicide notes these days, anyway? she'd thought bitterly as she banged it out, deleting the document afterward, a couple of nights before her grand plan. She made the note seven sentences, printed it out, folded it and stuffed it in the bottom drawer of his desk where he kept extra computer chargers. And what better way for him to be seen in death? So pathetically obsessed with someone who had rejected him, wishing peace to his wife whom he had grown so indifferent toward. He would hate that being his legacy.

In her bathroom, in front of the full-length mirror, she practiced her call to 911, which she would have to make in the dead of night once she began to smell sulfur. She modulated the pitch of her voice, rehearsed the pinch of fear between her eyes, the tears that would begin to fall once she "realized" what had happened.

The day of, she went to lunch with her friend Shirley. "God, you look as tired as you were when you left. What did you *do*?" Shirley remarked, sipping on a Chardonnay whose color reminded Odilie of a rabid dog's eyes. They were supposed to be discussing fundraising plans for some charity Odilie had already forgotten the name of.

"You know, my dad was in the hospital, so I spent a lot of time in there. It wasn't exactly a vacation, I'm afraid." She plucked the cloth napkin off the table and flattened it onto her lap.

"Oh, you poor thing. I'm sorry, was I being insensitive? Spending so much time with the kids lately has made me completely forget how to have normal conversation." Odilie shook her head.

"It's fine. You're fine." Odilie took a drink of her water, looking furtively around the room. Everything seemed to have a dull sheen to it; like the room of the restaurant, its inhabitants and furniture were covered in wax.

"How's Layla?" Odilie asked.

Shirley rolled her eyes. "Oh, you know, same old stuff. She was away most of last month. But then when she's here, she's really here, you know? I can't complain about that. She spoils the kids rotten, though. And seems to be really overly invested in sneaker collecting recently." She prattled on. Odilie liked Layla. She was a powerhouse with a highly demanding job. But she very clearly loved Shirley, in a visceral, profoundly ordinary way that had never surfaced between her and Tom, even on the best days.

"Tom hasn't been happy at all since I came home," she said

abruptly, during a short pause in the prattle. This was another part of her plan.

Shirley squinted, flicking her wrist so hard that her wineglass almost toppled. They were served their salads. When the waiter left, Shirley scrutinized Odilie once more. "What makes you say that?" She cut into her steak, the juices running bloody over the leafy greens.

"He's been acting odd. You know how Tom is, always very regular. Doesn't really diverge from his habits." Shirley nodded. "He's been more erratic recently. Maybe something happened when I was in Michigan." She dived into her own salad. The sautéed shrimp tasted like wax, too.

"Are you going to confront him about it?" The blue cheese in Shirley's salad was congealing in the juice from the steak.

Odilie paused for effect. "I'm not sure. You know, I just got home a few days ago. I haven't wanted to spring anything on him." Shirley nodded in agreement, finished off her wine.

"Well, I hope it's nothing. The last thing you want to deal with is a man who can't be alone for a little while. You need to be able to leave them without worrying that they'll wander off, you know?" Odilie nodded in agreement, downed her water. Her tongue, too, was waxy, stuck to the roof of her mouth.

When Odilie got home she took a tour of her own house, the last day she would inhabit it with his scent suffusing it. She twisted the tassels on the curtains the interior designer he'd hired had forced them to buy, licked the wall with the hand-painted trellis and fountain. She scratched the surface of the stupid kitchen island Tom had insisted they have installed even though neither of them cooked. She stared for a while at the jagged groove she'd made with a long-handled knife in the marble, tracing it with the pad of her thumb.

When she was finished surveying the house, she took a

glass of water and sat outside, in their back garden. It was such a lovely spring day. She didn't even need a jacket. She could hear kids from the school down the street racing home, shouting at each other in friendly, carefree tones. Soon, Penelope would be back from swim class with the nanny. Soon, Odilie would be able to smell the chlorine coating her little girl that somehow lingered even after she was bathed.

Then she entered his office, leaving the door wide open, allowing the room one last breath of air.

She had done her research at a public library in Novi, before she had even committed to the plan. Gas fireplaces, like the one Tom used, had a small sliding cylinder of steel called a combustion shroud, that could only be adjusted when the flame was off. All Odilie had to do was simply adjust this sliding cylinder, and once Tom turned on the fireplace, the appliance would begin emitting carbon monoxide. The only noticeable difference would be the color of the flames, yellow instead of blue, a change Odilie was certain Tom wouldn't be observant enough to discern; Odilie believed that he wouldn't try to leave, that the effects of the gas would hit him before that could become a problem. It wouldn't take too long for the gas to do its job and because of the room's sealed nature, with barely a sliver of space under the door, no other part of the house would be affected. The carbon monoxide detector near the bedrooms would be too far away to sense anything, but she removed the batteries just in case.

SNAPea had moved his computer, which was in the home office, because of the board's new rule about working out of HQ, and only HQ; Tom was waiting for some newfangled laptop to arrive. But surprisingly, this hadn't deterred him from shutting himself in there the past couple of nights. He told Odilie he was enjoying himself and working on a "tech-free secret project," a term at which she rolled her eyes.

After adjusting the combustion shroud with latex gloves on—no fingerprints—she ordered in dinner, a falafel pita sandwich. She heard Tom come home, the slam of the front door, the squeak of his shoes as they slid off. She hated that squeak. He poured himself a beverage, made a soft exhale the moment after he took a sip. She didn't want to engage with him. There was no need. She didn't have any parting words for him.

She put Penelope to bed, reading her *Make Way for Ducklings*, and petting her head as she watched her velvety eyes flutter closed. "What do you think of just Mommy and Penny and Baby?" she asked, stroking the bridge of her daughter's nose, the soft spot just between her eyes. But Penelope was already sound asleep, her breathing heavy and rhythmic.

Odilie went down to the second floor, waiting for the sound of that heavy office door's hinges being pulled open for the evening. After popping an antihistamine to take the edge off—she couldn't risk any real sleeping pill while pregnant—she just sat in the darkness and stared, seeing things in the dimness, outlines of the furniture dancing into different shapes before her eyes. She had no diversion; everything seemed unreal. She typed in her passcode, Vera's birthday, but even the phone didn't distract her. It seemed, instead, like a strange appendage strapped to her hand, jarringly loud and bright.

She was so poised for the sound of the office door's hinges, that every little scuffle downstairs was an explosion in her ears. Every creak he made around the kitchen amplified as he plated his chef-prepared meal, neatly tucked away in the fridge like a bullet in an ammo can.

And then, when the dancing fuzzy lines in the dark seemed to be coming nearer and nearer, finally, finally, she heard the door being pulled open, a tremor resonating throughout the house.

But sitting there, all that waiting, it made her impatient.

She wanted to quicken the job. Even though it hadn't been a worry previously, why risk Tom figuring out, from the yellow flames or the dizzying effect of the gas, what she was up to and wandering out of the office before the job was done?

She left her phone on the couch, went upstairs to the bedroom and pocketed the Ambien sitting on Tom's night table. Then she went downstairs, poured a glass of Stag's Leap pinot noir, watching it swirl into the bulbous glass Tom had insisted on buying. With the bottom of Tom's iPhone, which he had left in the kitchen, she crushed a pill, the powder almost camouflaged by the honed granite island. The powder sank to the bottom of the wine and she stirred it deftly until all those granules were floating seamlessly, invisibly, in the red liquid.

With the wineglass in hand, she walked to the office, almost pirouetted, in fact, as much as she could with her growing belly, her body loose and languorous from the antihistamine coursing through it, her mind already relishing the dulling, foggy effects of the pill. "Brought you some wine," she sang out as she opened the door, unaware that, behind her, the wobbly bar lock, the only thing that kept the door from locking since Tom broke the handle, had retracted into its casing as she stepped into the room.

But he was already sprawled facedown in a pile of papers, a blueprint, it looked like, for a horse enclosure. Like the one from the night they first met, those iridescent, spellbinding ponies. Unconscious already, dying, shallow breath escaping his slack, supple mouth. She smiled.

Then she heard the door click shut behind her.

EPILOGUE

I HAVE A date tonight.

He's a filmmaker, scrawny with red, thinning hair and glasses, perfectly unassuming. We met on the nonexclusive app, the one that anyone can join, postmen and models, bartenders and finance bros. Maybe even murderers. But as we know, those can be found anywhere.

I'm wearing a gray cashmere tank top, since it's supposed to be a little breezy tonight, black wide-legged jeans, platform sandals, a long, billowy, lime-colored silk Altuzarra overcoat. My first instinct was to try to look as inconspicuous as possible. It's hard to date when your face is known for so many different things now, splattered on everything from a sleazy supermarket rag to a $500 sneaker. But unassuming is not who I am. That was never who I am.

This date will have to be a brief one, though. Peri and I

are starting to dream up the second collection of SEPH and there's way too much to do. It's funny what having a career revitalization can do for you. Huda won't stop calling me to do a collab, but obviously, I'm ignoring her.

When Peri cornered me at my mom's, she told me that her next venture was art and fashion. That she'd dipped her toes into so many industries, tech and cars and food and oil, but hadn't discovered the right vehicle to make her dreams of aesthetic dominance come true.

Until she found me.

Peri had modeled in her twenties, but not very seriously, not for high-end designers or labels. When she'd broached the subject of starting a fashion label, of curating an art show, even with her current contact people had dismissed her. She was too low-rent for that, despite her billions. As many times as she re-created herself, she was still a working-class girl from Florida with an ample chest and good hair, who had scrabbled her way into this world by being the escort to a much older man. And besides, she didn't have the artistic talent.

Fashion, high art, they were the only professions in which people were still looking at her credentials, at her past. And because of this gatekeeping, she yearned even more to break into these fields to prove to everyone that she could smash obstacles, create original, unique products that would sell out in seconds and require waiting lists, that could be the next cultural touchstones.

Peri, armed with my collages, my insider knowledge and my technical expertise, knew she could finally achieve this, that she could launch herself into this world, that people would respond to her with respect and awe. And they did. With her money as a lubricant, my collage work ended up in Salon 94.

Then she launched SEPH; she's the "designer," creative director and CEO and I'm the COO. She's the face, I'm the person making it all happen, pulling the marionette strings, the one with the real power. The first line was inspired by my art, high-concept dresses and shoes, pants, too, made from prints based on my collages, not unlike other brands' collaborations with Kusama and Mickalene Thomas or the estates of Jean-Michel Basquiat and Keith Haring. We hired a ghost designer, recently let go from a Paris haute couture house, to formulate actual pieces.

SEPH's first collection sold out so fast last year that we had to contract another manufacturer to keep up with demand. This, of course, was after my gallery show went viral, when I had established critics from all over the world, including Peter Schjeldahl and Adrian Searle, calling me the next Rachel Feinstein or Niki de Saint Phalle. Compliments came, too, from Mark Ryden himself and his wife, Marion Peck. Everyone wants to see a woman's rage if it's beautiful, if it's safely contained to a twelve-by-twenty-four-inch piece of paper.

I've made Peri more money in a year than she initially thought possible and it's only full speed ahead. A beautiful, tragic woman with a redemption arc makes for a great heroine, especially when she's backed by billions. And anyway, isn't it trendy now to side with the supposed villainess, the woman who, in retrospect, was demonized unfairly by the media? Soon, no one will remember me as Tom Newburn's mistress. People are already starting to forget. Thanks to Peri, thanks to my own tenacity.

With that thought in mind, the next collection, the next exhibition, may go in a different direction, but we're not sure which. We're only now beginning to plot, to plan.

When Peri offered all of this over my mother's kitchen table, I couldn't pass it up. Here was a woman with the world on a string, who wanted *me* to help her do something I already loved, I already knew I was brilliant at, who could catapult me to heights I hadn't even considered when I was working for Huda. And the only thing she was asking for was my silence. It would have been stupid, naive, self-righteous to say no. I had wanted, from the beginning, to sell my collage work somehow; Peri was expediting that process.

In a way, Peri *was* a fixer. She told me that instead of giving me money, she was going to offer me a business opportunity. But first, I had to tell Quinn that I didn't want him to do the story about Tom, that something had shifted in me during my trip to see my mom; I knew he wouldn't complain due to his loyalty to me, due to the fact that it was my entanglement and rage that led to the article idea in the first place.

I told him that instead, he should write an article about Odilie's Instagram, the doppelgänger effect. How she'd been crazily, eerily, obsessed with me, she and her husband both. And that that obsession, inexplicably, led to their deaths through no fault of my own. Emphasis on the last part. It's an investigative piece, about social media and emulation and how, in the darkest circumstances, all of it can be deadly. Photos by Sam, as promised. And just to get the Pattersons off our backs, part of the story was about Page, how we became close friends, how we'd found support in each other through shared devastation. *Bullshit.* But who cares, as long as it looks good.

Page is fine, anyway; Peri easily paid her off, helped her with that vacation home idea of hers, which is actually beginning to take off. She has partnerships now with Sotheby's Realty and a Hollywood location scout. She's still with Jackson, shacking up with him in some ridiculously priced Tribeca loft. Thankfully, her hair is honey blond now. Though, occasionally, I see glimpses of her on Instagram wearing a dress I was spotted in, her nails coffin shaped and burgundy. It never ends, I guess. But at least now I'm sort of flattered by it.

Of course, I wanted Quinn to have his day. Peri promised she would work behind the scenes to make his piece go viral, too. It did, and now Sam is getting more and more recognition for their photography; last month the Ford Foundation commissioned them to develop a portrait series of survivors of intimate partner violence. Quinn and I have a podcast series, a movie deal. Peri has shielded us from any efforts SNAPea has made to squelch our ascent. And besides, no one is *talking* about SNAPea. Only about Odilie, social media, the dangers of making oneself public online.

Quinn seems content enough, but I suspect that part of him, a little molecule of himself that he doesn't like to share, is a little resentful, is upset that we didn't take down the Man. He wanted to eviscerate SNAPea, become a *real* investigative journalist, not remain a pop reporter.

In some ways I ripped some of his future from his hands with one click of a lighter. The moment I got back to Brooklyn from my mom's house, I snuck into his room, stole the photo, burned it and deleted all the digital copies.

He's smart enough, of course, to infer that I made a deal with the devil. He's never said it, but I'm sure he recognizes that my insipid protestations, my explanation for forgoing the SNAPea exposé, are categorically untrue and highly unlikely. He knows I'm working with Peri; he does *not* know that Peri was behind my gallery representation and the virality of his piece, though I'm certain that he has his suspicions. I told him that my first time meeting her was when she contacted me about collaborating on a new project, that our convergence wasn't shocking, since she *is* a contemporary art collector with a personal stake in my story.

Sometimes, though, in the quiet of the dark, when I'm thrashing around trying to sleep, I see Calypso's eyes in that photo, the terror in them. And for a moment, a very, very brief moment, I question what I'm doing, if entrusting myself to this woman will lead to inner peace, a lifetime of happiness; if at some later point I'll have to confront the true price of my zealous ambition. But those seconds, they go up in smoke like the picture itself, charred into oblivion.

As I step onto the street, on the way to my date, I wonder what iteration of me this guy knows, if he's googled me. But does it matter, really, if he does? Odilie, Tom, they're part of my story. A story that's beginning to give me the omnipotence, the influence, of which I'd always dreamed.

I head into the night to meet him.

★ ★ ★ ★ ★

ACKNOWLEDGMENTS

Wowee, another book!

I had an especially difficult time breaking ground with this one, so there are endless people to thank. First off, my agent, Stephen Barbara, who remains a god among men. I have the utmost gratitude for you and your championing of my writing. I am so fortunate to work with such stellar folks at Inkwell, including rock stars Maria Whelan and Alexis Hurley.

Thank you to my wonderful editor, April Osborn, whose thoughtful guidance and understanding of my characters have made this book what it is today. Thank you to the rest of the brilliant MIRA team for their tireless work getting this story into people's hands. I'm so lucky to have Justine Sha, publicist extraordinaire, and marketing mavens Ashley MacDonald, Ana Luxton and Lindsey Reeder in my corner.

Speaking of publicists, I am eternally grateful to the powerhouse that is Sandi Mendelson and her team, including the wonderful Caroline Connors, Sarah Payne, and the rest of the Hilsinger Mendelson crew.

Thank you to Stef Hammett for being the ultimate work wife and picking up the slack at my day job when I was losing my mind juggling all of my responsibilities. You are seriously the best.

I'm always in awe of the support I get from my friends. No author has had a better cheerleading squad than I! I'd like to give an especially big shout-out to Sabrina Tompkins, Michael Iselin, and Kelly Rissman for listening to endless voice notes about the inhabitants of Asterisk Land while I was deep in the throes of writing this book. You guys are so patient and helped move this baby along just by being there and listening to me monologue about my personal life.

Thank you to Meredith Grossman for keeping me sane! And much appreciation for Bob Hoven and Mark Abraham, both of whom helped with technical aspects of this novel.

And last but not least, thank you, thank you, thank you to my family, extended and immediate. Mom and Dada, I wouldn't be where I am without your support. I love you.